Harness and Hatches Secure

Harness and Hatches Secure

Bob Mowbray

The Pentland Press Limited
Edinburgh • Cambridge • Durham • USA

© Janet and Bob Mowbray 1996

First published in 1996 by
The Pentland Press Ltd.
1 Hutton Close
South Church
Bishop Auckland
Durham

All rights reserved.
Unauthorised duplication
contravenes existing laws.

British Library Cataloguing in Publication Data.
A Catalogue record for this book is available
from the British Library.

ISBN 1 85821 412 2

Typeset by CBS, Felixstowe, Suffolk
Printed and bound by Antony Rowe Ltd., Chippenham

This is a work of fiction, set against the background of the development of airborne Radar during the Second World War. Significant events and significant people are referred to under their correct names. When the fictional characters encounter the famed personages the actions and dialogue are invented to suit the narrative. Any resemblances shown by the fictional characters to actual persons living or dead are fortuitous and certainly not intended.

To Janet

Thanks are due to Joan for providing access to archival sources, to Graham for advice on Word Processing, to Catriona for providing Library resources and to Anne for smiling at the right time. David Landells helped on matters orthopaedic. Fiona Hale and Ian Leslie of the Library of the National Aviation Museum are to be thanked for their efforts in finding and supplying the copy of the chart from which the jacket was made.

EXPLANATION

The title is recalled from 50 years ago, from the list of checks made on an aircraft before take-off. The pilot began with an external inspection, looking at the obvious components in a clockwise walk round the aircraft. In the cockpit he carried out a visual check of the controls, fuel switch, settings for throttle, mixture and carburettor heat. He then checked brakes were on, the master switch was on and the ignition properly set. After ensuring that no one was in danger, he switched the engine on, checked the throttle action and the oil pressure at idling speed. There were further checks of the controls, then the engine was run up and the magnetos and carburettor heat checked at high revs, then at idling.

The final checks started with harness and hatches secure, ensuring that the safety harnesses and door hatches and covers were securely fastened. The elevator trim nut was checked for being tight, the mixture controls moving freely against the slipstream, gauges reading correctly, and the correct settings on the altimeter and compass ring.

The complexity of the ritual varied. In single engined aircraft the pilot could use a mnemonic to cover the necessary checks. In multi-engined aeroplanes, the second pilot or flight engineer would prompt from a printed sheet. Nowadays, in a commercial passenger aircraft, the lists make up a book.

CONTENTS

Part One
    Adam 1940–1943   1
Part Two
    Jock 1940–1942   97
Part Three
    Ether Atom 1942   131
Part Four
    Jock 1942–1943   155
Part Five
    Adam 1943–1985   213
Part Six
    An Ending 1990, 1995   273

PART ONE

ADAM

1940–1943

CHAPTER 1

It was June 1940 and Adam Robert Aitken was standing at the rail of the ferry steamer *Caribou* which linked the island of Newfoundland with the country of Canada. He was tall, sandy haired, with bright blue eyes and a firm mouth. In his uniform as a Pilot Officer of the Royal Air Force, he had attracted the attention of his fellow passengers, and with their polite, but persistent enquiries, they had tried to satisfy their curiosity about the presence of an English airman on a Newfoundland ferry miles and miles from home. He had explained that he was not English, but a Newfoundlander, born and bred in St John's. The most usual response was that they could tell that now they heard him, for he spoke like a townie.

The questioning had been most intense on the long train journey from St John's, right across the island to the ferry terminal at Port aux Basques. How did a good Newfoundlander get into the English Air Force? Wasn't he some young to be an officer? Where was his aeroplane then? He explained that he had been sent to school in England and had flown at weekends with an RAF reserve squadron. He had got his pilot's wings and had been commissioned. When he finished school he had come back to Newfoundland to work for his father while he waited to be called up.

He would be twenty-one years old in two months and was on his way to Montreal to get an aeroplane there and fly it to Britain. 'That's some hard, me son, there's many fine men been lost at sea, trying to get their air-machines to cross to England. Now me, I'd never go in a contraption like that. I'd go in a Newfoundland built schooner, though. You'd be safe enough in that. Now what line of work is your father in?'

His explanation that his father owned Aitken's businesses, which they had all heard of, and many worked for, evoked in them exaggerated ideas of the power and wealth of the 'Water Street Merchants.' The majority of Newfoundlanders were at a level of poverty such that prosperity meant simply being able to provide the necessities for themselves and their families. Adam's questioners had drifted away. They were too gentle and well mannered to be bitter, but they were embarrassed at the wide gulf between themselves and people like the Aitkens.

Adam started to reminisce. Growing up as an only child, he knew and accepted that he would one day run his father's business. It was daunting when he considered the many firms, agencies and companies in Newfoundland that came under the Aitken banner. He liked to travel to the outports with his father, when they visited fishing boats, fish processing plants, workshops, stores, offices and garages. His favourite establishments were the fish plants, and he loved to watch the deft, confident moves of the filleters as they wielded their sharp knives to ready the fish for the customers. He always had good memories of his childhood. He enjoyed being at the local school with many friends. There was poverty and hunger all round him, but his parents gave money to the poor. He heard that Wall Street had fallen somewhere in America, but had no idea how that could affect Newfoundland.

Adam had always been fascinated by watching the seabirds soaring above the cliffs and the waterfowl landing on the ponds. At the field where Old Colony Airways did charter flying, aerial surveys and occasional mercy flights, he watched the take-offs, approaches and landings of a de Havilland Gipsy Moth.

He had saved up his pocket money for his first flight in this aeroplane, and he could still smell, taste, and feel the sensations. He could also recall his lack of success in trying to convey to his father, 'Skipper' as he was known in the family and to his staff, his enthusiasm for flying.

On a school holiday in Toronto Adam attended a flying school. He soloed in 4 hours and did some bush flying to deliver supplies to Northern Ontario. He rapidly built up experience and used the cash he earned to learn the finer points of flying and build up the flying hours in his log book.

By the standards of the day he was an experienced pilot at sixteen. When he returned to St John's he tried to interest his father in this aerial approach to transporting goods and staff within the island. His father's first and only question was, 'Who will drive the machine?' When Adam told him he was now qualified the response was, 'Don't be foolish. You'll have the business to run.'

By the spring of 1938, Adam was in Britain, at Malvern College. His father felt that exposure to the British public school way of life would stand his son in good stead when he took over the reins of the family business. Adam was not overawed by the scions of noble families, many of whom shared his interests and outlook. However he was irritated by some of his more effete fellow students, 'chinless wonders' as they were termed, particularly those who seemed to believe that there was some merit in keeping themselves ill-informed. His greatest irritation arose from their indifference and ignorance of Newfoundland. He took pains to inform his fellow students that Newfoundland was the first British Colony. One disinterested seventeen year old earl drawled, 'Well, if you say you're a Colonial why aren't you black, what?'

Prowess in sports earned him some fame. His height and bulk made him a useful forward on the Rugby field, and a well placed jab in the first three minute round elevated him to the status of celebrity when he laid out the school heavyweight boxing champion. Academically his time was rewarding. An enthusiastic master got him interested in Shakespeare by encouraging him to look behind the eloquence of the dialogue and savour the plot. Another convinced him that Science was interesting if you thought about how the discovery was made and not just the end result. 'Feety' Anderson believed that his job was just to awaken the latent enthusiasm for Mathematics that lurked in every soul. Adam responded and found he was better than he thought in this arid subject, once he appreciated that trigonometry was the basis of navigation by Dead Reckoning.

'Feety' Anderson was also second in command of the local RAF Auxiliary squadron, and with more emphasis on his flying log-book than on his birth certificate Adam enrolled in the squadron and was gazetted as an Acting Pilot Officer. He spent his weekends flying a Hawker Hart biplane, and in this sturdy, machine he honed and acquired skills that were expected of a fighter pilot, tight formation flying, evasive turns, deflection shooting and navigating by following the local pattern of railway lines.

On one noteworthy Saturday, Wing Commander 'Bull' Sullavan flew down to let them see Hawker's successor to the Hart, the monoplane fighter, named the Hurricane. After letting them inspect this magnificent machine on the ground, Bull did a fighter pilot's take-off, retracting the wheels just as flying speed was reached. He stood it on its tail, climbed and put it through its paces, ending with a victory roll. He beat up the airfield, climbed, waggled his wings and flew off leaving the weekend fliers excited at the prospect of screaming round the skies behind the greatest of all aero-engines, the Rolls Royce Merlin.

These hopes were dashed when they were converted to Bristol Blenheims, twin engined multi-seater monoplanes, originally designed as low level light bombers. Their dreams of being knights on chargers were replaced by the prospects of being bus drivers going where the observer told them until they reached the target and then obeying his instructions to aim the bombs.

In early 1939 Adam left school and returned home to an executive position in the St John's Insurance office of the Aitken empire. His father admitted that he had arranged this to make sure that his son was well away from the impending war in Europe. Adam was determined to be in the war. He was sure he had not been given his flying training just to look at actuarial tables and write placatory letters to disgruntled clients.

The conflict between his duties to his father and the firm, and his commitments to fly aeroplanes in Britain was not resolved when war was declared and he was not officially recalled for service. He sat out the so-called 'phoney' war when nothing happened and everyone said it would be over by Christmas.

The Germans overran Europe with their Blitzkrieg methods. British troops were evacuated from Dunkirk. France gave in. In North America there was talk about Britain being finished. All Hitler had to do was to cross the Channel, and it was all over.

That had not yet happened, and Adam had at last received the official letter ordering him to report to Montreal. Aircraft from the neutral United States were being delivered into Canada to be flown to Britain and he was to join the unit which would make these transatlantic deliveries.

The letter was signed by a Squadron leader in charge of special posting and countersigned by Beaverbrook, the Minister of Aircraft Production, with the added flourish 'from one Aitken to another'.

Full secrecy was stressed but he showed it to the Skipper, his father, who was more interested in the fact that Beaverbrook had signed the letter. Max Aitken, a Canadian publisher, newspaper owner and entrepreneur, had become a multimillionaire in Canada then moved to Britain and as Lord Beaverbrook, became an important figure in British politics. When Churchill took over as war leader, he chose Beaverbrook to run the British Ministry of Aircraft Production because he got things done by cutting corners, and using unconventional ideas, disturbing the traditional British Civil Servants in the process.

Adam's father admitted that Beaverbrook was no relative but he liked to think he might have been. Beaverbrook's son, also Max, about Adam's age, had joined the Royal Air Force, and to Adam's delight the Skipper at last accepted that his son was going off to the war.

CHAPTER 2

In Montreal Adam was housed in a modest, comfortable hotel near the city centre. An Administrative Officer, who seemed to have memorised every regulation that had been written, told him that as a member of the RAF, not the Royal Canadian Air Force, Adam was entitled to foreign service pay and allowances. The sergeant in the pay office processed his forms and said that as a volunteer from Newfoundland he was entitled to wear Newfoundland shoulder flashes. A stores corporal just happened to have two sets of these. Heartened by being so well entitled, Adam asked for flying boots and a helmet. He was deflated when he was told that only flying personnel were entitled to draw flying gear.

He was given an office with his name written in pencil above a more permanent label which read 'Crew Selection'. His job was to review applications submitted by pilots, engineers and radio operators and to make up the crews to ferry Lockheed Hudsons across the Atlantic. Pilots were easy to find as a large number had applied. If they had sufficient hours on twin-engined aircraft, they could get some practice time on the Hudsons at the airfield at Dorval.

There had been few problems in recruiting flight engineers, but radio operators with aviation experience were scarce. If land based or marine operators could be persuaded to get into an aeroplane, never mind fly over the Atlantic, they required special training.

Adam was dismayed that he had simply exchanged one deskful of files in St John's for another in Montreal, but he buckled down to making lists of crews from the records on his desk. Some were aircrew from the RAF, the RCAF and from Allied forces; some were on loan from British Airways and the Canadian Department of Transport; others were American professional pilots, bush fliers, crop dusters, odd job pilots, even stunt pilots from the film industry. Don, he was told, would have the last word on the selection and composition of the crews, and Don wanted the crews to be selected for the first crossing in late August. At least once a day Don's name cropped up and Adam grew more intrigued to find out about this mysterious Don.

One morning an unfamiliar civilian appeared in his office. In a clipped accent the newcomer introduced himself as Don Bennett. 'I see we've got the same rank,' he said, 'but I've got a few years on you.' He handed Adam a thick folder. 'Here's my crime sheet for you to sort out.' His eye caught the volume at the edge of Adam's desk. 'Glad to see you've got Martin's book on Air Navigation. Read it well, for we'll have to be up on Dead Reckoning going across the water. The other thing you'll need is good radio procedure.'

Adam picked up quickly on these remarks. 'I am a pilot, but for over a week I've been a clerk. How do I get to fly here?'

Bennett snorted, 'You, of all people, ask me that. Make up a file for yourself with all your logged hours in it and give it to the officer in charge of crew selection. His name is Aitken. You know him well, don't you? I'm glad you're keen to fly. When I heard about you I thought you were Beaverbrook's son looking for a cushy job.' Adam vehemently denied this, but realised he had been shown a way out so he kept quiet on his suspicions that his own father might have organised the cushy job for him.

Bennett invited Adam to fly with him that afternoon. He was to check an Airways Captain on a Hudson and Adam could come for the ride. Adam accepted happily. Bennett left and Adam prepared his own file, including a copy of his posting orders with the covering remarks from Beaverbrook. He placed his file at the bottom of the heap, then thought better of it and brought it up to second from the top.

Don Bennett's folder told about a man who had set out to make himself the most complete airman that Adam had ever imagined. He was Australian, and had done his ab initio flying training with the Royal Australian Air Force, then held a short-term commission in the RAF and was currently in the Reserve with the rank of Pilot Officer. Hence his reference to the rank he shared with Adam. After his RAF service he flew with, then became chief pilot of Imperial Airways, and opened up a number of new air routes for this British company.

In the famous Mayo Composite experiment, Bennett had flown the small flying boat, named *Mercury*, which took off piggyback on a larger seaplane, *Maia*. Adam was thrilled to have met the man who had flown in this type of venture and who, in 1938, accompanied by a wireless-operator, had flown *Mercury* non stop for 6000 miles in just over forty hours. This record for distance flown was hailed as a landmark in aviation history. Bennett's exceptional experience at the controls was matched by his technical qualifications, knowledge and skill in navigation, wireless and aircraft engineering.

Bennett and Adam drove out to the airfield at Dorval. They found a middle aged man in the pilot's seat of a new Lockheed Hudson with the pilot's notes on his knee familiarising himself with the cockpit lay-out. A laconic exchange of greeting: 'Afternoon, Don,' 'G'day, Frank,' and Adam was introduced to Captain Frank Yetman, who had opened up many routes in Canada and Newfoundland as a senior pilot with Trans Canada Airlines.

During the flight Adam listened to the quiet interchange of two civil aviation giants going over the merits and demerits of each component and system of the aircraft. He had a chart before him and kept a running plot from occasional glances at the ground then at the compass and Air Speed Indicator. When Bennett suddenly asked him for a course to steer for home, Adam could oblige immediately. On landing, Bennett told Frank Yetman that he could take over as Instructor, and Adam would be his first pupil.

Excited at the prospect of flying, Adam removed his name from the office door, drew his flying kit and moved to the Dorval site the following day. During three weeks of glorious Montreal sunshine, Adam revelled in the full schedule of day and night flying. Following Bennett's example, he watched the fitters and riggers at work on the routine servicing of the aircraft, and haunted the radio hut to get up to date on equipment and procedure.

The crew lists for the first leg of the ferry operation were posted at the beginning of August. Bennett, as expected, was to captain the lead aircraft. For another aircraft Adam was listed as pilot and Kazlowski as Flight Engineer. 'Kaz' was a quiet, intense, lanky American, who had renounced his first name because it was unpronounceable. The Radio Operator was Michael McGeogh, a red haired Irishman who had been at sea with the Cunard Line, but had adapted well to flying. This trio worked well together on their practice flights.

However they shared in the frustrations at the delays in getting sufficient components to equip the eight aircraft for the first crossing. Bennett spent his time between the chart room, where he was working on a flight plan, and chivvying the suppliers on the telephone.

This delay led to a hold-up in the entry of crew members, hence a reduction in the amount of instruction required. As a number of his instructors had already left, Frank Yetman asked Adam to become an instructor, mainly to chaperon pilots in their first experiences with the Hudsons. He agreed, then spent his days pointing out the pros and cons of the Hudson to men who had ten times his experience. It was, he reckoned, a useful way of putting in time until he flew over to Britain and joined his squadron.

At the end of August Adam was promoted to Flying Officer and informed that he was no longer on deferred service, but now on active service. The following weekend he showed his thicker stripe proudly to his father who had come to Montreal on business. The Skipper reported that the economy of Newfoundland was beginning to improve, with the increased shipping activity in the port of St John's. No one would go near Water Street after dark now, with all these drunken sailors shouting and fighting and carrying on with girls. Ships came in with men wounded by gunfire or covered in oil. Newfoundland soldiers were over in Britain, and it was rumoured that some were going to be sent to Africa to fight. All that bombing of civilians in Britain must be terrible, and Adam must be grateful to be away from that. Adam was quiet. He knew how difficult it would be to convey his wish to fly in battle against the attacking bombers.

Being taken round circuits and on short cross-country trips by such a varied group of fliers was an opportunity for Adam to learn the lore of flying from experts. He was particularly impressed by the wisdom and airmanship of 'Shouter' Humphrey, a regular RAF Flight Lieutenant, whose claims to fame included having flown every RAF aeroplane in his long service, and being able to drink pints of beer while roaring out the headings for the pre-flight cockpit check, always emphasising ''arness and 'atches secure.' He admitted to being forty and had been a flying instructor for ten years.

One evening, in a despondent mood, Adam told Shouter of his despair of not flying against the enemy but just acting as nanny to pilots who could fly Hudsons better than he ever could. Shouter proved to be a good listener and Adam found himself talking about his difficulties with his father, in particular, the Skipper's expectations that Adam would prefer to be in business in St John's than in the RAF in Britain. In an uncharacteristic quiet tone of voice, Shouter pointed out that Adam's father was showing affection for his son. 'Look, lad,' he continued, 'you want your old man to stop trying to pull you into the business. But you want him to fix it so that you can go back to a squadron in England.'

Adam squirmed a bit. 'I only want him to help in some way.'

'He can't do that. Now can he really? Come on. Even Beaverbrook can't have that kind of influence. Everyone thinks that the decisions at the Air House are made by important blokes with chests full of medals and arms full of broad rings. Not true. The people who do things and get them done are faceless and nameless bloody clerks. They're the sort of bods who couldn't sell lavatory brushes in civvy street so came into the service to do administration. These are the lads that you, not your father, have to take on. That's point one. Not daddy, you. The next point requires another pint.'

When Adam had fulfilled the requirement, Shouter took a swallow and went on. 'You think the way to go is to get your Auxiliary chums to write the Air Chief Marshal Godalmighty to ask him to let you come and play with them. Right?' Adam nodded. Shouter went on, 'Wrong. Not your chums. You. That's point two, Adam my boy. And who do you write to?'

Adam replied doubtfully, 'The clerk who couldn't sell lavatory brushes?'

'The very man,' enthused Shouter. 'You can contact him as the Officer in Charge of the Posting section. Now we come to point three, when to write. All RAF records, going back to when Pontius became a Pilate, all that bumph is stored in files, in drawers, in cabinets, in rooms, in storehouses. Your file is lying quietly out of sight and, as you know, out of mind. Now the things that flush it out are promotion, demotion, too much pay, court martial, status changes, such as being made instructor. These things get your file on to someone's desk. That's when you have to make your attack and write your letter.'

Shouter gave a triumphant thumbs up when Adam told him that his promotion had come through just over a week ago. 'Then now's the time to contact them to say you're waiting for your posting to your squadron.' He ended with a sober warning that an instructor was likely to be stuck with the job for ever. Slapping Adam on the knee he said, 'There it is, then, advice from the ancient's mouth. It's up to you. No one else. You write to the Postings section.' Adam thanked Shouter and watched him head for the bar. The war cry rang out, ''arness and 'atches secure.' Shouter was himself again.

Adam drafted and redrafted the letter in his mind, then lost no time in writing describing his predicament in detail to the Air Ministry Postings section and placed it in the unit mail box. After lunch he was interviewed by an embarrassed Canadian Intelligence Officer who had helpfully sketched out a more restrained letter which would not reveal all to any German spy in the Air Ministry. A chastened Adam thanked him for his help, rewrote his letter in the form suggested and resubmitted it.

A few days later Bennett led the first group of Hudsons, one of which had 'Shouter' at the controls, on the first leg to Newfoundland. Adam saw them starting to taxi out as he shepherded a former crop-duster on to the down-wind leg of his approach. He sighed and then had to assure his 'pupil' that he was not criticising his flying.

With a regular, but never arduous stint of daily duties, Adam had plenty of free time in the evenings. On a suggestion from his father he got in touch with Mr Lamotte, a Quebec manufacturer of building material who supplied the Aitken construction division. He was formally asked to call at the Lamotte home for dinner *en famille.*

On the appointed evening he put on his best uniform and took a taxi to the address in the Mount Royal district. M. Lamotte was a small plump man with heavily oiled hair, wearing a dark business suit. Adam was intrigued to see he wore pince-nez, metal rimmed spectacles clipped on to his nose. He was meticulous in observing the social graces for the occasion, but Adam felt his host was showing more reserve than politeness might demand. He was then formally presented in turn to Madame Lamotte, to the son Giles, then to daughter Amélie. Giles was slightly older than Adam and had a supercilious attitude. Amélie smiled in a welcoming manner but said little.

At table, a delicious onion soup had just been served when Giles asked Adam his opinion on the conduct of the war in Europe. Adam replied that he hoped that the fall of France would not prove to be too much of a set-back for the British. This inflamed Giles for he accused England of having sold France to the Germans simply to gain time to escape at Dunkirk.

Adam had no time to muster a rebuttal when Lamotte senior broke in. 'You English can never be allies to anyone. You just want to save your own skin. Your navy killed more than one thousand Frenchmen when they destroyed the French ships in Algeria, at Mers-el-Kebir. Was that the action of an ally? No. You are taking American planes, from a neutral country, and you yourself right here in Montreal are training men to bomb French people and French cities. And you come to see us, proud in your uniform, knowing that your government believes that the people of France can no longer help you, so they can be sacrificed.'

Adam at last found words to respond. 'I cannot agree with your opinions. I apologise for wearing this uniform . . . No, I don't. I don't apologise for it even it if offends you. I would like to leave.'

He bowed to his hostess. 'Goodnight Madame,' and left the room, picked up his cap and went outside. He had reached the front gate when he heard footsteps behind him and Amélie caught his arm. 'I am sorry for what they said, but that cannot matter. Please let me drive you back to Dorval.' He nodded reluctantly and she ran to a small car in the driveway and drove up beside him.

He got in and half smiled at her. 'Perhaps you'll be one French person who's not an enemy.'

'*Touché*,' she said and drove along the road to the top of Mount Royal. She stopped the car and they sat quietly looking over the lights of the city. Adam broke the silence. 'Thinking about it, the most shocking thing tonight was the information you had on what was happening at Dorval.'

She shrugged. 'Easy. We read about it in the French language newspaper. I knew about you as the English pilot who came to Montreal to teach Canadians how to bomb Europeans. That to us means Frenchmen.'

'But that's not true,' Adam exploded. 'We're just taking the planes across the Atlantic.' He shut up quickly, realising he was breaching security. 'Dear God, Miss Lamotte, give me a minute to sort this out will you,' Adam pleaded.

'I will do more. I will now drive you to Dorval, and I will not be your enemy on the drive, and you, you will call me Amélie.' As she drove she asked Adam directly about himself. He tried to express his dreams about how aircraft would become a fast way of world travel.

She listened politely, then talked of herself. She was a University graduate whose ambition was to become a journalist who would be able to sway thousands of readers in their opinions, in English as well as French. Her articles would be written for women, not just for men. There was such a thing as a woman's point of view. Adam agreed, saying there should be magazines about fashion, recipes and housework. He had hit a sore spot. She shrieked, 'No, No, No! That's not it at all. That's just what men want to think about women. Women have a special way of looking at politics, even war, at business and commerce, at art and music, quite different from the man's point of view. My God, I have a lot to teach you.'

At the gateway to his quarters, she invited Adam to come out with her in two days time. She assured him that he would not be taken to her home. He agreed and she kissed him warmly, convincing Adam of her physical as well as her intellectual charms. On his way to the dining room to make up for the dinner he never had, he found the Security Officer still at his desk. Adam walked in and told of his surprise at how much the people of Montreal knew about what went on at Dorval. 'And where would they get this information from?' asked the Security Officer stuffily. When Adam replied they got it from the newspapers, he snorted, 'Rubbish,' and pointed to a stack of newspapers on his desk. 'Part of my job every day is to read the newspapers, morning and evening, just to find anything like that. There have been no leaks about our operation.'

Adam looked at the pile of papers and saw they were all in English.
He asked, 'What about the French papers?'
The reply was immediate, 'I don't read French.'

CHAPTER 3

After Adam had told him of this gap in security, Bennett quickly got the authorities to increase the police and security services and also to appoint a bilingual officer. This officer confirmed that blatant descriptions and guesses about what was going on at Dorval had been published. Ottawa imposed security restraints on classified information, and local editors agreed to co-operate.

Seeing Amélie regularly kept Adam from becoming despondent at his inability to get into the war. When they ate in one of their favourite small cafés her sparkle and a glass or two of wine lifted his spirits. Afterwards her small car became an arena for their amorous adventures, as he thought of their encounters. He had had adolescent sexual experience with girls in Newfoundland, but he could never have expected such wild embraces from a flower of St John's society.

After one blazing bout, she sat up suddenly and fastened her clothing deliberately. 'We are not lovers. We are not to be married. We must simply enjoy each other. We have no commitments, one to the other.' Adam realised that he was being inflamed to the point at which his self-control was fully tested. Evenings with Amélie began to contribute to, rather than to relieve frustrations. However, it was Amélie who ended the affair when she got engaged to the son of a business friend of her father. Adam was partly relieved, but sad that he was to be denied the excitement of her company.

The Battle of Britain had held back the expected invasion by Germany, but in September the Blitzkrieg bombing on London began. Civilians spent night after night in air raid shelters. Contrary to expectation, morale remained high. A letter from his squadron hinted they were engaged in defending against these raiders. The public were reading about 'cat's-eyed' pilots who flew in the dark to find and destroy the surprised German crews. It was revealed that a diet of carrots gave these heroes their outstanding night vision. The rumour, fostered as a 'smoke screen' to keep the development of radio direction finding equipment secret, backfired on the aircrew of one night fighter squadron who were served carrots at every meal, after the catering officer read of the amazing effects of a diet of carrots in a popular magazine.

Adam spent his Christmas leave at home in St John's. His parents hosted the annual large gathering of Aitken employees. Directors and their wives mingled with typists, accountants with truck drivers, and a callow office-boy was found in intimate play with a manager's wife. All in all a successful company party, it was agreed.

On his return to Dorval at the beginning of January, 1941, Adam was surprised to find Shouter Humphrey at the bar. He showed Adam the new two and a half rings on the sleeves of his well-worn tunic. 'You now have the privilege of buying a pint of wallop for Squadron Leader Humphrey.' Adam complied and got a half pint for himself. After Shouter had given the toast, he told of what had happened to him in Britain.

A 'bloody jumped up clerk' told him that he was too old to fly on operations, but he could become an air traffic controller. 'I told this twerp in no uncertain terms what to do with his suggestions. I thought about my mates in old Dorval. I thought about my Madame Dutemps, a comely widow woman, with her fine villa residence not a stone's throw from here. And I thought of her burning desire for Clarence Humphrey.' The bar exploded at this revelation that Shouter could have such a name.

Once he had silenced them by a steely glare, Shouter went on to detail his immediate plans. 'Later tonight I shall propose to my lady love, and with the bit of leave that's coming to me, we will be wed at the end of this month. Then a long drawn out honeymoon. Stop drooling, you lot of randy buggers. That'll finish my leave and I will take over from young Adam as the most revered Chief Flying Instructor. The powers that be have agreed that I can do the occasional ferry trip just to keep my hand in.'

Adam gave a yell of delight. 'Shouter, you're a gentleman. I will buy you another pint. To celebrate the occasion I shall also have a pint. No half measures tonight.' A party developed. To the surprise of everyone in the mess, Adam insisted on singing a Newfoundland song, 'The Kelligrews' Soirée'. This rollicking number was a hit in St John's but just as his audience began to tap their feet and bang their beer mugs, Adam stopped to explain the Newfoundland terms or to try to remember the words. His last action was to drain his fourth pint, while explaining seriously that cavalances were the same as calavances and they were both beans for making soup. Mumbling, 'my 'arness and 'atches are not secure, I fear,' he set his beer pot down carefully then passed out. He was carried off to his bedroom and put to bed by a well practised squad of his friends.

At breakfast the next morning he sat hunched over his coffee and toast until his blood caffeine reached a level sufficiently high to start the day for him. When he checked, he was on the list for the next flight to Gander Field, but there would be some delay in getting the components to ready the aeroplane for the crossing. He was listed as pilot, with his old friend, Mike McGeough as Radio Operator and a South African as Flight Engineer. He spent part of the afternoon composing a follow-up letter to the Air Ministry to hurry up his posting to his squadron.

The spare equipment turned up and was quickly fitted. However there was no clearance given for the first leg to Newfoundland. He had little local flying to do because of the snowy conditions in and around Montreal. He attended Shouter's wedding to Mercedes Dutemps, a vivacious chubby blonde woman whose blue eyes shone with love and admiration for her new husband. With his hair neatly combed and dressed in his best blue, Shouter looked like, and behaved like the epitome of a gentleman during the ceremony and at the reception. As he and his bride prepared to leave for their honeymoon, the real Shouter broke through. 'Think of me tonight, lads, 'arness and 'atches secure.' The bride's guests were bewildered, but the Dorval contingent cheered this exit line.

The first week of February was forecast to offer a window in the weather, sufficient for ten of the Hudsons to fly the first leg to Gander field. After an uneventful flight, as he circled to land, Adam saw large rolling clouds to the north. All the aircraft landed safely and were escorted to sheltered dispersal points, where the wings were guyed by strong cables to rings set in concrete and canvas covers were put on each engine. For the next few days winds of up to 80 miles per hour blew snow horizontally over the whole establishment. Once the storm abated, Adam joined a group digging the aeroplanes out.

A series of postponements of the Atlantic crossing left Adam with time on his hands. When his father telephoned to tell him that his mother had been admitted to hospital, he borrowed a floatplane to fly from Gander Lake to Quidi Vidi lake in St John's for a weekend visit. Adam had been brought up to accept that his mother's recurrent chest infections required her to be admitted to a specialised hospital several times a year. Matters were serious on this occasion, as she had developed pneumonia.

The Skipper was relieved that his son would be with him to give support, for he had been warned to expect the worst. To Adam's embarrassment, his self-assured, confident, strong willed father revealed himself to be unsure of his ability to cope with a personal crisis. He listened as his father told of his marriage.

They were wed in 1918. Lucy, Adam's mother, was the only daughter of a long established merchant family in St John's. Her two brothers who were to inherit the thriving business, had died in World War I, at Beaumont Hamel, when the entire Newfoundland Regiment was all but wiped out in one bloody day.

Archie and Lucy's wedding was the social event of the year, and represented not only a union of two prominent families but also a commercial amalgamation, which produced one of the largest business empires in Newfoundland. Archie was a dutiful husband, solid in his business transactions and staid in his social contacts. Lucy, his vivacious redheaded bride, revelled in her new status as a hostess of note, giving and attending impeccably conducted soirées, and taking part in charitable affairs, mainly those intended to help the large number of Newfoundlanders suffering from tuberculosis.

She suffered occasional bouts of breathlessness and pains in her chest. Her doctor worried that she may have contracted tuberculosis, but the tests showed her to be clear. A specialist in Toronto diagnosed asthma, and prescribed tonics and a linctus. When she became pregnant, her symptoms cleared up, and following medical advice she stopped taking the medicines as they contained alcohol. She had a healthy pregnancy and after an easy labour, delivered a bouncing Adam in August 1920.

Lucy did all the right things, including breast-feeding, in spite of the growing fashion of using commercial baby foods. Adam throve, and when he was one year old, a nanny was hired to give Lucy some time to resume her activities with her friends. A thirteen year old girl came from an outport settlement to live in. A staunch Roman Catholic, Bridget Murphy's child minding experience had been gained when she looked after nine younger brothers and sisters. She displayed an awe of Lucy and Archie and a proprietary attitude to Adam, to whom she chatted continuously in the outport vernacular. The child responded to her loving attentions, to an extent that he sought comfort and solace from her rather than from his mother.

Archie was pleased that his son was being looked after so well, but he became uneasy that Lucy was not properly occupying herself as a mother. Her bouts of asthma returned and she had to use an inhaler to get relief. For some time she would be active and cheerful about the house and at those times she would read to Adam, or play the piano for him, or teach him nursery rhymes. She would later begin to complain of being tired and lose interest in playing with him. Then she became aloof, and sometimes morose and uncaring to her son. 'The devil's working at her,' was Bridget's explanation of why his mother rejected Adam's affection. In the hope that fresh air would help her breathing difficulties Archie sold the town home and bought a house in the country, and Adam found he had no one to play with. This move made little difference to his mother's health. After a period of being happy and cheerful, she began again to lose interest in herself, her husband and her child. In these phases Bridget ended up looking after his mother as much as she did her small charge.

In the silence that followed his father's account, Adam realised how distant he had been from his parents and how little he had known of their private anguish. He had come to depend entirely on Bridget's love and devotion. Archie put his head in his hands and sobbed, 'Oh, Lucy, my Lucy.' Adam embraced his father and let his own tears flow.

After a time, Archie whispered, 'That was an awful thing to spring on you. I feel the better for telling you, but my relief is your grief. I'm sorry.' He shook Adam's hand and said quietly, 'You're my son. I'm very proud of you.'

Adam hugged his father. 'We've never got close. I've been afraid of you for years, but I never knew what you've had to put up with. I wish I had known.'

Bridget opened the door to remind them they should be leaving for the hospital. She seemed surprised at the intensity with which Adam embraced her. 'You'll feel better now you know the truth of it all,' she comforted him. Adam whispered, 'I know how important you've always been to me. Thank you for looking after me.'

CHAPTER 4

In the taxi taking them to the hospital, Archie placed his hand on Adam's shoulder. 'I'm glad you're with me, son. I'm dreading how we'll find her.'

A nurse met them at the door to the ward. 'You've brought young Adam to see her, God be thanked. She's always wondering if she'll ever see her son again.' She strode inside, bent over the slight figure in the bed and said gently, 'Here are both your men to see you.' Adam did not recognise the gaunt, white haired patient until a radiant smile spread over her ashen face. He kissed her gently. 'Oh it is Adam. But you're at the war, they tell me. Did you come back, just to see me? I've been sick, you know.'

Adam told her about his time in Montreal, the sights he had seen and the meals he had eaten. 'You've become the gentleman I always knew you'd be, ever since you were born. Let's all go home now.' The nurse reminded her that she had pneumonia and was still very sick. 'What nonsense. I'm well enough to go home this instant with my very own Archie and my son, Adam.' She tried to sit up, but burst into a bout of coughing and showed no resistance as the nurse guided her back on the pillow. Her face was flushed and her eyes glittered as she wrung her hands together rapidly. She held out her hands as if she wanted to grasp something. Archie took one of her hands. Adam took the other. She smiled and said, 'My own Archie. My own Adam.' Adam felt her hand flutter in his, then it lay still. Her eyes were half closed and she was smiling. The nurse felt for a pulse, then gently closed Lucy Aitken's eyes. 'She's gone, Mr Aitken. Just see how happy she looks.' Archie burst into great painful sobs. Adam gently released her hand, then kissed his mother goodbye. He stood behind his father while he kissed his wife, then helped him to stand up, and supported him back to the taxi and home.

The next few days were a blur to Adam. This was his first direct experience of death and he found Bridget to be a source of comfort and help with the interviews with doctors, the forms to be filled in, the arrangements with the undertaker, the viewing of the well made-up body at home, the flowers, the

Harness and Hatches Secure

visiting relatives, friends, the well wishers, the busybodies, the minister, the choice of hymns, the caterers, the cars to and from the cemetery, the thank you for your sympathy letters to be written. At the end of this he learned that his transatlantic flight from the Gander field had taken off with a replacement for him in the pilot's seat.

He spent another two days with his father, getting closer than he had ever been. As they said their farewells, Archie smiled ruefully. 'You'll be a Water Street merchant one of these days, Adam. At long last you're going to war. But make sure you come back. Not just because of the business, mind you. I think we should have some time together to really be father and son.' Bridget held him tight and said she was glad he had come closer to his father. 'Every night I ask Jesus and Mary, his Mother, to watch over my own dear Adam.'

Gander terminal was busier than before. Nine Hudsons were being serviced for a crossing, with Adam, Kaz and McGeogh listed for the following week. Kaz and Mike and several pilots he had checked out had already made two crossings. They had not yet encountered the German long range Focke Wulf Condors, and most agreed that the main hazards of the flight were boredom and cramp from sitting for the ten hours or so, looking at grey water below, grey clouds above and all too familiar instruments on the panel in front. The rumour was that formation crossings would soon be stopped in favour of flights by individual aircraft.

Having already missed a crossing, Adam was reluctant to move off the terminal as his flight date approached. He 'phoned his father several times, and was glad to learn that Bridget was to stay on as housekeeper and that the Skipper was involved in new business developments. Both of them wished Adam Godspeed and a safe journey.

On the appointed day the weather was good and the forecast for the next twelve hours was favourable. Adam took off and circled until the flight of nine aircraft was assembled. In a not too elegant formation they climbed from 1000 feet and turned on to the planned easterly heading for the crossing. Mike checked his transmissions and reception on the assigned channels. Kaz noted the dial readings on the instrument panel and listened to the drone of the engines. They gave each other the thumbs up sign and Adam settled down to the routine of watching his instruments, adjusting the controls, checking the compass reading, looking below and scanning ahead and up.

When he and Kaz went through the ritual of changing from one fuel tank to another the rate of fuel consumption was found to be as planned, with a margin for emergency. Shortly afterwards they entered thin cloud which eventually thickened until visibility was lost totally. Adam had some concern that there could be a mid-air collision, and concentrated, as he hoped the others were doing, on flying his Hudson straight and level. When they emerged into bright sunshine, he could only count a total of eight aircraft.

A call round identified the missing aircraft as being piloted by Tex Gruber, a quiet, likeable forty year old former barnstormer from Texas, whose throwaway sense of humour made him a popular figure among the ferry crews. Preflight briefing had emphasised that no search was to be made for any missing aircraft as delays could jeopardise the operation. This order had seemed obvious in the briefing room, but when the situation had arisen, no one was happy to comply. However, in spite of their reluctance, they all obeyed.

They flew on in continuous bright conditions, then began to let down with Northern Ireland to starboard. Over the Firth of Clyde they started their approach to the main runway at Prestwick. After they landed, they were told to go to dispersal points as quickly as possible. When they were parked with engines switched off, the crews got out to stretch and ask what was happening.

A Hillman van driven by a WAAF, a member of the Women's Auxiliary Air Force, drove up, and a portly Flight Lieutenant got out. He was wearing a steel helmet and carrying a revolver which he brandished alarmingly as he addressed them. 'There's a flap on, you know. A Gerry's flying this way, and we're on red alert.'

'What does that mean?' asked Adam.

'It means I can't give you transport to the mess until the flap's over. So be a good chap and get all your chums to stay where they are for the moment.' He tapped the driver on the shoulder and they drove off towards another dispersal site.

They stood around waiting and watching as a variety of vehicles raced from one point to another. Suddenly a plane appeared low at the end of the runway. The tubby warrior reappeared with a squeal of brakes. 'Here comes the bloody Hun! Take cover!' he roared, keeping the ferry crews at bay by gesturing with his weapon. They watched in silence as the aircraft touched down, then burst into cheers as they recognised Tex's Hudson.

At the dispersal point, the Hudson was surrounded by the cars and trucks which had been speeding up and down the runway. As Tex and his crew emerged on to the tarmac, the Flight Lieutenant asked him who the hell he was. In his best Will Rogers impersonation, Tex said, 'Give me a minute, boy. I gotta put a new battery in my hearing aid.' He then turned to the ferry crews who were all clamouring to know what had happened to him. 'Remember we all went into cloud. I wanted to get away from you half assed fliers, so I climbed just a touch. There was an almighty bang as we got hit by lightning. That blew the radio some, for we couldn't get any message out, though we heard you trying to raise us. I thought we should continue on our own, but the compass had gone off a bit. We just flew until we got over some high mountains. It looked like Bonnie Scotland so we just headed down the coast, until we saw all these Hudsons with their no-good crews hanging around doing nothin' at all. All the way down people were trying to find out who we were. But we couldn't say diddly to them, because our hearing aid wasn't doing what it should have.'

The Flight Lieutenant relaxed and put his revolver away. 'Gentlemen, I regret that I welcomed you so badly after your long journey. We were a bit trigger happy. You may remember that Rudolph Hess caught us napping when he landed near here. When the Observer Corps picked up an unidentified aircraft heading this way they did not know you were one short on your flight, and could only assume it was not friendly. Hence the shambles.' He turned to Tex. 'I'm glad you are none the worse for your misadventure. Welcome to you all. I suggest that everyone grab places in the cars and get down to the mess for a bath, a drink, a meal and a good night's sleep.'

Adam joined the Flight Lieutenant for the short drive. When he introduced himself, the reply was, 'Oh good, there's a posting signal waiting for you in my office. Are you by any chance Lord Beaverbrook's son?' Adam said he wasn't. The Flight Lieutenant smiled, 'Bloody good. VIPs, very important persons, always turn out to be ruddy nuisances.'

The signal simply directed Adam to be at RAF Ouston, near Newcastle, in three days time to join his squadron. The Flight Lieutenant who turned out to be the Station Administration Officer told him that he could get a seat in an Anson, leaving Prestwick in the morning of Thursday, and that after a night's sleep, he could have the day off tomorrow to have a look round Prestwick terminal. Adam mentioned he would like to visit the village of Fenwick, where his grandparents had come from. He was told that transport was not as easy as that. However he could get a bus from Kilmarnock, and there was sure to be some vehicle from the station going there in the morning.

After a good sleep and his first breakfast of powdered egg, Adam was driven in a small Hillman car with two Sergeant Air Gunners who were to catch the London train in Kilmarnock. Once they had been delivered, the car was to wait for two hours for an incoming train. The WAAF driver, named Valerie, was a vivacious redhead with a noticeable local accent and an infectious laugh. She decided that she would just run Adam to Fenwick.

On the way to Kilmarnock, Adam had been impressed at the tidy, small well-kept farms, with cattle and sheep mingled in fields bounded with walls built from stone. Climbing out of Kilmarnock on to moorland, there were fewer sheep, fewer trees and more rocks. 'This is the back of beyond. No wonder your granny and grandpa went to America,' Valerie observed. They reached a collection of houses, a church, and pulled up outside a general store. 'In you go to the shop. There's a man in there. He'll know everything about the place.' Adam put on his cap, got out of the car, straightened his tunic and entered the store to a loud clatter of a bell on a spring at the top of the door.

'Aye, Sir, what can I do for you?' asked the middle aged man wearing a long white apron and a cloth cap. Adam told his name and his family's connections with Fenwick. The shopkeeper introduced himself as James Ferguson and explained. 'There are no Aitkens living here now. They all seemed to leave the district at about the same time, some to Edinburgh, some to Glasgow, some to London and your grandparents to the Newfoundland across the Atlantic Ocean. I'm told that as a boy, your grandfather Aitken worked for my great grandfather in this very shop. I heard that he opened his own shop and prospered well in the new country.'

Adam explained the large number of enterprises in the Aitken empire, and James Ferguson was appropriately impressed. He called out to the back of the shop. 'Agnes come through here and say hello to our visitor.'

A small stout smiling woman with her hands covered in flour came in and shyly greeted the smart young officer. 'You are very welcome, Sir.' Her eyes clouded suddenly and she became distressed. 'Oh dear, have you brought bad news of our John?'

Her husband broke in quickly, 'Oh no, no, Agnes, you're always expecting the worst. The gentleman's from Newfoundland and his grandparents came from the village. He's an Aitken.' Then to Adam. 'John is our oldest boy and he's a pilot like you. He is in Lincoln somewhere and we think he flies bombers. He writes often, but never says what he does. Now Agnes, could you make something for us and that lassie in the motor car and I'll walk Mr Aitken to the churchyard and show him the old Aitken cottage.' She nodded delightedly and scurried out to invite Valerie inside.

Adam was impressed at the number of headstones recording the deaths of children, among them Aitkens. 'These were hard times for everyone, and illnesses like diphtheria could wipe out families of young ones. Many a child died because its family was too poor to afford medicines and too proud to take charity,' Ferguson said sadly. Adam remarked that similar hardships had befallen Newfoundland, and graveyards there told the same sad stories.

They continued past the church to an uninhabited cottage. A vegetable garden round it was divided into plots where the villagers were encouraged to 'dig for victory'. The cottage was in need of paint and repairs. 'This is the Aitken cottage and would have been home to your grandfather. We use it as the Headquarters of the Local Defence Volunteers. We patrol the moors from here to watch for German parachutists. Dear knows what we would really do if we came across one. But that's all that's left of the Aitkens round here. Are you by chance a reader of Robert Burns, Mr Aitken?' When Adam admitted he was not, Ferguson was disappointed. 'More's the pity. Burns made reference to your part of the world as "somewhere far abroad, where sailors gang tae fish for cod". A namesake of yours, maybe even an ancestor, a very skilled and famous advocate, one Robert Aitken, was named in Burns' very famous satire "Holy Wullie's Prayer".'

Mrs Ferguson and Valerie had set out a meal of slices of tinned luncheon meat and salad with freshly baked scones. They ate quickly as Valerie did not intend to be late and arrived in Kilmarnock in good time, to find that the train had been delayed. Two hours later they collected a bad tempered Group Captain, who appeared to be offended that they had only sent a Flying Officer to meet him. He asked Adam about the number of service personnel on the station and what rations they drew, and treated Adam's ignorance on such matters as deliberate evasions bordering on insubordination. Adam had to suppress his chuckles when he had a sudden thought that they had encountered Charles Laughton playing the part of Captain Bligh, and waited for the classic line, 'I'll hang you from the highest yard arm.'

After they delivered the Group Captain and were out of earshot, Adam burst out laughing. Valerie braked rapidly and joined in his laughter when he told her that they had just met Captain Bligh.

Outside his billet he thanked her for the transport and for being such good company. 'Think nothing of it. I enjoyed the day fine. Mrs Ferguson's a nice soul and I'll go back and see her again.' On his cot he found a note saying that his flight to Ouston would take off the following morning at 09.00 and he should report to the control tower at 08.30.

CHAPTER 5

Adam's reunion with his squadron was disappointing. Many of the pilots he knew had been killed or wounded in France, or posted away. 'Feety' Anderson and his crew were the first to die when their Blenheim was shot out of the sky by a German fighter. The replacement aircrew were from the regular service, but more were now coming from the Volunteer Reserve, signed up for 'the duration of hostilities only'. These Volunteers had just completed their training as pilots, observers or wireless operators/gunners and held the rank of Sergeant.

The squadron was still flying Blenheims on night patrols. 'Just stooging around in the dark trying to pick up a Gerry bomber,' explained the C.O., whom Adam remembered as a local accountant in their weekend flying days.

'We're just like Piccadilly whores, only we're not nearly as successful,' said a bored looking Flight Lieutenant, later introduced as Mike MacMorran, the squadron Irishman. He was the only man to have been within sight of a Heinkel bomber, but it broke away before he could do it any harm. 'They gave us RDF, Radio Direction Finding to them that reads books, but it doesn't tell us if the signals we pick up come from one of ours or one of theirs,' he continued with a scowl. 'I speak from the heart, because I got myself shot down by one of these new Beaufighters, fitted, of course, with Radio bloody Direction bloody Finding and with wings full of the nastiest machine guns you've ever heard. The dam' thing appeared from behind a cloud blacker than the Earl o' Hell's waistcoat and blew holes in my tail. I landed, showing my consummate skill as a pilot. My observer had a bit of his ear shot off and was bleeding like a stuck pig, and swearing something terrible. The worst part was that the CO of the Beau squadron sent us each a bottle of Scotch Whisky along with his letter of apology. He obviously had never heard of Jamieson, the patron saint of Irish drinkers.'

Adam felt an affinity with Mike's relaxed personality, which shone among the dispirited and despondent utterances of the others in the squadron. He warmed to Mike's accent which was akin to that heard in St John's. Someone was to point out later that Adam and Mike were the only two who could understand what the other was saying. In spite of Mike's blarney the squadron was a pretty dismal group.

After being checked out Adam joined in the night operations, but after a few months he found himself becoming as dispirited as the others. The crews' morale was at rock bottom because they could not engage the enemy before they had bombed British civilians. The popularity of the RAF, which had been high after the Battle of Britain, had plummeted. One sergeant pilot had been beaten up at a dance hall, by a group of soldiers who had objected to the Air Force types letting the Germans get away with their murderous attacks on British towns and cities.

Part of the difficulty was that the enemy were operating at night over a wide area of the country. Operations in the Battle of Britain had centred upon the use of Operations Rooms on the ground, from which Spitfire and Hurricane fighters were 'vectored' to the attacking bomber forces. In those days, the Controllers could use Radar bearings and Observer Corps sightings from over a large area in guiding the fighter pilots.

With the new airborne equipment nightfighter aircrew had to find their own targets, but the only information they could use had to be within the range of their Radio Direction Finding sets which were not yet fully reliable. Further, the observers were not experienced enough to detect and interpret the signals reliably. Efforts were being made to improve the performance of both gadgets and operators but these efforts had to remain secret.

On one patrol Adam noticed that he was picking up radio signals made up of repetitions of Morse Code dots or dashes. He learned that others had picked up these odd signals. One pilot had flown into an area where the signals were dots only, and when he altered course he got into an area of dashes only. When he circled he could get back to dots then into dashes again. It was possible that they had encountered the rumoured electronic beam that the German bombers followed to their targets. On their next patrol Adam and his crew were able to plot the bearing, the width and the frequencies used in this German 'secret weapon'. On two successive nights he asked other crews to take the same readings and he wrote up a report on the findings. Mike took the exercise one stage further. On his next sortie, he flew along the beam and successfully engaged and destroyed an incoming Heinkel bomber over the North Sea, just off the Humber.

Morale jumped up immediately as crews began to think of the enemy as sitting ducks and they each vied for a shot at a bomber. They had some success, but after two blank nights they realised that there must be more than one beam, or it could be moved. Three civilian scientists came down to visit the squadron to discuss the report that Adam had compiled. For some time they had known about the German beam system. The German bomber pilot flew along the main beam by steering between hearing dots and hearing dashes, until he received signals from an intersecting beam which told him he had ten minutes to target, then another signal from another beam which indicated he had reached target.

One scientist noted that the frequency of the beam reported by Adam matched the frequency of diathermy machines used in hospitals to give heat treatment to patients with muscular problems. These 'boffins', as the scientists became known, rounded up several old diathermy machines from hospital basements, and fitted them in Ansons, which could be flown alongside a beam and interfere with its reception in the enemy bombers.

Adam, together with an observer and a Radio Mechanic, flew an Anson along the area of the enemy beam at night, squirting out rude electronic noises to drown out the German signals. Their efforts were successful. Some stray Heinkels were picked off by Beaufighters well to the South of the Blenheim squadron territory, and the Germans began to change the system drastically. Once again the Blenheims were seeking for targets that never appeared and squadron morale slumped.

Unreasoning hatred of Beaufighters emerged anew as a topic of conversation. They were death traps, unstable in the air, liable to roll over on landing and could only be flown by the best pilots. Mike retained his irreverence and humour. 'If they can only be flown by the most skilful pilots, these are the machines for me and I only wonder that Winston himself has not given me one already. He must surely know that I am the second best pilot in Ballyjamesduff.' His words were prophetic in that two days later the CO announced that they were converting to Beaufighters and that one of these aeroplanes would be arriving after lunch to give them a chance to see and test it.

The aircrew were waiting by the control tower when the spanking new machine arrived with a roar, beat up the runway, did a climbing turn to the right then began its approach. They were all impressed at the way this machine performed, but agreed that it was being delivered by some top-notch pilot just to show them how to do it. The Beau came in at a high approach speed, then whispered on to the ground in a textbook landing. It slowed down quickly to turn and follow the signals into a dispersal site.

'Now we get to see the great flier,' said Mike. His jaw dropped as a small figure in white overalls came out from the hatch on the underside of the fuselage, dropped again as the pilot revealed long blonde hair as she pulled off her helmet, and dropped further still as he uttered, 'Jesus, Mary and Joseph it's herself.' To the surprise of the others he ran straight up to the visitor, hugged her off her feet and kissed her excitedly. One sergeant said admiringly, 'There's a fast worker for you.'

Mike, with his arm round her waist, led the girl to the group, both smiling excitedly. 'Gentlemen and other wretches, you have heard me mention modestly that I am the second best pilot in Ballyjamesduff. Allow me to present to you the first best pilot in that renowned village, my young sister, Deirdre, the queen of the Air Transport Auxiliary.'

Deirdre smiled at the attentive group of men, and her bright blue eyes twinkled. 'Let me hand the Beau over to your Engineering Officer and I'll come back and tell you about her.'

She joined them in the dispersal hut, and sat in the centre of an admiring throng of aircrew. Adam asked how many hours she had in Beaufighters. She chuckled as she answered, 'Fifty minutes. That was my first flight. Once you appreciate that the Beaufighter moves at a hell of a lick, she's a great machine. Mind you I almost wet my knickers coming in at over 90 mph, but there was nothing to it.' One young sergeant, still blushing at her talk of knickers was amazed that what they had seen was her first landing. She admitted she had seen them watching her, so she put on dog, just to impress them. She had heard of difficulties in landing the Mark I model, but she thought the change in the design of the tailplane had improved the elevator control. 'I had no worry about the Beau coping with my own usual sloppy landing technique. I envy you having her to fly. She's a dream, compared to a Blenheim.'

She entranced them further with a mixture of coquetry and technical assurance until the Engineering Officer stuck his head round the door to say that an Oxford had arrived to pick her up. She collected her gear, waved brightly to everyone, shouted it was nice to have met Mike's chums then left hand in hand with her big brother. They watched her speak to a squadron leader who had apparently arrived in the aircraft, saw her kiss Mike then get into the Oxford which taxied off.

They were still chattering about a Beaufighter being flown by a smashing girl like that when Mike returned with the newly arrived Squadron Leader whom he introduced as John Boswell. Someone heckled that he would rather have Deirdre. Mike silenced him by informing him that his sister was well and truly married to a Fleet Air Arm Lt. Commander and had two great children.

John Boswell would be with them for a week, as they took over more aircraft and began their familiarization flying. They noted that he sported the ribbons of the DSO, the Distinguished Service Order and the DFC, the Distinguished Flying Cross, while they could not muster a 'gong' between them.

He began his comments by confessing that he had piloted the Beaufighter that shot at Mike. There was an awkward silence, then a burst of laughter at the expression on Mike's face. Mike recovered his spirits, peered at Boswell's ribbons and said he was looking for the Iron Cross awarded by Hitler. Boswell laughed then said the Beaus were now carrying IFF, a method of identifying friend or foe, so there would no longer be an excuse for being shot down by, or shooting down a friend.

The excitement of the day was capped by the announcement that, with the exception of the Diathermy Anson, there were no patrols set for tonight. Formerly such an announcement would have led to an evening of gloom, complaining and backbiting, but the new outlook led to a spontaneous party, which reached its peak with Mike leading the company in singing of the astonishing charms of a famous Mayor's daughter, while Adam and his crew were droning back and forth in the dark Midlands sky.

In the week that followed, the Engineering Officer led the ground crews through the Maintenance and Repair Manuals and each crew of pilot and observer completed three circuits and a cross country at night. To a man their affection for Deirdre led them into making more and more exuberant claims for the benefits of the Beaufighter. Boswell remarked to Mike as he left that the squadron morale had recovered, all due to a competent landing by Deirdre. Mike remarked that it was a lucky accident that she had been detailed to deliver that aircraft. Boswell admitted that he had arranged for her to make the delivery as he had heard of the kind of remarks the squadron had made about Beaufighters. He knew of her skill as a flier, and bet that her example would silence their objections.

CHAPTER 6

In the five months he had been with the squadron Adam had flown night patrols in Blenheims and in Beaufighters, and became as adept as the others at complaining at being kept away from contact with the enemy. He had logged almost as many hours in the Anson on diathermy patrol. The boffins were convinced that what he called 'driving a noisy truck up and down' had led the Germans to change their plans, so the interference runs were gradually diminished.

One lunchtime he saw a Hudson land on the airfield. A single figure got out and hailed an airman who pointed in the direction of the mess, then saluted. Adam knew that jaunty walk and the atrociously battered hat. He ran to welcome 'Shouter' Humphrey, and ushered him up to the bar. True to form, the pint was raised and out came, ''arness an' 'atches secure'. The Shouter was more rotund than before, but was still his outrageous self. Adam asked after his wife, Mercedes, and Shouter lowered his beer with a dreamy expression on his face. 'She's great. A treasure to me. She's getting slimmer and I'm putting on the beef, and loving it. Another inch round here and I won't be able to fasten the dam' harness, never mind make it secure.' The loud snort, then guffaws of laughter brought the Senior Steward, Flight Sergeant Caldwell, out from his office.

Always a dignified person, Caldwell addressed Adam formally. 'Sir, I must ask you to permit me to buy your guest the pint he already needs.'

Adam was astounded, but Shouter suddenly roared, 'Leading Aircraftsman Cadwallader Caldwell, that's who you are. You served me piss rotten beer in Aden in 1937. You're still up to that I'll bet,' and he flung his arms round his former comrade.

'You were a Warrant Officer in those days, flying a Wildebeest,' reminded Caldwell.

'And I did it bloody well, don't forget. I was Lord of the Desert, remember. I'm still flying, you know. Still fit aircrew. Must be the beer.'

Caldwell smiled at Shouter, then turned to Adam. 'I'm sorry I broke in on your conversation, Sir, but I got excited at seeing Mr Humphrey again and looking so well.' Adam smiled at him and Caldwell grasped Shouter by the hand, 'Cheerio, Sir. Look after yourself. There are too few like you left.' Shouter hugged him and said softly, 'Cheerio, mate, keep up the life of crime.' The Senior Steward's eyes glistened as he turned on his heel and went back to his office.

Shouter wiped away a tear, then composed himself with an almighty swallow on his pint. He had hitched a ride from Prestwick just to say hello. He was leaving that night to head back to the merry-go-round at Dorval. He had laid on an Anson to pick him up in half an hour. 'So tell me what you're up to.'

Adam walked him into the empty anteroom and told him about his disappointment that there had been so little action. Shouter listened sympathetically, then said, 'I might be able to do something for you. There's an old mate of mine, a bit toffee-nosed, but he's all right. I taught him to fly. He's a Group Captain in charge of a hush hush operation and he hinted he was looking for pilots who could do bush flying, like you did. I'll phone him tonight and tell him to get in touch with you.'

Adam pointed out that he was once more indebted to Shouter. He asked if Shouter had volunteered to do the Instructor job to let him get into the war. 'Only partly right, young Adam,' was Shouter's response. 'I found something to keep me in Montreal, remember. Mercedes, my wife. I never knew that the feeling of security I always looked for could come from being with her.'

Shouter looked serious then continued, 'You know my silly toast about 'arness and 'atches. That phrase impressed me when I was a kid looking for something to hold on to. My Mum was a charwoman. My Dad had been in the Army during the first war as a stores clerk, but he couldn't hold down a steady job. They were always having rows, and they would knock each other about. Two or three times I ran away, but I was brought back, given a hiding, and the whole thing started over again. When I was thirteen, I was a big lad for my age, and I thumped my father when he went for my mother late one night. Mum sent for the police and gave me in charge. I ended up in a Borstal home for delinquent boys. I was in a mess. There wasn't a blind thing in my life I could hold on to. One teacher in that Borstal was interested enough to push me into RAF Halton as a boy entrant, the best thing that could have happened to me.'

Shouter thought for a moment. 'You know, it's funny. Being shouted at by corporals and everyone else just meant that someone really knew I existed. I didn't have to be confused. There were rules to follow, even if they were stupid, and I knew what would happen if I didn't stick with the system. After I got accepted for pilot training, the whole idea burst on me, that I was able to cope with complicated things. When I got my pilot's wings and my sergeant's tapes, I was so proud of myself that I went back to let my Mum see what I had done.

'The old man had done a bunk, and she was living with a fat layabout who never did a hand's turn of work. She was still charring. Fatarse said I wasn't coming to live with him in his house. I put my fist in front of his face, reminded him that I had done a job on my father, but could do a better job on him because I was now bigger and tougher. I told him to sod off. He did. I gave my mother seventy quid that I'd saved up for her, told her to keep it out of the hands of that fat slob, and marched out of the house, and never went back.

'I came to realise that the preflight checks, all the things you had to do to find out if the plane was fit to fly, were just like looking round at the way you lived, and making sure of things that would give you support. When you came to 'arness and 'atches secure you were just checking that you were in the system.

'There you are, young Adam, that's what I'm all about. A Squadron Leader Borstal Boy who shouts out how secure he is every time he starts on a beer. I'll have a pint, now. I'm just a passenger going home tonight.'

Two other officers had entered the anteroom and their talk turned to reminiscences of Dorval. Adam was surprised to hear that Don Bennett had joined the RAF again, with the rank of Wing Commander, and had been given a squadron in Bomber Command. It was soon time for Shouter to leave and Adam forgot all about his friend's old mate, the Group Captain.

Shortly after this, he was sent on attachment to Trangarwyth in Wales, ostensibly to try a new version of the Beaufighter fitted with Rolls Royce Merlin engines. On arrival he was interviewed by a senior member of the Security Branch, who took him solemnly through the Official Secrets Act and asked him to sign an acknowledgement that he had been fully informed of the nature of the Act and the consequences of infringing it. He then discussed Beaufighters with pilots on the local squadron, read the Pilot's Notes and flew the Beaufighter Mark II with the Squadron Commander in the Observer's seat behind him. On landing he expressed his delight with the performance of this new version, with Rolls Royce engines.

He met other pilots who asked about his bush flying in Canada. He was sitting in the mess with three pilots when a slightly built Group Captain in a well tailored uniform joined them. The newcomer, with sharp-cut features and bright blue eyes, was introduced as Group Captain Rampton. Adam was surprised when Rampton showed him the hook on his right hand. 'I lost this in France. On mess nights, and only on mess nights, I answer to "Hooky".' He smiled and turned to the others at the table. 'Aitken and I share the privilege of being friends of the great Shouter Humphrey, who taught me to fly in 1935 when I was a sprog Pilot Officer and he was a Flight Sergeant. Shouter told me about this colonial with bush flying experience, but warned me never to let him sing if he has had more than one pint of wallop.'

Rampton told Adam that they had been vetting him for an unusual posting. The station housed an Operational Training Unit of the Special Operations Executive (S.O.E.) in an isolated corner of the airfield. 'This is why we got you entangled in the Official Secrets red tape,' Rampton explained. 'We are impressed by your wider background than most service trained pilots. After lunch we'll put you up in a Lysander just to see how you like it. Now, we're far too hush hush to mingle with this lot. Let's go to our place, for a SOFL, a Special Ops Frugal Luncheon that is.' He gave a snort of laughter at his joke then led them out to a truck in which they were driven to a barbed wire enclosure. At the gate they were each carefully checked in by a Sergeant Station Policeman.

The Westland Lysander was known to Adam in name only. The 'Lizzie' was a chunky high wing monoplane with a single Bristol Mercury radial engine and a sturdy fixed undercarriage. It was originally designed to carry a pilot, an observer and a gunner and to serve as a fighter. As such it went on service in France, but like the Fairey Battle and the Blenheim it proved to be too ponderous for fighter duties, and no match for the German Messerschmitt fighters.

It was reliable and could take off and land in relatively short areas, due to an unusual wing shape and a specially designed system of landing flaps ('A miracle of flappery and slottery' as it had been described). Its excellence in slow flying, a defect in a fighter, became a virtue in Army Co-operation, artillery spotting and moving personnel around battle zones, where only rough and ready landing strips were available.

After lunch Adam was taken on a check flight by the Flying Instructor, Flight Lieutenant Garth Trethewie, a soft spoken Cornishman, who had flown a Lysander in France and had shot down two German bombers. As he taxied out Adam felt he was driving a tank on stilts. When he opened up the throttle for take-off the aeroplane rose like a kite and the clumsiness fell away. At a safe height he tried a stall, which proved jarring and rough without flaps. With flaps he found that the stall was a long time coming but the nose dropped smoothly. With this knowledge and with Trethewie's reminder about attitude and height above ground he tried a landing. He felt the wheels bite firmly but the tail was still up for some way along the runway. He was ordered round again and next time succeeded in a three point touchdown, stopping in a surprisingly short distance.

After a further set of landings and take-offs, Trethewie had him head some distance past a small village. There was a farmhouse, nestled in a clearing in a forest and a small meadow beside it, ringed by trees. 'That's Brewer's Meadow. Land there, but be ready to climb up quickly if I lose my nerve and scream,' the instructor said calmly. Adam looked at the meadow, he saw nothing to entice any sane airman down there, but noted wheel tracks diagonally across the field. He went round, losing height on the downwind leg, and approached using half flap to let him keep his momentum in case he had to lift over the trees in the corner. Once clear he tried full flap, got his tail down nicely, coming to a stop with more than half the diagonal of the field to spare. When he turned round on the ground to take off again, the turning circle appeared to be better than that of the family car at home. Back at the airfield, he grinned at Trethewie and told him he liked the Lysander very much.

Later, when Hooky asked what he thought of the Lysander, Adam admitted that he had enjoyed flying it and thought it was an easy plane to fly, but he guessed it might be difficult to fly well.

'Good for you. Some pilots can only think of it being so ponderous that they would hate to fly it for any length of time. One chap told me it was like driving a London 'bus. I got snooty and asked him if he had ever driven a London bus. He said yes, he had done so for two years before joining up. He now flies Sunderland flying boats in Coastal Command. Have you any idea what we're up to here?'

Adam paused. 'You've talked about hush hush, but I haven't any idea of what there is to hush about. When we landed in Brewer's Meadow I thought you might be smuggling supplies into awkward spots.'

Hooky nodded. 'Half right, my dear chap. We're training experienced pilots to use Lysanders to set down and pick up British and French agents as well as to deliver equipment to the Resistance in enemy occupied territory. Would that kind of thing interest you?'

Adam's reply was an immediate yes. Rampton smiled. 'Glad to hear it. We started these missions in late 1940. While everyone wanted to know when Britain would start to take the fight to the enemy we were doing that all the time. We flew only 22 sorties last year but we'll probably do 100 this year. It's a dicey job but you'll enjoy running your own one man show.'

During dinner Adam met a number of instructors, many of them civilian. On the following morning he flew the Lysander solo and made a cross-wind landing in Brewer's Meadow. His day ended when he and Garth Trethewie were driven to this same field and waited until a pilot about to graduate did a night landing on Brewer's Meadow, dimly lit by bicycle lamps. To simulate the conditions of picking up agents, they scrambled aboard, and watched the pilot's every move intently as he took off with more weight than he had landed with.

He was back with his squadron for only a short time when his posting to Trangarwyth came through. When his fellow pilots asked about it, he told them it had to do with the diathermy flights. They were sympathetic. 'Hard luck, old man. You'll miss all the action when we take our Beaus down South any day now.'

Mike MacMorran was going on a weekend leave to see if he could help Deirdre. Her husband was missing in action and she had received no word of what might have happened to him. Adam asked Mike to add his best wishes to all those from the members of the squadron.

CHAPTER 7

When he reported to Trangarwyth Adam found he had been promoted to Flight Lieutenant. On the course with him were two Squadron Leaders and three other Flight Lieutenants. All were older than he was. In the squadron, Mike McMorran and he, at age 22 had been among the oldest of the active aircrew. Adam admitted that he was a bit stuffy, but his colleagues had not changed from the schoolboys they had been two or three years earlier. They seldom discussed technical matters and only at a superficial level. Having a bloody good piss up or getting a hand into a girl's knickers were the main subjects. The more senior officers on occasions let their hair down and joined in the adolescent horseplay. While Adam could sympathise with these deliberate attempts to let off steam, he was too inhibited to join in readily.

On this course Adam was with a widely experienced, relaxed and sedate group of fliers, content to talk shop among themselves about the charactcristics of aircraft and how to handle them. They all seemed to reflect the adage that there are bold pilots and there are old pilots, but there are no old and bold pilots. Adam realised that by temperament he was covered by this generalisation.

Like Adam, Squadron Leader Lawton and Flight Lieutenant Barlow were scheduled to operate with Lysanders. The other three were training for operations with bombers, which could deliver supplies and ammunition and drop agents by parachute in German occupied territory further away than France.

In addition to their flying training, the pilots were lectured on the social, economic and political conditions in German occupied territory, the organizations involved in the Resistance movements and the political rivalries between different factions, notably in Yugoslavia and in France. This information helped them understand the environment in which the agents had to operate.

To prepare them to cope with being stranded behind enemy lines, they were trained in survival techniques by a Sergeant Major from the Scots Guards. When he taught them woodcraft he was a quiet spoken Scout master, but he underwent an alarming personality change when he taught them how to kill fellow human beings with or without weapons.

Adam's schoolboy French and his time in Montreal enabled him to read the language, but he was discouraged from speaking it as Canadian French pronunciation was uniquely different from that used in the streets of the towns and villages in France.

Morris Lawton, the Squadron Leader from Nottingham had flown Hurricanes in France and in the Battle of Britain. His CO in France had been Wing Commander Sullavan, the hero of Adam's schoolboy days. Adam was interested to hear that while most regular officers had been promoted twice over their pre-war ranks, 'Bull' still bore the rank of Wing Commander, due to his irreverent attitude to and disinterest in anything that did not get him into the air.

As a pre-war fighter pilot, Lawton had no difficulty in handling the Lysander, but found it difficult to navigate on his own in the cockpit without being monitored and vectored by a ground station. As he could not feel confident at using only his own resources to set and maintain his course he asked to be returned to conventional squadron duties and Rampton agreed readily. Bert Barlow misjudged the sudden change in wind speed on his first night landing in Brewer's Meadow and ended up tail high in a ditch. The broken arm and the cracked ribs he suffered put him in hospital. Adam was thus the only replacement to fly Lysanders. Secretly he was relieved at this decision as he had heard that his many hours on Hudsons had suggested him as being suitable for posting to a squadron which used bombers on Special Operations, but he looked forward to undertaking one man operations.

On a long weekend leave in London Adam met up with Mike McMorran and was pleased to find that this Irish broth of a boy in the mess really shared his own indifference to the frenetic round of booze ups and girlie shows preferred by the others. Mike had the use of a flat in South Kensington and he gave Adam a vast bedroom with a four poster bed in which the owner, a Duchess no less, was reputed to have entertained visiting cellists when they came to play at the nearby Albert Hall. He took Adam to a number of museums and small galleries in the district.

Deirdre joined them at a lunch time piano recital given by Myra Hess and took them for lunch afterwards. She was in high spirits as she had just heard unofficially that her husband was alive in a German Prisoner of War camp. To celebrate she sang an outrageous version of Tipperary at the top of her voice as they marched arm in arm along the crowded Kensington High Street. Two haughty ladies registered their well bred shock when they heard 'That's the wrong place to tickle Mary' from someone who obviously should have known better.

In spite of the German blitz attacks and disturbed sleep Adam felt relaxed as he caught the train to join the Special Duties Operational Unit in Sussex. Like the training unit, the operational group was housed in a remote corner of Tangmere airfield, sequestered behind a barbed wire fence, with a 24 hour guard and the personnel were discouraged from mixing with members of the other groups on the station.

The agents were housed in a cottage at a distance from the compound. The flying personnel were not told anything about the agent or why he or she was being sent into France. Pilots would meet their passenger or passengers in the briefing room just before take-off. At these briefing sessions the weather conditions along the route were forecast, the code signals of the day were given, the charts were discussed and the surrounding terrain was described, as well as the type of load to be delivered e.g. arms, ammunition, money or wireless sets. The pilot was introduced to the agent using code names only and he explained the various aspects of the flight including the short take-off and landing distances.

The pilot and his passengers were searched meticulously for small pocket rubbish such as railway tickets, theatre or cinema stubs, or restaurant receipts which could inform enemy captors that the peasant they were interrogating had recently travelled on a London 'bus, eaten at the Savoy, or watched the statuesque girls at the Windmill. At the aircraft the passengers were shown the best way to climb the ladder fixed outside the rear cockpit, a thoughtful modification which had overcome many difficulties for agents unused to the many undignified ways to get into, or out of, an aeroplane.

Replacements for Morris Lawton and Bert Barlow had not yet been selected and there were only a few experienced pilots involved in the French operations. Thus Adam found himself accumulating flying hours at a faster rate than he had expected. After several missions he had found a number of favoured routes. If his destination was Brittany for example, he kept well North of Portsmouth, left the coast with the Isle of Wight to port, and darted over the English Channel avoiding all Royal Navy ships, as they were known to be trigger happy. When he was out of 'friendly' range he kept clear of German stationary vessels which could warn defending fighters or anti-aircraft guns of his approach. He swung wide of the Channel Islands then headed straight for the French mainland, flying low under the cliffs on which the German Radio Direction Finding

Stations were located.

Most of his flying was at night and by the time he had carried out over 20 operations he had become confident in his ability to get the passenger agents to their destination, deliver the goods to the Resistance group and return safely with agents and/or material to the South Coast base. On returning to Tangmere, once his load had been whisked away and he had handed the aircraft over to the maintenance crew, he would report to the Intelligence Officer on any unusual conditions or problems he had encountered. At that time he would pass on verbal messages from the Resistance leaders dealing with matters such as the effectiveness of the equipment or rumours of the Germans' intention to change identity passes or to modify security procedures.

After one delivery and pickup of two of the agents he had taken over on earlier flights he was interviewed by a new WAAF Intelligence Officer, much younger than Flight Officer Birkenshaw, the efficient ex-headmistress who usually put him through his paces. He gave her details of the flight and commented that the new landing field was good for their purposes as it was set in some really bleak countryside where the enemy could not easily lay an ambush. He was surprised when he was asked if it was as bleak as Fenwick Moor. He began to respond that it was just as bleak, when he stopped and looked closely at his interrogator. She smiled and gave a familiar laugh at his perplexed frown and open mouth. 'You're new, but I know you,' he concluded lamely.

'Flight Officer Birkenshaw is on special attachment. I'm Valerie who drove you to see your ancestral home just after you arrived in Prestwick.' She explained that at that time she had been waiting to be commissioned. She had now completed her Intelligence training and this was her very first posting, right in the thick of hush hush. Adam congratulated her. She displayed her one thin stripe. 'Assistant Section Officer MacKay, if you please, Sir,' she exclaimed proudly, 'and you're my first customer. Isn't it great? But we have work to do.' She took him through the list of routine questions. At the end, she asked 'Did I cover everything?' Adam reminded her that she had not asked about the weather conditions. The pilots were expected to provide information to the meteorologists on which to base their predications.

Later they met in the mess and chatted easily, like old friends reminiscing about old times, although in their case they had shared only a few hours. She had gone back twice to see Mr and Mrs Ferguson in Fenwick village. Their son had finished his second tour and was now instructing on an Operational Training

Unit. Valerie suddenly said, 'Do you remember Captain Bligh, that terrible man we picked up at Kilmarnock Station?' Adam remembered the corpulent, grumpy Group Captain who had been offended when he thought that only a lowly Flying Officer had been sent to meet him. 'Well,' Valerie continued, 'he was only at Prestwick for about three days. I don't know what he was supposed to be doing, but he offended everyone and they told him to leave. Next day when I drove him back to Kilmarnock, he complained that no one would cooperate with him. I never said a word the whole way as I didn't want to spoil my chances of getting a commission.'

The next few months went smoothly for Adam. The flight came up to strength when two pilots joined as replacements. Although the routine flying was akin to driving something between a taxi and a delivery truck, he enjoyed the freedom to set and fly his own course. There was a spice of danger in being over enemy occupied territory but he acknowledged the greater danger the agents faced. On one occasion one agent to be returned to Britain had somehow been rescued from the Gestapo. He had to be lifted bodily into the aircraft and on the return journey kept shouting that he could not remember any more. In helping him out of the aircraft, Adam saw that his finger nails had been drawn out and his face was covered with burn marks.

On another occasion, André, a resistance leader he had come to know quite well, informed him that the dark haired vivacious young girl he had delivered ten days previously had been betrayed to the Gestapo. She had been raped by her jailers, then was tortured every day in such a manner as to mutilate her. She had not told the Gestapo what they wanted to know and the torture was to continue. A member of André's resistance group had infiltrated the prison and given her a cyanide pill as the only real help that could be offered to a colleague.

An easy friendship sprang up with Valerie. They would cycle around the area, or visit Chichester. They found a secluded shingle beach which had not been littered with tank traps and barbed wire where they enjoyed reading and picnicking and simply being in each other's company.

They talked of their hopes for after the war. She described her conviction that tooth care was important for the future health of a child, and that she should become qualified as a children's dentist to do work in prevention. He told of his commitment to go back into the Aitken empire, not in insurance, though, but in other parts of the business where some enterprise on the part of management could generate financial benefits for the employees. He was thinking of something like profit sharing. To do that would require some way of managing risk. Adam felt that risk management was the most important technique for an up and coming business executive. He wondered about the Aitken group starting in the commercial aviation field, but he would have to have information on the potential market for passenger and cargo carrying before he decided how risky this new venture would be.

Valerie turned over on to her front. 'Adam Aitken. You are the world's greatest stick in the mud.'

Adam sat up indignantly 'I am not. Wait till you meet my father.' He grinned. She smiled, turned over and lay back. He leaned towards her and pronounced slowly, 'Valerie MacKay. You are a flibbertigibbet.'

She was up in a flash, her eyes blazing. 'I am not. I have never flibbertigibbeted in my whole life. Besides I don't know what the word means.'

'Neither do I,' retorted Adam.

She pinched his cheek. 'Come on Newfoundlander. It's time to get back. I have to wash my hair tonight. And do you know what I'm going to use on it? Flibberdiwhatsit.' He laughed, and they cycled back to the station.

CHAPTER 8

A few days later Adam and his Commanding Officer, Wing Commander Goudie were summoned to a special briefing. They faced two RAF Group Captains, a Royal Navy Commander, a dapper French Officer wearing a square hat, with an elegantly cut tan tunic, breeches and gleaming riding boots. A tall, willowy, officer from the Women's Royal Naval Service was introduced as the secretary and a small, pompous civil servant ignored the presence of the Commanding Officer of the Unit and announced that he, an Under Secretary and the Cabinet representative, would take the chair. Adam glanced at 'Goodie' Goudie and saw him frowning in disbelief at this discourtesy.

The exile French Général de Gaulle had made a demand to have a French Admiral brought over to Britain. The War Cabinet had consented, and had constituted this body to arrange the transport. Their two previous attempts to evacuate the Admiral by sea had failed, resulting in the loss of a mine-sweeper and a submarine and over a hundred survivors in German Prisoner of War camps. The powers that be were smarting at the 'gigantic balls up', as the rescue attempts had been termed by someone high up in Government.

The Admiral was now in the hands of the Resistance, but the leader of the Resistance group did not want to have to take responsibility for such a valuable person much longer. The complications were first that the Admiral was wanted by a rival Resistance group, all ardent Communists who had no respect for high ranking officers or their class privileges; further, they blamed him for having forced French labourers to work in the U boat repair yards at La Rochelle. The second complication was that several of these forced labourers had committed acts of sabotage in the submarine pens. The Germans held the Admiral responsible and wanted to get their hands on him to exact vengeance. He was in double jeopardy and obviously the longer he remained exposed in France, the greater were the risks for him and anyone who shielded him.

The leader, code named Tirebouchon, had contacted a British agent on another mission in France, and had been advised that the only way to rescue the Admiral was by an air lift. No aircraft had ever landed in their territory before, but they had a very good field, well away from German patrols. The Admiral would be at the field at 16.00 the following afternoon. They did not want to arrange the pick up at night as they would be better able to defend against a daylight attack by the rival Resistance workers.

The Under Secretary indicated that the group should now formally discuss the rescue mission. He would begin by putting the problem into perspective. Adam had no interest in participating in a long drawn discussion of what was to him a straightforward mission. Heads were still nodding in agreement with this traditional Whitehall approach as Adam spoke up. 'I presume that I will be flying this mission, gentlemen, so let me have a say in it. I take it that you're all agreed that the Admiral is to come over here?' There were murmurs of agreement. 'And he is to be brought over tomorrow afternoon?' Again the agreement. Adam stood up, 'Then the only problem is to get there in one piece and get back with a passenger in one piece, and that's my job. Four o'clock in the afternoon is as good a time as any. In fact it's preferable to operate in daylight as the landing field will be a new one for me. And it should be an in and out job. No brass band. No ceremony of any sort.'

The Cabinet representative interrupted, 'Of course we will require film of the Admiral arriving here.'

'Goodie' Goudie, cut in, 'I agree with Flight Lieutenant Aitken. No pictures here. We cannot have that or any kind of publicity. Flight Lieutenant Aitken will bring him back here and then you can take your Admiral away from the field anywhere you want and get as many photographs as you like. But certainly not here.'

One of the Group Captains grunted his agreement. The Under-secretary insisted that he and his group would be on hand tomorrow as the welcoming committee. 'No cameras of any sort,' interrupted Adam. It was the under-secretary's turn to scowl but he conceded grudgingly that they would take the Admiral to some other airfield for the official pictures. Adam smiled to himself, thinking, 'Where's your stick in the mud now, Miss Flibbertigibbet?'

Having ascertained the procedure for confirming the identity of the Resistance Group and of the Admiral, Adam prepared to leave the meeting. The under-secretary asked when he would return to brief the group. 'Goodie' butted in quickly 'We will not be briefing you on this or any other mission. Flight Lieutenant Aitken will make his arrangements. I will supply the back up arrangements for him. But we don't announce them to all and sundry.'

The Group Captain who had grunted previously spoke up. 'Quite right, Goudie. You and your pilot have to run this show. God knows what we old farts are doing here.' The secretary smirked and made a note in her pad. The under-secretary looked uncomfortable. The French officer said that it was an important mission for General de Gaulle and they should wish the Wing Commander and the pilot all luck in their venture. 'Yes, that's right. Make a note of that, Madam Secretary.'

'Goodie' dealt the last blow. 'I'm afraid we can have no notes or any minutes floating around here of what has been discussed. I shall make a formal complaint to RAF security that you were not formally cleared before coming here.'

'But we were authorised by Cabinet to come here,' the under secretary blustered.

'I was not authorised to receive you,' retorted 'Goodie'. The Group Captain said he would try to sort things out and left to telephone some higher authority.

Adam left to organize the mission. The signals officer put him in touch with Tirebouchon, who spoke excellent colloquial English, so that Adam could instruct him in clearing the field, laying out a wind direction marker, and having the Admiral, code named Reynaud, ready to move quickly to the plane whenever he signalled. He learned that Reynaud would be accompanied by a British agent, Ariadne.

Next he checked with his ground staff flight sergeant to make sure the aircraft would be serviced. He then headed for the map room to find the charts and to the Intelligence Section to read any files which Valerie could find for him.

The proposed airfield turned out to be a version of Brewer's Meadow located in the Monts d'Arrées to the East of Brest. Photographs showed a bare patch of turf surrounded by a forest of old trees in the middle of what had once been hunting land. The chateau, along with several servants' cottages, had fallen into disrepair. Access was by woods tracks only and there were no main roads nearby, no towns or villages to house German troops. The updated information was that no German troops were stationed within 10 miles of the landing airfield.

He asked Valerie to check if there were any more recent signals so that he could reduce all risks to a minimum. They were going through the most recent log sheets when the CO knocked and entered. 'May I interrupt your work for a moment, Miss MacKay?' Goudie asked. 'I wanted to congratulate Flight Lieutenant Aitken at putting the Under Secretary to the Cabinet in his place this afternoon. I doubt if anyone has ever spoken to him like that. I must confess, Adam, that I felt I would end up by saying "Yes Sir, no Sir, three bags full" until you spoke up and told him what was what. After you'd gone, he asked for your name. When I told him, he scowled and said, "Christ, not Beaverbrook's son?" I had to tell him I didn't know.'

Adam shook his head, 'I'm glad to say I'm no relative of the Minister of Aircraft Production.'

He expressed his concerns at the way in which their tight security had been breached. As a pilot, this was the first time he had heard the story of the mission. The security blunder by these bungling outsiders had occurred over twenty-four hours before the mission, plenty of time for the enemy to find out.

'Goodie' said that he had spoken to the visitors about the need for top security, but he was uneasy about possible leaks, although they all swore they had not told anyone about this operation. The Group Captain reported that Headquarters Security had cleared the operation but confirmed that no photographs were to be taken or written accounts to be made. 'Goodie' had contacted his superiors at Group about calling the whole thing off but had been told to continue as the operation was of the highest priority to the War Cabinet. He wished Adam good luck and left.

Valerie exclaimed, 'Will you never learn the right way to behave, you colonial clodhopper? Why can't you be more of a stick in the mud.' She reached over and took Adam's hand. 'Make sure you look after yourself and come back in one piece.'

'Right, me old trout,' said Adam in a fine outport accent, chucked her under the chin and went to interview the met officer who gave him a prediction of fine clear weather for Northern France, with frost expected at nightfall. A ten mile an hour westerly wind would hold until sunset when it would go northerly at about five miles per hour. This prediction was repeated the next morning and again as Adam made his preparations in the afternoon.

At the hangar the Under Secretary and his group were there to shake Adam's hand and to wish him good luck. 'This is an important mission. It could be a political bombshell if it didn't come off. Charles de Gaulle, you know, can be a bit difficult.'

Adam responded with an imitation of Mr Pilowsky, his tailor in St John's. 'Now don't you worry about anything. Not a thing. Leave it to me, Sir. I've done it before and I'll do it again.' He resisted the temptation to add the Newfoundland colloquial, 'me son, me son'. The Cabinet representative looked suspicious for a moment then shook Adam's hand again. The others called out their good wishes, and the French officer kissed him on both cheeks and saluted with a swagger.

Adam put on his flying jacket and headed for the Lysander. A cheerful red-haired rigger who helped him get settled in the cockpit asked if the French Officer was his fiancée. Adam scowled. 'I hope you'll both be very happy,' Ginger grinned infectiously. Adam laughed and gave him the classical two finger gesture then began the start up procedure.

He took off and climbed to 3,000 feet. As he throttled back he could see the spread of the coast of the English channel. There was a convoy guarded by the notoriously trigger happy Royal Navy, so he kept inland, with the Channel to port. As he passed Poole, he mused that many of the early Newfoundland families had come from this area, and, with Torquay to starboard, he put his head more South towards enemy territory. A few miles off the shore of France he flew high over a fishing fleet until he reached a promontory when he came down to sea level below a large gun emplacement with a powerful wireless transmitter beside it.

Out of sight he came to a small stream flowing on to the beach. He climbed over the shore line and identified a road leading to a row of cottages. He could see Brest in the distance, and, after a short time on the course he had worked out in the map room, he found the clearing and circled it to get a good look at the conditions.

The grass was smooth and there no bushes, sheep, cattle, or goats, wires or fences to obstruct his landing. White sheets were laid out to show that the wind was from the West. He began his approach to use as little of the field as possible, in case he had to take off in a hurry. Everything seemed quiet and deserted until a group of about twenty men carrying rifles emerged from the woods and stood quietly. He touched down, braked and taxied back to meet them.

CHAPTER 9

The leader of the Resistance Group introduced himself, using the agreed codeword 'Tirebouchon'. He was a tall, bespectacled, earnest young man, wearing a dark suit, blue scarf and black beret. As he accepted the two packages which Adam had been asked to deliver, he said 'Ah, money,' and talked of the various expenses he had to meet. When Adam congratulated him on his excellent colloquial English, he explained he had been at college in England for eighteen months.

Adam noticed a group of people surrounding a little old man, all engaged in heated argument. The little fellow was flinging his arms about shouting '*Non*' and trying unsuccessfully to free himself from the grasp of two burly labourers and to attack his tormentor, a peasant woman, wearing a black headscarf, black dress and an apron made from an old canvas sack. Tirebouchon identified the old victim as the Admiral Reynaud, and the aggressive peasant woman as Ariadne. As this group moved slowly and noisily toward the aircraft, Adam was surprised to recognise the harridan yelling at the unfortunate old chap. It was Flight Officer Mavis Birkenshaw, the Intelligence Officer from the Special Operations Unit.

The prim and proper Mavis was now a down to earth peasant woman, dressed in rough black clothing, with a basket slung over her arm. She acknowledged Adam brusquely. 'Hello Aitken, we've got ourselves a right balls up here. The bloody Admiral doesn't want to go up in an aeroplane. I gave him some Cognac to take his mind off flying, but he's swigged the whole lot and now he's unpleasantly sozzled. To add to the general fun and gaiety there's a swarm of local Communists in the woods looking for him to blow his head off. They'll be here any minute to shoot the lot of us.'

Tirebouchon confirmed Mavis' analysis of the situation and felt that Adam should take off as soon as possible. He joined Mavis and the two labourers in screaming at the Admiral. Shots fired in the woods indicated that the pursuers had caught up with them. Adam shouted at Mavis to get up the ladder into the aircraft then got one of the labourers to stand on the middle rung. His colleague on the ground passed the Admiral to him, then Mavis pulled while he pushed the Admiral aboard, none too gently. Adam scrambled into the cockpit and started the engine. Several armed men appeared out of the woods behind them. Tirebouchon waved his men into cover behind bushes at the edge of the wood, and they opened fire.

Adam needed no urging, and opened up the throttle. He checked the gauges as the aircraft started to move and was reaching behind for his safety harness when he heard shots and a crack appeared in the canopy. He felt a blow on the side of his face and left shoulder, and he lost feeling in his left arm. The Lizzie was trundling forward, gaining speed and, in order to gain height he draped his useless arm over the control column, and leaned back gradually as he set the throttle. With more bangs from further hits, the aircraft rose and Adam headed North to return to base.

At 2,000 feet and on course, he throttled back to cruising speed and adjusted the trim to accommodate for the two passengers. He then took stock of his own situation. He had no strength or sensation in his left arm but he could fly by bending and twisting his body to move the control column held tightly under his armpit. If he released pressure on this arm, it became painful and began to bleed. He explained the position to Mavis. He heard some shouting from the back, the Frenchman making a fuss again, then a short peremptory command from Mavis which seemed to do the trick. Then she passed him a pad saying, 'Fold this under your armpit. It'll do as a cushion and as a tourniquet.'

Adam found this provided relief so that he could fly straight and level. The sun was still above the horizon on his left, and he realised he could just get home in daylight. Mavis picked up the chart and followed him as he pointed out the Channel Islands on their right. Straight ahead was the English coast and she said she could see Dartmouth with the moor behind. He started to explain that they would carry on along the coast, but never finished. His head fell forward and the aircraft went into a shallow dive. He woke with the scream in his headset. 'Wake up, Adam, you can't go to sleep.' He grabbed at the controls, groaned at the pain in his arm, and eventually resumed his previous method of control. Mavis said, 'I will keep talking to you to keep you awake. Tell me what you are doing. Come on now.'

Adam thanked her and pointed out that he was regaining the height he had lost when he had passed out. He asked how she had got things so quiet in the back. 'I gave the wretched man some of my brandy, and he flaked out just about the time that you did. I think you can hold this course. I can see The Isle of Wight dead ahead.'

'Thank you, navigator,' Adam said as he confirmed the heading on the compass and they kept up a conversation about the course, the weather and the absence of other aircraft, friendly or foe. Mavis explained that she and her family had done a lot of sailing from the Isle of Wight, so she knew this part of the Channel. Twice Adam felt he was going to pass out, but he was jerked back to reality by a stern command from Mavis. Once he crossed over the coast he headed directly for his base with Selsey Bill to starboard and radioed that he had the necessary parcels to deliver, but he was wounded. He didn't want to be diverted to a satellite field and was going to come straight in, so would they please clear the field for him.

After two further episodes of near fainting he had the airfield in view and was cleared to land. Mavis told him for the last time to stay awake. He murmured, 'Yes, Mavis,' then warned her to hold tight. He took the direct approach with full flap to lose height then sideslipped the last few feet to land firmly and roll up to the official welcoming party. He heard Mavis say, 'You did well, Adam.' He throttled back, switched off the engine, then fainted. He was dimly aware of Mavis telling people to look after the pilot first, then he blacked out completely.

Adam came to with someone patting his face firmly and telling him to wake up. It was not Mavis, but Paddy Reilly the unit Medical Officer, who smiled and asked, 'Who the hell is Mavis? You've been calling me Mavis for a long time.' Adam explained who it was and Reilly asked if she had given Adam the tourniquet which had done the trick. When Adam affirmed this he was told that he should be very grateful for having exactly the right pad for the job.

Paddy reported that in the two hours that Adam had been out they had given him a blood transfusion, sutured the wound in his shoulder, and taken a preliminary X-ray which had shown up two bullets in the scapular region. However they would have to check the X-rays again once Adam was able to co-operate a bit more in the examination. For the moment, everything was up to date and the shoulder had been immobilised. An orderly was standing by to tidy him up and then he could have the visitors who were waiting to see him.

The first visitor was 'Goodie' Goudie, who, after enquiring how he felt, asked about the possible reasons for the ambush by the hostile Resistance group. Could they have been informed by someone from the Under Secretary's group? Adam was not sure, but he felt that Tirebouchon was a bit too inexperienced to be aware of any possible leak in his own security.

The Wing Commander then relaxed. 'Do you know I'm sorry we didn't let them have a film camera on the tarmac as you taxied in, just to get the expression on the Under Secretary's face. He had spent the whole time rehearsing his speech, you know, "*Bien venue en Angleterre, mon Admiral*". In his mind the distinguished sailor would draw his sword and they would kiss each other's cheeks. Old Charlie de Gaulle would be happy to have his comrade in arms looked after in such a civilised way. He would praise chummy's efforts to Churchill, and there would be a knighthood in the next Honours List. I'm sure that's what he had in mind.'

Goudie smiled at the recollection. 'The shambles when you stopped was hilarious. Mavis had everyone engaged in getting you out. She was a tower of strength, looking like a farm servant with vomit all over her skirt and roaring out commands like a drill sergeant. The Under-Secretary asked her about the Admiral and was told, 'Just keep out of the way, you silly little man!' He did. When the medics had you under control, she brought the Admiral out, almost by the scruff of the neck. That poor Cabinet fellow's face fell a mile, when he saw the drunken little sot. He had wet his trousers and had been sick over himself as well as over Mavis and he reeked of brandy. He hadn't a clue what was happening but just stood there mumbling to himself. Mavis showed him no mercy. She held him by the scruff of the neck and told us he was the wretch who kept you hanging around because he didn't like to fly. He got you ambushed and he got you shot.

'The French officer whisked the Admiral off to a car and the rest of the party got into theirs and they all scuttled off with their tails between their legs. I never heard the speech of welcome.' Goudie guffawed and Adam smiled.

After he had made the expected offer to help in any way, the Wing Commander told Adam he had put up a good show then left. The next visitors turned out to be the Unit's total Intelligence strength, Mavis and Valerie. Mavis, back in uniform, and smelling of carbolic soap, shook him cordially by the hand. Valerie kissed him warmly. After telling them about his state of health and what had been done to him, Adam expressed his surprise at coming across Mavis in France. She agreed it was unusual for a member of the Unit staff to go into the field, but she had hiked and camped in the district and had met the Admiral when her husband served under his command before the war. 'I never guessed what a miserable toad he could be. Father Pierre suspects he really was a collaborator, you know, and he wanted to tell you, but we had to leave in a hurry, when the shooting started. I hope the good father wasn't harmed in the fight we left behind.'

Adam looked blank, so she explained, 'You met Father Pierre as Tirebouchon, the Resistance leader. He did part of his training as a priest near Manchester.'

Adam suggested that Father Pierre's suspicion should be included in a report about the Admiral. Mavis said she had already done so in her report, sent as a priority, with copies to the Under-secretary and all the members of the group who had been down to meet the Admiral. She blamed the Admiral for the mix up in the mission, resulting in the wounding of the pilot, who had nevertheless managed to get them back in one piece, showing bravery and skill. She was getting warmed up to her eulogy of the blushing Adam, when he interrupted. 'Hold on, remember you did the navigation for me and kept me awake, as well as keeping our gallant Frenchman in order. And what's more, the doctor tells me you gave me the best tourniquet I could have been given.'

Mavis' expression froze, then she blushed and, giving a lame excuse at having to go on duty, she left the room hurriedly. Valerie was smiling. 'Adam, you can be a silly man, can't you?' Adam was not aware of any recent silliness he had committed. In some puzzlement he asked, 'Did I offend Mavis? I didn't mean to. I just wanted to thank her for saving my life.'

Valerie shook her head and smiled. 'Mavis gave you a sanitary towel. She was bringing over some French ones for our female agents to carry in their handbags when they were sent to France. If they were stopped and searched, they would be in trouble if they were carrying spares with English written all over them. She was embarrassed that you might think it was one of hers. She is of the old school who would not admit to menstruation and most certainly not to a man.' Adam was now embarrassed, and asked Valerie to get some flowers to convey his thanks and apology to Mavis.

The orderly came in to send Valerie packing and to prepare Adam for his evening meal. The next visitor was Ginger, the fitter who had been cheeky about him being kissed by the French Officer. Ginger proudly confessed that it was his blood that Adam had got. He then presented Adam with a well-thumbed paperback of Kipling's *Captains Courageous* which was written about Newwhatsit. 'That place you come from. All the maintenance wallahs wrote their names in it and wanted to be remembered to you, because you're a good bloke.' Adam was too overwhelmed to object to this maltreatment of the name of his island birthplace. Paddy Reilly came back and asked Ginger to leave. Adam told Paddy that Ginger had to be treated with respect as he was now a blood brother. Ginger gave a thumbs up and a wink and went out.

Paddy said he wanted Adam rested as the next morning he would be going to an Orthopaedic Unit at Beaulieu, a former country house converted to a hospital, where he would undergo more intensive X-rays and be examined by a famous Harley Street specialist.

CHAPTER 10

Next morning, at Beaulieu, he was posed in front of several large X-ray cameras, then spent the rest of the morning in bed and feeling gloomy until Sir Wilfred Chinley appeared. He was a short, stocky, bustling man who seemed to revel in taking control of situations. He had a North Country accent, and began by addressing Adam slowly and clearly. Once he realised that this Newfoundlander spoke and understood English, he doubled his rate of delivery and let forth the vernacular. 'You're bloody lucky, I say. Bloody lucky. Oh, I know you don't think so. You're asking yourself "What's this daft bugger on about, eh? Here am I, you're saying. A bullet in me shoulder that wasn't there two days ago. What's so lucky about that"? You're bustin' to ask me that question if I would only keep me mouth shut for long enough. Right then I'll tell you. You're bloody lucky because the bullet stopped where it did. If it had gone on it would have torn your neck about and you would have been empty of blood in no time at all.' He stopped long enough for Adam to register his message.

When he reckoned Adam was about to speak he started up again, 'In a sense you're just as unlucky as you were lucky. The bullet stopped because it hit tough hard bone, and it smashed off a long thin splinter. That's what looked like another bullet when your doctor took the X-ray yesterday. This broken bit of bone could interfere with the action of the ball and socket arrangement at the top of your arm and give you a useless shoulder.' Adam felt and looked crestfallen, and was about to ask about treatment when Sir Wilfred started off again. 'Cheer up, son. I told you that you were lucky, didn't I? Have you ever known me to lie? Course you haven't. You're lucky because you're in the hands of the best shoulder man in the business. That's right – me.'

Adam had heard of snake oil salesman, but felt he was in the presence of a master. Sir Wilfred's spiel continued. 'See, there you are smiling, and you've every reason to do so, young Adam. The things I can do in and around the shoulder are miraculous. I often think I should become a Catholic so that the Pope can make me a Saint. Saint Wilfred. They could call a railway station after me. Like St Pancras.'

Adam's spirits soared as he realised that in spite of the mountebank performance, he had been told the hard truth and reassured at the same time. Sir Wilfred explained that in three days, Adam would be transferred from the general ward to the special surgical unit where he and his surgical team would remove the bullet and splinter. They would then debride the wound, getting rid of the fragments of shattered bone. After that his whole shoulder would be immobilised and remain so for several weeks. Then physiotherapy at a rehabilitation centre, then leave, then back to the RAF as good as new.

Things went along as Sir Wilfred decreed. After all the procedures had been completed, Sir Wilfred gave him another 'you're bloody lucky' lecture. This time he told Adam there had been a risk of him ending up with a useless arm at one stage of the proceedings, when some odd infection had blown up in the wound. 'But you were bloody lucky to be in the hands of Jessie Rodgers, a nurse who doesn't put up with nonsense like blood poisoning.'

Adam recalled two or three days when he felt listless and dispirited and his shoulder throbbed like hell. That was when the formidable Sister in charge of the Orthopaedic Unit had been unusually concerned and solicitous about his progress. When he improved she returned to being the martinet he had come to know.

At the end of six weeks Adam was allowed to take his arm out of a sling long enough to attend Buckingham Palace to have the Distinguished Service Order bestowed upon him by the King. Shortly after this he was summoned to the unofficial French Embassy. His skill and daring were proclaimed by the elegant French Officer who had kissed him farewell on his trip to pick up the Admiral, who, incidentally was not at the ceremony. General de Gaulle invested him with the *Croix de Guerre* and kissed him on both cheeks. Adam had an irreverent thought of what Ginger's comments might be, and it was his smile at this thought that the photographer caught for the official record.

After these ceremonies, he went on leave with Valerie to her family home in Troon on the West Coast of Scotland, a few miles away from the Prestwick ferry terminal. Valerie's mother and father made Adam feel at home with them once they had stopped being overawed by him as a wounded hero. They had to be persuaded not to help him with tasks involving his left arm and hand.

Linda, Valerie's twelve year old sister, was starry eyed and said little in his presence until one meal time she asked him to pass the salt. Adam complied with her request, but the salt was to his left, and that meant a complex procedure.

He could not extend his arm spontaneously, but he had been shown how to use finger movements on a flat surface. He placed his fingertips lightly on the tablecloth and began to walk his hand toward the salt shaker, like some five legged beast. When he reached the shaker, he grabbed it firmly and snatched it back to his right hand, then passed it to the wide eyed Linda. Every one at the table had watched this extraordinary performance in silence until Linda burst into giggles and announced that after all that palaver, Adam had passed the pepper pot. Adam joined in the general laughter and at all subsequent meals he was ribbed about Newfoundlanders who didn't know pepper from salt.

He found it easy to be within the MacKay family group, sharing in the banter, and easy conversation. Colin, Valerie's brother, was not at home. He was serving as First Lieutenant on a destroyer on Atlantic convoy protection duty, and occasionally telephoned from Northern Ireland when he ended a run in Londonderry. Adam recognised the MacKays' deep love when they talked of their son with strong pride showing on their faces, followed by a fleeting frown of worry as they thought of the dangers he faced. He felt some regret that he had not had a relaxed family life like this.

One evening Valerie took him to the Orangefield Hotel just beside the Prestwick Terminal. She thought it would be best if they wore uniform as the bar would be filled by others in uniform. Mrs MacKay whispered to Adam, 'She just wants to show off her new uniform to her friends there.' In the lounge bar, Adam ordered a Pimms for Valerie and a glass of lemonade for himself. By the time the drinks were served their table was filled by a group of girls, most of them in uniform, all ignoring him in favour of keeping up a barrage of questions to Valerie. One girl in civilian clothes saw his arm in a sling and asked him how he had hurt it. He told her it was an accident. She asked him about Newfoundland, and was that where he came from. Adam corrected her pronunciation. 'New Finland? Isn't that near Russia?' said the young lady and turned away to join in the chatter.

Looking round the lounge, he saw a familiar face and recognised the tall craggy figure of Kazlowski, standing at the bar. He excused himself but no one paid attention as he walked over to the Flight Engineer with whom he had flown the Atlantic. 'Well, look at you, a new stripe, a sore arm and medals for shooting down hundreds of Krauts. What are you up to now?' Adam said he was on Special Duties and Kaz grunted and changed the subject. He was still crossing the Atlantic as Flight Engineer, but now on Liberators. 'Everyone is bringing these heavy bombers over now. I reckon they're going to really start plastering Germany with high explosives, any day now.'

Adam asked how Shouter was doing. Kaz drained his glass slowly. 'I forgot, you couldn't know. He was piloting a Liberator with three ferry crews back to Gander. Halfway across he radioed that he had been jumped by a Focke Wulf Condor and no more was heard of him. That was three weeks ago. He's on the books as "Missing believed killed," but he must be a goner.' Adam fought back his tears. There was no reason why such a lively boisterous man should meet such an end, and his shout never again be heard in a tavern. He looked at Kazlowski. 'Let's drink to Shouter.' He got them a pint each. They both raised their beer. A nod and they let rip with ''arness and 'atches secure,' then drained their pints, unaware of the sudden silence that had fallen on the lounge bar. 'I don't think Shouter could have done it better,' said Kaz.

Two men pushed their way through the crush at the bar. They greeted Adam and Kaz with enthusiasm. One of them said, 'We know that shout. We served with him before the war. Any friends of Shouter Humphrey are friends of ours. What'll you have?' Adam was about to refuse their offer when he was gripped by his bad arm, winced and gave a groan as he was pulled round to face an irate Valerie, who was shaking his arm vigorously. 'How dare you behave like that? I wanted you to meet my friends and you sneaked off to get drunk and make an exhibition of yourself with this . . . person here.' Adam was bewildered.

Kaz was equal to it all, 'Lookee here, captain lady. Adam is not drunk. I've seen him drunk and it's the most boring thing you could imagine. Adam and I have lost a friend called Shouter. That's because he always shouted. And we have just shouted Shouter's favourite shout to pay our last respects to him. He wore the same uniform as you and Adam and I wouldn't want you to sour our memory of him.'

Valerie looked at Kaz who smiled encouragingly. One of the strangers looked at Valerie then turned to Adam. 'We'd best be off. Thanks for doing that for Shouter. Christ, mate. You look bloody awful. Is it your shoulder?'

Valerie turned quickly to Adam was supporting his left elbow and was obviously in pain. She was contrite. 'I forgot about your shoulder. Oh Adam I'm sorry. We'll get the doctor to have a look at it. Oh I'm awful sorry. I thought you were drunk.' Adam wished Kaz good luck. 'I think we did Shouter proud. You did well with Valerie. I never heard you say so much before.' They shook hands and Adam joined Valerie who had been explaining to her friends that her escort was not drunk.

The doctor turned out to be a next door neighbour who readily agreed to look at Adam's wound. He was intrigued by the site and size of the incision scar and particularly the intricate stitching. He found that there had been some muscular strain and a slight tear but no major damage. He advised Adam not to exert the shoulder for a day or two. Valerie thanked the doctor and she and Adam went next door.

Before they went in, Valerie stopped Adam gently by the gate. She put her arms round his waist and looked up at him. 'I was awful tonight. I was showing off to my girl friends, and left you on your own. I wanted to show you off, because I'm so proud of you and what you've been doing. But when I heard the shouting I thought you were just a noisy drunk. I didn't know about your friend being killed. And then I forgot about your arm and pulled it like that. Oh, Adam.' She burst into tears. Adam patted her clumsily on her head, kissed her gently on the cheek, then offered his clean handkerchief.

They went in and met Mrs MacKay on the way upstairs. She saw her daughter's swollen eyes, but kept quiet. In the morning she told Adam that Valerie had given her a full account of the previous night's events. She was glad that it was a misunderstanding. Valerie was really ashamed of her behaviour. Adam replied that he understood and he had accepted her apology. Mrs MacKay changed to a bantering tone. 'Come on now. I've got a real egg for you. You get dressed and I'll get you a proper breakfast, porridge, then a boiled egg and oatcakes.'

After breakfast Adam accompanied Valerie and her parents as they played golf, enjoying the brisk, clear morning, the invigorating sea breeze and the views of the Firth of Clyde. He could see the island of Arran and the dumpy rock of Ailsa Craig, landmarks he remembered from the briefing for his Atlantic crossing. He felt far removed from the war until he saw aircraft taking off or landing at Prestwick, or a group of young Army commandos running along the beach.

At the end of the day he realised he had spoken very little with Valerie. Mr MacKay had noted the distance between them and when the ladies were engaged in hemming up a dress for Linda to wear to a school party, he asked Adam what had happened. Once he learned that the issue was no more than a misunderstanding, he introduced Adam to the quiet pleasure of whisky. Jack MacKay had retired as head of quality control from the Johnnie Walker Whisky company in nearby Kilmarnock and he had developed a respect for the appropriate use of his company's product and a cautious attitude towards its abuse.

Jack's comment was, 'You should always remember that as well as doing harm to you, whisky can relax you when you're worked up about something, and stimulate you when you're down in the dumps. But you have to learn when you've been relaxed enough or stimulated enough by the dram and you'll find you can stay a moderate drinker. It's a matter for your judgement.' Adam was unsure of the taste but at the end of the evening found himself more relaxed than he had been for a long time.

CHAPTER 11

At breakfast on the last day of his leave, Linda asked Adam to pass the salt. With no hesitation he reached out his left hand and in one smooth movement, picked up the salt cellar, made sure it was not pepper, then passed it to Linda. She realised what had happened. 'Listen everybody, we've trained Adam at last.' She planted a kiss on Adam's cheek, then sat back, red faced, in an awkward silence, as the others in the family offered their congratulations to Adam.

He and Valerie travelled together to London where she caught her train to Chichester and he stayed to spend the night at the Commonwealth Club to keep an early appointment with Sir Wilfred Chinley. After his examination, Sir Wilfred thought that he would be fit to fly in the long run, but that was up to the medical board which was to meet the next day.

At the Air Ministry Adam was shown into a waiting room with three other pilots waiting to hear their fate. A Flight Lieutenant with an artificial hand was ill at ease as he sat screwing his appliance half off and on again. A Squadron Leader with an empty trouser leg and crutches beside him was trying to chat to a fair haired Flying Officer, whose face had been obliterated by a criss-cross of scars. He sat with his hands to his sides, but he made a movement that showed that in two of his fingers the exposed bones gleamed white against the dark discoloured skin.

The pilot with the artificial hand was called in first. He spent about quarter of an hour in the interview room, then emerged to collect his hat. He was more relaxed than he had been. He simply said, 'They grounded me, thank God. Good luck to you.' He nodded to them then left.

The Flying Officer with the burn scars watched him go, then said, 'I hope to hell they don't ground me. There's a Hun out there I want to shoot down in flames.' He was called next, and returned quite quickly, smiling. 'I'm to fly again after I get more grafts on these hands. Hope things work out for you.'

The Squadron Leader was then invited to go behind the massive door and Adam was alone for almost an hour, until the interview was over. The verdict from the departing and delighted Squadron Leader was that he was off Lancasters altogether, but once his artificial leg was fitted, he would be given a chance in a new light bomber.

When it was Adam's turn, he found himself before a Group Captain, two Wing Commanders and a Squadron Leader, all wearing the Caduceus collar badge denoting Medical Officer. The Group Captain introduced himself as an Orthopaedic Surgeon, one Wing Commander as a Psychiatrist, the other as a General Physician and the Squadron Leader as a Neurologist. 'So you see, we've got you pretty well covered, eh.' Adam smiled politely.

The Group Captain was brief. 'I trained under Sir Wilfred, so I know that his report is entirely sound. I assisted him the very first time he used that technique of repairing a shoulder. What's your impression of the operation?' Adam told of the unusual infection but the subsequent uneventful recuperation and the quick return of smooth movement. The Group Captain observed that he had had a couple of patients who showed similar signs shortly after surgery. He wondered whether it really was infection or the body system objecting to the strange bits of stuff that were stuck in during the long initial stages of the operation to prevent infection.

The others then asked questions on the amount and speed of recovery of function and the degree of pain. Adam told them he was disappointed at his lack of strength in his left arm. The Neurologist tested his grip and pull and agreed that there was still more restriction in lateral extension.

The physician broke in. 'Hold on a bit, Algy. It's early days. We're seeing this chap just a couple of months after the operation and it takes that long for everyone to recover just from meeting Wilf Chinley, never mind his surgery.' Adam joined in the laughter. The psychiatrist then asked if Adam really wanted to fly again, after the crash. Adam interrupted quickly. 'Oh, it wasn't a crash. I was wounded on the ground, but I was able to take off and fly back to base, with the help of a passenger who kept shouting at me not to pass out. I'm afraid I can't say too much about it as it was a hush hush affair. But I definitely want to keep on flying.' The chairman assured him that they had all the information about the mission and they too were bound by the Official Secrets Act.

The psychiatrist came back. 'Would you go back to taking agents over to and bringing them back from France?' Again Adam answered that he would. He enjoyed carrying on a one-man-show and having to make decisions on his own. But his arm had to be right. 'They trained me in unarmed combat to prepare me to behave like a soldier if I got stranded in France. But I would come off second best now if I had to fight a girl guide.'

'Should I question you further about that?' the psychiatrist asked with his eyes twinkling. Adam smiled and said, 'No thanks.'

The physician took up the interview. 'You could instruct.' Adam replied that he had done so in Montreal and felt that once you became an instructor you were likely to be stuck with the job. He explained that he was happy with any form of flying, but in wartime the only appropriate flying was against the enemy. He found himself articulating a thought that was only half formed in his mind. 'I would like to find some way of flying on operations, not necessarily as pilot, for long enough for my arm to recover fully. Even though I am not service trained as a navigator, I have passed the Guild of Air Pilots and Navigators examination, and I've got a lot of flying hours doing my own Dead Reckoning Navigation.'

The Neurologist chimed in, 'That has something to be said for it. This board can, in fact, recommend passenger status for you on operations. But I have another thought. I know someone who's working on airborne radio navigation, and he admits it will need a specially trained type of aircrew to operate it. You could go and see him at the Scientific Branch Office. In fact I could drive you there after this seance is over.' He reminded Adam that he had signed his assent to the Official Secrets Act and could not divulge anything he might learn from this scientist. Adam agreed.

The chairman summed up. 'We are agreed, then, that Flight Lieutenant Aitken be given a further period of three weeks sick leave. He could go home to Newfoundland if an air crossing can be arranged. After that he will be examined on our behalf by Dr Baxter.' The neurologist nodded his agreement. 'If there is no progress Mr Aitken will be brought before this board again. If progress is satisfactory he will be graded temporarily by Dr Baxter as suitable for passenger status on operational flying and seconded to RAF Scientific Intelligence for training in the newer forms of navigation. Arrangements will be made for Flight Lieutenant Aitken to be put in touch with . . .' He turned to the Squadron Leader, who replied, 'Professor Barlock.' There was a general murmur of assent among the panel, and Adam was asked to go back to the waiting room.

After a short while, Squadron Leader Baxter led him downstairs, saying, 'Join me for a quick lunch at the RSM, the Royal Society of Medicine. The food is usually good for wartime, and then I can take you to meet Peter Barlock, before I go back to my wards.'

As they handed in caps and coats at the cloakroom of this world famous Medical institution, they were accosted by Sir Wilfred Chinley. 'Ah, Baxter, I hope you were able to appreciate my masterful surgery on this young Newfoundlander.' Baxter laughed and admitted Sir Wilfred's genius, which went hand in hand with his modesty.

The surgeon winked at Adam. 'Is he treating you all right, my young colonial?' His eyes twinkled. 'Did you know that if you laid out all the neurologists in the world head to toe, they would still not be able to reach a decent diagnosis?' Baxter shook his head resignedly. Sir Wilfred guffawed and shook Adam gently by the elbow, wished him good luck quietly, then turned Baxter around and carried out a conversation out of Adam's reach. He eventually nodded, clapped Baxter on the shoulder, waved to Adam and joined a group at the entrance to the dining room. 'We've received the accolade from on high,' said Baxter and led Adam in.

After lunch they went to Broadway where they met a tall ungainly and untidy man who was eating an ice-cream cone while puffing a pipe and contemplating a circuit diagram on a blackboard. Baxter introduced Adam to Professor Barlock, who raised a finger before acknowledging their presence and asked them why a heat shield should be such an unstable source of magnetic radiation. Adam looked at Baxter who looked just as blank, but managed to reply, 'You tell us.' Barlock looked puzzled and retorted, 'That's just what I cannot do, yet.'

He invited them to sit and, having finished his ice-cream, smoked his pipe contentedly while paying full attention to Baxter's report of Adam's situation. After getting the basic information, the Professor broke in, 'When he's finished his leave send him over to us at the Scientific Branch. He could learn about our Radio Direction Finding stuff in the air and use it for navigation. The Bomber people are very impatient for us to get our new equipment so we have to get on with it.'

Adam interrupted, 'Isn't there a gadget that allows the bombers to fly a preset course over Europe by following radio signals from fixed bases in England?'

'Yes, there is,' Barlock replied then turned quickly to Dawson. 'Is our friend here covered under the Official Secrets Act?' When he was reassured, he continued to Adam, 'What you are talking about is called "Gee". We developed it. Radio signals from three bases give the navigator an immediate fix on his position. It is complicated to operate. The curvature of the earth limits its range to about 400 miles for an aircraft at 20,000 feet, and, most importantly, the radio beams can be interfered with.' Adam smiled and told about his diathermy flights.

'Probably you inspired the Germans to do the same for our Gee boxes,' said Barlock. 'What we're working on now is a device that is self contained within the bomber. No need for any beams from the ground. We want to produce a receiver like Watson Watt's television that will give the navigator a picture of the ground they are flying over, even through cloud. We've nearly reached the first stage. The image we get needs very high voltage to give it clarity. That means heat inside the equipment, and heat makes for unstable frequencies so the picture is not stable enough for use in practice, so . . .'

He stood up suddenly, upsetting a pile of books. 'Ah, I've got it. The answer is to use two heat shields, one spaced from the other at a distance which is a fraction of the wavelength. Now what's the name of that Bomber fellow in Lincolnshire somewhere?' He picked up a battered ebony ruler and rattled it noisily along the heating radiator. A comfortable smiling middle aged secretary appeared immediately through the open door and told him the name he was looking for was Bennett. She also handed him an offprint of a scientific paper.

She was told to let Bennett know that Barlock's new recruit, Adam Aitken, was going to start training on Airborne Radio Direction Finding in a few week's time and would soon be up to see him. Baxter took his leave to get back to his hospital duties, wishing Adam good luck and reminding him to come for examination when he returned from leave.

Barlock waved his hand vaguely and returned happily to his pipe and blackboard. Adam waited in the secretary's office until she prepared a rail pass and an authorization for entry to Bomber Command Headquarters at High Wycombe. She had these papers prepared and she said, 'One last thing. I put a call through to Mr Bennett's assistant to tell him about you joining Peter's team. I also asked when you and he could meet. She promised to get back to me in five minutes, and that time is now up . . .' the telephone rang, 'and here she is.' She picked up the 'phone, listened for a moment, then asked Adam if he was free the next day. When he confirmed he was available, she spoke into the 'phone again. 'Right I'll have him at your railway station at 8.20 in the morning. Can you get someone to pick him up? That's good. Bye, bye.' She had a rail warrant ready in his name, added the date and time of departure, saying that was everything he was likely to need and wished him goodbye.

Armed with these official papers Adam took his leave of this highly efficient lady and passed through Barlock's office on his way out. The Professor was still jubilant. 'D'you know why it was so easy to solve that problem?' he called out, holding up the scientific off print that his secretary had given him. 'I had already solved the problem in 1935 when I wrote this paper on magnetic radiation in metals under varying levels of heat. Amusing, isn't it?' Adam nodded wisely and left.

CHAPTER 12

Bennett had put in his share of operational flying with his Halifax squadron. He was now organising the formation of Pathfinder squadrons, a special target finding force within Bomber Command to improve the accuracy of the bombing. Thus he welcomed Adam not only as a former colleague but also because of his interest in serving as a navigator.

It was August 1942 and 'Butch' Harris, had been Air Officer Commanding-in-Chief of Bomber Command, for about six months. His reputation as a leader, as his nickname suggested, arose from his ability to make tough decisions and carry them out. He had made great strides in introducing order into the preparation for and the conduct of bombing missions, and was convinced that persistent 'area' bombing with heavy loads of bombs would eventually break the enemy's morale.

At first Harris had been suspicious of Bennett's idea of achieving precision bombing using a select group of experienced aircrews including the most skilful navigators with the most up to date electronic aids. Bennett gained the support of other senior officers who, like himself, had recently flown on Bomber Command operations, and eventually Harris accepted their suggestion with good grace. He promoted Bennett to Air Commodore, and gave him command of the new Pathfinder Force (abbreviated PFF).

'This'll interest you,' Bennett told Adam, as he walked him down a corridor. 'This first thing I did was to appoint a crew selection officer. Come and meet her.' He led Adam into a large room filled with filing cabinets, and occupied by two WAAF, a large cheery Sergeant with flaming red hair and an elegant officer. Both stood up as the Air Commodore entered and were introduced as Sergeant Blodwen Caraig-Jones and Flight Officer Leslie Duncarron. Adam found himself blushing like a schoolboy at the sight of the tall, slender and stunningly beautiful officer who had removed her tortoise shell reading glasses to reveal bright flashing blue eyes. Bennett excused himself on the grounds that he had to meet the Air Vice Marshal and told Adam to put his name in as a volunteer for lead navigator. He shook Adam's hand, nodded to the two girls then left, only to put his head round the door seconds later to ask Leslie if she would take Flight Lieutenant Aitken to lunch. She said she would be delighted. Adam was thrilled.

Blodwen explained the first stage of the selection process, assessing the files of aircrew who had volunteered for Pathfinder duty. Those who had served their tour successfully with no complications were placed in one pile for the Air Commodore to interview. Files which had unusual features, such as occasional periods of sickness, breakdowns in equipment, difficulties with members of their crew or with colleagues were set aside for further investigation by the Air Commodore. Adam smiled to himself when he recalled the days in Montreal, when every decision had to be made by or approved by Don. Leslie then explained that she looked more closely at the applications from navigators. They were high priority, as the success of Pathfinder missions was dependent upon the preliminary force getting to the right target and dropping the markers in the right place. Her information could be gleaned from the intelligence reports at the end of the raids as well as from comments on the navigator's performance made by skippers and other members of the crew. Adam wrote out an application to join the Pathfinder Force as a navigator, giving details of his injury and his coming training with Barlock's Airborne RDF group.

At lunch he was starting to tell Leslie about the city of St John's when she said she had been there in 1937. She had crossed the Atlantic with her parents and her two sisters, in a freighter belonging to a company in which her father was a director. Their destination was Montreal but before they reached the Gulf of St Lawrence they had to divert to Newfoundland to have a seaman admitted to hospital. They spent two nights in the Port of St John's and had visited the cathedral, but had found the whole place to be dirty and smelly. She recalled seeing three of the largest policemen she had ever seen bringing drunken sailors back to the ship. One of them was actually carrying a drunk under each arm. They had no desire to go ashore again. 'After all, we didn't know anyone important there,' she ended. They finished their lunch in an awkward silence. Adam left to catch a train to London.

During the train journey he felt despondent that he had fared so badly with such an attractive girl. He admitted he had been riled by her unfavourable memories of St John's, but she lacked the capacity to elicit warmth of feeling in another person. In contrast he thought of Deirdre and her bubbly elation when she found out her husband was safe.

He telephoned her when he got to Victoria Station. She had heard no further word of her husband's home-coming. The children were at her mother's, and she had no ferrying commitments for the next three days. She was fed up and if Adam had 'phoned up to take her to dinner, she would be delighted. If that was not his intention then she would take him out to dinner. Adam laughed. She said that was just what she wanted – to hear someone laugh. They agreed to laugh some more at dinner.

The head porter at the Commonwealth Club told him of a quiet traditional restaurant that could still rise to a good cut of roast beef and a very drinkable house claret. It was just around the corner and he was advised to call in person to book a table as soon as the place opened. This he did and his request was courteously granted by Charles, the owner. An hour later the same owner was on hand to welcome Adam and Deirdre when they arrived. His face beamed when he saw Adam's partner. 'Welcome, your ladyship. I should have known that you were coming when the Flight Lieutenant ordered roast beef and our own claret.'

Deirdre smiled and clasped the owner's hand between hers. 'Charles, that's exactly what I want, if you will spare a little Stilton to go with the last of the bottle.'

As they sipped the first glass of wine, Adam asked. 'What about this ladyship business?' Deirdre was matter of fact in her answer. 'Mike and I are the offspring of a bog Irish peer, the fourteenth Earl MacMorran of Duingaugh. Daddy is a very good farmer in Southern Ireland and we were both brought up as farmer's kids, cloth caps and Wellie boots. I am the horsy one. Mike is beef cattle. We go around looking like tinkers. In fact we have tinker friends who protest that we're so scruffy we give the tinkers a bad name. But we're filthy rich and live in a great comfortable barn of a mansion. It's always full of noisy relatives and chums, including a dotty great uncle of ours who still has the Bristol fighter he flew in the First World War. Occasionally he gets a couple of lads from the village to fix it and tune up the engine.

'He taught Mike and me to fly it, but only when mother was away as she had the screaming nadgers if she knew we were airborne. We were told what to do on the ground then tried to remember it when we were in the air, doing circuits sitting on Uncle Horace's knees. I can claim to have soloed after ten minutes dual, and that at the age of twelve. Mike took all of twelve minutes before he soloed. That's how I became the first best pilot and Mike the second best pilot in Ballyjamesduff. That's a place near our house.'

Adam laughed and Deirdre joined in. Her eyes were twinkling. She clasped his hands. 'Let me tell you about castor oil. The Bristol used castor oil and when the engine heated up it sprayed all over the place, mainly backwards over the pilot's face. When we landed we had white where our goggles had been and oil marks on nose and chin. We also swallowed some, so we were never constipated. Bless you, you oldest British colonial, dear Adam, for getting me to laugh.'

The roast beef was carved at the table and served with roast potatoes, Yorkshire Pudding, green peas or carrots (which Adam, as a former night fighter, hastily declined) and freshly made horse radish sauce. Stilton cheese arrived with the last of the wine. Adam found this cheese to be the perfect ending to the meal but wondered how something with such an unappetizing smell could taste so right.

As Adam was paying the bill he overheard Deirdre tell Charles that tonight he and Adam had really helped her get out of the blues. There was still no word of the Commander, but she could only keep hoping. 'As soon as he gets back, bring the Commander here for dinner and I will serve you this menu.' Deirdre kissed the proprietor on the cheek and slipped her arm through Adam's.

They walked back to her flat, happy that the nightly raid had not started yet. She invited Adam in for a nightcap of Bushmills. Adam declined saying, 'It's not because of the Bushmills, which might be very nice. I think I'm in love with you, but I wouldn't want to take advantage of your husband being out of circulation.'

Deirdre wrinkled her nose. 'Adam Aitken, you're a darling stuffy man and I won't forget how you raised my spirits tonight.' She kissed him briefly then hugged him tightly and went inside. At the club the head porter asked if the dinner had been successful and was delighted with the pound note Adam gave him.

At breakfast next morning Adam was called away from his plate of porridge to take a telephone call. It was Deirdre. 'Adam, the most marvellous thing happened last night. Roger got back at midnight. He got a lift in a bomber from just outside Lisbon and landed in Bedfordshire somewhere. He'll be home tomorrow!'

Adam thought it must have been Special Operations who delivered him. He caught her elation. 'That's great. You must be very pleased.'

'I'm over the moon,' she said then paused. 'There was a moment last night when I wanted you to make love to me. But you were gallant. I'm really a prudish little maid, in spite of the act I put on. If you had taken me to bed, I would have been riddled with guilt when Roger phoned this morning. Thank you, Adam for being a true gentleman. Keep in touch, will you please.' She rang off and Adam thought about what a miserable swine he would have felt if he had made love to her. He sighed as he concluded he was a reluctant knight in shining armour, and went back to tackle his porridge.

He went to the postings section in the Air Ministry, to get his present status sorted out. An intense bespectacled Flight Lieutenant confirmed that he was officially on sick leave and was due to report in three weeks time to Squadron Leader Baxter at the National Hospital, Queen Square for reassessment.

When Adam asked if he could go home on leave, the official answer was that he was expected to do just that. A brief glance at the file, brought the comment that he could not get home and back by boat. Adam suggested that if he had travel authorization to Prestwick and ferry to Gander he could arrange the trip himself. The reply was, 'There and back, I presume.' Adam assured him that was the case.

The next statement from the postings officer was a surprise. 'They're short on fliers out there to do the Wings For Victory tour. Would you be willing to go to Montreal and Toronto to talk to service clubs and a couple of factories. You know the sort of thing – how the conduct of the war depends not only on the soldiers, sailors and airmen, but on the men and women who work in the factory. That would give you official status.' Adam agreed and the posting officer seemed pleased. 'Give me forty-five minutes to lay it on, then come back to Room 337. My sergeant should have the timetable and the passes ready for you by then.'

To his delight the WAAF sergeant had Adam booked on a sleeper overnight to Kilmarnock, thence by local train to Prestwick, where he could phone up for a car. He should then report to the Dispatch office for another overnight trip across to Gander. She then showed him the documents for both the outward and the return flight. Mr Noseworthy, in St John's, would arrange his speaking engagements in St John's, Toronto and Montreal. Adam expressed his gratitude for her help. She blushed and smirked.

On his way out Adam had a sudden thought. He opened the Postings officer's door and waved his handful of documents, crying, 'It's all fixed. Thanks for your help. Do you mind if I ask you what you did in civilian life?' Shouter would have been disappointed at the officer's reply. He had been senior route planner with the London, Midland and Scottish Railway. Adam nodded then closed the door, leaving the officer looking perplexed.

CHAPTER 13

Adam spent a day sightseeing in London then slept soundly overnight in a sleeper out of Euston Station and awoke just after Carlisle. He got dressed but could not get any water to wash or shave. At 6a.m. in Kilmarnock station he splashed cold water on his face and joined the Ayr train for Prestwick. When the railway lines met the coast he saw the crisp morning light over the Firth of Clyde and at Troon he identified the links where he had walked round with Valerie and her family. As he left the train at Prestwick station, the sun was strong and the sea breeze bracing.

He shared a car which was waiting for another officer bound for Prestwick aerodrome, and he was soon breakfasting in familiar surroundings. He got himself listed for a Liberator crossing due to depart that same evening and met some of the ferry crews he had known in Montreal. They all expressed their sorrow at the loss of Shouter but he could not get any news of Shouter's wife, Shouter's widow, he corrected himself ruefully.

On an impulse, he telephoned the MacKays, who insisted he should come to lunch. He was welcomed at the front door by a red-haired man whose resemblance to Valerie was so strong as to convince Adam that this was brother Colin, who had just arrived and was on leave for another few days. Valerie had arranged a weekend pass and would be home the next morning. Adam's room was ready for him and it was a great thrill for the MacKays to have this reunion. Mrs MacKay was so excited that Adam was saddened to tell her that he had to be back at the terminal this evening.

Mr MacKay mentioned that Linda had not seen Colin yet and did not know that Adam was coming. She was due home for lunch and Adam and Colin could just catch her coming out of school, and give her a real surprise. Colin went and put on his tunic and Mr MacKay took great pride in pointing out to Adam that his son also wore the ribbon of the Distinguished Service Order. The two officers in uniform were greeted by a number of shoppers as they walked to the school and a squad of soldiers gave them eyes left at the stentorian command of a drill sergeant who flashed up a dazzling salute. Adam and Colin tried to be dignified but only succeeded in looking sheepish as they responded.

Colin talked of his Atlantic crossings, escorting convoys. His destroyer was one of the fastest ships of the line, and had been in at the kill in five submarine hunts. It was being repaired in Belfast after a torpedo had damaged the engine room and the steering system. Hence his leave. Colin usually spent time ashore in St John's at the end of their outward journey. In contrast to Leslie Duncarron of two days before, he had been impressed by the buildings in the older part of the city. He mentioned the generous interest and kindness shown to the Royal Navy sailors by the citizens.

They were by the school gate swapping names of people in St John's when Linda came out the school entrance in a crowd of children. They saw her eyes widen, then heard her shout of 'It's Colin' and she was running down the path when she stopped and stared until she recognised Adam. She bit her lip and whispered 'Adam,' rushed into Colin's arms then turned to be kissed by Adam, and burst into tears. When she recovered, Linda walked hand in hand with them and responded to Colin's questions about school. When she was explaining the complexity of her relationship with her best friend, she stopped and asked Adam if he still knew how to pass the salt. 'I am the best salt passer in the whole Air Force,' he replied solemnly. She turned to Colin, 'I had to teach him how to do that.'

Before lunch, Adam went quietly into the dining room and made sure that the salt cellar was well to his left. When Linda asked for the salt he reached out in one smooth movement to make the pick up, passed it hand to hand, then with a flourish, placed it in front of the delighted Linda. The rest of the family congratulated Linda on being such a good teacher, and Adam felt again the strengths of the bonds within ordinary family life, which had opened up to include him.

Conversation turned to Valerie and her work in Intelligence. Mrs MacKay told Adam that Valerie's senior officer, Mavis, had been awarded the Order of the British Empire. Adam was pleased at the honour awarded to Mavis, and recalled her coolness, bravery, her protective attitude to a wounded pilot and her prudery.

After lunch they all accompanied Linda to school then walked back along the beach road. The sun was strong and sparkled on the gentle waves on the incoming tide. Adam remarked that the tough Commando troops seemed to be missing. Jack MacKay thought they must have left three or four two days ago, but there were no rumours where they might have gone.

They talked of the progress of the war. Things seemed to be turning round for the better in North Africa. The RAF and the US Air Force had started a pattern of day and night bombing of German targets. The U boats had been driven into deeper waters by Coastal Command's new methods of detecting submarines, and they were attacked from the air when they were coming out of or returning to base. Jack MacKay thought that the war in Russia had taken Hitler's attention away from the Atlantic campaign.

Mrs MacKay remarked that Valerie was distressed that she had not been able to make amends for the quarrel at the Orangefield Hotel. Adam tried to explain his feelings. He looked on her as a dear friend, but until he had a definite future and would survive he could not ask Valerie to be anything other than that. He told of his aunt in Newfoundland, widowed in the First World War, who had never regained an identity in the family or community other than 'that poor widow woman'. He was sorry if he appeared callous or indifferent to Valerie's feelings, but he liked her, respected her too much to place her at risk of becoming another Aunt Margot.

His embarrassment was ended when Linda returned from school, proudly sat on the couch between Colin and Adam and regaled them with the school news. Eventually Colin announced that he still had a tankful of pre-war petrol in his motor cycle and offered Adam transport to the Prestwick terminal.

During the goodbyes Mrs MacKay apologised contritely for meddling in Adam's affairs. Adam kissed her warmly and thanked her for letting him into her family and asked her to give his best wishes to Valerie. Mr MacKay insisted that Adam should visit them and stay as one of the family when he returned to Prestwick. Linda solemnly asked him not to forget how to pass the salt and they were off on a hair raising ride on the back roads, past fields where harvest was being taken in by elderly farm-hands and volunteer Land Girls. As they said goodbye, Colin said he understood Adam's position. He felt the same way about a girl-friend of his, but if Adam ever decided he would marry his sister it would be a great pleasure to him, even if it meant having a brother-in-law in the junior service. They both smiled and shook hands warmly.

The Liberator had a complement of nine passengers and a crew of four. In spite of the uncomfortable canvas stretcher bench on which he sat, Adam fell asleep until he was awakened almost ten hours later by the rumble of flaps and wheels as they went into circuit for the Gander field. His shoulder was painful so he replaced the sling. One of the returning pilots took his bag for him.

As he entered the make shift hangar, which also housed the arrivals office, he saw his father and Bridget waving frantically at him. They had made the drive on a road which was only a track in places to welcome him and drive him home. The transport officer told him they had been there since early morning, sitting quietly and determined not to miss their boy. The old lady had told everybody of Adam having been decorated for bravery by the King himself, and also by the French General. The Skipper just sat beaming with pride.

When he left the arrivals office, Adam made a beeline for his father and Bridget, and stopped as a round of applause rang in the building. Mechanics, cleaners, clerks, waiting aircrew were adding their welcome to the returning hero. Adam blushed and waved then embraced his father and Bridget. Both looked well, having put on weight since he last saw them. He drove the car on the journey down, and he was alternatively bombarded with questions about the war and informed about the state of the economy in Newfoundland. Three of his boyhood friends had been killed and one had been returned home having been completely blinded in a gunnery accident in Britain. 'Never got to fire at the enemy,' was the sad conclusion.

The port of St John's continued to be busy with Royal Navy vessels arriving after crossing the Atlantic, or assembling to act as escorts to a convoy for the return crossing. The Aitken household was involved in providing hospitality to some of the sailors on Sunday evenings. The Skipper proudly announced that Bridget had insisted that they would entertain the other ranks, while his stuffier colleagues received officers only.

The American forces had brought boom conditions to the city on a scale never before imagined and they had set up several base camps, including one beside Quidi Vidi Lake on the outskirts of the city. They were currently building a hospital on this base, whose walls were, it was rumoured, thick enough to withstand a direct hit from a bomb.

For the first few days in St John's he visited familiar parts of the city and met up with some old chums. He visited his blinded friend, who was waiting at home to be sent to a training institution in Ontario. The victim was suffering from an over-protective mother who insisted on being present during their conversation and interpreting the plight of her son to Adam. At one point, for example, Adam had thoughtlessly used the phrase 'I see,' to indicate his understanding. She broke in, 'Of course it upsets him when people say things like that.' Her son could contain himself no longer and burst out. 'For Christ's sake, mother, I know that other people can see and I don't expect them to pretend they can't.' She sighed and shook her head. 'See how upset he gets.'

Mr Noseworthy, the organiser of his tour, had been Adam's English teacher in High School. When he retired he had taken on the job of coordinating the Victory talks as part of his war-effort. Adam addressed the St John's Business Club in their premises on Water Street. The audience, composed of his father's contemporaries and fellow merchants, as well as 'Skipper' himself, listened gravely to his account of service and civilian life in wartime Britain.

He told of some of the more harrowing aspects of the bombing attacks against civilians. He ended on an optimistic note, drawing on his conversation with the MacKays before he left Prestwick two days previously. The Army was beginning to take the advantage in the North Africa campaign. The Navy was experiencing few losses of merchant shipping to U boat attack, and the RAF and Dominion Air Forces by night and the United States Army Air Force by day were bombing German targets round the clock. This could well be the beginning of the end for Germany.

In his vote of thanks Mr Noseworthy thought that Adam might be too optimistic too soon. He asked if Adam had heard of the Dieppe raid in which Combined Operations, under the command of Lord Mountbatten, had crossed the English Channel to engage the enemy. The British had some experienced Commando troops in the force, and Adam thought of the Commandoes he had seen training in Troon. However, the majority of the troops were untried Canadian soldiers who had been hanging about in Britain waiting for action. The operation was not a success, with 4,000 casualties suffered in 11 hours, all to little strategic point other than to 'blood' the Canadians. Adam was embarrassed to admit that he had not had this information, which Mr Noseworthy had received from the overseas service of the BBC just that morning.

The next few days were spent in visiting friends and relatives in and around St John's. He realised that there was a dynamic in the economy of Newfoundland which had not been present in the immediate pre-war, post-depression days when Newfoundland had run up a huge public debt, and could not pay the interest charges. The war had brought riches to Newfoundland from Canada and the United States, mainly to finance the construction of military bases and installations. Hundreds of millions of dollars poured into the economy and for the first time ever there was no shortage of jobs. The Commission of Government even found itself in a position to lend or give money to Britain. Thus Adam found a confidence, even a cockiness, in the Newfoundlanders which he had not encountered before.

CHAPTER 14

Following Mr Noseworthy's arrangements, Adam picked up a flight to Toronto in a Douglas Dakota. He spoke at a factory which was assembling Lysanders so he told the workers at a lunch-time meeting in the canteen a little of the operations he had flown with their aircraft, praising its sturdiness and manoeuvrability. The girls were fascinated by his observation that a large number of the agents he had flown in and out were women. One girl, neatly dressed in the regulation coverall and headscarf, asked if women were allowed to fly Spitfires and shoot down the Germans. He admitted this had not happened yet, but there were women ferry pilots who flew everything from Spitfires to Lancaster bombers and delivered them from the factories to the squadrons. When the questioner asked how she could become a pilot like that, he pointed out that these Air Transport Auxiliary fliers were people like Amy Johnson and Jim Mollison who had done a lot of flying before the War began. He boasted a little of knowing a ferry pilot who was a titled lady who had learned to fly at a very early age. The girl looked crestfallen. Obviously her dream had been shattered and she burst out bitterly, 'Well, stuff you. You want only women with a lot of money and privilege to be pilots.'

Before Adam could recover, the sour looking man next to the outraged girl was on his feet. 'It's a capitalist war you're running. I've been to Newfoundland and I know all about you Aitkens, and their business. You're agents. You take your cut off everything that goes on to the island, food, furniture, booze, everything. You just stand around with your hand out getting rich. Bloody spongers, living off the needs of the working classes. When are you going to help Comrade Stalin and open up the second front, eh?' Adam muttered lamely that neither he nor his family had anything to do with making war policy, and the meeting ended with a discontented audience and a bewildered Adam.

He vowed to be more circumspect at the evening meeting with the Board of Commerce. Accordingly, he played down the naïve hopefulness of the ending of his address in St John's and made no mention of a titled lady. He agreed with a questioner that the end of the war could only be talked about seriously, once the Allied troops had landed in Europe. A banker asked if he thought that the expense of modern warfare was excessive. Adam thought he agreed, but could not think of how to cut down on expenses, apart from ending the fighting.

The city of Toronto was bustling and the shops were well stocked. All this and no blackout made the war seem far away. He met acquaintances, but no friends and he was glad to move on to Montreal and visit the Dorval Ferry Unit which now rejoiced in the acronym ATFERO (Atlantic Ferry Organization) and had become part of RAF Transport Command. He was interested to learn from one of former 'pupils' that the RCAF was charting air routes across Canada to ensure that the increased amount of air traffic could be controlled under safety regulations.

Mme. Humphrey was still devastated at having lost Shouter. 'I often wonder, Adam, what "'arness and 'atches secure" means.' Adam explained how Shouter had found security in the RAF way of life and that phrase, from the pre-flight check, was his way of being thankful he was secure. 'But when I last saw him, he told me he had found real security with you,' Adam told her quietly. Her eyes filled with tears, but she brushed them away and smiled. 'He remains always in my heart. We loved each other as young people do. I can never forget him. Do you know, Adam, he once said he wished he had a son just like you.' She rose suddenly and left the room, returning with Shouter's disreputable hat. 'Please have this to remember him by.' Adam was overwhelmed and accepted the hat and wore it proudly back to the Dorval mess.

His talk that evening was held in a lecture theatre at McGill University. The chairman made much of the fact that Adam had been decorated for gallantry not only by the British, but also by the French. Adam disarmed the audience by starting off his talk in recognizable French then switched to English. He shared with them some of his own experiences ferrying agents, without revealing details which could infringe security regulations. He told of the hardships of civilian life in war-time Britain, of the setbacks in military operations, of the rationing of food and clothing, but also of the overall optimism of the British in adversity. As he ended he saw a familiar face in the audience.

Amélie Lamotte sat quietly, just waiting, unlike the intense, wound-up, restless girl he remembered. After he got free of questioners she hurried up to him. 'Adam, I have a great favour to ask of you. Will you come and meet my parents?' Adam hesitated, and Amélie explained that her brother, Giles, had been wounded at Dieppe and was in a British military hospital. They had no idea how badly he had been wounded. Her father had tried to 'phone the hospital, but was told there was no such place. Adam reassured her he would try to help. When he explained that he would be late at the reception, the chairman eyed Amélie, gave a Gallic shrug and said, 'Of course.'

On the way she explained that Giles had joined the Army, and was a Lieutenant in the Fusiliers de Mont Royal. Like other Canadian regiments they had been in England waiting to go into action for almost a year. Dieppe was his very first encounter with the enemy.

M. Lamotte apologised for his conduct when they last met. Since then, his, and the attitudes of many Quebecers to the war had changed. He handed Adam the official notification of Giles' wounding which was formal and gave no hint of how badly he was affected. Adam noticed that Giles was in the Orthopaedic Unit at Beaulieu Military Hospital, where he had been treated by Sir Wilfred Chinley. In his diary he found the telephone number and the extension for Sister Jessie Rodgers the senior orthopaedic nurse, and announced that, even though it would be late there, he was going to telephone the hospital, pronouncing it 'Bewlay'. He had been a patient and would get in touch with a senior nurse to get information about Giles. M. Lamotte interrupted to give the French pronunciation. Adam reassured him that the English pronunciation was different.

M. Lamotte looked relieved. 'When I telephoned England no person knew this hospital. It was, now I think, because I said the name wrong.' He spread his hands wide to his wife.

After a delay of about two minutes, Adam heard the familiar crisp voice saying, 'Sister Rodgers here. Who are you? Speak up. We've got a bad line.' Adam smiled and identified himself.

A surprisingly short pause, then, 'Are you on the 'phone at midnight to tell me you've made a mess of the shoulder we worked on so hard?'

Adam denied that emphatically and explained that he was calling from Montreal and he wanted to know about Giles Lamotte. She answered, 'Then I'll not waste any time chatting. Your Lieutenant is one of five French Canadian casualties admitted under Sir Wilfred's care. That was two days ago and we're still doing the preliminary investigations. I think he is going to lose a leg, but his spirits are quite high.' There was a muffled conversation then Sister Rodgers voice came back again. 'I'm told I should let you hear this from the horse's mouth, so here he is.'

Then there was a great roaring from Sir Wilfred. 'We've just stabilised young

Lamotte and he is no longer in mortal danger.'

Adam placed his hand over the mouthpiece and told the Lamottes 'He's no longer in danger.'

'What's that?' shouted Sir Wilfred.

'I was speaking to his parents.'

Sir Wilfred lowered his voice, 'The next bit's not so nice. He's got to lose his right leg. If I had to do it right away it would have to be a high amputation. That's an awkward one for fitting a good artificial limb so I don't want to do it unless I'm really forced. If I wait until I get some reasonable healing and good flesh I can do it below the knee. Easier fitting and easier for the poor chap to cope with afterwards. We can't save the leg, but if we take it off now he'll be really handicapped. If we get him to heal a bit he'll only have a slight limp. D'you understand?' Adam said he did. 'So that's why Sister Rodgers and I are going to keep him here to make sure we can do the best job possible on him. That's what we did with you, remember. Now you explain that to his parents. We could have him started on his recovery in seven or eight weeks. During that time I will find somebody in Montreal to look after his rehabilitation. But I bloody well won't rush it. How's that shoulder of yours, eh?'

After further explanations and a promise to visit Beaulieu when he returned to Britain, Adam saw that the Lamottes were in no position to talk to Sir Wilfred, so he asked for the Lamotte's love to be conveyed to Giles and hung up.

Mme. Lamotte burst into violent sobs and Amélie took her gently to a sofa. M. Lamotte stood wringing his hands with tears running down his face. Adam patted him gently on the shoulder and he raised his head and managed to smile. He then explained what Sir Wilfred had told him, taking care to assure them that Sir Wilfred was the best in his field. Because Giles was in no danger of dying it was unlikely that special arrangements could be made for one or all of the family to go to Britain to visit him. The news about Giles having to lose his leg was more difficult for them to accept, but they became reconciled to it and followed the reasoning that the lower amputation would be less of a handicap than the high operation.

Adam said that he would soon be back in Britain and would make a point of going to see Giles. He would telephone them with the news in just over a week's time. Adam noted to himself that his promises carried the proviso that Giles would have to be more kindly disposed towards him than at their one and only meeting so far. Amélie reminded him he had to go to the Mayor's reception. A kiss from Mme. Lamotte, a firm handshake from M. Lamotte and he was bustled into her car by Amélie.

On the ride to the City Chambers she thanked Adam for taking the trouble to help her and her parents. 'That was a nice quiet thing you did, just like an English gentleman.' To avoid the topic Adam asked Amélie about herself. She said she was working as a journalist, reporting news about women's roles in the war effort, but she had not had a proper opportunity to crusade for her views on women's special roles in society. She had married the son of her father's friend, but he had turned out to be less than a man. Adam did not understand this, until she explained that he was homosexual and could not consummate the marriage, but continued to have a succession of male lovers. As a Catholic she could not divorce him, but had the marriage declared null as he had been unable to respect the primary purpose of marriage, 'the procreation and education of children'. 'Now I have a succession of male lovers,' she said defiantly. Adam was sorry that someone as passionate as Amélie should have been frustrated by an unresponsive husband.

Back in St John's, he spent his last two days at home, receiving visitors or visiting around the town. On his final evening Bridget persuaded Adam and his father to accompany her to the cinema to see Nelson Eddy and Jeanette MacDonald's latest film, and they all three enjoyed a good cry. As he said his farewells the next morning, the Skipper asked if he would leave the RAF, arguing that his two medals were proof that his contribution to the war effort was outstanding. Adam admitted that if the medical board were to ground him from all flying duties, he would ask for a medical discharge, but he still wanted to fly. His father was disappointed, but wished him luck. Bridget promised to keep saying the rosary for his safe return.

During his return trip to Prestwick, Adam took a spell at the controls of the Liberator in order to get an idea of how ready he was to be returned to flying duties. The pilot remained on hand to sort things out, if necessary. Adam got the feel of this large aircraft quickly, but found that he could not adjust the trim correctly for comfortable handling. After two hours he felt cramp in his left shoulder and was glad to hand over the controls.

At Prestwick he got an immediately flight to London at 6 a.m. and did not want to disturb the MacKays at that unwelcome hour. He was back in the Commonwealth Club in London by 11a.m., facing a late breakfast of powdered eggs and cursing himself for not having appreciated real eggs while in St John's.

CHAPTER 15

At Queen's Square a young physiotherapist put him through a series of arm raising and lowering exercises. At first she was ill at ease, but as he was grunting while hefting her copy of Gray's Anatomy above his shoulder, she relaxed and broke into a smile. 'I'm sorry, but you looked so funny, scowling with your face all red.'

Adam countered, 'I was having a tough time with your damned exercise. All I've been doing so far is walking my fingers, and my greatest achievement to date is passing the salt. I admit I once got the pepper by mistake.' He smiled at the memory.

She laughed. 'I'm glad to see you can smile anyway. When I read about you doing secret service work, I thought you would be tight-lipped about it all. Besides I could hardly open a conversation by asking if you had heard any good secrets lately, could I?' It was Adam's turn to laugh. She asked him about Newfoundland and he told her about the origins of the Colony while grunting with the heavy volume. She was a good listener, and after ten more painful minutes, she asked Adam to dress then sit outside while she prepared her report for Dr Baxter.

As he sat, he realised how easily he had been able to talk with this girl once the ice had been broken. By the time she had completed her report and come out to give Adam the sealed envelope, he had made a decision. 'Will you have dinner with me tonight?' he asked her, having in mind a return visit to Charles' restaurant where he had entertained Deirdre.

'I think it would . . . oh no I shouldn't. Why not? I would love to. Thank you very much, and my name is Eleanor Scrivener, and I'm a widow, and I'm just getting over it.'

It was Adam's turn to be confused. 'Oh well perhaps . . . would it be too much . . . I'm very sorry . . . but I mean . . . I never knew.'

She placed her hand on his and smiled, 'I told you that to save you being embarrassed later on. Will we really go to dinner?'

'Yes please, and my name is Adam.' They made arrangements to meet later and Adam went back to the Outpatient Office for his appointment with Squadron Leader Baxter.

Baxter opened his remarks with no frills or gambits. 'Your X-ray shows good healing from the surgery, but Mrs Scrivener is a bit worried that you still have a residual weakness in prolonged testing. But you're looking very well. You must have enjoyed your stay at home away from the war. But we can talk of that later. Let's see what her report meant.' He also had a heavy weight copy of Gray's Anatomy and it ended up in Adam's hand above his left shoulder. After three minutes, Adam dropped the book and tried to ease his painful shoulder. He told Baxter of his experience piloting the Liberator.

Baxter listened carefully and responded, 'We've not been aggressive enough in getting your muscle tone up to snuff. Walking with your fingers doesn't challenge your muscles a hell of a lot, and I'm going to have you see Mrs Scrivener every day for the next ten days. Then we can set up another Board and try to bring your case to what Sir Wilfred would call "a splendid termination". Come to think of it, it might be an idea to get Sir Wilfred to look at you now and after the exercise programme. Hold on a moment.' He lifted the telephone and asked his secretary to get the earliest possible appointment for Sir Wilfred to see Flight Lieutenant Aitken.

He asked Adam about his trip and was interested to hear of the conditions in Newfoundland and Canada. Adam had just told him of his phone call to Sir Wilfred about Giles Lamotte, when Baxter's phone rang. He picked up the receiver again, listened for a short time, then asked Adam, 'You're at the Commonwealth Club, aren't you?' Adam nodded. Baxter relayed this to the caller, listened again for a brief moment then put the receiver down with a smile. 'You're getting the de luxe service, my dear chap. Tomorrow morning at 7.45 ack emma Sir Wilfred will pick you up and take you to Beaulieu to see the chap you've just told me about, and examine you for the record. He'll have you back in London by lunchtime. So don't get up to excesses tonight. I want you bright eyed and bushy-tailed first thing tomorrow.'

Adam grinned and told of his dinner engagement. Baxter was delighted. 'She lost her husband last year. He was a Surgeon Lieutenant on the *Ark Royal* when she was sunk in the Atlantic. I think she's been moping too much. She hasn't had an evening out since then, I'm sure. You'll be as good for her as she'll be for you with her copy of Gray's Anatomy.' Adam grimaced at the prospect.

Harness and Hatches Secure

On his way back to the Club, he called in at the restaurant and found Charles tidying up after lunch. He was delighted to have a chance of serving Adam again and promised roast beef and Yorkshire pudding with Stilton to finish, and the house claret. He reported that Deirdre and the Commander had not yet been in to celebrate his return. He knew that Deirdre had told her husband that her sense of humour had been rescued by Charles and an oh so gallant Colonial RAF officer.

'We may have to do the same again tonight, Charles. I shall count on your help once more, this time with a girl whose husband was lost at sea.'

Charles clicked his heels and gave an elaborate salute. '*Oui, mon colonel.*' Adam burst out laughing, for Charles had given a perfect imitation of the pompous French Officer who had sent him off on his disastrous mission to France.

Eleanor had taken trouble to dress up for the evening out. She wore a light blue hat with flowers on the brim, and a flowered dress to match. Blue was her colour for it matched the brilliance of her eyes to contrast with the pink in her cheeks brought out by excitement. When they arrived outside the restaurant, she gasped. 'Jimmy and I always had an ambition to have a meal here, but we never could afford the time or the money.'

Inside they were greeted by Charles, who bowed. She said, 'My husband, my late husband, and I always wanted to come here.'

Charles took her hand. 'And I, madame, have always wanted you to come here.' He raised her hand and kissed it gallantly, intensifying the pink in her cheeks and the sparkle in her eyes.

Adam could not help smiling as they sat down and she looked all round the room taking in every detail, and exclaiming, 'It's lovely. It's our dream come true.' She sighed happily. 'I suppose it's rude of me to talk of Jimmy when I'm with you, but I'm never going to forget him. I'm determined to make a life for myself though. You're helping me to take the first step. Why have you been grinning at me ever since we came in here?'

'Because I enjoy being with someone so pretty and who is having such a good time, without expecting to be fussed over. And I don't mind hearing about Jimmy.'

She looked down at her left hand and he saw that she wore her wedding band and engagement ring. 'I'm not ready to stop wearing these yet, but I don't wear them to work as they pinch my finger.'

'Serve you right for torturing unsuspecting victims like me,' Adam joked.

She laughed out loud, a chuckling infectious laugh, then quickly clapped her hand over her mouth as an elderly lady at the next table gave a long stare. Adam mused that his recent experiences with women, with Deirdre, with Shouter's widow and now with Eleanor, had identified him clearly as a man who could make women laugh.

Eleanor talked of her background. Her father was a Chartered Accountant in a small agricultural town in Derbyshire. She had wanted to be a nurse, but her mother had insisted that she should study for physiotherapy, which was more suitable for a well-brought up young lady. While she was training she had met Jimmy who was working at anything that would pay him to get through medical school. His father was a carpenter in a neighbouring town and Eleanor's mother was distressed that her daughter was attracted to a young man with no family background at all. 'Mummy has a thing about disastrous marriages to men with no background.

'We got married when Jimmy graduated and came to London so that he could do his post graduate training in chest surgery at Hammersmith. I landed my very good job at the National Hospital, and he had finished the first part of his Fellowship when war broke out. He could have been exempted but he felt he had to do his bit, so he joined up, had a few weeks in Portsmouth then was posted to the *Ark Royal*. He was lost last November, on the thirteenth, unlucky for him and for me.

'I find it easier to be away from home. I don't get on with my mother-in-law either, because I lured her son away from home. If he had stayed with her, he could have been a school doctor, and not got himself lost at sea.'

Her head was bent and she was pushing her wedding ring up and down her finger. Adam reached over the table put a finger under her chin and raised her face up. 'Where is the smile, where is the laugh, where is the sparkle in your eye, where is the pink cheek? If they don't return immediately I shall get Gray's Anatomy and you know what that means, now don't you?'

The smile came, her eyes shone, her cheeks grew pink, she laughed quietly and pleaded, 'Oh no, Sir, not that. I beg you.' Her laugh pealed out suddenly and she looked quickly at the next table. The lady and her escort had finished their meal and were coming to their table.

Adam scrambled to his feet and acknowledged them, 'Sir, Madam.'

'Young man, your young lady has a delightful laugh and you must do all you can to make sure she uses it. My husband and I have enjoyed hearing it tonight. It has lifted our spirits in a time when there's not very much to laugh about. Thank you and bless you, my dear.' She bent down and kissed Eleanor gently.

Her husband shook Adam's hand and nodded to the ribbons on his tunic. 'You've had a good war, I see. I've never flown. It must take a lot of courage just to go up there, never mind getting shot at. God bless you, Sir.' He turned to Charles who had come up quietly to ensure there was no problem. 'Thank God there are young people like that around, Charles. It means there's a future for us.' Charles smiled and showed them out.

He returned to Adam and Eleanor. 'That was General Sir Oliver and Lady Brander. I hope you weren't embarrassed. They were being quite sincere. They lost two of their three sons in the Battle of Britain and their youngest was killed in March in a bombing raid over Germany. They don't talk of their losses. I admire them greatly. Now I have good news for you both. I am instructed, nay commanded, to capture you with claret and Stilton and not to let you leave. If I don't obey, a certain lady will, as she so charmingly puts it, have my guts for garters.'

Eleanor looked puzzled and Adam explained how he had met Deirdre and had dined her here when she was at a low ebb. Her husband had now returned from being a prisoner of war. Adam hesitated wondering whether Eleanor would be upset that Deirdre's husband had survived but Jimmy had not. Eleanor guessed this and assured him that this would not upset her in the least.

He was explaining Deirdre's background when the door of the restaurant opened and Deirdre burst in, calling, 'Where is he, my own Colonial gentleman flier?' She left a tall dark coated figure being greeted by Charles and made straight for Adam. She kissed him excitedly, and with her arms still round him, turned to Eleanor, 'Isn't he a real sweetie? I told Charles to let us know if Adam ever popped up here again. We're delighted. Bring Roger over, Charles.' She continued quietly to Adam, 'He lost both his eyes. That's why the Germans weren't keen to keep him prisoner and shipped him out.'

The tall man with a badly scarred face and wearing dark glasses followed Charles with a hand on his shoulder. Deirdre introduced him to Eleanor and Adam. 'At last I get to meet the famous Adam who saved my wife's sanity.' Adam exchanged a brief glance with Eleanor.

Roger felt for the edge of the table then the chair and sat down. 'Let's have some of Charles' great claret. I've just worked out a way of pouring wine without spilling too much.' Charles set a glass before Roger who felt gently for the rim with his left forefinger. He brought the bottle in his right hand down gently until it touched the rim, curled his finger into the glass, and began to pour. When the wine touched his finger tip, he stopped pouring, set the bottle down, then declared, 'Now we're tickety-boo,' and toasted Adam and Eleanor. The others drank in response.

Deirdre asked Adam about his recent trip, and he told them about the contrast between the Canadian scene and wartime London. After a while Deirdre announced she was going to the Ladies room, Eleanor went with her. Adam wondered at this particularly female social custom. Roger dismissed it as one of life's mysteries. He then asked if Adam thought the recent Canadian losses at Dieppe had made the Canadians bitter. Adam felt there was some bitterness, but there was also a sense that Canada was now committed.

Roger spoke quietly, 'I was involved with Dickie Mountbatten in earlier planning for this raid. He was led on by General Montgomery, another publicity hound, into thinking that all he had to do was to go round the Canadian troops telling them how good they were and they would be as good as the fully trained British Commandos. I wasn't convinced the Canadians were ready for that kind of swashbuckling operation.

'As part of the planning I was sent to do photo-reconnaissance of the beaches around Dieppe, flying a Blackburn Roc of all things, and was shot down, had a hell of a crash landing, knocked my face about and literally lost my eyes. I couldn't see to run anywhere, so I got captured. The Jerries were good to me in hospital but the guards in the prison camp were real swine. They took great pleasure in telling me about the large number of casualties they had inflicted at Dieppe. I thought they were lying until I heard the BBC here.'

'I heard a figure of over 4,000 casualties for a one day operation,' said Adam.

'That's about it,' Roger agreed. 'Remember it was all to gratify Mountbatten's desire to get into the history books.'

Adam had harboured this awful suspicion and Roger had confirmed it. He was upset and changed the subject by asking Roger what he was going to do now. 'I get sent to the best school, old boy, St Dunstan's,' was the answer, 'and there I learn all sorts of ways of not falling over the furniture, how to read Braille, how to pee straight, perhaps get guided by a dog and how to operate a telephone exchange. The telephone business seems to be the most favoured, but I don't see me making a career out of it. Once I get house trained at St Dunstan's I'll think of something a bit more daring. Can I ask you a favour, old man, although I really don't know you?' Adam agreed.

'Deirdre thinks the world of you, you know. She's going to have a hard time of it with me. She wouldn't take help or advice from any old chum, but she would from you.'

Adam broke in, 'You'd like me to keep in touch and keep an eye on her and offer any help I can.'

'Spot on, old chum, especially the keeping the eye on her bit. I haven't got one to spare.'

Adam winced, recalling his blind friend in St John's. He frowned, 'Of the two of us you're grounded, I'm sure. I'm the one likely to get the chop,' was Adam's reply.

Roger shrugged, 'In that case I'll offer to help Eleanor. I hear the ladies coming out of the loo, so put the bottle beside my glass, and I will pour myself another, then you can serve yourself and the girls. Come and see my trick again, Eleanor.'

He poured until the wine rose to touch his finger again. 'There we are. Tickety boo once more. Drink up darling and we'll haul Eleanor and Adam round to the flat to damage that new bottle of Bushmills you bought for me.' Adam explained that he was having a medical examination in the morning and had been told to be bright eyed and busy tailed. Eleanor had to be at work and she had to leave as well.

They parted promising to keep in touch with Deirdre and Roger. It was a pleasant autumn evening and London was quiet, still waiting for the nightly blitz to start. They walked slowly without exchanging a word for a while. Eleanor broke the silence, holding Adam's arm as she spoke. 'I'm glad that never happened to Jimmy. His whole life would be ruined and I would not know where to start helping him. That's what Deirdre feels at the moment. She told me all this in the Ladies' room.'

Adam stopped and turned to her. 'My plan was to give you a pleasant evening out to welcome you back to life, not to have a new set of problems paraded before you. I didn't know about Roger, but I'm not too happy about him going to St Dunstan's. I know nothing about the place, but he seems so cynical about it.'

Eleanor explained that St Dunstan's was a major charity in Britain, founded to help blinded ex-servicemen and their children, and operated with no government funding. Adam frowned, 'It's not St Dunstan's. It's the way that Roger talks about it.'

As they reached the entrance to Eleanor's flat she clasped his hands. 'I never expected my first evening out to be so eventful. You fulfilled a wish when you took me to Chez Charles. We laughed at silly things. You diverted me from a bout of self-pity. I've never met such courageous people as the Branders. I think Deirdre is a strong person, strong enough to cope with Roger being blind. I hope so. Tomorrow night I want to get to know you and to let you get to know me. We shall meet at Queen's Square at 4.15. You will be my last patient for the day, and we shall have fun and games with Gray's Anatomy.' She stifled Adam's groan with a kiss then ran inside.

CHAPTER 16

Adam was at the front door of the Commonwealth Club, when a gleaming black 1933 Bentley rolled to a stop, and a grizzled haired chauffeur jumped out to open the rear door. Sir Wilfred was sitting reading *The Times*, wearing an Air Commodore's uniform, with a row of First War medals under his RFC pilot's wings. 'Had your breakfast? Good. Now I talk my head off the whole bloody day, but not in the mornings, until I get indignant at something in *The Times*. Here's a couple of pages to keep you quiet for a bit.'

Adam settled back to read the report of a discussion of fat stock prices in the House of Lords. After a time, he heard the remainder of *The Times* being crumpled up and Sir Wilfred grunting and grumping at an editorial which cautioned Bomber Command against becoming twentieth century Vandals and Goths. 'This is the kind of thing that the Bishops are always on about. Don't they know there's a bloody war on?'

Adam changed the subject. 'I never knew you were a flier, Sir Wilfred.'

'Only for about a year at the end of the First World War. I flew a Handley Page bomber. It looked like and flew like a pair of park gates, but I was very proud of being chosen to fly it. Still am. Got an M.C. for dropping bombs on the Huns. Suppose that *Times* fellow would have called me a Vandal.

'I've got my uniform on because some Frenchies are coming to see the six French Canadians we've got on the wards, including your chum. I remembered you had got a *Croix de Guerre*, so you'd be a good man to have on my side today. So tell me what you did on your leave and how your shoulder shaped up.' Adam told him and expressed his concerns that the shoulder was not improving quickly enough. Sir Wilfred proceeded to ask probing questions about the mobility of the joint and the quality of sensations.

To Adam's embarrassment he had to take off his shirt and be prodded and poked by Sir Wilfred. During this examination, several cars happened to draw alongside and the drivers and passengers were intrigued or shocked by the conduct of one of His Majesty's serving officers in the back seat of this magnificent vehicle. His examination ended as they reached the stone pillars of the Beaulieu estate. Adam was fully dressed by the time they had stopped at the back entrance to the mansion. 'I can't clear you fully for flying, you know. There's a hell of a lot of work to be done in strengthening all the neck and shoulder musculature and I will recommend that you have some fairly strenuous exercises.' Adam explained that this had already been started.

Sister Rodgers was delighted to see Adam. She reported that Giles and the other Canadian patients were doing very well. Sir Wilfred asked, 'Could we to get Lamotte into theatre in two weeks time?'

The Sister nodded. 'And the limb fitter is standing by to do the measurements once you've seen him this morning.'

'Good. Now do you have enough of your digestive biscuits for me to invite young Aitken here to have tea with us?' She led them into her sitting room where morning tea was set.

When Adam visited Giles, the apprehensions about his reception were unjustified. The flabby sullen young man who had gone out of his way to be offensive in Montreal was now slimmer, brighter, and very much in control of himself and his feelings. He had received a letter from his parents, so he thanked Adam sincerely for his help. 'Well, here I am, a changed person from the one you met who hated the English. I joined up and got my commission quite quickly. To my surprise I began to like Army life, largely because I was so proud of my soldiers. We always did very well in the training exercises, and I wanted to show the world how good my Fusiliers were. We were like children when we arrived in England, wanting to go and fight the Germans right away. We hung around, did exercises, but did not fight.'

Adam smiled. 'I know the feeling. I flew night patrols in the North of England while German bombers came over the South of England. What was it like at Dieppe?'

Giles shrugged. 'Dieppe was to be our introduction to battle. Lord Mountbatten told us we were ready for action and tough, and we believed him.' Adam remembered Roger's comments on Mountbatten deliberately misinforming these raw troops.

Giles continued with his account of the Dieppe landing. He and his fusiliers were held offshore in a landing craft. They were to be sent in to mop up any resistance from the few Germans that were expected to remain in the town. Accordingly they only carried light arms to allow them to move rapidly through the streets. Giles sighed. 'One of Napoleon's wisest generals said that the only thing that can be expected in battle is the unexpected. At Dieppe the unexpected was that German Waffen SS troops had been exercising in the area and we Canadians found ourselves facing a hardened enemy.'

When Giles and his fusiliers were sent ashore, they got no further than the beach before they were pinned down by heavy machine-gun fire. 'As one sweep passed our position, I led my men to the foot of a sea wall and we dived into shelter beside a group of British Commandos who had just finished "doing a bit of damage to Gerry Headquarters".' Giles laughed. 'That's the way their commanding officer talked, all la-di-dah. He called me "old boy", but they were very experienced fighters and had been in and out of the town with only one casualty. Six of my men had been hit in about 15 minutes.'

Giles shook his head and continued, 'The English officer asked if we would like to join in their attack. I agreed, for anything was better than lying low with our heads down. He took a dozen of his "lads" back into the town through a sewer drain, and at 17.30 I took my fusiliers along the wall towards the pillbox. The rest of the commandos made a diversion by running one by one to hide behind a burnt out troop carrier vehicle on the beach. I lobbed a grenade in front of the pillbox and my men followed suit. As the explosions died off we heard shots from the town side as the commandos began their attack. I led over the wall. There were some rifle shots coming from our right. I did not expect that. I was hit in the leg and went down hard with a number of my men going down beside me. I could not raise myself to fire my rifle. The Englishman rallied his men to go to the flank. Suddenly the pill box was silenced, and he came back to me to find out how I was. My two second lieutenants had been killed. Most of my senior NCOs were casualties, and I could not walk. He got the wounded collected under cover, did appropriate first aid then had us moved quickly down to a field station on the beach. Before he left he shook me by the hand and said how well we had fought. "You're real soldiers," he said as he and his men moved off. I never saw him again. I am proud of my men and I want all Montreal to know they were real soldiers. I, who once hated the English, was with English soldiers in battle, learned about fighting from a la-di-dah English officer and now I'm being looked after in an English chateau by an English Sir.'

Giles then asked Adam an unexpected question. 'Do you think it better to have my leg off below the knee or above the knee? I am sure Sir Wilfred thinks my leg has to come off. The infection below my knee is very much better. If it heals up, I could have an artificial leg below the knee, which would be easier to put on and to walk with. I hope to raise it with Sir Wilfred.' Adam said he was not qualified to have an opinion, but Giles' reasoning sounded good.

Giles asked how his parents had been when Adam saw them in Montreal. He expressed anger at how Amélie had been let down by the little rat she had married. Adam agreed, but thought she was tough enough to get over the disappointment. At that moment a nurse came to say that Sir Wilfred would like to see Adam. He said goodbye to Giles, promised to telephone his parents to tell that he was in good spirits and returned to the sitting room.

Sir Wilfred looked grave. 'I've decided this is the day I tell young Lamotte that his leg has to come off. This is a job I hate doing. I know I should be all tactful about breaking the news, but you'll agree that's not the kind of chap I am.'

Adam smiled. 'I think young Lamotte has been screwing up courage to tell you that his leg has to come off. He also has an idea that if you wait for the flesh to heal below the knee, it would be better to have it off lower rather than higher.'

Sir Wilfred laughed. 'Well, I'll be buggered. Did you put him up to this?'

Adam shook his head. 'No. He's just been telling me about it, in the hope that I might hint at it to you.' Sir Wilfred shook his head, and stumped off down the corridor.

Sister Roberts took Adam along to the reception room, where several of the staff were waiting to greet the visiting French delegation. Sister Roberts was introducing him to various doctors in uniform, when the French party entered led by Lieutenant Colbert. Adam recognised him immediately from the botched up attempt to rescue the Admiral, and his investiture with the *Croix de Guerre*. Colbert went straight up to Adam, saluted and stepped forward. Adam stepped back, fearing another kiss. Colbert turned on his heel and addressed his colleagues rapidly. Adam got the gist of what was said and blushed.

Colbert then turned to the staff and spoke in English. 'Ladies and gentlemen, I have just said that the Lieutenant Atking fought bravely for France in a highly secret operation, and he is recognised as a wounded hero.' He bowed, then joined the others who were leaving to visit the French Canadians.

Adam stayed behind and was joined after a short time by Sir Wilfred, who declared he had found Giles in good heart and they had settled on a below the knee amputation for the week after next. Sir Wilfred went on, 'I found just the chap in Montreal. He did his training under me and he'll be able to keep an eye on the results of my handiwork and get young Lamotte's rehabilitation off to a good start – better than yours turned out, I hope. You've met the Frenchies. I've met them. So our duty to King and country is now over. You sit and down and read the paper, and I'll do the notes and the letter about you. Then we'll go and have a free scoff with the visitors, and head home early. I'm taking my wife out to dinner and I won't change out of uniform. That'll please her. She says I cut a romantic figure like this. I think I ought to be outside a cinema, getting people to queue up in an orderly fashion.'

At the end of the lunch Sir Wilfred stood up. 'Right then, we've had a fine time. I propose a toast to the *entente cordiale*, the French, the French Canadians, the lad from Newfoundland, the Scots, Welsh, Irish and English and, of course the Yorkshiremen, including myself.' On this note of magnanimity the party finished and he and Adam were soon in the stately Bentley bowling back to London.

Later that afternoon Adam told Eleanor Sir Wilfred's views and she showed him no mercy. She invited him to accompany her to hear a Chamber concert given by the Boyd Neel quartet. He had never heard Chamber Music before and was transported by the perfect blend of the string instruments, each played by a maestro.

At her flat they listened to a record of chamber music. When she got up to take the record off, he stood up too. He put his arms round her gently, then kissed her for a long time, trembling as new sensations spread over him. She sighed deeply then led him to her bedroom. They undressed each other.

The trembling excitement increased in him and he tried to say something. She silenced him, 'Don't speak. I want you to make love to me.' She lay down and he stretched over her. She sighed and moaned 'Yes, that's it. Yes, Yes,' as they reached a climax.

Afterwards he lay back and said ruefully, 'I hope you won't think badly of me.' Eleanor burst into a giggle, 'That's what the girl is supposed to say. We're just two people who broke down our inhibitions and enjoyed each other.'

Adam confessed it was his first time, and he was slightly afraid at how intensely he had felt. She turned to him, placed a finger over his lips and moved her hand slowly down his body. In the morning she rushed off to work and he walked back to the Commonwealth Club.

On Professor Barlock's advice, he got a special ticket to the Reading Room of the British Museum and read about Electricity and Magnetism, Transmitters and Receivers, and built up the ideas of sending and receiving signals which were derived from smooth wave forms at frequencies within the range of the human ear. The emphasis was on minimising distortion in favour of smooth forms consistent with fidelity. He felt that he had made some great discovery and tried to explain it to Eleanor by pointing out these distortions on her gramophone. She was not impressed.

He went to Beaulieu to visit Giles, who had had his leg off and was to return to Montreal in ten days time by the Atlantic ferry. The news from Montreal was that Amélie was writing a weekly feature on women at war, and his parents were excited at the prospect of having their son back. Giles excitedly pulled out a magazine from under his pillow. 'You remember I told you about the lah di dah English Officer at Dieppe. Here he is. He is Lord Lovat and he was there with his number Four Commando.' There was an article on Lovat's Scouts at Dieppe and a picture of this famous soldier on the beach talking to his men, with a hunting rifle slung over his shoulder. Adam returned to London, pleased that Giles was in good heart.

The Medical Board confirmed Adam's passenger status on operational flying. The special course of instruction on airborne Radar would take about six weeks, and would be held at Number 7 Radio School in a small classroom in the College of Art in South Kensington. Adam would be one of a group of ten aircrew, selected for this special training.

PART TWO

JOCK

1940-1942

CHAPTER 17

Scotland's River Clyde gained an international reputation in shipbuilding from the yards, factories and works which developed on the seaward side of Glasgow, before the river broadens into the estuary and then the Firth of Clyde. Inland on the east side of Glasgow, the river rises in the Leadhills of Lanarkshire then flows towards the city through the fertile Clyde Valley with rolling farmlands, nursery gardens and greenhouses, producing flowers, fruits and vegetables. To meet wartime needs, these smallholding operations had been expanded under the 'Dig for Victory' policy, with government control of both production and distribution of the harvest.

Andrew Davidson was a mid-level grade civil servant, in his middle forties, who headed the Inspectorate of the Lanarkshire Division of the Ministry of Food. His efforts to ensure that small-scale farmers and market gardeners adhered to the Ministry's guide lines were not popular but he accepted the opprobrium of the local growers as part of his war effort.

He owned a solid stone built two-storey home on the outskirts of Hamilton, a prosperous agricultural centre and market town for the area. He was a Sergeant in the Local Defence Volunteers, and, like other volunteers, found it embarrassing to explain how their endless drills with broomsticks fitted into the country's defence tactics.

Edith, his wife of 20 years, was proud that her husband had achieved security and high standing in the community. This status, with her personal commitment and energies, helped her to assume leadership in the local Women's Voluntary Service. Her present duties were centred on a canteen at the railway station which served tea and sandwiches to servicemen passing through. She wanted to start a club for servicemen who were permanently stationed in the area, a place where they could relax, write letters, meet and make friends and be entertained by each other and by the local people. The ideal place was the Church Hall, but she could not persuade Mr Craig, the parish minister, that it would not become a centre for sin. In her arguments with him, she displayed a ready wit and an ability to put over heavy sarcasm with a light touch, designed to avoid offending all but the oversensitive.

Robin, her elder son, a 17 year old, had inherited her ready wit, but did not yet display the diplomacy which made it useful in debate. His teachers at the Glasgow Technical College, she had been told, had been forced to improve their performance after this brash first year student had taken one of them to task for a sloppy explanation of something technical. Two years before that, the Reverend Mr Craig had been challenged by Robin on the inadequacies of superstition as an explanation of the divine aspects of the life of Christ. He had admitted to Robin in private that the idea of resurrection was perhaps illogical. The following Sunday he had been appalled to be loudly heckled by the indignant 15 year old Robin in his own church when he had referred to resurrection as the single most important basis for Christian belief.

The family meal had just finished. As she looked at Robin, over the supper table, sitting next to his younger brother, William, she contrasted their looks. Robin, stocky and always ready to respond to some challenge, William the dreamer, tall and shy, but able to respond in kind to Robin's assertions. She remembered how William had pointed out to Robin that his cheap debating trick might have been at the expense of the Reverend Craig's public embarrassment. Robin had gone and apologised, but she had never heard whether this apology had provided any solace to poor Mr Craig.

'I'm off to the Air Force. I've to report to Padgate in ten days time,' Robin said producing the buff official envelope which had arrived for him by the morning post. 'I'll tell them at the Tech tomorrow. They know about it anyway and they'll be keeping my place for me.'

Edith fought to keep her tears in control and looked at her husband. He realised she was expecting some response from him. He cleared his throat. 'That's where the recruit pilots go. It's near Crewe station, I think.' The expression on his wife's face clearly indicated that she expected more, so he continued lamely, 'We'll keep your place here of course.'

Edith burst out 'I don't want you to join up!' and with a sob rushed out of the room.

Andrew said quietly 'I'd better go and see she's all right. We knew this day would come when you volunteered. I don't want you to go either, but . . .' He trailed off, then left the room quietly.

Robin watched him go. 'Once more Davidson has stuck his great foot in it,' he said.

William shook his head sadly. 'Will you never learn?'

The next few weeks were filled with unfamiliar activities, saying goodbye to friends and neighbours, persuading his mother that he did not need to buy a good suit, travelling a long distance on a crowded train to England, being shouted at by corporals and living in a hut with many other young men from all parts of the country.

The most disturbing part of this group living was the 'dawn chorus' from the smokers who woke up coughing, lit a cigarette 'to clear the tubes, you know', then burst into ear shattering hacks, harrumphs and long drawn out gasps, their eyes bulging, their faces crimson. Robin continued to be a non-smoker, but occasionally joined the other recruits at a pub, only to drink fizzy lemonade. Occasionally he attended dances with them.

He did his ab initio training in a de Havilland Tiger Moth, a biplane built in 1936 which rattled as a result of the thousands of bounced landings it had made. He learned that the Tiger Moth was a better flier than he was, and was advised that if he got into trouble with his hands and feet, he should let everything go loose and the Tiger would correct herself.

After four hours of instruction, he told his sergeant instructor he could fly this machine anywhere. When the Chief Flying Instructor, a tired looking Warrant Officer, was told of this, his first response was a noncommittal grunt. Then he asked the sergeant if Robin was worthwhile keeping on the course. On hearing the sergeant's positive 'Yes', he leaned forward and said, 'If you want to save him, here's what you should do.' As he spoke a hopeful grin developed on the younger man's face.

Next morning Robin was asked to climb to five thousand feet. At this height he was asked to name all the cloud formations in sight. While he was doing this, the sergeant suddenly cut the engine and hauled the stick back with the port wing down. The resultant spin gave Robin a feeling of alarm which he had never experienced before. He got some control, but did not restore power to resume level flight until he was under two thousand feet. The instructor, who had remained silent while Adam was wrestling with the Tiger Moth, took over and landed. 'You made a right botch of that. You forgot a lot of things from the last few lessons up there, but worst of all you didn't show any respect for being in the air.' Robin opened his mouth to argue, but wisely closed it then mumbled, 'I'm sorry.'

Two days later, after he had diligently learned to get into and out of spins, he had a check flight by the Chief Flying Instructor, then was told to do a circuit on his own. He felt elated but tense, remembered and carried out all the pre-flight checks and procedures. As he lined up on the strip and began to push the throttle open, he spoke to the aeroplane. 'Now come on, wee Tiger, you've only got one man to carry now. That's it. Your tail's up. Now bring your nose up. Wasn't that nice? See you could do it. Now we'll climb and then we'll go round. A nice smooth turn.' Talking to the Tiger Moth the whole way round, he flew his first solo impeccably. When he landed, taxied to the flight hut, and switched off, the chief instructor shook his hand and told him he was a good pilot, but he would be a good flier when he had some self discipline.

After his passing out parade, he wore his wings and his sergeant's tapes on his long weekend leave at home. He was aware of the quiet bursting pride of his father and mother. William was agog to know when he would be flying a Spitfire. At his mother's insistence he attended a Saturday night dance at the Church Hall Canteen, which the Reverend Mr Craig had eventually come to accept as a valid way of helping those young men and women in the Armed Forces. Mrs Davidson, with her volunteer helpers, served behind the refreshment table, glorying in the comments about how handsome her Robin looked in his uniform.

After Robin had danced the Waltz Valeta with Fiona, the red-haired girl from next door, Mr Craig came up to him, congratulated him warmly on his success and diffidently said that he would pray for him and all the others who had gone to war. Robin hesitated then thanked the Reverend, adding, 'I'm sure I'll need your prayers.' He was as surprised as Mr Craig at the sincerity with which he said this.

His mother had returned home before the dance ended, so in the local parlance Robin saw Fiona home. As they walked slowly through the blacked out streets, the excitement of the evening had made him talkative. He solemnly explained the theory of flight to Fiona as they passed from the shopping area to the tree-lined avenues of the suburbs.

At one point Fiona burst out laughing, put her arm through his affectionately, and said, 'Robbie, we've known each other all our lives and this is the most you've ever said to me. And I don't understand a word of it, and I don't care. I just enjoy being with you.'

He hesitated and wisely decided not to repeat his explanation of lift and drag. 'I would like it fine if I could write to you,' he said guardedly.

She squeezed his arm 'And I would like to write to you. I'll be nursing at Killearn from next week on, but just send your letter to my home and give me your new address.'

The next day Robin travelled to Lincolnshire for advanced training, initially on Miles Magisters, then on Airspeed Oxfords. The conversion to twin-engines Robin accepted as destiny, pointing him to bombers rather than fighters. He admitted to himself that the steadier, but more complex handling required of a multi engine aircraft was more in keeping with his temperament.

His first operations were in Handley Page Hampdens, dropping leaflets over German cities. However these relatively slow aircraft proved to be little match for the Luftwaffe fighter pilots. Robin was eventually posted to an Operations Training Unit then to a Wellington squadron where the number of Volunteer Reservists, like himself, was about the same as regular RAF personnel.

His squadron was housed on a station, built before the war. Solid living, eating and recreational quarters were located beside a variety of structures which held offices and stores and paraphernalia for the complex web of skills and practices required to put a dozen or so aircraft into the air, to drop bombs on a distant target, run the gauntlet of fighters, anti aircraft and other hazards and return to have the aircraft serviced and repaired and the crew fed, housed, entertained, get haircuts, have laundry done, get paid regularly, have their health and welfare monitored, socialise with their fellows, worship and play sports, all in this village known as the station.

At first he was confused, but found refuge in his own room in the sergeants' mess. It was small, sparsely furnished with a plywood table, two folding wooden chairs, an iron bed, three brown canvas covered 'biscuits' which together formed the mattress, a pillow and a pillow case, blankets and sheets, all duly signed for in stores. This was his place to think, to read, to dream and to write to Fiona.

The phoney war was still on, and the Wellingtons were expected to attack only military installations and shipping. In Parliament an exhortation by one member to bomb the Krupps munitions factory in the Ruhr was countered by the Air Minister who pointed out that this could not be done as it could result in damage to private property.

From June 1940 Europe was closed after the Germans had captured France and the Low Countries. British bombers now had to cross 200 miles of German held territory to reach their nearest targets. In contrast, German bombers just had to fly across the Channel to reach theirs.

CHAPTER 18

Robin had several shake down flights with his crew in his new Wellington. The only officer was the Navigator, Flight Lieutenant John Walker, with the obvious nickname of 'Whisky'. A career officer, he had served for over 10 years, most of the time in the Middle East. He was a quiet earnest family man with a wife and two schoolboy sons living in Shropshire. His age and experience made him the anchor for the crew, in providing advice on the service approach to things, saving money and avoiding trouble. Apart from ensuring that the aircraft reached the target he set the bombsight, directed the pilot to the aiming point, then released the bombs.

The Second Pilot, Sergeant 'Digger' Drodge was a tall rangy Australian who had been a railway clerk in Melbourne. He had come from Australia to join the RAF. His performance on Wellingtons at Operational Training was not up to standard, but it was expected that operational experience would allow him to overcome his difficulties and get him a command of his own. He had acquired a detailed knowledge of airframes and engines and their mysteries and could hold his own in technical discussions with the maintenance crew, so Robin looked on him as his technical expert. Robin suspected that he overplayed the Australian, with his slang terms and phrases.

The flamboyant member of the crew was Sergeant Brian Evans, the upper gunner, who was always addressed as 'Taff'. He was a restless energetic dark haired 25 year old who had been a gymnastics instructor at a teaching training college in Cardiff before he volunteered. He had a wide selection of topics on which to harangue an audience and was always out training hard for some coming Rugby football match. He had in fact represented Wales in international Rugby for three seasons and had played for his country in the first war-time international.

The Wireless Operator was a small bow legged man, who, with his ruddy complexion and bright blue eyes could have been nothing but a jockey. Despite appearances, Sergeant 'Jimsey' Wittleton had been an assistant stage manager at a London Theatre. When he introduced a reminiscence, his audience expected more than they ever got. Once an intense discussion on whether airwomen should be allowed to climb ladders wearing short skirts was halted by Jimsey's disclosure that something worse happened to a girl who was in *Lady Windermere's Fan*. Everyone stopped talking and waited for the juicy morsel of back stage gossip. They only got a banality. 'She got a boil on her neck the next week.'

The rear gunner came from Leeds and was a furrier by trade, working with his father and two brothers. Sergeant Abie Isaacson was an orthodox Jew, who viewed the war as a grudge match between himself and the Nazis. He realised that becoming a prisoner was a greater hazard for him than for his fellows, but he wanted to punish the Germans for what they were doing to their Jewish citizens. Basically he was a quiet, well spoken, well read young man who could put over many of Bing Crosby's songs with the characteristic casual phrasing, resonant voice and slight lisp.

In their first operations Robin and his crew faced the hazards of daylight sorties over Germany. The simple methods of navigation, the lack of co-ordination or planning of the raid or selection of target, the presence of German fighters and anti-aircraft batteries led to a series of uncertainties, not just about the effect of the bombing, but whether it actually took place at or near the target.

The transition from daytime to night operations reduced some of the uncertainties but the haphazard conduct of the raids was a shock to Robin. His canny nature had led him to expect that details of take-off time, height to fly, route to the target, arrival time, time to release the bombs, would all have been worked out beforehand and specified at briefing. On the contrary, at briefing, the target was stated and the surrounding terrain described, with an intelligence officer estimating the likelihood of anti-aircraft and fighter resistance, and a meteorologist predicting the likely weather en route. Other details of the mission were at the discretion of an individual skipper. On two occasions Robin elected to go over the target at about 10,000 feet. The first time he felt that the lower height gave him the better chance to put the observer in the best possible position to release the bombs. On the second occasion he and his crew were too distracted to aim accurately by bombs being dropped just behind them from one of the squadron aircraft at twice their height.

At the briefing session on returning Robin told the scandalised Intelligence Officer that he objected to being 'shat' on from a great height. A Flight

Lieutenant in the next chair advised him never to go below 20,000 feet. 'Too dicey by far, you know. All sorts of nasty things happen down there. Get to the target at 20,000 feet, let your bombs go and get the hell out of it. That's how I stay fit.'

This was all too amateurish and reminiscent of the 'Dawn Patrol' heroics of the First World War for Robin. He exploded, 'But what about the target? We're supposed to get there and bomb where we were told to, not just blatter at anything and everything without seeing it.'

The Flight Lieutenant looked surprised at being taken to task by a Sergeant. 'Look, laddie,' he interrupted, 'I offered you good advice in a friendly manner. I don't like being told what to do by some jumped up Jock.' Robin kept his tongue under control as the officer snorted and moved away. From that day on, Robin was known as Jock.

As they flew sortie after sortie Jock came to know and respect not only the men with whom he was taking the fight to the enemy, but also the Wellington which carried them. The squadron letter, D, was allocated to their split new aircraft and the crew had decided after long deliberation to name it D for Dumbo after a favourite story book character of Taff's three year old daughter.

When Jock reflected on things, he conceded that he was still a boy. He had not reached the age of 21. He did not have a licence to drive a car yet, but he had been given a very expensive aeroplane to fly. As a schoolboy he had watched Brian Evans score two dazzling tries for Wales against Scotland in an international Rugby match. Now he was skipper of a crew with this celebrity in it. The lives of five other men who flew with him, two with family responsibilities, had been placed in his hands. It was even more strange that they deferred to him in the air as skipper of the aircraft, even though he was the youngest and the most junior in rank.

He raised these issues with Flight Lieutenant Walker. The navigator assured him that status on the ground and in the air were different things. Each member had a contribution to make to the operation of the aircraft, but a final decision could only be made by one person, the pilot, not by a committee. There had to be a leader. Jock thought about that then asked what leadership was. Whisky said that it arose from having experience and exercising judgement on the basis of that experience. Leadership was the way that other people responded to your decisions with trust. You were a leader when you found your crew asking no questions when you decided what was to be done.

Jock was surprised to realise he and his crew were among the longest surviving members of the squadron and that he had earned the accolade of being a 'lucky skipper'. The superstition had grown among the crews that if you survived the first two or three sorties, the next hurdle was the thirteenth. If you survived that, then you could count yourself among the 'lucky' ones because Dame Fortune smiled more readily on your skipper than on other skippers.

Jock noted that just before the thirteenth mission his crew was showing signs of irritation with each other's childish jokes, expressing concerns that the aircraft was no longer in good shape. On one occasion on the warm up before take-off, Taff said he thought the port engine was running rough and it might not hold out for the raid. Jock checked the dials, ran through procedures with Digger, found everything in order, then told Taff quite sharply that he should get on with his own checks as there was no reason to get out of flying that night. After a pause Taff said, 'Sorry, skipper,' and they took off.

Some members of the squadron were showing obvious signs of the stresses of operational flying, such as shrugs, blinks, winks or other unusual forms of behaviour. None of Jock's crew seemed to have developed a 'twitch', as these mannerisms were known, but he had found himself automatically reciting the days of the week forward on the run up for take-off, and saying them backwards on the run in to target when he had to follow passively the bombing directions given by Whisky Walker.

In contrast to the initial stages of the tour, the special hazards in the last two or three missions were rarely talked about. Jimsey pointed out that this was just like the theatre, where superstition held that you did not talk of the success of the show you were in. Rather than tempt fate by wishing someone luck in a new role, you cheated the Devil by doing the opposite and telling him or her to break a leg. Taff thought about that for a moment, then pronounced it stupid.

The crew of D Dumbo appreciated Lady Luck's contribution in that Bremen, lightly defended against air attack, was selected as the target for four of their last five missions of their tour and, on each occasion, the weather proved to be ideal for bombing and night flying. The last flight of their tour was yet to come.

CHAPTER 19

Kiel was the target for the last mission of their tour. After the briefing and other preparations, Taff and Jimsey went to collect the 'picnic' for the whole crew, three vacuum flasks of tea and three of Bovril, and six paper bags each containing a sandwich, glucose sweets and a piece of chocolate. Their next stop was the shed where a pretty WAAF issued their parachutes, favouring Jock with an alluring smile.

'You want to watch her, Jock,' whispered Jimsey. 'She's the "station chopper".' This unpleasant title was given to a WAAF who had been friendly with several aircrew who had later got 'the chop', the slang for being killed in action. Jock shrugged.

The usually quiet atmosphere of the short drive to D Dumbo's dispersal point was marred by a niggling argument between Taff and Jimsey. On previous visits to Kiel, flak and fighter cover had proved to be more troublesome than dangerous. This prompted Taff to predict that their mission would be a 'piece of cake'. Jimsey objected to this flaunting of their luck. Whisky Walker had inflamed matters when he reported that at the Navigator's briefing he had been told that Kiel had become one of the more vigorously defended targets.

'What did I tell you? You've spoiled our luck already, you Welsh git,' was Jimsey's final contribution. Taff glowered.

On the outward leg the weather was clear and the moon was bright enough for them to identify landmarks from their cruising height. Jock and Whisky would have preferred a deep cloud or two to duck into, as it was easy for an enemy fighter to spot them.

They crossed the enemy coast unchallenged and ahead of Whisky's original estimated time of arrival. On their run in everything remained quiet and Jock brought them down to below 10,000 feet to make sure they got a good view of their aiming point. On the perimeter of the target as Whisky was readying his bombsight, all hell broke loose from the ground in a steady wall of heavy noisy flak, which rattled and banged on D for Dumbo's fuselage. A few pieces of shrapnel penetrated Dumbo's skin. Fortunately there was no significant harm to the aircraft or its occupants.

This flak seemed to last for a long time. Whisky announced they were coming up to the target zone, and they were immediately caught in a cone of three searchlights. To get out of the trap, Jock put the nose down in a power dive, turned sharply to get back on course. He came to straight and level then held at a lower height and waited until he detected a lull in the shower of shrapnel. He dived the Wellington again to lose another thousand feet and to get out of the way of the Messerschmitts, which he guessed would be the next irritation.

No fighters appeared but they ran into another bank of flak, and in carrying out a violent evasive manoeuvre he caused Taff to crash his head against a strut of his turret. The intercom resonated with Welsh obscenities for a bit, then Jock heard his navigator call, 'Come riiiight. I see it. I see the dock area and the target. Bomb doors open.' Then the usual rumbling and creaking. 'Slowly now,' Jock throttled back to get a good level run in. 'Riiiiight.' Jock ruddered her round slightly until he heard, 'Now straight. That's good. Steady. Steady.' Whisky droned on, 'Steady now, straight and level. We can hit it nicely on this run. Steady, skipper. Steady . . . steady . . . steady. Bombs gone.' A judder as the aircraft shed its load, and a thump as the bomb doors closed then Whisky's usual epilogue, 'And that, my fine fellow fliers, ends tonight's lesson for Adolf. Bomb doors closed. Full throttle, please. Take us home, skipper.'

Jock opened up the throttles and started a climb to port until Whisky yelled, 'Wrong way!' He took a hard turn to starboard until they were clear of searchlights. Whisky explained, 'We had three Wimpies coming in just above us to port and you know what they were going to do.' Once away from the friendly Wellingtons keen to drop their loads, and climbing steadily, Jock took D Dumbo round again to confirm that their bombs had been first at the target and had straddled the target building. As they flew off they saw the other three Wellingtons, now below them, dropping their bombs, again to good effect.

The flak had stopped, so Jock told the gunners to watch for fighters. He turned on oxygen again and climbed to 15000 feet over the moonlight panorama. He asked round the crew for a check on the damage they had sustained, and was pleased to learn that no damage to persons had been sustained although Taff reported he had a lump on his head from hitting the strut. All the systems seemed to be intact, even although Dumbo's skin had been peppered, and the noises through the holes produced eldrich screeches, groans and bangs. Digger said it was like Jock playing the bagpipes.

Jock throttled back to cruising speed, and took the course for home from Whisky. He just had time to swing on to the heading, when Taff, in the upper turret, reported three Me 109s closing from behind. Abie confirmed he had them in his sights and enticed them to come closer. 'Come on, my beauties.' They accepted his invitation.

The first attack was a deflection approach from starboard, one German slightly behind and below the other two. Dumbo's fuselage was raked by bursts of machine gun fire. While the crew members were ducking and putting on safety belts, Abie was concentrating on the attacker who came in from the rear then dived below the reach of the tail gun. D Dumbo's belly was raked by a short burst from below and pieces of shattered equipment flew round dangerously in the enclosed space. The wireless console was smashed and the navigator's table was knocked from its mounting. Taff yelled that he had been hit in the head, and started groaning. Whisky called out that he would attend to Taff's wound.

Abie reported that the Messerschmitts were regrouping behind them, and that these were experienced fighter pilots whose tactics were difficult to predict. Jock anticipated an attack from the port side and was dismayed when they came again from starboard and his evasive turn presented the fighters with a side on target. He swore as this flank attack shattered the instruments in front of him. Abie was firing and cursing at the attackers as they followed each other and regrouped, like wolves looking for the kill. Dumbo's controls were sluggish, but still operative.

As the Me 109s came behind for their third attack, Abie held his fire for the middle one, whom he felt sure was going underneath them again. It did and he was rewarded by seeing his bullets smash the pilot's canopy and tear pieces from the tailplane. Digger up front saw the Messerschmitt continue its dive under no obvious control. The other two fighters climbed swiftly and turned back to take up positions on D Dumbo, one on the port flank, the other to starboard. They began their attack from 45 degrees, one raking from behind forward, the other from front to rear. The only evasive action Jock could take was to corkscrew and, as he went into a dive to starboard, he yelled 'Corkscrew' then announced over the intercom each roll, dive or climb to port or starboard as he started to execute them. The two German pilots were good enough fliers to keep up with him and continued their hellish damage as he traipsed all over the sky. In a particularly steep dive to port, the speed built up, and D Dumbo started squealing. They were no longer being hit, so he eased out of the head long plunge. The silence in his head set as he called for a report on the attackers made him realise then that the intercom was out of action.

Once he was straight and level Digger Drodge shouted that the attackers had gone and the aircraft was 'a bloody shambles', but the crew was intact. The only casualty was Taff who still had a bump on the head. The blood from his head wound had been nothing more than warm tea from a broken flask.

Jock was surprised to find that this whole damaging encounter had lasted only three or four minutes. The controls were still sluggish, but D Dumbo was climbing, admittedly slowly, to a cruising height, the engines were still turning and no apparent damage had been done to the fuel system. Whisky Walker had sorted out enough from his damaged charts to offer a course for the English coast and had estimated three hours to get to base, with their speed reduced considerably.

They had lost radio contact to the outside world as well as intercommunication within the aircraft. The Air Speed Indicator was out of commission, but the Altimeter was still reading. The engines, throttled down to cruising speed, were firing well. The fuel gauge was showing enough to get them home. Temperatures were a bit high after the aerobatics, but they were settling down.

The pilot's compass was shattered, but Whisky brought forward a bearing compass from his station. He thought the only thing needed for more precise navigation was a fix on some landmark to get an idea of speed and some estimate of the effect of the wind on the course they were making. He seemed oblivious to the tattered state of the aircraft as he expressed his navigational concerns. Jock was impressed at Whisky's calm, cool and collected attitude but felt more worried about keeping the aircraft in the air than about the finer points of Dead Reckoning.

'We're in great shape,' said Digger. Jock did not argue, but confessed that he was worried about the sluggish controls and about the hydraulics for the undercarriage. Digger cautioned against trying to get the wheels down at this stage. If they got them down and couldn't get the bastards to lock or to come back up, they could end up in worse strife than they were at the moment. He then looked at the engine gauges and nodded his head wisely. 'In the absence of any information to the contrary, Skip, you should assume that the bloody wheels are working.' To his surprise, Jock laughed. Digger gave him thumbs up and went off to look at the control cables.

Taff came next to tell him that the sky was quite clear of enemy aircraft. The upper turret had been damaged and could not be operated automatically. It could be hauled round manually, but it would take two men to do this, never mind fire the gun. The rear turret was completely jammed, and they had needed the special gear to get Abie out of it. He was sitting just outside his useless turret nursing a great hatred of the enemy who had broken his weapon. When Jock asked him how he felt, Taff said he felt a bit of a Nellie, making all that hullabaloo about getting a faceful of warm tea.

Jock told Taff to get each crew member to come forward individually, satisfied himself that they had not been wounded and asked each about the others, but got the same reply. 'We're all right, skipper.' He shook his head and smiled, as he reflected that he had all these fellows sitting in a great pile of scrap metal, nearly three miles up in the air, and they were, to quote the expert, in great shape. Bloody hell!

He became aware of an ache in his right knee, the site of an old sports injury. He recognised this as being a symptom of oxygen depletion and realised that the automatic oxygen supply was not working. He carefully lowered the nose and reduced height to 10,000 feet to prevent the crew suffering from anoxia.

They droned on, whistling and banging, alone in the sky and useless for battle. The lookouts were still keeping a wary eye open for fighters, but they were over the Heligoland Bight and fighter activity was not usually a hazard on this part of the flight. Off the Dutch coast they could expect a stray fighter or two to take an interest in them, but until then he had to think out his options.

Whisky gave him a revised estimate of their progress. If the good flying conditions held, they could make East Anglia in two and a half hours on the given heading, but he would still like to make a check on their drift to confirm their track over the ground. The opportunity presented itself as they got within visual distance of the Dutch coast and the first signs of dawn let them see a large lighthouse some miles to port. On a previous trip Whisky had identified this building on his chart so he could take a series of bearings on it as Jock held the course. After doing the sums he came up with a change in the course to fly and a revised estimate of their time of arrival.

Jock acknowledged these and changed heading. He talked his thoughts out to Whisky. They could still turn north to do an emergency landing in Denmark, but he was not sure what kind of reception they would get. He could turn in toward the north coast of Holland and they could all bale out. There were tales of airmen being helped to return to Britain by the Resistance force, but there were also tales of airmen being dumped into German POW camps. He felt that Abie would be treated badly by the German guards.

Whisky thought for a moment then said he would have a word with the others. While he was gone, Jock felt a sudden freeing of the controls and Digger returned to report that all he had done was to lever out a broken support from the navigator's table which had been jamming the cables to the controls. Jock smiled and thanked him, adding, 'We're in great shape, cobber.'

'Too right, mate,' was the laconic reply, and to Jock's embarrassment, the Australian patted him on the shoulder and shouted, 'Good on yer, skip.'

Whisky reported that the crew preferred to sit quietly where they were, rotating the look out duties while their skipper took them home. 'Right, that's what we'll do then,' said Jock, then added, archly. 'Didn't you tell me that in a bomber you couldn't do things by committee?'

Whisky grinned. 'I'm wise but I'm not always right.'

The speed was much reduced from normal because the engines had to push a collection of ragged holes through the air. Digger reported that things were going well. They knew where to go, could maintain flying speed, had fuel enough to get home. On the other hand it was flaming cold at this height and could the driver take them down a bit to where there was less bloody ice about. Jock took D Dumbo down gingerly to under 6000 feet and Digger claimed the draughts through the holes were much warmer than they had been.

The flying was less strenuous and Digger sat at the controls while Jock stretched his legs. Whisky came to tell him that Taffy could see faint outlines of coast. They were dead on course and could start to set down as they crossed the shoreline. Jock returned to his seat and he and Digger began to discuss the problem of the landing wheels. They decided the only test was to do it and if the wheels clonked down and they felt the aircraft slow down, they would accept it as being good enough to land on. They continued their slow descent and soon began to make out details of the coastline as the clear white light of the moon was tinged by the first blush of the sun rising behind them.

Within quarter of an hour Digger had let down the landing wheels. The noise level was too high to hear if the wheels had locked down, and there was no light on the panel, but they felt they had lost some speed. Jock went on to a down wind leg over the runway to let the control tower staff see the state his aeroplane was in. He was pleased to see that some of them were using field glasses and he knew that if they noticed anything wrong with the landing gear, they could warn him off with a red Verey light. There was no such signal. He completed his leg, and started his landing procedure having warned his lookouts to watch carefully for other aircraft. He could not get full flap so decided to use the full runway and keep off the stall as long as he could. He creamed over a hedge, and got his wheels on less than a hundred feet from the beginning of the runway.

He throttled right back and the tail came down in what would have been a perfect landing if the whole tail assembly had not chosen that instant to come off. He undid his harness clip and stood up on the brakes and held the control column rigid as the Wellington sped down the runway leaving its tail and gun turret at the other end of the tarmac. The screech of metal as the fuselage scraped along the tarmac was deafening inside, and the ambulance, crash wagon and fire tender raced beside the sparking, speeding and disintegrating aircraft.

The end of the runway was visible, and Jock tried to slew D Dumbo round in a ground loop to avoid hitting an armourer's hut. He then realised that the required controls were about a mile behind him. A burst tire gave him the manoeuvre he wanted and Dumbo skidded sideways to a halt. Jock and Digger switched everything off, shook hands, then with the others stepped quickly on to the tarmac from the back of the open fuselage, wary of the great heat which friction had built up.

The fire truck moved in and within minutes had a coating of foam over the remains of D Dumbo. The Medical Officer and his orderlies stood open mouthed, looking at the bullet riddled aircraft and the crew who were in no obvious need of their attention. No one spoke for a moment or so, then Whisky thanked Jock for the best flying he had ever seen. The others followed suit. Jock impatiently shrugged them off.

They were then whisked off to Sick Quarters where they were pronounced fit to attend the briefing session. This was conducted by an Intelligence officer who had put on uniform over his pyjamas and resented being awakened just to interview these late comers, who had been written off as one of the three crews missing in the action. His final question was, 'Did you sustain any damage to the aircraft?' and he was outraged when they burst into gales of laughter.

As they left to go to bed Jock told them that he had been impressed by their decision not to abandon the aircraft. There was an awkward silence, then Taff broke in. 'We had very little option, boyo, for the parachutes were all shot up by that second fighter.'

As Jock composed himself for sleep, he clasped his hands as his mother had taught him years ago and whispered, 'I don't know why you did it or how you did it. I just want to thank you, God, for saving us up there.'

CHAPTER 20

The following morning Jock felt more relaxed than he had for some time. He reasoned this was because he had finished the tour, and he expected to get some time away from flying on operations. He also suspected that the peace he had found the night before had helped to calm him down. He decided to ask the chaplain to explain prayer to him.

After breakfast he went down to the runway and saw the wreckage of D Dumbo being winched onto a trailer for transport to a scrap yard. Flight Sergeant Woodson, the ground crew chief, came to congratulate him on his feat of flying. Jock thanked him and praised D Dumbo.

'She did her job. She got you all back, lad. That's the main thing,' was Woodson's sincere answer.

An airman came out of the Section office to say that Jock was wanted in the Squadron Commander's office. As he entered the administration building the squadron chaplain, greeted him with hearty enthusiasm. 'Your name's Davidson, isn't it? You put up a good show last night, a wizard prang in fact.' He put his hands on Jock's shoulders. 'That's the way to biff the Hun,' and he continued with this schoolboy drivel until Jock said he had to leave and decided he would never ask that padre anything.

Wing Commander Thomas was in his office with another officer, whom he introduced as Flight Lieutenant Dobson. Jock recognised the officer as the one he had offended at the briefing some time ago and said coldly, 'Aye, Sir, we've had words.' Dobson's eyes twinkled and he shook Jock's hand and congratulated him on getting back. 'There's too much fuss about all that. I was very lucky. I could have put the airfield out of service. But I felt that my best chance to save the crew was on an airfield I knew,' was Jock's laconic reply.

'Will you let me make one more fuss, Sergeant?' asked the Wing Commander. 'What you did this morning had nothing to do with luck. You showed good judgement as well as good flying. I think your feat of airmanship must be written up in the squadron records.'

Jock's answer was typical. 'Aye, maybe, but I wouldn't be too keen on that. That kind of thing is better for somebody who wants to make a permanent career in the RAF, but I certainly don't.'

The Squadron Commander began to realise how difficult it was to make light conversation with a dour Scot, and looked at Dobson to take an initiative.

He took the plunge, 'Last night, over Kiel, three of us, the Wing Commander here, Squadron Leader Merton and I decided to follow your example and go in low. We saw you over Kiel even lower than we were. After you had bombed, you slipped off to port then jinked to starboard and took some of the flak with you. We homed in on your bomb bursts and got some dam' good hits. That was the first time I didn't feel uncomfortable at the return briefing, for I could point to the area where I had seen our bombs strike, not just to where we had let them go. I want to apologise for being short tempered with you at that briefing.'

Jock squirmed and hummed a bit, then held out his hand and smiled.

As others had found, a smile from Jock could prove to be disarming and Dobson was no exception. 'Can I shoot a line to you, Sergeant? My first operation was in the very first bombing raid of this war, on the day after war was declared. I was a new Flying Officer with a new Wellington and a new crew. The target was Wilhelmshaven and we were to bomb German capital ships in the port. We were a force of thirty aircraft, half Wellingtons, half Blenheims. It was raining with a cloud base of 500 feet, the worst flying weather, so bad that ten aeroplanes had to turn back as they could not find the target. One other bombed Esbjerg in Denmark, a mistake that took a lot of international fixing and compensation. Three others nearly bombed ships of the Royal Navy, until they recognised the signals of the day. They returned to base with their bombs. I got to the target but two of my bombs failed to explode and the others caused only slight damage. The German anti-aircraft shot down five Blenheims and two Wellingtons. It was a real shambles and we haven't learned a damn thing from that first operation.'

'That must have been terrible,' said Jock sympathetically. 'But maybe we can learn now.'

Dobson handed back to Thomas. 'Your tour is finished, Sergeant,' the C.O. started, 'and it would be appropriate for me to recommend you for a commission.'

Jock broke in, 'Thank you, but no, Sir, I don't intend to stay in the Service and being an officer would not appeal to me at all. But on that subject of a service career I would like you to get a Distinguished Flying Cross for Flight

Lieutenant Walker. He is a regular and has been a great navigator on every raid and a good influence on the younger fellows in the crew – like me. Last night he was outstanding.'

The Wing Commander nodded and promised he would do something. 'While I'm on it, Sir, Digger, that is Sergeant Drodge, deserves a medal too. I don't think he would want to go back to being a railway clerk. Maybe a commission for him as well would be right. Abie Isaacson deserves a medal. He's got the most guts of any of us and he's done well as our tail end gunner. He's Jewish, you know, and he would be badly treated if he ever got into the hands of the Nazis. He'll go back to the family business, so he'll not need a commission.' The squadron commander suppressed his smile at this young skipper's confident recommendations and returned to the question of tactics and planning of raids.

Jock needed no prompting. There were still too many skippers going in as high as possible, getting rid of their bombs and then beetling back to base. The majority of the bombs fell nowhere near the target. He hoped that the top brass at Headquarters could improve the bombing.

He stressed that going in low over the target was successful because the aiming and release operations were more direct. It was also a good idea to get to the target early. The flak was less of a trouble because the German anti-aircraft batteries were not set up for intruders at that altitude. 'Mind you, if more of us attacked at that level, the Gerries'd waste no time in changing the elevations of their guns.' He stole a sideways glance at Dobson. 'There's another advantage in being early. The high fliers in the squadron haven't arrived so they can't loose their load on you.'

Dobson smiled and bowed his head, 'Guilty as charged, your honour.'

Dobson and Thomas were hopeful that Bomber HQ would soon be receptive to ideas as 'Ginger' Harris was rumoured to be taking over as Chief of Bomber Command. This name meant nothing to Jock, but the two regular officers held him in high regard. After Jock had left, Dobson shook his head and smiled. 'I've just had a thought. Why don't we send Jock up to tell Harris face to face about his ideas on bombing? I can't decide whether Jock or Ginger would meet his match!'

Jock's reputation as a 'lucky skipper' held as he finished his first tour with his original crew intact, even if his aircraft was destroyed. Whisky Walker was awarded the Distinguished Flying Cross and Distinguished Flying Medals were awarded to each of the others including himself. He and Abie were promoted to Flight Sergeant. Digger was to be posted to an Operational Training Unit to do a conversion course on twin engined light bombers.

Once more Jock refused to be commissioned. In addition to his previous reasons, he suspected that a change in his status could change his luck. He could, however, find no reason to refuse promotion to Flight Sergeant.

He had a week of relatively light duties on the station, the highlight being playing rugby for RAF Bomber Command in the same team as Taff in an exhibition match against an Army XV. He recognised many of the players in the two sides as internationals he had seen in action or read about. He found himself marking a 'hard man' on the Army team, a thick set bull of a man who seemed tireless in doling out punishment to anyone who tried to stop him once he got possession of the ball. Jock was told to make sure that this man did not get past him, for he had a phenomenal tally of points scored.

The hard knocks he received from this opponent convinced Jock that he was pitted against the evolutionary missing link. The eyes were small and deep set beneath a tangle of wiry black hair, there was a heavy five o'clock shadow of a beard and a large gap where his front upper teeth should have been. His chest and thighs were massive and he had an extra hard skeleton which he used to punish opponents who dared to thwart his progress towards the goal line. Jock's upper torso and shoulders were bruised, but he kept his resolve to control this subhuman adversary.

Towards the end of the match he had to make a do-or-die flying tackle on this hard man to prevent a score. He succeeded in bringing the hard man down, but as they both crashed to the ground Jock's head was jerked back and hit his opponent unintentionally on the nose. The match ended a few moments later and Jock went up to apologise for the accidental injury he had inflicted. The victim was trying to staunch the flow of blood and it was difficult to understand what he was saying.

After the traditional noisy and rowdy shower baths, all the players, back in their uniform, enjoyed meat paste sandwiches washed down with beer or shandies made from beer and lemonade. Jock was chatting to an Army Sergeant who had played on numerous occasions for Scotland, when he was interrupted by a quiet voice asking if he might join them. The newcomer was a smartly uniformed major, newly shaved, with his denture in place and his dark hair controlled by hair dressing. He wore the paratrooper badge, and to Jock's astonishment he also had on a clerical collar. He recognised the bruised nose and the two black eyes. Jock stammered his apologies again and asked after the injuries. The victim assured him that it looked worse than it felt. He greeted the sergeant with familiarity as 'Corky'. 'I knew you wild Scots were tough, but I never knew you were lethal until I was set on by this young ruffian here.' He winked at Jock but ended up with a painful grimace.

'Holy Holt, don't you dare cast aspersions on my trusted skipper,' burst in Taff from the next group. 'He flies an aeroplane lovely. He's not a bad rugby footballer, now is he? And you'll put him up for Scotland won't you, Corky? He has talent, good enough to be a Welshman.' Jock found himself in a small group giving and taking banter in an easy manner.

It turned out that 'Holy', otherwise Major Holt, held over twenty international caps for England and was a regular Army Chaplain. He was one of several padres who had done parachute training to be able to carry out their duties wherever the men went. The paratroopers, just beginning to be recognised as a significant military force, were to hold their Church parade at Sandringham the next day and Holy Holt had been given the honour of preaching before the King and Queen. Jock tried to blurt out his apologies again, but Holy dismissed him good humouredly. 'When the King asks me tomorrow who made such a mess of my good looks I shall tell him it was a wild Scotsman. He will have you in the Tower on a charge of defacing a national treasure.'

Taff roared out, 'What national treasure? The King's never seen you coming from the back of the scrum intent on damaging a sensitive three quarter like myself. Frankenstein's monster in a bad mood – that's what you're like. You're just as ugly now as you were before young Jock got his hands on you.'

Jock chipped in, 'Not my hands, Taff, the back of my head.'

When he and Taff returned to the station, Jock realised that the day's sport and his acceptance into an élite group of top sportsmen had marked for him a rite of passage, a transition from schoolboy dreams to adult attitudes, duties and responsibilities. He thought it strange that the change should have come about from the not too mature cavortings on a rugby field.

A visiting Air Vice Marshal arrived to present their medals. A journalist and a photographer from the popular magazine *Picture Post* had been invited to attend by an official of the Ministry of Information. They already had photographs of D Dumbo as she had arrived at the scrap yard and insisted on taking a group picture of her crew in flying gear in front of someone else's Wellington. Jock gave the reporter the quote to start his article. 'The credit's not due to me or even to the crew. It should go to the men, aye and the women, who built our Wellington for us.'

At noon the whole station was paraded under the direction of Mr Grimes, the Station Warrant Officer. In the guard room he inspected the crew to make sure they were shaven, properly barbered, neat and tidy in dress, with buttons and shoes shining, then marched them on in single file to the front of the parade. Taff asked him if he would not get a medal if his buttons were dirty. Mr Grimes put his face close to Taff's and gave him a steely glare. 'We want to show the Air Vice Marshal, don't we, that an operational station can still put on bags of swank. Right?'

Taff nodded. 'Yes, sir.'

The SWO gave them the command to stand at ease, then begged Whisky, 'Try to keep this lot in order, Sir, particularly the Welsh comedian. It's just for a little while.' He then stalked off.

Taff was silent for a suspiciously long time then he burst out, 'My brother-in-law now. There's a comedian for you. He is called Dai the Pru because he works for the Prudential Insurance. He wanted to know who to get in touch with to sell the RAF insurance policies on their aeroplanes. I told him to go and see Winston Churchill and even gave him the address. I'd like to see his face when he sees the picture of D Dumbo and thinks of all the money he might have lost for the company.' They were saved the discomfort of holding back their laughter by a stentorian roar from Mr Grimes commanding the whole parade to come to attention. The ceremony began.

That evening to their surprise Jock joined the others in a celebratory drink at a local pub, sipping a half pint shandy, and refusing their offers of pints. He solemnly told them that they had not missed a mission. 'That means we got our medals for perfect attendance. I got prizes at Sunday school for perfect attendance when I was a wee laddie.'

Taff roared with laughter, 'You're still a wee laddie,' and Abie pulled Jock on to his lap, and sang, 'Climb upon my knee, Sonny boy.'

Jock glowered initially, then he caught the spirit of the evening. He stood up and sang 'Loch Lomond' in a clear tenor voice, which penetrated the hubbub of a crowded bar room, stilled the audience and drew out the chorus quietly from them. 'Ye'll take the high road and I'll take the low road. And I'll be in Scotland before ye.' When he had finished he left to return to his room to write to Fiona.

With a new crown above his chevrons and his medal ribbon with blue and white diagonals just below his wings, he went home on leave. He was idolised by William, who was planning to be a Fleet Air Arm pilot in two years time. Jock allowed himself to be persuaded to attend a meeting of the Air Cadets, in which William was a corporal, and tell the young enthusiasts about flying training. Inevitably he was asked how he got his medal, and he found himself describing operations. One young lad, whose uniform was new and too big for him, asked how they knew that they had hit a target if it was night time. Not wanting to disappoint the boys by telling them that they didn't know, Jock found himself saying that they took photographs. The next question was whether they took sandwiches with them on the raids, so the matter ended.

While shopping with his mother he was hailed by several of her friends as 'wee Robbie' and told how much he had grown. He found out the truth of this when he had to borrow clothes from his father. He called on the Reverend Mr Craig, but did not manage to ask about prayer as Mrs Craig insisted on serving tea and kept the conversation at the level of chit chat. As he left, the minister promised to keep on praying for him. Jock thanked him sincerely and told him his prayers were working very well.

The local newspaper had picked up the official announcement of his decoration so he had to get back into uniform to have a picture taken with the rest of the family in their uniforms for the front page article in the weekly *Advertiser*.

Fiona had a week off from her duties as a staff nurse in the ex-service wards at Killearn Hospital. While they were walking in the High Street she confessed it was hard looking after some of the cases who had been in the hospital since the end of the First World War. She was glad she could do it, although at first it was appalling to think of men being helpless for so many years. Jock made one of his characteristic assertions that it would have been better to put these fellows out of their misery, as they did for wounded horses. For the first time ever he witnessed a truly angry Fiona. She stopped and stamped her foot. Her eyes blazed. 'Don't you ever say that. Don't you ever dare even to think it. They're not animals. They're brave men who had terrible things done to them by other men. They're worth all the care and respect that I, aye, and you can give them.'

Jock was taken aback, and oblivious to the shoppers around them he pulled her to him and kissed her full on the lips. He moved his head back and looked her straight in the eyes, no longer blazing. 'Och, Fiona, you know me,' he said. 'I always shove my foot in my mouth. I'm sorry I upset you.'

A passerby broke in, 'So you should be, Robbie Davidson. Upsetting a nice lassie like Fiona. Would you want to lose her?'

Jock stammered, 'No, I wouldn't,' to Mrs McKelvey, a smiling neighbour who had been forced to walk round them.

He then realised he still had Fiona in his arms. 'I said that without thinking, and that was wrong,' he said.

'You kissed me without thinking and that was right,' was her retort.

An Army Corporal gently pushed them apart, 'You were always in the way, Robin,' and they spent a few minutes chatting with this school friend who was about to go overseas with his tank regiment. As they chatted, Jock found himself looking anew at the girl he had known all his life. Fiona's eyes were sparkling.

'You're in terrible trouble now, Robbie,' she said when they were alone. 'Mrs McKelvey saw it all.' Jock caught her mood.

'Aye, lass. I'll marry you, but not till I get settled down in a steady job with prospects. We could get engaged now, though. I've got enough in my Post Office Savings to buy a nice ring, I think.' She took his arm happily and led him to the display window in the High Street jeweller' shop.

CHAPTER 21

When he reported back from leave Jock found that the operational activity of the squadron had intensified. Wing Commander Thomas had completed his second tour and Dobson had taken over as Squadron Commander with the rank of Squadron Leader. Arrangements had been made for Thomas and Jock to meet a member of the Scientific Intelligence Group. They flew to High Wycombe in a Miles Magister and reported to Professor Barlock. Since meeting Adam the Professor wanted to have more contact with the aircrew who would use his devices.

He was tall and angular and wore a crumpled suit whose jacket, trousers, and waistcoat did not match in size or colour. When he was standing he had a disconcerting habit of rising on the soles of his feet, as if he were about to race off somewhere. Once seated he produced a blackened briar pipe and cleaned the stem with a feather, scraped the bowl noisily with a well worn knife, rubbed tobacco between his hands then filled the pipe.

He waited until Jock had aired his concerns then lit his pipe with obvious contentment, and asked, 'We get reports on our bombing from our agents on the spot but they take weeks to reach us. So how can we find out immediately if the bombing has been effective?'

Jock mentally blessed the Lanark Air Cadet. 'We take photographs.'

'Yes, we could. We could take photographs.' Barlock nodded his head and smoked happily. 'But that is only an aspect of the problem, Mr, er,' he added groping for a name. Robin supplied it, 'Jock.'

The Professor thought about it 'Yes that's it. Jock. And you're,' turning to Thomas who stammered, 'Oh, I'm Geoffrey.'

Barlock remained pleased then announced triumphantly, 'My name's Gaston but everyone calls me Peter. You see, Jock and Geoffrey, the idea of photographs is good, but it only records the errors after they've been made. It doesn't prevent the errors from being made.'

Jock burst in, 'But the photos will give us how much we've missed by and if we get better, they'll tell us how much better.'

'Right, Jock, but the problems are of navigating to the target, identifying the target from a reasonably safe height, dropping the bombs with some certainty that they will land where they're supposed to, then navigating back to the aerodrome. Would photography help us there?'

Thomas, whose disclosure of his first name had helped him to relax into this informal atmosphere spoke up. 'Yes, we could have a special aircraft on each raid, fitted with cameras to take pictures as the raid was in progress.'

'But it's dark,' interjected Jock.

Barlock took his pipe out of his mouth and pointed it at Geoffrey who immediately came back with, 'We use magnesium flares.'

Barlock gave an incongruous high pitched giggle, 'Wasn't that nice? We were together like one big brain. I presume magnesium flares will work?'

Geoffrey shrugged his shoulders, 'I think they might, but I have no way of knowing,' he admitted.

Barlock was rubbing the still hot pipe up and down the side of his nose. 'Young Jock, there is a very famous aphorism from someone from your part of the world, John Hunter.' Jock knew of the reputation of the eighteenth century brothers, William and John Hunter, in medical science and practice, whose birthplace was within miles of his home. He knew one well quoted saying by John, a dedicated student of anatomy, so he offered it, 'Don't think, try the experiment.'

Barlock beamed, 'That's it and that's what we'll do. I'll set it up. A target for night flying. An aeroplane to carry cameras and magnesium flares. Oh, did you know that the magnesium in magnesium flares isn't really pure magnesium at all? But never mind, we'll also need a dark night.' He picked up the horn of a cylinder dictating machine, switched it on and shouted into it, 'Get dark night, aeroplane, cameras, magnesium flares and place to drop them.' He set the horn down and stopped the cylinder. 'Well, now, wasn't that all simply splendid,' said Barlock as he terminated the interview.

As they walked to their aircraft, Thomas expressed his concern that Barlock was a very odd character. Jock wryly said that he had thought Barlock was all right; he was just English, and all the English were like that. The Wing Commander looked at him. 'For that cheeky remark, Flight Sergeant Jock, you can fly me home. I shall lounge in my seat and savour your distinguished flying.'

'Oh, I forgot – didn't I just! Thank you for getting all of us our medals,'

Jock blurted out.

'You earned them,' added Thomas.

A week later they were surprised to be summoned to meet the Professor at an airfield in South Wales. They were even more surprised to find an American Flying Fortress there, complete with an American crew, a cigar-smoking pilot, a navigator and an engineer. Barlock explained that this was a visiting aircraft from neutral America with a supposedly civilian crew. The crew had all been taken on operations by Bomber Command and they offered themselves and their aircraft for any purpose the RAF wished. The War Cabinet knew there would be a hell of a row if it was known that the Fortress was engaged in hostilities so they offered it to the 'hush-hush' boys.

The Professor told the American crew the nature of the experiment, dropping practice bombs and flares and taking photographs, both still and moving, of their trajectory and impact. He introduced Flight Sergeant Davidson and Wing Commander Thomas as operational pilots who would fly with them. A Warrant Officer Wireless Operator would also be on board to make sure they used proper wireless procedures. He regretted that he was not allowed to fly. Geoffrey Thomas briefed them on flying on a moonless night over the Atlantic, and dropping practice bombs and flares. The bombardier asked how they would know when to drop the bombs. 'When I tell you,' was the crisp answer.

They ran through the procedure in the aircraft and inspected the bomb racks, which were accessible from a hatch behind the second pilot's seat. An RAF armourer primed the magnesium flares just before they took off into a pitch black night. The Wing Commander acted as navigator and Jock sat in as second pilot, interested in finding out the differences in layout from the RAF aircraft. Over the target area he went into the bomb bay to check that the release of the magnesium flares went smoothly.

Using a pre-arranged schedule of times, Thomas made a note of compass heading, speed and height then instructed the bomb aimer to press the three switches that started the cameras, released the flare and then the practice bomb. At first things went well, then the fourth bomb jammed in its rack. Jock could not release it by hand but tried to kick it loose, holding on grimly to the struts on the platform. It came partly loose, but as it fell the bombardier let go the next flare which jammed between the rack and a support. Jock shouted for him to stop and tried to disconnect the cable which carried current to the rack to ensure that the remaining six flares did not go off. He was too late. There was a massive flaring in the bomb compartment and a release of acrid fumes. The bomb doors were still open and most of the fumes were drawn out from below. Jock was blinded, but shouted, 'Fire!' as he inched his way to the hatch into the flight compartment. Just as he reached it, it was forcibly slammed shut and he could find no handle to get out.

The heat was intense and his eyes were stinging from the fumes, and he was concerned that he would slip and fall over 10,000 feet into the Atlantic. He hammered and kicked on the metal door. By the time it was opened and he was freed, the second pilot was able to deal with the flames with an extinguisher.

Jock was trembling in shock as he heard the Wing Commander give the peremptory command to the pilot to turn on the reciprocal heading and to start losing height.

Jock felt himself being stripped of his singed flying gear. 'It's all right, it's Geoff here. We're getting you to a hospital.' The RAF wireless Operator raised an airfield which he knew had a good hospital nearby and soon had them standing by for an emergency landing. Flying control gave them heading and height and promised a few minutes of landing lights when they were on final approach. Thomas stayed close to Jock and told him every step that was involved.

Jock was sweating yet he felt cold. His pulse was racing and he wanted to get away and be on his own. His breathing became fast and shallow and he needed air. He wanted all this to be stopped. He couldn't stand it any longer. He didn't know how to control it. He had never felt like this. He must be dying. He cried out, 'Oh, Christ I'm dying. I can't see anything. I'm blind.'

He got an extraordinary response. He heard Thomas say, 'You're an opinionated bloody Scotsman, and I'm a Wing Commander and you are bloody well not blind until I say so. Do you understand? Do you?'

Jock sobbed, 'Yes.'

'Yes, Sir,' was the relentless reply. 'Come on, say it.'

Absolutely cowed Jock whispered, 'Yes, Sir.' He felt hurt that he should be treated like this, but realised that his resentment was helping him get control of himself.

On landing, Jock was whisked quickly into sick bay. A cooling drip was administered to his eyes by the Medical Officer while the remainder of his clothing was cut off. The stinging pain in his eyes gradually diminished and he could see light and shade but nothing more distinctly. He felt a sharp prick in his buttock and he fell asleep. When he awoke his eyes were fully bandaged and his nose and cheeks were covered in gauze. There was some greasy stuff on his lips which made them feel puffy. His hands felt like balloons. He heard a chair creak and the familiar voice asking how he was, no longer hectoring as it was last heard. 'I don't know, Sir,' he mumbled through his useless lips.

'Oh Jock, I'm sorry. I heard you shout fire, but didn't realise the second pilot had slammed the door on you. The pilot was all for bailing out, so I had to settle him down. By the time I got to you, you were starting to panic so I put on my Wing Commander act to stop you. I recognised what was happening to you because I once panicked in a fire in the air. The only thing that stopped me was a good right to the jaw by my observer. Last night I couldn't punch you because of your burns, but I delivered a shock to your pride and you didn't lose your head.'

Jock mumbled, 'But I'd just gone blind and that's the worst thing I could imagine.'

Thomas replied, 'They tell me that the chances are good that you're not blind. The heat gave you a lot of mucous on the covering of your eyeball and this mixed with the chemicals from the flares put a layer of gunk between you and the world. They're sure they got rid of it all. They'll be taking your bandages off soon.'

Professor Barlock was there too. However skilled he was as a theoretical physicist, he was a clod in a sick room. 'You are a mess aren't you. I suppose we won't be able to use you in any other experiments, if you're blind. But all is not lost, you know. When I was telling these extraordinary Americans my short cut for calculating the incremental effects of gravity on a falling object, I realised an even simpler way of expressing it, and of course of calculating it.' Thomas ushered the Professor out of the room, suggesting that Jock should get some rest.

Snatches of the Professor expounding his formula floated into the room while Jock tried to compose himself. He realised that he had begun to panic in the Fortress and that Thomas had stopped him just in time. The anger he had felt about being dressed down when he was in the worst mess of his life, was replaced by gratitude that he had been helped, even though the method had been drastic.

He heard people come into the room and stand round his bed. A touch on his shoulder. 'I'm a specialist in burns,' a voice told him, 'and I've just heard your tale. You were playing silly buggers in some hush secret operation up in the sky, when you got burned by magnesium flares. Snip these things off, Sister.' He felt the bandages being taken off his right, then his left hand, and the mild relief that followed. 'If that's what we're dealing with, it's all very hopeful, now isn't it?' There were various murmurs of assent from round the foot of the bed.

Then fingers were moving gently over the bandages on his face and he heard the curtains being closed. The specialist spoke again, 'He has a little bit more severe burning on his face than on his hands. Now help me with these pads, please, Sister, and we'll wait for the patient's verdict.'

Jock gasped as the pads were lifted off. There was a great glare of light and he screwed his eyes tightly shut and began to open them very tentatively. He saw a large man in a white coat bending over him. There was still some glare so he closed his eyes.

'I can see,' Jock whispered. He felt the tension in himself, and in the room, deflate, and he thought he was going to cry. He bit on his lip, but the specialist smiled, 'You know, your own tears would be the best thing for washing out your eyes. We'll leave you and come back later.'

Jock lay back on his pillow, let his tears run and sobbed his relief. Eventually he relaxed and lay, just looking at everything in the room. His hands were red and a little puffy, but he could move his fingers and there were blisters on the back of his left hand where some sparks had landed on him. 'I'm in great shape,' he thought remembering Digger's pronouncement in D Dumbo.

After a week of regular meticulous washing of his eyes and his hands and face being painted with Gentian Violet, he was asked if he wanted to go on leave. He refused because of his appearance. He had gone to the local cinema two evenings previously, feeling that the darkened premises would be ideal for him to spend two hours. He had forgotten about the interval when the lights went up. A little motherly lady took one look at his face completely covered in blue except where tufts of his beard were showing, then she and her friend moved away hurriedly, saying that the management should not let people like that into their cinema.

He opted to return to the station and applied for a posting until he started his second tour. He met on occasion with Wing Commander Thomas and Squadron Leader Dobson. Headquarters had paid some attention to their views, and selected aircraft were now carrying cameras to record the results of bombing. The analysis of the photographs simply confirmed the inaccuracy of the bombing. The morale of the crews was not helped by finding out how bad bombing and poor navigation had simply wasted the efforts they had made.

Jock's request for posting was answered quickly when he was sent to London to attend a special course on Radio Direction Finding. Professor Barlock convinced him that the six weeks would be well spent and by the time his face had healed, he found himself housed in a bare flat just off the Exhibition Road in a part of South Kensington which seemed to have been commandeered by Number 7 Radio School. The special course was to be held in a studio in the Royal College of Art.

PART THREE

ETHER ATOM

1942

CHAPTER 22

Adam gave up his room at the Commonwealth Club and moved in with Eleanor. He had suggested this arrangement as her flat was nearer to the Royal College of Art, and his billeting allowance would more than cover her rent. Other than this, there had been little discussion of this step, although they both appreciated how much of a commitment it signified.

He had thought that they would attend concerts, visit galleries, theatres and the like, but they preferred to stay at home, as he had come to think of her place, reading or listening to music and enjoying each other in bed. During the day London still offered plenty of interest. At night the city took on a different look. Fewer people moved on the streets. They scurried around debris from previous air raids and listened for the banshee sirens that played the overture for terror and destruction. Air raid wardens, firemen, rescue workers, first aid workers, Salvation Army mobile canteens and special police stood by ready to respond to the destruction to come. Dimly lit double-decker buses slowly zigzagged between the piles of cleared rubble, with taxis or cars following their lead.

Below the blacked out streets, men, women and children gathered with their bundles of bedding, thermos flasks and sandwiches on the cold platforms of the Underground stations. In the early days there had been spontaneous sing songs and parties with strangers from all walks of life joining in 'Knees Up Mother Brown', 'My Old Man' and other cockney ballads. This camaraderie reassured them that they could 'take it'. After a year of uncomfortable, sleepless nights amidst coughs, sneezes, snores, belches and farts, then rising to grey mornings to find out if homes or workplaces were still standing, scanning casualty lists, facing shortages, rationing and restrictions, the party spirit wore thin. They could still take it, but they were now taking it quietly and determinedly.

In addition to Adam, the course at the College of Art was made up of three other pilots, four navigators and two wireless operators. These latter two flight sergeants seemed to be at ease with the basic ideas that Adam had struggled to get to grips with in the Reading Room of the British Museum. The navigators, all Flight Lieutenants, were serious academics, who would have little problem with the theoretical aspects of the course.

Of the other three pilots the senior man in rank on the course was a Squadron Leader who had been flying Catalinas in Coastal Command. Another Flight Lieutenant had piloted a Beaufighter photo-reconnaissance plane. The fourth was a dour Scots flight sergeant with a DFM who had finished his first tour in a Wellington. He had studied Engineering and had some inkling of how wireless worked.

In the first session a Wing Commander reminded them that they were bound by the Official Secrets Act and that the developments in which they were participating were highly secret and could not be talked of, or even hinted at outside these walls. They were allowed to take notes or do calculations, but only on a child's toy 'etch-a-sketch' or 'magic scribbler' which had to be erased every evening and could not be removed from the classroom.

The first two lectures gave Adam a reprise of the material he had gleaned from his library researches, namely that conventional wireless reception depended on methods of refining, stabilising and amplifying signals. So far so good, but after lunch, Mr MacIsaacs, a small bespectacled Scot, began with the shattering assertion that all the conventional principles stressing fidelity of signals were irrelevant.

'Radio Direction Finding that some call Radar,' and the rrrrrs in his speech came out like a drum roll, 'depends for its operation on distortion more than fidelity. It functions, it thrives on square waves, rather than on smooth curved forms as in the wireless set that brings you Henry Hall and his dance band. Square waves and distortion, gentlemen. Add to these ideas the use of very high, radio frequencies and you have the three basic elements of Radar. The first thought I want to instil in your minds is "short sharp bursts of radio frequency". Savour it. It's as near poetry as you will get from me, and it will guide you to an understanding of how wee machines can extend the input of information to you further than you could even guess.'

The Scots Flight Sergeant had his hand up. The teacher smiled broadly. 'Och, it really is you, Mr Davidson. I thought I recognised a kent face. I should tell the rest of you that it's not so long ago that Robin Davidson and I were sparring partners at the Technical College in Glasgow.'

The Flight Sergeant was impatient, and burst in with, 'What you're telling us is that this machine of yours can work at very long range, a long way from the ground transmitter . . .'

'No, no, no,' interrupted Mr MacIsaacs. 'I will be telling you something else, not now but next week.'

Davidson was silent with his mouth open for a short time, then he burst out, 'Ah, but how can you . . .?'

'Next week, Robin. Next week.' Robin smiled and shrugged.

At the end of the class Adam and other students milled round their classmate who knew enough already to ask questions. They introduced themselves, and Robin told them that in his squadron he had been known as 'Jock'. From this first contact Adam was impressed by this direct, if laconic, person who endeared himself by pronouncing Newfoundland properly and telling how, as a youngster, he used to give his Sunday school penny to Dr Grenfell's medical mission. He added that he had seen pictures of Newfoundland that looked just like Scotland. Adam agreed and said he had found Fenwick to be like the barrens just outside St John's. Jock said that he had once camped on Fenwick Moor, and, with some experience in common, they had taken the first step in getting to know each other. By the end of the first week they had developed an easy relationship on first name terms.

Adam ended up sharing Jock's concerns about what they had heard so far. High voltage for the transmitter would have to be generated in an unusually small space to fit in an aircraft, and getting stable radio frequency signals would be a new technical feat. Mr MacIsaacs stubbornly avoided answering these questions, however.

At the beginning of the second week the Wing Commander who had welcomed them returned, accompanied by two thick set men in civilian clothes. He introduced these gentlemen as former police inspectors, who were now his assistants. He reminded the class about the Official Secrets Acts and the commitments they had already made to the terms. He then spoke gravely about imprisonment as a consequence of breaching the act.

His next announcement made the group sit up suddenly. 'We have discovered a breach of security from this class.' He paused to let that sink in, then continued, 'A German agent whose signals we have been monitoring, identified a group of RAF aircrew meeting in this College. He had no idea what they, that is you, were up to, but he found out it involved using short sharp bursts of radio frequency.' Everyone looked at Mr MacIsaacs, but the Wing Commander assured them their teacher was not the culprit.

He went on, 'We were led to a public house, the Wheatsheaf, quite near here . . .'

'Christ, mate, it's us,' one of the wireless operators burst out.

'Right you are,' replied the Wing Commander gravely. 'You have been in there a few evenings and told the barman you were on a course at the Art College. You didn't tell him what the course was about, but you were heard on three occasions, to say 'short sharp bursts of radio frequency . . ."

The second Flight Sergeant protested, 'Oh come on, it was a joke between us. I was just imitating Mr MacIsaacs. It was harmless . . . a bit of fun.'

The Wing Commander interrupted, 'The German agent didn't think so. He was bright enough to put two and two together, so we had to put him away in prison before he got any more information to send to Berlin. That means we lost an agent who was under our control because we knew what he was telling the enemy. Now we have to look for another one, damn it, because of your bloody stupidity.'

He addressed the rest of the class, 'I have raised this matter publicly to make you others realise that loose talk is dangerous. Even the most innocent things. For example, one of our own agents was keeping an eye on a factory in Germany that was famous for making toys. He hung about a pub and one night heard two of the workers joking about their charge hand who had been sacked for having matches in his overall pocket. Our agent thought this odd for a toy factory, so got himself a job and found they were making incendiary bombs. The factory was bombed and is now out of action.'

He turned back to the Flight Sergeants. 'I now ask my assistants to arrest you under the Official Secrets Act and to detain you until a full enquiry can be mounted.' In a strained silence, each Flight Sergeant was named and cautioned by an inspector, then led from the room. The Wing Commander reminded the remaining eight that the arrests they had just witnessed were also covered under the Act and should not be made known to anyone outside the room. He left them feeling uneasy and trying to make sense of what had happened. One of the navigators tried to get them indignant about the democratic rights of the individual being overlooked, but no one responded.

Mr MacIsaacs said he was sorry about this incident. He had been told to avoid giving top security material until the investigators had done their stuff. 'Now,' he continued, 'I can tell you the answers to some of the questions you and Mr Aitken raised, Robin. Radio frequency pulses can be achieved by an entirely new type of radio valve known as a Magnetron. It gets its name because the flow of electrons inside it is controlled by an external magnetic field, and it contains a number of cavities or chambers, which can resonate at given frequencies. I'll tell you later how it works,' he added quickly as he saw Jock stirring in his chair.

He continued, 'Your next question was where do you get the very high voltage needed to run a transmitter? The boffins have developed a large diode valve which is the heart of a rectifying system to amplify electrical power, and can be put in a box small enough to be carried on an aeroplane.'

Jock and Adam nodded at each other and Adam said, 'You'll be telling us about that later as well, Mr MacIsaacs.'

The teacher smiled and nodded. 'Right you are, Mr Aitken. All I'll tell you now is that you will be flabbergasted at the huge number of watts that can be generated by a small piece of equipment. The last thing I will be telling you about is how the microwave frequencies are kept stable by a system known as Automatic Frequency Control.'

He spent the rest of the afternoon introducing them to the principles of operation of these very new and secret inventions. Afterwards, walking through the streets, Jock and Adam tried to explain their own concepts to each other and became so engrossed that a brand new Pilot Officer who saluted Adam was surprised when his salute was returned with a wave and a greeting from Adam's companion.

They eventually found themselves able to follow Mr MacIsaacs as he pieced together the ideas he had presented to them. The last bits of the puzzle seemed deceptively simple. The transmitter sent out very powerful high frequencies which could bounce off targets and be reflected back to a receiver, the 'echo' effect which could be displayed on a Plan Position Indicator. This let the observer know that there was something out there. The time taken for the signal to travel from the transmitter to the receiver gave a measure of how far away the something was.

As they neared the end of the course, Adam found Jock's innate brightness and his existing knowledge, plus his willingness to expound his concepts in everyday language had been of immense value to him. Eleanor was glad that he had found a male chum and suggested that Jock should be invited to dinner on the following Sunday.

Right on time Jock appeared, carrying a bowl of hyacinth bulbs which he solemnly presented to Eleanor. She saw that his inscription on the card was signed 'From Jock' and addressed to Mrs Aitken.

Jock opened the conversation, 'You must find things very different over here, different from Newfoundland, Mrs Aitken.'

She smiled at him, 'But, I don't come from Newfoundland, Jock. I've never been there. I come from up North.' Adam intervened to rescue Eleanor from further embarrassment, and explained their situation.

Jock listened attentively, his eyes moving from Adam to Eleanor then back to Adam. 'I can see that's a very convenient arrangement from your point of view, Adam. But what about Eleanor?' Before either could interrupt he went on, 'In a week or so you and I will be finished down here and we'll be posted. Will Eleanor go with you, eh? I doubt it. I hope you thought of that when you set up this arrangement.'

He broke off when he saw that Eleanor was holding back tears. 'Och, Mrs . . . Eleanor, I'm being an awful fool, gabbing on like this, like some prissy Sunday School teacher. I was always like this, but I thought the RAF had civilised me a bit. I respect Adam and like him as a man. I should respect you and come to like you as a person because you . . . live with him . . . Would you forgive me? . . . Would you want me to get out of here?' His expression was so contrite and doleful that she moved forward, put her hands on his shoulders and assured him that she did not intend to waste a whole weekend's work in preparing the meal. She smiled and Jock responded with a beam.

The dinner was a success, as Jock turned out to be a hearty and appreciative eater and put Adam to shame by asking for more Brussels sprouts. He drank milk rather than wine, saying he had never tasted it. After dinner he refused a cigarette that Eleanor offered and the glass of whisky that Adam produced.

The rest of the evening went well, with Jock talking about his family and home life in Hamilton, and his fiancée, Fiona. At ten o'clock, he stood up, announced he should be leaving and thanked Eleanor warmly for being a good hostess. After he left, they both set about clearing dishes silently, avoiding anything that would demand communication.

Adam spoke first, 'I'm sorry about Jock. It must have embarrassed you to hear him spouting off like that. I never guessed he was that sort of chap . . . If I had known I would never have brought him here . . .'

She shrugged. 'It wasn't Jock. He happened to be right about us, about you and me. I was too besotted with you to think further than the next night's sex. I think you were the same. We just never owned up to it. What will happen when you are posted back to a squadron? I have my job to do and it's more important to me than being with you.'

Adam held her close. 'I love you but I can't think more than a day ahead about what will happen to us. Will you marry me, Eleanor? Maybe that's what we should do.'

'No, no, no. Don't think like that. Our being married would only stop Jock from moralising about us living in sin. That's not a proper reason for us getting married. I don't even know if I want to marry again.'

Adam shook his head. 'I'm afraid I can't think much further than getting posted to a squadron . . .'

She put her hand over his mouth and said, 'That's it then. We enjoy each other until you're posted, then we will part friends.'

For the last two weeks of the course Mr MacIsaacs instructed the class on the actual equipment that had been devised. They then spent a final weekend flying in bombers that were already fitted with experimental Radio Navigational Aids. When they returned to the Radio School their postings were handed to them.

Jock and Adam were listed as pilot and navigator respectively of a Wellington aircraft which was to be picked up at a Bomber Station near Cambridge and flown to a location in South Wales. They were to report in 48 hours time. Adam would take command of the operation with an aircrew which included an observer and a wireless operator in addition to Jock and himself, and a specially trained ground crew which would deal with fitting and calibrating the instruments. The Unit was given the official title, 'Experimental Airborne', abbreviated in the phonetic alphabet to Ether Atom.

For their last night together Adam took Eleanor to Charles' restaurant. She chided him for being too sentimental, but he claimed he did not want to be morbid about their parting. 'Nor I, dear Adam,' she assured him. 'I want this to be my celebration of how you have brought me back to being a real person again. I shall always remember you fondly for that. Remember I'm grateful to you, but I don't love you. And I'm sure you don't love me. You did a lot more for me than I did for you with Gray's Anatomy.'

As they left the restaurant, Eleanor thanked Charles and asked after Deirdre. 'She is still desolate at the loss of the Commander.'

Adam immediately asked what had happened, and was shocked to hear that Roger had committed suicide at St Dunstan's two week's previously. He had been doing well and had just had his first day of instruction in operating a telephone switchboard. He seemed happy enough so everyone was surprised when he shot himself. 'Oh God,' thought Adam as he recalled his suspicions during his brief conversation with Roger in this restaurant, and he remembered Roger asking him to look after Deirdre.

He immediately phoned her, expressed his and Eleanor's sympathy, and asked what he could do to help. She said she did not want any help at the moment, but she asked him just to keep in touch occasionally to be a support to her. He promised and returned to Eleanor who was in Charles' office weeping for Deirdre. He comforted her, then they walked slowly back to her flat.

Once inside, she stood still, clenched her fists and said vehemently, 'What a bloody, bloody thing this war is. There's me. Now Deirdre, and a million other wives with great gaping holes in their lives, all because our men have to go and be heroes. Now that's what you want to do, Adam.'

In bed they lay side by side, holding each other, sleeping fitfully. In the morning she kissed him goodbye as she left for work. He picked up his kit and set off to take part in Ether Atom.

CHAPTER 23

Next morning at the railway station, Jock noticed Adam's despondency. Adam assured him that he was in the dumps because of the death of a friend and that he and Eleanor had parted amicably.

'Och, I really hope you'll forgive me.'

Adam smiled and shook Jock's hand. 'There's nothing to forgive. You were a bit blunt about it, that's all.'

In the train, the lady sitting opposite Jock shyly asked if he minded her feeding her baby. He smiled and shook his head, but blushed when she opened her blouse to offer her breast to an obviously thriving infant. 'We're going to meet his father, and I wanted to have him quiet and peaceful. My husband's just back from the desert, and he's never seen his son.' Adam smiled at her and the baby.

Jock and Adam chatted about the peaceful view they were having once the train had emerged from the grime of London. Occasionally there would be reminders of war in convoys of Army lorries on the roads beside the track or glimpses of airfields, but they enjoyed the sight of villages with cottages around a green, a pub, a church and a manor house.

At Stansted, Jock took the baby while the mother stepped on to the platform. Adam carried her case. A burly sergeant rushed up, embraced her, took the baby from Jock and the case from Adam. He thanked them. The mother waved goodbye and the young family moved off down the platform. Jock was delighted at having seen the tender expression on a mother's face as she fed her baby. He would see this expression on Fiona when she fed their babies.

The other passengers had left the compartment, but two had boarded while Jock and Adam were on the platform. When they re-entered the compartment, Professor Barlock was seated in the far corner. The Professor raised his eyebrows. 'There you are, Jock Davidson. So you're not blind after all. And your shoulder's well I hope, young Aitken. I'm on my way to meet you two to tell you what we're up to. It's exciting stuff, isn't it? Hush hush, though. We should watch for spies everywhere,' and he narrowed his eyes at the thin weedy elderly clergyman opposite, who shifted in his seat uncomfortably.

Barlock thought for a moment. 'Did you ever meet Watson-Watt? A most opinionated Scotsman. I've always held Scots to be opinionated. Jock, you're a bit that way yourself aren't you. But Watson-Watt beat the cake . . .'

The previously uncomfortable clergyman broke in, 'That's mindless twaddle on your part, Sir. To be opinionated about the opinionated is the height of bigotry, unworthy of any man who would claim to be a scholar.'

Barlock countered, 'I have never claimed to be a scholar. I am a scientist, and a bit of a tinkerer in mechanics, but I am not a haunter of libraries like some academics I know. I prefer the laboratory. Perhaps you will permit me the luxury of a conversation with my young colleagues.'

The elderly cleric extended a bony hand to Jock then to Adam. 'I'm Bishop Sievebert, and I had the misfortune to be Barlock's moral tutor at University. From your knowledge of him, you will realise how badly I failed.'

The four of them had the carriage to themselves, so Barlock grew expansive. 'Sievebert is in Scientific Branch too, as a cryptographer. As a Bishop he has always had too little to do, so he did crosswords, and composed them. He was also College chess champion, and played competitive bridge. He now works on translating coded messages from the Luftwaffe, all dealing with our bombing tactics and possible counter-measures they could take.'

The Bishop interrupted. 'I'm very proud that at my age, I can have a direct part to play in the air war.'

Adam questioned him, 'But isn't it your duty as a clergyman to speak out against attacking German cities by dropping bombs and killing people?'

The Bishop inclined his head, 'I distinguish between greater and lesser evil, and pray that our efforts to be precise about where we drop our bombs will lessen the killing and maiming of innocent German people and reduce our lesser evil still further.'

Jock smiled. 'I'd be with you on that, and I hope to find out if it can be done in the next few weeks.' Barlock pointed out that they would begin the discussion in half an hour or so.

At Cambridge a staff car was waiting to take them to the unit specially prepared for them. When they were seated comfortably in an ante-room, with a Station Policeman posted outside the door to keep everybody else out, Sievebert told what his intelligence section had gleaned of the German version of the Scientific Branch activity. 'They know we're up to something but they can't fathom out what it is. Their strongest guess so far appears to be that the RAF is trying to devise a system which will prevent the bombers up top dropping their loads on those in the lower layers.'

'They must have heard Jock,' Barlock burst in with a guffaw. 'When I first met him he was indignant about this very hazard.'

The bishop nodded to Jock. 'Tomorrow morning I'll take you to meet my motley crew. It'll be a thrill to all of us to be associated with Ether Atom and to talk to the chaps who are actually doing the flying on the new equipment. Now I'm going to have my nap.' He bowed to each of them and left the room.

Barlock looked after him as he closed the door. 'Now to business. This is the first time we have had an experimental unit entirely composed of currently serving RAF personnel. A specialist ground crew will set up a workshop on the dispersal site which we have requisitioned for you. You will test H2S under different conditions and find out how best to train navigators to operate the system. Your first test flights will be to find the best positions for the aerials. Just follow the instructions of a sergeant and a corporal who are experts in this field.' He finished, 'You will meet all your team tomorrow, and I hope you find them to be the good fellows I believe they are. After you have met them you can visit the Bishop's set-up, then you test the aeroplane, and if it holds together you sign for it.'

Next morning they met Flight Sergeant Storey, the Observer, and Sergeant Kagan, the Wireless Operator, both of whom seemed to be unusually restrained about the venture they were about to undertake. To Jock's delight, the ground crew was led by an old friend, 'Chiefie' Woodson, who had kept D Dumbo in fine fettle until she came to bits after her trip to Kiel. He came to attention and saluted Adam when he was introduced then brought forward two fitters, a rigger for the airframe, two engine mechanics, and a sergeant and corporal who were both signals specialists in the design, fitting and adjustment of wireless aerials. With the exception of these last two, Jock recognised the team as being part of Woodson's empire, and beamed when they addressed him as Jock.

The aerial experts were in Woodson's words, 'A horrible scruffy pair of airmen, but I'm told they know their stuff about this secret business.' Corporal Shipleigh seemed to know Professor Barlock well, for he immediately drew him to a blackboard and chalked up a formula which they both proceeded to change bit by bit. He had been one of the Professor's graduate students, and Sergeant Birkmyer had been the associate editor of a respected wireless publication.

Barlock spoke to the group on the history of Radio Direction Finding. Bomber Command needed a navigation aid which would get the planes to the correct target and make sure they released their bombs at the right place. H2S had been designed to overcome these limitations in previously devised systems. There were no beams to be interfered with, as the transmitter was carried in the aircraft. The curvature of the earth did not limit the range of the operation and they were taking special steps to produce highly trained operators who would be less likely to be confused by the judgements needed in the present systems. The job for Ether Atom was to test the gadget in practice to see how far the ideas of the backroom boys could carry into real life.

When he finished, someone asked why the system was called H2S. The Professor smiled. 'It's a bit of laboratory humour, really. At one of the early briefings on the project the comment of the senior scientist was "it stinks". Someone thought it should be called "the stinker", but someone else remembered his school chemistry and called it H2S, which you will know as Hydrogen Sulphide, the foul smelling stuff that was put in stink bombs. The name stuck.'

There was a ripple of laughter, then a Squadron Leader informed them that as a unique unit, Ether Atom would be based at St Antle Maintenance Unit in South Glamorgan. One Welsh voice was heard to say that his home was nearby. The interjection was ignored. They would be housed in a separate site, consisting of a dispersal point, workshops and sleeping quarters. They were all under the Official Secrets Act, and there could be no opportunity for even day passes.

Further, they would be expected to keep themselves to themselves by not mixing with other airmen, or airwomen on the main parts of the station. Nor could they mix with the locals, particularly in the pubs, for the expected period of six weeks. They should all keep addressing their letters as they were doing at present, and there would be special deliveries to South Wales. Turning to the now disappointed fitter he said, 'I know this will be hard on you, but it will have to be enforced if we're going to keep this caper secret.'

After their visit to Bishop Sievebert's Unit, where they were overwhelmed by cryptography, Jock and his crew went over the aircraft with Flight Sergeant Woodson, who had carried out his full inspection earlier that morning. When Jock had finished his checks, they took off for an hour's local flying. On their return, Kagan reported a faulty transmitter switch which was replaced immediately. The aircraft was signed out as fit to fly the following day.

On reaching St Antle, Jock parked the Wellington at the designated dispersal point, and they unloaded their kit. Adam walked round the perimeter track.

The airfield was relatively small and appeared unused, but the fencing was new and there were recent repairs to the concrete on the runways. There was a bustle of activity in and around the large hangars to the south of the airfield, like a factory in full production. This, then, was the maintenance unit.

In the Administration Building, he met the Station Commander, a middle aged Group Captain wearing a pilot's brevet and ribbons from the first World War. He laid down his pipe and rose to welcome Adam warmly. 'I'm Charteris. I don't know what an atom is, never mind an ethereal one. So what will you be up to here and how can we help you?'

Adam explained that his group were going to test some new navigation equipment, first of all on the ground, then with low level flying locally in daylight, and, if they got it right, longer range night flights. Charteris seemed pleased. He explained that the Maintenance Unit was running well, but he preferred having aeroplanes that flew in and out of his station, rather than coming and going on the backs of lorries.

Adam's group would be housed altogether in a Nissen hut beside the dispersal point. There was a workshop next door, well isolated from the other parts of the station. Meals would be brought down for them. Security would be provided by having two Station policemen on duty at all times. Adam expressed his satisfaction with the arrangements and took his leave.

CHAPTER 24

Chiefie Woodson had indicated that the first task would be to fit sensor aerials in the wings. With time on his hands Adam decided to look for likely places to lead the connector cables from the wings to the display unit inside the aircraft. He pulled a trestle over, removed his hat and tunic and put on a brown dust coat.

He was on the trestle with his head inside the wheel space when he felt a sharp tug on his trouser leg and a gruff voice giving the traditional military greeting, 'Let's be having you,' followed by 'laddie.' A short, thick-set Warrant Officer was standing by the wheel. He appeared to be angry at something and ready to be angrier yet.

Tapping the insignia on his sleeve, the visitor said, 'These didn't come off a syrup tin, laddie. I'm Station Warrant Officer Lobban and you'll call me Sir and you'll tell me sharpish just what the hell you're up to, laddie. First of all, who's in charge, then?'

Putting on his tunic Adam said that he was and added, 'Sir.' Lobban did not flinch.

'You're a Yank, so you can't be expected to know about etiquette. You have to display rank badges at all times . . . Sir.'

Indignant at the display of ignorance of his home, Adam put on the accent he had acquired at Malvern College. 'I am not a Yank, laddie. In fact, laddie, I am from Britain's oldest colony and I don't intend to be taught etiquette by a lout, like you, laddie. And don't ever call me laddie. Sir will do fine.' Adam, astonished at his own temerity, continued, 'Talking of etiquette, you are now in a security area, so unless you have official business I want you out of here. Right now.'

Lobban sneered, 'The Station Commander detailed me to find an orderly for you. I've got just the bloody orderly you fly-boys need. Just wait and see.' With that he walked off in a stiff legged manner.

To control his anger, Adam walked to the billet to find out where he would take his bags, but Jock had already laid his kit on a bed next to the stove, and was sitting on the next bed writing to Fiona. Telling Jock about his encounter with Lobban helped him to settle down. A tall, burly figure in flat hat, armlet, revolver and shiny boots appeared at the open door. 'Corporal Weymouth, Sir, reporting with Station Policeman Jenkins for guard duty.' They moved outside to inspect the area to be guarded. As they spoke a van drew up and a young airman alighted with a box of cleaning supplies. He laid the box down, saluted Adam and reported that he was Aircraftsman Fairstone detailed by Mr Lobban as the hut orderly.

His duties were to keep the hut clean and tidy, arrange for laundry, set out meals delivered from the cookhouse, clean the lavatory and so on. He appeared restrained and deferential in his speech and manner, so much so that Adam made a mental note to tell Jock and the others to avoid the personal banter and insult that passed for conversation with them.

Corporal Weymouth looked at Fairstone's back as he went into the hut. 'That young airman's having a hell of a time. The Station Warrant Officer has got a real down on him. He was posted here, graded LMF – Lack of Moral Fibre. I saw his records when he arrived. He is regular Air Force and was a Sergeant Wireless Operator on Hampdens. On his first tour his plane was badly shot up and crashed on landing. He was the only survivor. He finished his tour with another crew, and was transferred to Wellingtons for his second tour. About half way through this tour they were shot up over the target. The pilot was wounded, but managed to ditch in the Channel. Luckily they were all rescued quickly, and young Fairstone was commended for his work in looking after the wounded pilot in the dinghy.'

Weymouth shook his head, 'He asked not to fly again, and they sent him to a specialist, who said he lacked moral fibre. He was bumped down to aircraftsman second class for general duties and sent here into the clutches of our SWO, who is ordinarily a fair, if strict, man, but has certainly got his knife into this young lad.'

Adam had noticed lighter patches on Fairstone's tunic on the sleeves where his chevrons had been and above the left breast pocket where his brevet had been. This was the lesson that Lobban had promised, a fly boy who had gone wrong. Weymouth continued, 'Lobban's view is that LMF means cowardice in the face of the enemy, and he gives that youngster all the dirty tasks he can think of. He says that Fairstone's going to wish he had been put in front of a firing squad as they did in the first World War.'

In the middle of the afternoon the trucks arrived carrying the ground crew with their special equipment, spares and stores. Flight Sergeant Woodson took charge of the billeting arrangements, and Adam found that his belongings had been repacked and all his gear moved to a small single room by the entrance to the hut. 'I'm sure you'll find it much more appropriate there, Sir, away from the men.' It's also away from the stove, thought Adam, but he accepted Chiefie's judgement on what was seemly and made no comment.

Sergeant Birkmeyer and Corporal Shipleigh, 'the aerialists', as they became known, spent the next three days fitting different kinds of arrays of antennae on the wings and attaching them to equipment inside the Wellington. The transmitter and receiver aerial for H2S were housed in a dome on the underside of the fuselage. To test that the transmitter was operating the tail of the aircraft was raised on a trestle to keep it level. A helper was asked to crouch down holding what appeared to be an ordinary electric light bulb. In fact, the bulb contained a gas which glowed when it was in a field of Radio frequency when the Radar transmitter was switched on . . .

One day Fairstone was asked to hold the bulb and burst into excited laughter when the light went on in his hand. He asked a series of questions about what was going on. Corporal Shipleigh answered all his questions readily.

Adam was surprised when he was approached by an animated Fairstone, who asked about the possibility of him returning to aircrew as Radar Operator. Adam gave his assurance that he would find out how this could be done.

He asked how Fairstone had learned what the Unit was up to. Fairstone's open admission that Colonel Shipleigh had told him all about it was unsettling to Adam. He asked Fairstone to protect Shipleigh by not telling anyone else how he had come to know about the work of Ether Atom. He then took Shipleigh to task, but Shipleigh observed that Fairstone was in the same uniform, and in the same secret unit as he was, so he assumed he was part of the group. He had not thought a great deal about the security and was contrite, but Adam asked him to do nothing.

A telephone call to the Station Commander obtained permission for Fairstone to sleep on the Ether Atom site, rather than leaving every evening to return to his barracks. The Station Administrative Officer arranged to explain the Official Secrets Act and to get Fairstone's signed consent to abide by the conditions. He mentioned that the Station Warrant Officer would have to be informed, but tactfully offered to tell Mr Lobban himself. Adam encouraged Fairstone to write an application to the Station Commander.

When the ground tests were completed, air tests were conducted at different heights. Adam noted that at 12,000 feet, he could get a clear picture of some villages along the coast road, clear enough to confirm the position on the map. At lower heights, the pattern of light and shade on the oscilloscope was changing too quickly to give a picture which could be interpreted with any confidence. Both Adam and Jock were able to relate the position indicated by the H2S signals to the position on the chart, and to the topography of the ground over which they were flying.

However neither Flight Sergeant Storey, nor Sergeant Kagan could make this identification, even after explanations from Adam and Jock. Eventually Jock said, 'Remember, we didn't get it the first time, either. You took longer than I did. Why was that?'

Adam thought for a bit. 'I saw things clearly after I had about five minutes just looking at the display, not trying to get anything special.'

'Then that's what we'll get them to do,' said Jock putting the aircraft back on a reciprocal course.

When told just to watch the pattern, Kagan then Storey eventually saw a meaningful picture that they could match to the ground and the chart. Fairstone, now an official member of EtherAtom, was the quickest to interpret the signals and was intrigued that details on the screen matched the details on the chart.

Adam was finishing the report of his first ten days testing, all of which had been conducted during daylight with good visibility, when he got a message from the Station Commander, inviting him to a meeting in the Administration Block. He found the Group Captain, the Senior Administration Officer and the Station Warrant Officer already seated.

Charteris handed a letter to Adam. 'The others have seen this, so take a minute to read it. Then give me your views.' The letter was from Fairstone, written in a formal style, requesting that he be returned to aircrew status with a view to seeking training as a Radio Observer.

Adam expressed his surprise that such a category as LMF should ever have been introduced. Charteris admitted that he had shared Adam's views and had raised the issue at Headquarters. The justification was that bomber crews were all volunteers under intense pressure to fly long and dangerous missions night after night. To prevent aircrew simply refusing to fly there had to be a very strong deterrent. The public humiliation of being graded as Lacking Moral Fibre was used to shame aircrew out of refusing. It was illogical, unethical, but it kept the Bomber Force intact. 'But God knows what effect it is having on these young lads,' Charteris ended.

Adam related how Fairstone had brightened up once he got some idea of the methods of Radar and hurried through his menial tasks to spend some more time picking up information about the system. Fairstone had flown with them on several of the tests and had not shown any signs of nervousness or tension in the air. Both he and Jock felt that he would be a useful crew member with his Radio Observer training, and strongly supported Fairstone's return to aircrew.

Station Warrant Officer Lobban agreed. 'Mr Aitken and I have had our differences but these should not get in the way of helping this young fellow getting back his aircrew status. I will put in a favourable report on the way he did all the scut work I shoved at him, all without complaint. He took a hell of a lot from me without losing his rag. I don't think he lacks moral fibre, whatever that is. He's got plenty of guts.'

Adam smiled at Lobban and nodded his agreement. The Group Captain closed their meeting by saying that he would get the Medical Officer to set up the official review panel and asked for reports and recommendations on Fairstone's application to be on his desk the following day.

Lobban offered his hand, asking Adam to accept his apology. Adam shook gladly and explained his touchiness with people who misidentified Newfoundland. After the others had gone, Charteris told Adam that Lobban had lost his only son at Dunkirk, and he had remained bitter at the rumours that the RAF, his service, had not provided air cover for the retreating forces in France. Mrs Lobban had been severely depressed at her son's death, and had recently been admitted to a mental hospital to receive the new Electric Shock Treatment. Lobban had been very upset by her admission, and the sudden arrival of Ether Atom had not helped his outlook. However, his wife was responding to the treatment and Lobban was more his usual self.

In the next two days the weather changed to overcast, showery days which Adam felt were ideal for the second phase of their daylight testing. They flew well above the low cloud, and at ten minute intervals, entered their location on the chart as given by H2S. Jock then took them round again below the cloud ceiling to fly on the same heading at the same speed to get visual confirmation of their positions from H2S. The agreement confirmed that the system was accurate, and that the degree of accuracy was a matter of individual acuity. Fairstone was good at it, Jock less good but better than Adam, with Storey and Kagan the worst of the group. Adam made this a central point in his second report.

The third series of tests were carried out at night under conditions nearer those of the bombing missions for which the equipment was intended. With the co-operation of the coastal and naval authorities, they flew out into the Irish Sea and headed back towards various targets. Although they were not allowed near Bristol, Cardiff proved to be a good model for the dock targets that Bomber Command would be attacking. After one such exercise they were returning to base when they were told that a fog bank had moved in earlier than had been predicted. A ceiling of below 1,000 feet was reported.

Jock elected to try H2S as an anti-fog device. Having been assured that there were no other aircraft in the vicinity of the St Antle airstrip, and with Fairstone at the H2S box giving him readings of the coastline, he broke out of cloud at 800 feet with the aircraft's nose comfortably lined up with the runway.

Jock's blind approach suggested that H2S might be useful at lower heights, and a modification to the receiver led to displaying the height in numbers. They were asked to test this system below 100 feet. Jock maintained that the equipment itself was too sensitive for the pilot and aircraft to respond to the quick changes in altitude required for such low levels. 'But,' he ended with a melodramatic gesture, 'we press on regardless. Ours not to reason why.'

There was an escarpment which had a fairly even flat top stretching for over seven miles. The land owner had already brought his sheep down to lower ground for lambing. Flying blind behind a blackout screen all round his seat, on a calm morning, Jock took the Wellington down to a reading of forty feet above the ground. He wanted to maintain that height for as long as possible on the radar altimeter alone. Adam was fidgeting in the right hand seat, seeing all too clearly what was happening but steadfastly resisting his impulses to pull the aircraft's nose up. Kagan was monitoring the airways at his console, well away from a window. Storey was reading a paperback at the navigation table.

A puff from a thermal gave some unexpected lift. Jock over-corrected. While the instrument registered the loss of height faithfully, Jock was slower off the mark and the propellers and the underside of the fuselage struck soft earth with a bang, sending a great shudder through the aircraft and scattering dirt and gravel over the windscreen. Adam tried to recall the procedure for a belly-landing recommended in the Pilot's Notes. The devout Kagan crossed himself and began to say the Rosary, while preparing his equipment to send out distress signals. Storey dropped his novel and clutched the side of his table, knuckles showing white as he scanned the chart to get a position to report their plight.

Jock had enough presence of mind to let the aircraft bounce up for a few feet before starting to regain height gradually. Both engines were running roughly and noisily and the din and vibration reminded Jock of D Dumbo's return from Kiel, so much so that when he told Kagan to inform base of their mishap and possible damage, he ended by saying, 'We're in great shape.'

They landed without mishap and taxied noisily to the dispersal point, escorted by the fire wagon and ambulance. Before they could leave the aircraft the ground crew was crowding round looking at the propeller blades which had been badly bent on impact. Fortunately the Maintenance Unit had the equipment to straighten out and realign the propeller blades, and could provide mechanics to help 'Chiefie' Woodson's crew do inspections confirming that engines and airframes were not damaged significantly to have the aircraft declared unserviceable.

That evening Jock and Adam were asked to report to the Group Captain. Charteris looked grim as he said he had received a complaint against them. He then smiled at their crestfallen expressions. The landowner, whom he knew personally, had telephoned to ask if he would remind his pilot of the etiquette of golf and ask him to kindly replace the divots. He also wanted to congratulate his pilot on a very good piece of flying and recovery. Jock grinned, bowed his head and confessed his golfing sin.

Their pessimistic assessment of Radar as a low-level altimeter was confirmed ten days later when another Wellington crashed in Scotland, while testing out the same low level technique. No one survived to tell what had happened. Another group in South Wales were trying out H2S, flying a Halifax at high altitudes, consistent with the heights at which bombing raids would be conducted. Contrary to previous policy, six civilian scientists were in the Halifax to conduct a test under realistic conditions. Following a routine message from the Halifax, there was no further communication. The wreckage was finally located in wooded countryside, but there were no survivors among crew or boffins. No record was recovered of the results of the equipment test.

This was a devastating set-back to the plans for Bomber Command, and, to prevent a slump in morale, the public was not informed of the accident. The Scientific Branch were under strong pressure to restore the progress that had been lost and get H2S operational for Bomber Command as quickly as possible. Adam and his team switched to high altitude flying in their Wellington and confirmed that the apparatus could allow a high flying aircraft to bomb through cloud.

The Ether Atom group was disbanded at this point and Adam was posted back to Pathfinder Force. Jock was promoted to Acting Warrant Officer (second class), sent for operational training on heavy bombers, then posted back to his squadron, now equipped with Lancasters. Dobson was still in charge of the squadron, but was keeping up his operational hours. Geoff Thomas had been promoted to Group Captain and had moved on to Bomber Command Headquarters.

PART FOUR

JOCK

1942–1943

CHAPTER 25

Jock enjoyed being back in familiar surroundings in the Sergeants' Mess. Although many of his cronies had become casualties, some were still with the squadron. The crew of D Dumbo had all been posted away. 'Whisky' Walker was now a Squadron Leader in charge of a Navigation School. 'Digger' was commissioned and flying intruder missions in a Martin Marauder light bomber. Abie, Taff and Jimsey had stayed together in a crew in a Halifax squadron. Their aircraft had been shot down over Germany and they had been officially posted Missing in Action.

Jock's new crew, like himself, were Volunteer Reservists. They came from another squadron, after their pilot, a Regular Squadron Leader, went sick with jaundice. Compared to the Wellington, the Lancaster operated with a crew of seven. The second pilot had been replaced by a Flight Engineer who watched over the engines, fuel, extinguishers and electrics during flight. He also assisted the pilot during take-off and landing and could act as pilot in an emergency.

The role of the Observer in aiming and releasing the bombs had been handed over to a new member of aircrew, the Bomb Aimer. This category was rumoured to be the brainchild of the Chief of Bomber Command, 'Butch' Harris himself. In Iraq in the 1920s he had advocated lying facedown in the nose as the best place in which to guide the pilot over the target. The Bomb Aimer could back up the Navigator in his computations and in operating other navigational aids, such as Gee.

Flying Officer Forester Graveley, the Navigator, hailed from Canterbury and readily let everyone know that he had been an undergraduate at Cambridge, headed for the practice of Law. Jock found him to be a bit cocksure about his background. The Bomb Aimer, Flying Officer Boris Sancerre, had been articled as an accountant before he began training as a pilot in Canada, in his native province of Alberta. He had failed the pilot's course, but had shown sufficient talents on the special bomb aimer's course to be commissioned on passing out.

Pilot Officer William Prober, the Flight Engineer, was a Yorkshireman, a trained motor mechanic with an intuitive reverence for Rolls Royce engines. The Mid-Upper Gunner, Flying Officer Jonathan Rice, was a schoolmaster from Sussex and had been an instructor at Gunnery School before joining the squadron. The Wireless Operator, Flight Sergeant David Gray, was a big, burly son of a Lincolnshire farmer whose ruddy face and beaming smile made him seem younger than his thirty years. The Tail Gunner, Flight Sergeant Trygve Selsund, was a Norwegian who had been a merchant seaman on an Armed Fishing Boat in the North Sea. He had been involved in carrying agents to and from enemy occupied territory before transferring to the RAF.

The basis for team-work had been well laid for this crew. They were quiet and restrained in the air, compared to the chatter and insults aboard D Dumbo. Jock had to admit that he missed Taff's inanities, or Abie's crooning on the intercom. He wondered whether the restraint of this new crew was due to their realization that their first operation with him would be the thirteenth of their first tour.

On this thirteenth operation, they were attacked by five Focke Wulff fighters on their way to Hamburg. Sightings were passed on quietly and clearly, with occasional staccato interruptions such as, 'Break left, skipper.' The fighters were kept at distance by effective machine gun fire, and only three of the enemy were involved in the last of their six passes, one with smoke pouring from the engine cowling. The enemy withdrew, having made only a few hits and Rice and Selsund agreed that the German pilots must have been novices.

When the attackers disengaged, each crew member called in to report what little damage had been done. Reassured that there was no significant damage to crew or aircraft, Jock thanked them all for their good work then asked for the course to steer. As he said 'Thank you, navigator,' he realised he did not know if they had nicknames. None addressed him as 'Jock', preferring to use 'Skipper'.

Flak over the target was bursting at a safe distance, and did not interfere with their bombing run. After the bombs had gone and Sancerre had handed the aircraft back to him, Jock did a half circle to allow them to inspect the railyard. The glare from the incendiaries showed that a large area of the sidings had been damaged. He set course and had a clear run home. During the return flight, Jock mused that the whole raid had been conducted rather like a game of whist at home on a Sunday night.

On the next stand down, having his usual half pint shandy in the pub, he asked his friends about the crew he had inherited. One of them explained, 'They're good, because their skipper trained them the old fashioned way. He's a regular Squadron Leader who played God in the air and on the ground. Compared to him you're just a Johnny jump up, Jock, but they're overawed by the lad who flew half a Wellington home from Kiel to save his crew. You are known to be a lucky pilot, but they don't know if and when your luck's going to run out.'

Another chipped in, 'This lot is good and they'll do everything by the book, but they'll be a bit shy of you for a while.'

Jock nodded thoughtfully and looked up as a smiling WAAF sergeant joined them, saying, 'I've got good news for you, Jock. Even you will buy me a beer when you hear it.' Amid cries of 'You'll be lucky!' she sat down and told them that the Station Commander had received a signal to say that Taff, Abie and Jimsey were in a prisoner of war camp in Germany somewhere. Jock stood up, hugged her and ordered beer all round, including another shandy for himself.

When the landlord delivered the drinks and learned the reason for Jock's generosity, he refused to take the money, saying it was his treat. 'There you are. What did I tell you? You're a Scottish jammy devil that gets free beer,' was the final comment from his colleagues.

Later Jock talked to the crew about his so-called luck. He told them how impressed he was by their efficiency and skill, and hoped that having him squeezed in would not be too much of an upset of their routine. This effort embarrassed him, but at least they started to address him as 'Jock'. He was still uncomfortable at the superior altitude displayed by Forester Gravely and the patronising style he adopted to Prober and the two Flight Sergeants. He could not find words to articulate his concerns, or to diffuse the stiffness in their contacts with each other. Their tour continued successfully and smoothly, always reaching and bombing the target, dealing with fighter attacks, searchlights or flak by the prescribed means.

After their seventeenth operation they attended a special briefing with two other experienced crews from the squadron. Very long range missions were to be tried and these three crews had been selected to carry out the first raid. When Jock asked about the targets he was told about oil fields in Eastern European countries, which were supplying fuel, and heavy industrial plants in Eastern Germany producing armaments for the German war effort, but no specific target was named at this stage.

Their Lancasters would be fitted with extra tanks to increase their range to over 3,000 miles. The combined payload of bombs plus fuel would be just over 26,000 pounds, and they would spend the next week doing take-offs, and local flying with this weight aboard.

An Australian skipper, Flight Sergeant 'Blue' Murphy, pointed out that with all that fuel aboard a 'crook' landing in training could end up with a strong smell of burning intrepid aviators. He was assured that there would be no extra fuel or bombs aboard for these practices. The heavy weight of the aircraft would be made up with sandbags.

The greatest hazards on the mission itself would arise in getting back to base if they were damaged in any way. The briefing officer explained that an aircraft in difficulty could head for one of several airfields in Russian territory. The snag was that Russian troops did not speak English and preferred to shoot first and then ask questions. 'There is a solution,' he exclaimed dramatically and, with a flourish produced a garment like a bib with an RAF roundel on it. 'On being challenged by Russians, you unbutton your flying suit, display this roundel, and put your hands in the air, and shout *Angliski*.'

An objection was raised in a broad Glasgow accent. 'No me. I'll shout Scotsiski, eh.'

Another Australian voice broke in 'That means Blue's a goner. He never learned how to undo his buttons. Least that's what his girl friend tells me.'

The Intelligence Officer looked pained, but decided to go on with his demonstration. He opened his tunic to reveal the roundel bib, put his hands up and said the magic word, '*Angliski*'. Squadron Leader Uwe Klarman, the Canadian skipper stood up in the front row, aimed an imaginary rifle at the target and shouted, 'Bang.' Jock asked what genius had thought up this fancy dress. The Intelligence Officer admitted he was responsible and Jock's laconic, 'Oh, aye,' confirmed his fears that his idea had fallen like a lead balloon. Nevertheless he opened a cardboard box and solemnly handed each of them a folded roundel.

To change the subject he told them that Group Captain Thomas from Bomber Headquarters would fly with W/O Davidson. Jock shrugged, wondering what that might mean. The Intelligence Officer explained that the next briefing would be after they had got used to flying their overweight Lancasters and a target would be given. Uwe Klarman put the final question before they shuffled out. 'Do the Russkis know we're coming and do they know about the targets on our chests?'

The answer was as reassuring as the concept. 'Not yet, but they will be given plenty of notice, never fear.'

'Famous last bloody words,' was the Canadian's retort.

Harness and Hatches Secure 161

Jock was free from flying until the modifications on his Lancaster were complete, so he was pleased when he was told to report to Pathfinder Headquarters. When he arrived he was taken to see Adam, who asked how much he knew about the Pathfinder Force. Jock admitted his knowledge was scant other than that Bennett intended to get some order and discipline into bombing raids. Adam nodded. 'That's how Bennett found out about your views on the sloppy bombing so far. He wants to meet you in ten minutes.'

Jock interrupted, 'Why would he want to do that?'

Adam smiled at the typical Jock response. 'He wants to have you in the Pathfinder Force.'

At interview Bennett began by pointing out that Jock held the highest NCO rank, even though he was still young. Jock shrugged, but held his tongue and stared pointedly at the Air Commodore's broad band worn by his interviewer, who was just over thirty years of age. Bennett noted Jock's stare, but went on and asked why Jock had not been commissioned. Jock admitted that the offer had been made but he had declined. He repeated his views on commissions being appropriate for regular airmen, rather than for 'hostilities only' people like himself. 'Besides,' he added, 'I don't think that being an officer would make me a better flier, and I'm sure you're looking for good fliers, so I would just say no, maybe even no thanks.'

Bennett raised his hands to dismiss the subject. 'Thomas told me that you were pretty vocal about the way in which the raids were conducted. Did you ever drop your bombs short of the aiming point?'

Jock replied immediately, 'Certainly not deliberately, on the first tour and so far not on the second.'

'Glad to hear it. I've been bawling out these "fringe merchants", who drop their load and turn back before they reach the target. I get a Beaufighter or a Mosquito and check up on them over the target. Last week a Halifax let its bombs go thirty miles short of the target on a perfectly clear night. I was home before them. At the debriefing the bomb-aimer solemnly claimed they had only had an obscured view of the target, I called them liars and ordered them off the squadron, off the station, off the Group by the next morning.'

'You don't mess about, do you?' Jock started, then quickly added, 'Sir.'

'I certainly don't. Not while this war's still to be won,' and Bennett was off explaining his ideas on the Pathfinder approach to bombing. 'The essential thing is to have crews with known records in getting to the right targets, and being able to get accurate results from the bombs they carry. There is a sequence in every raid. The heavy bomber force is preceded by Mosquitoes, some of which drop coloured marker-bombs to show up the turning points on the route to the target. The others drop incendiaries into the city centre. Once these fires get hold they suck in oxygen and become a conflagration, then a holocaust. The firestorm is a target marker for the heavy bombers, which drop their high explosives round the perimeter. Their damage prevents movement into and out of the city centre. This is how you can obliterate a city, not just factories or marshalling yards.'

Jock was squirming and burst out, 'What you call a target is a city. And cities have people in them. Are you really and truly attacking German civilians? That must be against the Geneva Convention.'

Bennett held up a hand to stop him. 'You just think that's true. I'll bet you've never looked at the Geneva convention. Now have you? There's a Geneva Convention for the conduct of war on the land and one for war on the sea, but there's no Geneva convention for war in the air.'

Jock burst back, 'Oh that's just cheap debating. You should never attack civilians. It's . . . morally wrong. If you were thinking I might want to join your Pathfinders, don't bother yourself any further. I cannot approve of it.' Jock stood up fussed with his cap, eventually put it on, saluted and left the office. He sat down on a chair in the corridor breathing hard through his nose and scowling at the floor. Bennett came out of his office and stopped in front of Jock. Jock stood up quickly. Bennett seemed to want to say something but could not. He waved a hand and walked along to the end of the corridor.

Back in Adam's office, Jock described Bennett as having as much sensitivity to human beings as a polar bear's bum. He cooled down enough to tell what had gone on in the interview, and Adam agreed that Bennett was not a great humanitarian, and perhaps that was an advantage in wartime, especially in Bomber Command. Jock burst out, 'He is planning to kill German women and children as well as men. But I don't intend to kill anyone.'

Adam shook his head, 'If you aim a bomb at a building and it falls on top of some poor German he is just as dead as if you had aimed at him. A bomb cannot distinguish between a human being and a munitions factory.'

Jock got angry again, 'Aye, the bomb can't distinguish, but I can, and that's the point.'

Adam continued in a quieter tone. 'This place is a hotbed of moral indignation, protest and confrontation. We had a Cabinet Minister who proposed that any flier who had moral objections to bombing Germany should be excused from going on a raid. That fell flat. We all knew there would be very few aircrew for operations. The arguments we have here are about how best to use bombers, not whether to use them.

'For example, Bennett spends a lot of his time squabbling with Sir Ralph Cochrane, who is Chief of 5 Group and every bit as dedicated a flier and as cold and austere as Bennett. Cochrane wants high level approaches and low level bombing. Bennett wants to stick with high level bombing. Bennett wants Mosquitoes to do the target marking only, Cochrane wants them to do the bombing as well. The Air Officer Commanding, 'Butch' Harris, has to act as referee at their meetings, and it's a thankless task having to deal with two very talented aviators who have no noticeable sense of humour, and no insight into how ridiculous their behaviour can be. 'Butch' also gets criticism from bishops, politicians, professors, academics, amateur strategists, journalists and the public. I think he made a mistake in letting the press use his RAF nickname. It was a tribute to him for being a tough administrator, but it became a millstone round his neck when the public changed it slightly and began to call him 'Butcher' Harris.'

Jock thought for a bit. 'I'm not sure that I could ever come round to your way of thinking, but I'm a bit more sympathetic than I was.' He paused. 'Aye, but not sympathetic enough to join Bennett in his terrible plans.'

Adam said he had seen Eleanor the previous weekend. Her work was going well. She was fit, but was fed up with the blitz night after night. He was trying to get her a post outside London at Beaulieu, but had not heard if it could be organised. She had done a good job on his shoulder and he would have to face another Medical Board soon. 'Candidly, I might like to keep my Navigator status in a Mosquito,' he added.

Jock winked, 'Does that mean you might have to leave B Group and transfer to 5 Group? You'd desert your local ogre to join Cochrane's mob?'

Adam groaned, 'You're still the soul of tact, Jock.'

CHAPTER 26

The modification to Jock's Lancaster had been completed, including, to his surprise, the addition of a radome on the underside of the fuselage. A quick look inside showed him the H2S receiver beside the navigator's 'office'. Neither of the other aircraft had radomes.

As he walked to the mess he passed Flying Officer Graveley who was standing talking to a WAAF officer. He nodded, bid him, 'Good evening' and walked on. Graveley ran and held him by the elbow. 'Don't you think that on the ground, you should respect my commission and salute.'

Jock was menacing, 'Take your hand away. I'm in no mood for nonsense. I presume you're drunk.' He walked on.

A night's sleep helped and he was down at the hangars first thing, as the mechanics arrived with their stained mugs of tea. Jock had a quick look round the aircraft and noted some new rings bolted to the floor of the fuselage. Chiefie explained these would take the webbing that would hold the sandbags in place for the take-off tests.

He was asked to go to the Commanding Officer's office. Dobson and Thomas were both there. He saluted them both in regulation style. Squadron Leader Dobson said, 'My God, Jock. What's happened to you? I never knew you to be a bull merchant.'

'Och, I'm sorry. It's just that I got told off by a crew member last night for not saluting him, and I decided that from now on, I would salute only to show respect.' He smiled and walked forward to shake Group Captain Thomas by the hand. 'I'm glad you will be flying with us on this mystery cruise. You're looking great for a man who spends his time in yon madhouse I was in yesterday.'

Thomas laughed, 'Would it be Flying Officer Graveley who rubbed you up the wrong way?'

Jock nodded. 'The very man. I've been doubtful about his attitude to the others. They just don't seem to mix well.'

Thomas frowned, 'Last night Graveley kept on about how his life as a scholar had suited him to be a navigator. When he said he wanted to talk to me man to man, he reminded me of my father when he misinformed me about the facts of life. But Graveley's idea was to have all officers dine in once a month, black tie, mess kit, best silver, port and toasts. I told him I'd had enough of that and my mess kit wouldn't fit. Strange fellow. Anyway I'm looking forward to flying with you.'

Jock told him the H2S had been fitted. 'That's good. I wanted to try that on this special operation. The boffins fitted a camera to take pictures of the Plan Position Indicator during the raid and the armaments fellows put a detonator inside so that we can blow it up if we have to make a forced landing. So, we're all set. We'll have a quick meeting at noon today then we'll go and practise taking off with all the sandbags for the next couple of days.'

'What's the target?' Jock asked.

'Pitesti,' was the answer.

A pause, then Jock asked guardedly, 'Where the hell is that?'

'In Roumania, of all places,' Dobson answered, moving to a map of Europe on an easel. 'Here's Bucharest and here's Pitesti to the North East. There's a new oilfield with new large storage tanks, which supply the Wehrmacht. That's our target.'

Jock thought about it then asked, 'What about their defences?'

'We don't honestly know. I asked our Intelligence people, but I'm not sure how much they know.'

Geoff Thomas explained, 'This will have to be secret until the pre-operational briefing in two or three days time, depending upon the weather forecast.'

Jock said, 'Aye, it's big stuff all right. I'll keep quiet about it. Now I'm off down to do my take over checks with Chiefie Woodson. It's been great being with the pair of you again, just like the old days.'

Prober was in conference with Chiefie when Jock arrived. It took about twenty minutes for Chiefie to explain the modifications, including the procedures for changing from the auxiliary to the main tanks. Chiefie then stood by while Jock and Prober did the external inspection, the cockpit check, and the check on the tarmac. Eventually Jock signed the acceptance form, acknowledging the work that had been done and they set off to the Education Block where the day's meeting was to be held.

The Station Commander welcomed Group Captain Thomas back to his squadron. Thomas explained he could not give them their target yet, but it was a long way to go. 'No, not Tipperary,' he assured a heckler. This afternoon they would fly with full crew aboard to the auxiliary airfield. The sandbags would be loaded into the cabin and the cargo would be secured by webbing straps. Dobson said that he had once taken off in a Lancaster that was grossly overloaded. Well before it got to take-off speed the Lancaster started to swing on the runway.

A Flight Sergeant Flight Engineer called out, 'I remember that.'

Dobson smiled in recognition, 'Of course, it was you, Nobby. We both ended up hauling and shoving on the control column . . . a most undignified take-off. My advice is not to let the swing start.'

In the afternoon, with the sand-bags aboard, both Jock and Uwe Klarmann found it difficult to control the swings until Blue Murphy, the red haired Australian Flight Sergeant told them to use as much trim as they could get. By mid-morning of the second day all three could cope with the extra tonnage and the exercise was declared successful. The sand bags were unloaded and the maintenance crews carried out the daily inspections. Night Flying Tests were done on the equipment and fittings on the way back to the main airfield. As each aircraft was now ready for operations, it could be armed before the briefing at 17.00 hours.

Jock and his bomb aimer, Boris, went down to see how the bombing up process was going. Their Lancaster had been pulled out from the sheltering wall to give as much clear space as possible all round. The serviced machine guns were fitted into the turrets and the ammunition belts fed into place. The bomb doors, nearly thirty feet in length, were open and a WAAF tractor driver skilfully backed a train of bomb trolleys to a specified point below the cavernous opening. The dark green missiles were 500 pound general purpose bombs with heavy steel cases and a relatively small amount of explosive inside. It was expected that a high percentage of them would be duds, more likely to have an effect on morale than on buildings.

The high capacity bombs were ugly 8,000 pound dustbin like canisters crammed full of explosive. These were designed to be used against buildings, and one could destroy a significant area of the target. In addition to High Explosives bombs, the load included incendiaries, containers packed with ninety 4 pound sticks of magnesium which would burn with a spluttering white flame and ignite almost anything it touched. Jock remembered its effects on him and grimaced. Before being placed on the trolley, each fin had been straightened and the casing washed so that no dirt or mud could throw the bomb off balance as it fell.

The Armaments Officer had worked out the position each bomb would occupy in the bomb bay to prevent the sudden loss of weight affecting the Lancaster's centre of gravity. The bombs were winched slowly and carefully from the trolley into the bomb bay.

As the empty trolleys were being driven off, Jock whispered to Sancerre, 'This is the bit I hate.' The Sergeant Armourer, a small wiry man, pulled hard on each missile, and ended with his feet off the ground clinging to a heavy explosive canister, grinning to his audience. He jumped down and reported that everything was fine to the Armaments Officer, who then signed the clearance.

At the briefing the earnest Intelligence Officer showed them the location of Roumania, then Bucharest then Pitesti, lying about 150 miles south of the Transylvanian Alps. The main centre of the Roumanian oil industry was Ploesti, but it was too heavily guarded. Their targets for tonight were the newly built refining plant and oil storage complex to the west of this major oilfield.

An Air Commodore then told them the aim of their mission was to make a mess of Roumania's contribution to the German war effort. 'A sneak attack by your three aircraft could succeed without alerting too many defences around that area. To be truthful, we know damn all about the sort of resistance you could expect. But I wouldn't think they've had too much practice. Our American and Russian friends want to have a go at the main field at Ploesti, but I'd like to see us get first crack at Pitesti, which only began producing last year.'

On the route map the tapes stretched across the Channel to north of Brussels, then across the Rhine between Cologne and Coblenz toward Schweinfurt, then to Nuremberg, on to Linz, south of Vienna to Budapest then south-east and over the Transylvanian Alps until they crossed the Ort, a major river. They continued that heading until they came to a junction of two rivers where Pitesti was located. The Navigators were all taking notes, of the headings and route changes. Group Captain Thomas commented, 'We all know the first part of the route and it's got plenty of anti-aircraft and fighter bases, but Cologne and Coblenz are going to be attacked by Pathfinders just about the time you arrive between them. With these diversions, you, I mean we, should be able to slip through unnoticed. We don't know what kind of welcome will be waiting in Austria and Hungary, never mind Roumania.

'We should have fuel enough to return following roughly the same route. We'll be back at Coblenz and Cologne about five or six hours later, but they'll be too busy. We'll have less of a load, and can keep a good cruising speed at

20,000 feet. As it begins to get lighter, watch for contrails. They'll let old Fritz know where to send his fighters.'

Another question was raised from the floor. 'We know you're going with the flying Scot, Sir. Can you tell us what you're going to do? Maybe you're going to teach him how to fly.'

Thomas answered, 'I had hoped just to sit back, read *The Times* and drink brandy, but I'm going to try out the new H2S system, which has been installed in Jock's aeroplane. The chances are that the visibility will be lousy over the target. If it is cloudy and rainy, I am going to see if I can identify the target before and after bombing with my box of tricks. The Pathfinders are mad keen to get their hands on these gadgets, but I think we should get our hands on them first.'

The meteorologist said that conditions in Northern Europe would be fair to good, with the moon coming up to full. Winds would be 10 to 15 knots from the south-west, changing to south, below 10 knots on the last leg. There would be rain in the area of Pitesti, reducing visibility. The Station Commander quietly wished them Godspeed. The Flying Control Officer asked them to be ready for take off at 2100 hours.

The eager Intelligence Officer jumped up and reminded them about unbuttoning and saying '*Angliski*'. All the crews stood up, aimed their imaginary guns and shouted 'Bang, Bang!' The Wireless Operators went to get their frequencies and recognition signals. The Navigators were called to their special briefing. Jock went to his room to write to Fiona.

The pre-flight formalities were quickly dealt with as theirs was the only operation that night. The picnics were larger than usual, with two thermos flasks per man and undoubtedly extra chocolate. Jock had suffered in the past from having an undigested meal in his stomach for such a long time, so he refused the dinner in the mess but drank a little milk and ate a jam sandwich, 'a jeely piece', which Doris, a Glasgow waitress, prepared specially for him.

On reaching the aircraft Jock had words with Chiefie and heard his report. He remembered he wanted to warn the crew about the new bolts but he was too late. Selsund had already stubbed a toe on a ring bolt, and Jock learned that Norwegian swear words were remarkably like English. He completed his external check and joined Boris at the bomb doors. Boris solemnly asked him to open them so that he could climb on one of the canisters.

Jock started to object then noticed the grin on the Canadian's face. 'You nearly aborted the flight on the grounds of the state of the pilot's underwear,' he joked. He clapped the bomb aimer on the back, then signed the Form 700 accepting the aircraft from the ground crew, and climbed aboard.

Once the intercommunication system had been tested there was a quiet period as everyone settled in to try out their equipment. After completing the cockpit checks, Jock and Prober ran the engines, watching the oil pressure. Jock was to be first off and at 21.05 hours he got the signal to go. He opened up the throttles and forced the roaring monster out from the dispersal point to crawl its way round the perimeter track to the end of the runway, with Blue Murphy following his tail and Uwe Klarman following Blue.

At the end of the runway, Jock's code number was flashed to Control. The aircraft was pointed straight down the runway and the engines were throttled back. A large group of ground personnel had turned out to see them off. Among them, standing side by side were the Station Commander and Doris, his guardian angel in the Sergeant's mess. He knew that she was at that spot night after night, and seeing her with the Group Captain reminded him of a close family gathering making their farewells.

At last he got a green light and he revved up the engines, with the brakes fully on, to build up sufficient power to get his heavy load to move. He released the brakes, conscious that they were loaded well beyond the design limit. 'Quiet, lads,' he said automatically and unnecessarily.

He turned the trim wheel until it stopped. His right hand pushed the throttles firmly, twisting his wrist in order to counteract the swing due to torque from the propellers. The navigator was calling out readings from the Air Speed Indicator by his desk. 90, 95, 100, 105, as Jock got the tail up. The propellers gripped the air and the aircraft strained to rise. As the wheels left the tarmac the rumbling noise diminished and Jock raised his hand. Immediately Prober's hand slid under his to take the throttles. This allowed Jock both hands, together with his arms and shoulders on the control column to haul the overweight Lancaster into the air. Prober made a slight correction on the port throttle setting.

Jock nodded his thanks and called, 'Climbing power.' Prober set the throttles appropriately and answered, 'Climbing Power.'

Then 'Wheels up,' from Jock, repeated by Prober as he pulled on the lever. The dull thump assured them the wheels were fully retracted. 'Flaps up,' from Jock was repeated by Prober after he had closed the flaps with a grinding noise from the wings. At the top of their climb, the final part of the dialogue was Prober responding to, 'Cruising Power,' from Jock, by drawing back smoothly on the throttle levers, keeping an eye on the gauges and readjusting the mixture controls. The nose dropped a little and the engines took on a quieter, deeper note. Prober gave him thumbs up. Jock reset the trim and looked around. Everything was operating and the gauges all pointed to the right places, the trim was set. With Prober on the throttles, he began a steady climb to their ceiling of 20,000 feet, at 12,000 feet asking everyone to use oxygen.

Once he had reached height he adjusted throttles, mixture and carburettor heat. Then he switched on automatic pilot and loosened his harness to ease his shoulders, promising himself, as he always did, that he would spend more time in the gym.

From the rear, Selsund's soft voice with its lilting accent informed him that the other two aircraft had made it successfully and were following behind. He then went on, 'I wonder if they are surprised like we are still to have wings on.'

Jock was about to thank him when a sharp voice broke in, 'Navigator here. As senior officer in this crew I would ask the tail gunner to devote his time to keeping a watch, not to schoolboy humour.'

There was a stunned silence which Jock broke in a harsh voice, 'Skipper here, Mr Graveley, we've got a real senior officer aboard, so if I want anyone to pull rank, I'll get him to do it. Back on the tarmac you can do your Officer Training Corps stuff, but not in my aircraft. Now give me the course to steer for the first leg.' When he got it, he altered course, and reset the automatic pilot.

Later when he asked for a position, there was a pause then Graveley said the winds must have been wrong for they were further south than they should have been. They should have been skirting to the north of Brussels, but they were well to the south of the city.

'Are you all right, Navigator?' Jock asked impatiently.

'Well I'm a bit upset at being insulted in front of the NCOs.'

Jock let out a snort of exasperation, 'And it was an NCO who insulted you. Now, can you fly this mission or not, Mr Graveley?'

Thomas came on the intercom, 'I'm going to see what's what with this chap, Jock. You fly your course. I'll let you know soon.'

After a little, the Group Captain came back on. 'Jock. Geoff here. Your navigator made an error in taking the Gee fix and is way off course, I'm afraid. Steer 085, please and that'll get us back on track in 15 minutes or so.' Jock acknowledged and made the necessary correction, then sat wondering what nonsense he was facing now, knowing that his flying could be affected by the anger he felt building up.

Geoff Thomas came back on, he said he suspected that Graveley had taken drugs and could anyone in the crew confirm it. Jonathan Rice said he had known for some time that Graveley took stimulants and had warned him they could be harmful. Graveley had dismissed this on the grounds that he only took enough to make him feel good, and he never would take drugs when he was flying. Prober broke in to say that he had once shared a room with Graveley and had seen him taking white pills. He said they were to give him energy, but all they seemed to do was make him irritable. Geoff Thomas broke in, 'Thank you. That fits in with what I thought when I saw his eyes dilated. I think he's taken too many. I've found a tin of them in his pocket and have taken them away.'

Jock came back, 'We've sorted Graveley's problem, but can we continue the operation? If you can do the navigation, Geoff, we will go on.' The Group Captain agreed and suggested that Graveley should be formally relieved of his duties by the skipper and he would log this and the time. Jock was a bit tongue-tied, 'Flying Officer Graveley, as of now, you are relieved of your duties. You must not take any further part in the operation of the plane or in the duties being carried out by the crew. Do you understand?'

'Of course I bloody understand, and I protest . . .'

'Protest all you bloody well like, but only after we've landed. For now shut up, sit still and stay still, and let the rest of us get on with our jobs,' Jock snapped. Geoff Thomas accepted formally and reported that he had made the entries in the log.

The Norwegian accent came in. 'I'm with you, Jock.' Then support came from all the other members of the crew. Jock thanked them, then raised his voice 'Bloody hell! We're going on like weans at a Sunday School party. Let's get on with the war. I'm going to lose five thousand feet and put on speed. Mr Engineer, what about fuel? Mr Navigator, get me a course to steer. Mr Bomber and Gunners look out for the enemy. And no more bloody committee meetings.'

CHAPTER 27

Over the moonlit Rhine at 20,000 feet, to their left they saw a glow with clouds of coloured smoke above. The Pathfinders were over Cologne. Similar pyrotechnics were visible to the right, presumably at Coblenz, and, as hoped, there was no fighter activity directed at them. When he gave Jock a heading to keep them clear of Frankfurt, Geoff announced they were back on schedule.

Quarter of an hour later, Boris spotted two aircraft dead ahead. Jock decided not to use IFF (Identification Friend or Foe) as the Germans could lock on to that frequency and locate them easily. Instead he asked Boris to flash the letters of the day just before they got within their firing range. Shortly Boris reported that both had returned the correct signal.

The three Lancasters continued to fly together, keeping a distance of about 200 feet between wing tips. Prober took over while Jock catnapped in the right hand seat. He sat up and stretched after half an hour, got back into his seat and asked for a position. He was pleasantly surprised that they were over the White Mountains between Brno to the north and Vienna to the south. The wind had been more favourable than anticipated and they had gained almost 20 minutes. He congratulated Prober and asked if he ever answered to Bill. It was Bill who acknowledged with a thumb up, and reported that they were well off for fuel.

Jock then called round the aircraft asking for reports. Everyone reported being in good spirits. Trigger asked about Graveley. Geoff reported that he had been difficult for a time but David Gray stopped him leaping about and restrained him with one of the belts that had been left from the practice runs. Graveley was now in a deep sleep.

Jock had just altered course slightly to follow Geoff's new heading when Trigger called out, 'Fighter closing from five o'clock.'

'I see him,' Jonathan Rice said quietly, and his guns started chattering, as X-ray's starboard side was raked by machine gun fire.

'It's an FW 190 and he's coming round for another go at us,' Trigger warned then asked Jock to break left and fired a short burst.

A whoop from the mid upper turret, 'There you are, Fritz!' as Jonathan added his fire power to Trigger's, then, 'We got him, Trigger. See him stall. He's retired hurt. Enemy has disengaged, Skipper.'

Jock checked round for damage to crew and fittings. Both gunners had been sparing with their ammunition. Trigger reported that he was in a hell of a draught as a perspex panel had been shot out and he was freezing. Dave reported his radio was not damaged and he had not been hit. He then called 'Oh Christ, Graveley's been shot in the head. He's dead, I'm afraid. Must have been a stray. Nothing else around here's been hit.' Geoff confirmed Graveley's death and announced that he and Dave would put the body on the rest bunk in the rear. Boris went into the nose and reported the bombsight was functioning properly. Geoff, back at the navigator's table announced his gadgets were OK. Jock tried the controls and found them to be operating smoothly. Prober reported that the fuel supply seemed to be intact. As he spoke the oil pressure gauge for the port outer engine flicked a couple of times. He supposed it could be just a damaged instrument, but it might mean that oil was not getting to the engine. He stood up to look over Jock's head, then sat down quickly and announced fire in the port outer.

He switched on the extinguisher, asked Jock to shut down the engine and feather that propeller and stood up again to watch. At last he sat down and said he thought the fire was out, but he wanted to keep an eye on it as it was too near number three fuel tank. With this engine off, the generator for Gee and the rear turret pump would not work. Geoff confirmed that Gee was not working. Trigger was indignant that the loss of the engine had lost him his pump. His guns would still fire and could be moved up and down but his turret was stuck amidships. If the Germans would only fly straight toward their tail, he could shoot them down.

Jock called up Geoff and told him that they would press on, so he and Boris should plan to continue the raid. Boris went to the navigator's 'office' where he and Geoff conferred over their charts. Boris announced their mode of attack, stressing that so far they had great visibility, which was good for him, but bad for a test of H2S. Geoff would take them in to a point south of Pitesti where they would turn north and fly over the city to the target. Ideally they could pick up a railway line and follow it over two rivers until it joined three main railway lines and they could start their run in, with the H2S going from that point.

'Sounds good to me,' was Jock's reply, and he made a slight course correction suggested by Geoffrey. He looked across at Bill doggedly staring at his instruments and asked if everything was OK.

'Everything's in good nick. We won't need to switch tanks for over an hour yet, on our way home,' was Bill's response. Jock gave him thumbs up.

Boris settled down in the nose, the bombsight ready and his chart marked and folded, watching the slow moving landscape beneath them. 'I'm looking for that railway line. Ah, got it. The moon's glinting right on it. Hold that course, Skipper just as you are. What's the new course going to be, navigator?' Geoff gave the northerly heading. Jock acknowledged and set the compass ring in readiness. Boris came back, 'When I count from five and say turn, the navigator will switch on his machine and we will both start our stop watches. Skipper, you come smoothly on to that heading and keep on it.' Jock acknowledged. He felt the excitement rising as they flew, waiting for the word. The signal seemed to be a long time coming.

On the command he turned smoothly and could see glimpses of the railway line they were following on the ground, then a different metallic sheen from the first river. Across this and back to the thread, then another broader stretch of river. Boris announced, 'Bomb doors open,' as they crossed over the railway junction. Then the southern part of the city was beneath them, a conglomeration of small buildings, perhaps houses with several flickers of light as householders with no blackouts turned on their lights on being awakened by their droning. Then the northern fringes and Boris whooping as he saw the tanks. 'Come right, Skipper, riight . . . riiight . . . riight . . . That's it. Very nice. Now Steady. Steady.' A long pause. 'Bombs away!'

The aircraft bucked as she was relieved of her heavy load. There was the expected rumbling and thump and the announcement that the bomb doors were closed. Jock went round in a left hand circuit, with everyone watching as the bombs exploded. The effect of the incendiaries left no doubt that they had hit fuel tanks. There was a gigantic burst of flames from each tank as the explosives opened them up. Jonathan Rice reported two aircraft coming in just below them. He had just identified them as the two Lancasters when a battery of search lights ringing the field was switched on.

Jock veered off and circled to the right to watch as L for Lousy, Uwe's Lancaster, flew steadily in a cone of light. The Canadian dropped his bombs just as the anti-aircraft guns started up, and began a wild corkscrew to get clear of the light that was tormenting him. A steep dive took him out of the trap and he too joined the right hand circuit out of the glare. His bombs were more to the north and they ruptured something which set off another massive fire.

Harness and Hatches Secure 175

Thermals from this huge oil fire were buffeting Jock's aircraft.

The third Lancaster went in below the searchlight cones but it was soon picked out and exploded from a direct hit. They watched sadly as bits of the aircraft twisted and spiralled and fell straight down into the flames. There was no sign of anyone even trying to escape.

'Oh damn, damn, damn,' said Bill. 'That was Blue.'

Jock was brusque, 'Let's get the hell out of here.'

Geoff gave the heading to fly back, and with Uwe's L Lousy to starboard they settled down for a long leg. After they had passed Budapest and were on a heading to skirt Vienna, Jock managed to catnap while Bill sat in the pilot's seat with the automatic pilot on. When he awoke he called round the crew. Trigger reminded everyone that he was still being frozen, then added, 'Skipper, I would not like Graveley to be court martialled now that he is dead.' Jock agreed, but pointed out that Graveley had put the whole crew at risk, so they would all have to agree not to report it. They all consented readily, Bill Prober pointing out sadly that those who knew about his drugs had been wrong in failing to report it. Geoff was willing to change the entry in the log.

Jock was pleased that they had not shown any bitterness or rancour although they had reached the stage at which the discomforts of flying in the Lancaster were beginning to be felt. While it was a magnificent workhorse, a strong and reliable weapon of war, Roy Chadwick, its designer, did not have aircrew comforts high on his list of priorities. Vibration hammered the temples, shook the teeth, and drummed on the bones so that even after the most uneventful flight the crew reached an advanced stage of fatigue.

Scalps became itchy under the helmet and faces grew numb from wearing the mandatory oxygen masks and the microphones and headsets needed for communication. The Lancaster was also vulnerable to the condition of the air through which it flew. There could be a sudden smack into a hard wall of air or a sickening drop into an air pocket. Under these conditions, it was impossible to relax even for a few moments without being thrown about as the aircraft bucketed, rolled or yawed. The gunners found it difficult to concentrate on covering the sky in their watch for enemy aircraft. Making entries in a log was exasperating, and emptying one's bladder or having a hot drink ended up as an undignified activity. The pilot needed strength to wrestle the machine which, at times, fought to break out from his grasp. He sometimes needed all his own, and someone else's brute force to heave the control column around.

Jock asked Bill Prober if anything could be done to give Trigger a bit of heat. Bill went off to investigate. The weather was still clear in the bright moon, and there were tinges of light over the horizon to the east as Geoff gave him a course for the north-east of Nuremberg, and confirmed that they were on schedule. Boris, as usual, went down into the nose for a spell. He always liked to do a watch 'from the office'.

Dave Gray reported that he was getting German chatter. They were saying something about '*zwei Tomi*' and it sounded like a ground controller vectoring fighters. Jock altered his crew and waggled his wings to bring Uwe in closer. Uwe got the message and took up position to starboard and slightly below Jock. They had not long to wait. Bill quickly returned to his seat and reported that he had tried something to get more heat to Trigger. He would check later.

Boris suddenly yelled, 'A 110 beneath us!' Then Jock was alarmed to see tracer from L Lousy's upper turret going beneath them. An explosion in the rear, then another in the nose of X-ray and finally a great whumph of sound from outside as L for Lousy rolled away from them and blew up. A black painted twin engined Messerschmitt 110 was highlighted for a few moments, diving away from them. Jock regained control and tried to peer through the smoke that filled the cockpit.

Bill Prober was slumped forward in his seat. He did not respond to Jock's touch. Jock shook him then felt an excruciating pain in his right shoulder. With an effort, he pulled Bill back. The whole front of the Flight Engineer's chest had been blown away, and the dull black nose of a cannon shell was sticking obscenely from a bloody mess of bone and tissue.

Jock wanted to vomit and had to restrain himself from ripping off his face mask. He was relieved to hear Dave Gray's quiet voice on the intercom. 'A shell came through the fuselage back here and broke the Group Captain's left leg and left wrist. There's a lot of bleeding from his scalp, and below his ear. He's unconscious at the moment. Could you get down lower a bit so that I can take off his mask, and have a look for other injuries. What about your end?'

Jock reported, 'Bill is dead and I'm sure Boris must be dead too, but I can't move to find out.'

Jonathan Rice cut in, 'I'll come forward and give you a hand. Can you keep watch, Trigger.' When Trigger answered Jock was relieved that there were still some unscathed crew members left. He took the aircraft down below 15,000 feet as Rice went into the nose to check on Boris. He came out shaking his head, lifted Bill and laid him in the nose on top of Boris. Jonathan sat in Bill's seat and plugged in. 'What about you?' he asked Jock. Jock told him that he had lost feeling in his legs and he had sharp pains in his right arm and shoulder. Rice said, 'I'll get Dave.'

He left and Jock tried out his legs on the rudder pedals. He found to his relief that he could move them but had no awareness of how far they had moved unless he watched them. He decided that things could stay that way until he figured out a way of looking down the whole time to check when they were straight.

Dave came forward. 'The Group Captain isn't going to be in any condition to help you fly the plane. I've got his bleeding stopped and I've stitched up his face. If he recovers consciousness he might help with the navigation. That's why I haven't given him Morphine to knock him right out. But let's have a look at you now. Can you put this thing on automatic?' Jock did so and was pleased to find it was still operative. Dave confidently loosened Jock's flying suit and felt under his pullover and shirt over his chest and back. He got Jock to stand up holding on to a strut while he went over the lower back, crotch, thighs and upper legs.

He guided Jock back into the seat, unzipped the legs of the suit and checked what he called the lower extremities. He helped Jock to readjust his clothing then gave his verdict. 'There's no superficial wounding that would produce bleeding enough to worry us, but you have at least six entry wounds in your right shoulder, two or three in the right lumbar region, and a couple in your right buttock, and I would suspect there are more bits of metal inside you. What I can't tell you is whether you are haemorrhaging internally. All we can do is make sure you don't make any unnecessary movements.'

Jock thought for a moment. He was in no great pain and if he could remain like this for the next four or five hours he could get back, but if he passed out because of the inside bleeding that would be the end. He had a wounded Group Captain who had some important information to get back, but could not use a parachute. He himself could not use a parachute. He switched on his intercom. 'Bill and Boris are dead. The Group Captain and I are in no condition to jump. At the moment I feel I could take us home, but I might flake out along the way. You can jump if you wish, but I would suggest waiting until we get further north. You would have a better chance of getting picked up by the Resistance.'

Dave's answer was immediate, 'I'm staying. I've got Groupie propped up at his desk and I could get him to mark his chart with all the turning points set out. I could fill them in on your chart and walk between the two of you, occasionally listening in on my receiver.'

'I'll stay and join in with you, Dave,' Jonathan Rice broke in.

'And I will stay too. I have no wish to jump,' came from Trigger. Jock remembered a previous occasion and asked if the parachutes were still intact. The immediate answer was that they were fine.

'Good for you and thank you. You can always change your mind later on. Now let's see what's what,' Jock said as he took back the controls. The speed was well below 200 mph, but the amount of fuel was reassuring, so he let things stand at that. He warned that he was going to climb again, so oxygen would be required. Dave came forward to give him climbing power. As they got higher the holes in X-ray produced a great deal of drag so they settled for 18,000 feet.

Jock turned to Dave, 'You seemed to know what you were doing when you examined me and stitched the Group Captain.'

'I should, for I had been a veterinary surgeon in my own practice for three years before I volunteered for this lark,' was the surprise answer.

Jock laughed, Dave joined in, 'All I did was treat the pair of you as if you were my best customer's prize bulls. I haven't told the Group Captain my secret yet.'

'You have now,' came Geoff's voice.

Geoff gave the headings to take them round Nuremburg at a safe distance. Jock estimated a maximum speed of 190, and a cruising speed of around 160 mph at this height and the condition of the fuselage. Once they were settled on course, Geoff said, 'I've been thinking of how we got hit by that Messerschmitt. There were two of them, one for each of us, and they used a new and obvious tactic, an upward firing cannon. Our one came at us from below, right into our blind spot, our underbelly. He crept into position, matched his speed to ours and fired straight up. Uwe's chap hit a wing root and burst a fuel line, and up went the bomber. We couldn't see the one that got him because he was lower than we were. But Uwe's upper gunner saw the one under us and put him off his aim by firing at him. Bloody good luck for us, for some of us anyway. Bloody bad luck for Uwe and his lads, though. We should tell the Intelligence people about that. Incidentally our H2S is no longer working. I presume the aerials were smashed.'

Trigger spoke from the tail. 'Dawn's up, Skipper, and good visibility all around. No sign of anyone.'

Dave asked how his prize bulls were faring. Geoff said he had pains in his leg and shoulder and had been seeing double for some time. Dave told him he had been concussed and should get his calculations checked by someone else. Jock reported pain in right shoulder and just beneath the shoulder blade. He was still completely numb from the waist down but could use his legs on the rudder pedals, as long as he looked to see where they were. He assured them that so far he was still all right to fly. Jonathan Rice returned to his upper turret, and Trigger came forward to sit beside Jock.

Mercifully there was some low cloud cover, for they were flying in increasing sunshine, and a German dawn patrol would have an easy time finding them. Shortly after skirting Frankfurt they saw some dark smoke rising through the cloud. They identified this as Coblenz, still smoking from last night's raid and gave it a wide berth to starboard as they headed for Belgium. He suggested to the crew that they might like to jump in this area, and offered to fly lower. Once more, the three of them did not hesitate in saying they would stay.

Between them they had worked out a schedule of a listening watch on the radio, look out from the upper turret, assisting Geoff with the Dead Reckoning plot, and sitting beside Jock ready to switch to automatic if he should flake out. Geoff observed that not having H2S any more was an advantage as the powerful coastal Radar system set up by the Germans could not pick up their transmissions, and set more fighters on them. They droned on.

CHAPTER 28

As they reached the English Channel and cleared the enemy coast, Jock asked Dave to send out their identification signal and to inform control that they had casualties and some damage and would land on the auxiliary runway. Trigger was with Jock to help with the approach and landing. Secretly, Jock was glad to have the rear turret empty in case they had a repetition of D Dumbo's return to earth when the turret broke off. Dave reported that the runway was being prepared, and the crash services were alerted. The cloud base was 1000 feet with drizzle and sleet under it. The wind was light from the north-east.

Jock approached in cloud, holding the aircraft steady. They came out of cloud over a factory, with the arriving shift waving to them, and touched down with a long clear runway ahead. Jock had difficulty with the brakes, but eventually brought the aircraft to a halt. He clapped Trigger on the shoulder, thanked him and asked him to cut throttles and switches. The final exertions had produced a great deal of pain in his neck, shoulder and upper back, and he had no sensation below the waist at all. He sat looking glumly at the bodies of Boris Sancerre and Bill Prober in the shattered nose of the aircraft.

The Medical Officer and his orderlies were quickly aboard. Dave explained the nature of the injuries suffered by Jock and Geoff. After an examination by the M.O. Geoff's arm and leg were splinted and he was taken out on a stretcher. Jock's head and neck were immobilised to a back-board, an analgesic was given and he was cautiously transported to the ambulance. The three canvas covered bodies were lifted into the back of a van and driven off quickly. Trigger, Jonathan and Dave shook hands with Jock and Geoff and wished them good luck.

Jock was only vaguely aware of being undressed, having a light shone in his eyes, being struck by a rubber mallet on his elbows, but not feeling anything on his knees, being manhandled on to his left side and a number of X-ray pictures being taken. He heard people speaking but could not grasp what they were saying. He was asked questions loudly, knew the answers but could not say the words.

Suddenly his teeth began to chatter then his upper arms, forearms and hands, were shaking. His lower body was not affected. He heard someone say 'shock' and he was bundled up in extra blankets. He wanted to curl up but he could not get his knees to bend. He found himself swimming in and out of consciousness, being bewildered that someone was talking to him about something strange, then floating away. He thought that his mother and father and Fiona were there. His mother was crying and his father was comforting her, and his mother was telling someone that her boy was too young to die.

Fiona looked at him sadly and stroked his hand, but that made his hand sore. Then his neck was stiff, his throat was blocked and he had to breathe hard to get air. There were nurses all round and someone was doing something to his throat. He could get his breath at last, but could not speak. He slept again.

When he awoke there were clicks and wheezes and someone talking at the foot of his bed. He heard the word tetanus mentioned and tried to ask a question, but he found it difficult to speak as there was something over his mouth. In a half awake state he automatically reached up to switch on the intercom, but his hand was moved aside gently but firmly. 'It's all right now. It's just to help you breathe. I'm glad you're awake at last. We're all very glad to have you back with us. Let me clean you up a bit.'

The mask was removed and a cool wet pad was passed over his face. 'That's nice, thank you,' he smiled. 'Isn't tetanus the name for lockjaw? Is that what I've got?'

The nurse who had cleaned his face looked at the foot of the bed and a white coated older man came up and took his pulse. 'You had tetanus and we thought we were going to lose you, but you decided otherwise. You've got over it and we don't know why. We were discussing that when you woke up. What do you remember?'

Jock was silent for a while. He felt so weak that it was difficult to concentrate. Then it came back. 'Five of us got back. Three were killed. Two were injured.' He thought a little more. 'There were two other planes, Blue's and Uwe's.' Tears welled up. 'Seventeen were killed. I knew them all.' The nurse squeezed his hand. He tried to sit up in bed. 'I don't feel anything but I must go to the bathroom.'

The doctor was beside him. 'Not now, old chap. We've put a tube in you so you don't have to get up.'

Jock turned his face slowly. 'I can't feel my legs. Now I remember. I can't walk. When will I be able to walk?'

The doctor was firm. 'It's taken a team of doctors and nurses weeks to get you over tetanus. You'll have to recover from that before we can start digging out all the odd bits that are inside you. Then we can find out about your walking.'

Jock looked crestfallen and was about to ask another question when the nurse put her hand gently over his mouth and said, 'Hush, Robin. You're being worked too hard for a man who's been so terribly sick.' Her tone hardened as she turned to the doctors, 'Off with the two of you. Go and bother some healthy person. I want to get to know my star patient and tidy him up.' They nodded, smiled at Robin and left.

'Now Robin, I'm Sister O'Beirne and I am the Senior Orthopaedic Nurse. The man who just left is the general physician who is in charge of your treatment. He's delighted with you because you are the first known case to recover from such a bad bout of tetanus. The other young fellow is Dr Scott, the Surgical Registrar. He comes from Glasgow and you'll be seeing a lot more of him. He's going to be a fine doctor. He took his turn with the nurses in sitting night watch over you to make sure everything went well.'

She pressed a bell, removed a drip needle from his arm, opened the ties on his gown and slid it off his shoulders. Two nurses came in, one carrying towels and a steaming wash bowl, the other a stack of bed linen. After the introductions were made, the gown was removed and the young girls gently raised his buttocks and slid a rubber sheet under him. The formal ceremony of a bed bath was begun. An orderly came in and shaved him with a wicked looking cut-throat razor. Then the two girls combed his damp hair after discussing where his parting should be. The rubber sheet was removed and the sheets and blankets were replaced.

The nurses left and Sister O'Beirne handed Robin a mirror. He was shocked. His face had never been so thin and he had puffy dark circles under his eyes. 'In a couple of weeks time, once we have fed you up, just remember what you are like now. You've been getting liquids through a tube. You'll start solids today, and while I'm at it, do you know what an enema is?' Jock nodded in an embarrassed fashion. 'We will use an enema on you, and with a catheter in your bladder, you will not need to worry about getting up to go to the toilet.'

After three days Sister O'Beirne allowed him visitors. Geoff Thomas appeared in a wheel chair with his left leg in plaster. He was being pushed by Dave Gray and escorted by Trigger Selsund and Jonathan Rice. There was an immediate gaggle of greeting and handing over of a bag of apples that Dave's mum had sent from the farm's orchard, a guide book to Norway in Norwegian from Trigger, a small pocket book of quotations from Shakespeare from Jonathan, and then Geoff handed him a flat parcel wrapped in brown paper. They all watched eagerly as Jock unwrapped a silver-framed studio photograph of Fiona.

Geoff explained, 'I've been keeping in touch with your Mum and Dad telling them of your progress. To get Fiona involved I asked her to have this picture taken. We, your crew that is, chipped in to get the frame.'

Jock looked at the inscription at the foot. It read, 'To our skipper, Jock Davidson from his crew. January 1943'. Their names were listed. Jock tried to give his thanks but he was overwhelmed and broke down.

The others stood around awkwardly until Sister O'Beirne swept in, 'The man's very weak. That's why he's weepy.' She castigated them for upsetting her patient and banished them. She picked up the photograph, saw the inscription, 'All my love, Fiona'. She said, 'She's lovely. Do you know what? That's my name too, but it's spelled the Irish way, with two n's and gh at the end.'

Some of Jock's spirit returned, 'Then that's what I'll call you – Sister two n's and a gh.'

Sister O'Beirne actually smirked, but recovered, 'I'm not going to allow you any more visitors today. Go to sleep now. You'll get some supper soon.'

A quiet night and a bland breakfast, followed by an enema given by the dignified and humourless orderly who had shaved him, then his first visitor, the Commanding Officer of the Hospital. Colonel Hawkins congratulated him on his miraculous recovery from tetanus, then informed him that the King had been graciously pleased to award W/O Davidson the Victoria Cross for conspicuous gallantry. The King and Queen would travel from Sandringham to visit the hospital in two weeks time. During this visit, the King would bestow the highest military honour on W/O Davidson.

Jock really did not know what to say. He hummed and hawed. 'We were doing our job. If there were any heroes, it was the whole crew.' The Colonel assured him that they were to be decorated. Group Captain Thomas was to be given a bar to his Distinguished Service Order, Flight Sergeants Selsund and Gray the Distinguished Flying Medal and Flying Officer Rice the Distinguished Flying Cross, their investiture to be held at Buckingham Palace in a month's time.

Jock wondered if his family and fiancée could be at the ceremony. The Colonel told him they had been invited. 'In fact, to celebrate your recovery, they're going to travel from Scotland overnight to be in the hospital tomorrow morning. There's a train at lunch time to get them back home tomorrow night.'

The next visitor was Geoff in his wheelchair. After mutual congratulations on their decorations, Geoff said he had written to the families of Bill Prober, Boris Sancerre and Forester Graveley. He had not heard from Alberta yet, but the Probers had said how proud they were that their son had done his part in this dreadful war. Graveley's mother had actually come to see him in hospital. She was a downtrodden embittered soul whose husband had left her some time ago. She doted on her only son who had done so well in becoming an officer in the Air Force. She knew he did not want to go back to his job as a clerk in Canterbury Municipal Office.

Jock interjected, 'But wasn't he a student, a scholar, at Cambridge?'

Geoff said, 'Apparently not. I think that was all made up just to impress us.'

Jock shook his head. 'Oh the poor silly sod,' he said.

They began to talk of the mission to Pitesti. The Intelligence people had been impressed by the pictures of the raid itself. They confirmed major damage from photo-reconnaissance the next day. The boffins found the pictures of the H2S Plan Position Indicator screen too grainy to be of use for detailed observation. Bomber Command were pleased enough and had issued Path Finder Force Stirlings and Halifaxes with H2S for their first raid using target marking on Hamburg a week ago.

Geoff went on, 'I've had a hard time trying to explain to the Intelligence people about how we got damaged and Uwe got blown up. They chose to believe the report of an Engineering Officer, who said that the damage to X-ray was entirely consistent with flak. Unfortunately the medical people didn't keep the shell that went into poor old Prober. I got angry at the Intelligence Officer, who turned out to be the clown who wanted us to put on his silly waistcoats. I am telling any bomber aircrew I come across to be aware of sneak attacks from beneath. I think I've persuaded Dobson to warn the squadron.'

After lunch Sister O'Beirne came in carrying a bundle of mail which had been forwarded from the station. He greeted her as 'Sister two n's and a gh'. Her eyes twinkled as she said, 'Away with you. I think I preferred you when you were unconscious. You weren't nearly so cheeky.' She helped him to sit up and tidied up his bed.

The bundle contained a number of Christmas cards, and made him realise that he had been unconscious for the whole of the festive season. There were letters from his family, copies of the local newspaper, and a formal letter from the Scottish Rugby Union inviting him to play in a trial match, and meet the selectors in Edinburgh on New Year's Day. His family had asked some American service men for dinner on New Year's Eve. William was busy preparing to sit examinations for the Scottish Education Department Higher Leaving Certificate. His father was now a Lieutenant in the Home Guard. Fiona was very disappointed that he had been unable to be home. He thought of the hell they must all have gone through, having seen him during the time he was unconscious, and being told that he might not live. But he was going to see them tomorrow.

When his nurse came in, he asked for pen and paper to write to the Scottish Rugby Football Union apologising for not turning up at the trial match in Edinburgh and hoping to be considered for a future trial when he got out of hospital. He found he could not hold the paper steady and after several attempts he pushed the whole thing aside. When the nurse returned she saw the attempts he had made. She found out what he wanted to say in his reply, picked up the invitation then bustled off. A short time later she came back with a neatly typed letter which she held while he signed. She explained, 'Before I joined up I was a private secretary. I just borrowed a typewriter in the Colonel's office.'

He thanked her, 'You're spoiling me rotten.'

She smiled, 'I'm enjoying it.'

When Sister O'Beirne came in and started to tidy him up he knew he had another visitor. This time it was Adam, looking dashing in his best uniform with Squadron Leader rings around his sleeve, and the Pathfinder eagle between his wings and his medal ribbons, the whole spoiled slightly by Shouter's disreputable hat which he was carrying.

Robin grinned, 'Look at you, young Adam. I turn my back for a little while and you've got yourself promoted without my help. Have you no shame?' He ended up wincing as Adam shook his hand vigorously. 'Bloody hell, one half of me feels nothing, this half feels too much, and you've just found the worst bit.'

'Oh Jock, I'm sorry. I had heard you were sorry for yourself. I couldn't imagine you like that. So I got excited when I found you cheeky as ever. I hope I haven't done you any harm.'

'Och, I'm fine. I had been thinking I should go back to being Robin again, but I like being called Jock by the people I knew on the squadron, and in Ether Atom. Any news of the bods who were with us?' Adam mentioned that Storey and Kagan had gone to the Middle East. The two aerialists had gone to Malvern College to work with Professor Barlock.

Adam produced a letter and asked Robin if he remembered Fairstone. 'Certainly, he was our orderly, a Wireless Operator who went LMF and got keen on being a Radar Observer. He wanted to get his aircrew status back.'

Adam handed him the letter to read. It was in neat, careful handwriting from Station Warrant Officer Lobban and informed Adam that young Fairstone had got his wish and had got back on operations in a Wellington. He had completed eight missions. On the ninth he had to note the frequencies at which German fighters and their ground controllers transmitted and received. They had been attacked by five Messerschmitt 109s and he had coolly noted the frequencies as the Wellington was shot up all round him. When his radio set was damaged, he learned that the rear gunner was severely wounded, and had been moved out of his turret. Fairstone took over the turret and succeeded in damaging two of the Me109s which withdrew, with smoke coming from their engines.

Lobban had enclosed a clipping with a photograph taken at the gates of Buckingham Palace. Standing between his proud parents, Fairstone was holding the Distinguished Flying Medal, which had just been presented to him. The clipping quoted his citation which mentioned his conspicuous gallantry under fire, gaining information on enemy activity, and his success in damaging two enemy fighters. Robin smiled, 'That's good. We were sure he didn't lack moral fibre, and he proved us right.' He turned over the page and read on.

While at home on leave, Flight Sergeant Fairstone had put on his best uniform and his medal, gone out for a walk and then jumped from a railway bridge right in front of an express train. This was described officially as an accident, but he had left a note for his parents saying that he had proved that he was not a coward but he could not face ever having to fly again. The note ended, 'I know it's selfish of me to hurt you like this, but I wanted to be someone you could be proud of. The sad thing is that I cannot be proud of myself. Thank you for being my parents. All my love.'

'Oh God,' Jock sobbed, 'the poor bugger went through hell just to prove himself to his mother and father.' Adam patted Jock's arm gently until he got himself under control again. 'It's just that I cry very easily now. But thank you for letting me read the letter. We certainly misunderstood old Dobbin Lobban, didn't we.' There was an awkward pause between them, then Adam said that he had managed to get Eleanor out of London to a job at Beaulieu. She had tested his shoulder and he had taken her out for lunch. She was seeing a young doctor who had been an Army surgeon, who had been discharged after losing a leg in a minefield in North Africa.

Adam asked about Fiona. Jock frowned slightly. 'I'll be seeing her tomorrow. She is still keen to marry me, but I'm even less sure what use I'll be to her as a husband. I'll not be flying. I might not even be walking. I don't really see me as a civil, or maybe an uncivil engineer. I've got some hard thinking to do, and if you can think of something that would be challenging to me and would feed a wife who's a good eater, then let me know.'

Adam thought then asked, 'Would you consider going into business?'

Jock's answer was immediate, 'No, never. I could never sell things to people. I would just get angry at them.'

Adam laughed. 'I'm sure you would. I'll try to think of something else.'

CHAPTER 29

When his mother and father and Fiona arrived they were delighted to find him 'sitting up and taking notice' as his father put it. William had stayed at home to work for his exams but was going to attend the investiture. After the conventional enquiries about his progress, his father said, 'When people ask us how you got your medal, we feel a bit stupid when we have to say we don't know. Can you tell us?' Robin told of the long distance raid, and how three aircraft set out and only one came back. He lost three of his crew when they were attacked by fighters. He was wounded and the navigator was too concussed to take over, so he had to carry on. 'I suppose I got the medal just for doing my job.'

His mother asked, 'Is the navigator the man that telephoned to give us news of you, Mr Thomas? He just said he was a member of your crew and to call him Geoff.'

Robin nodded. 'That's right, Mum. He's a kind man. See, his name's on the frame.' He showed them the photograph of Fiona.

They talked of the everyday events in Hamilton. Fiona had a long list of friends who wanted to be remembered to Robin, and they recalled episodes involving these friends. In the midst of this, Sister O'Beirne brought in tea. Robin introduced her as 'two n's and a gh' and asked her to meet 'one n and no gh'. He explained to his bewildered mother the distinction between Fionnagh and Fiona. Sister O'Beirne played up well, commiserating with the family having to put up with such a cheeky blighter, and, turning to Fiona, 'To think you're going to marry such a terrible young man.'

Fiona looked at Robin and said tenderly, 'There's nothing I want more.'

Robin's mother and father left the room. Fiona took his hand and began to stroke it. 'I remember you doing that to me when you were here before. My mother was saying I was too young to die. I wanted to tell her I wasn't going to die, but I couldn't speak. I must have been getting the tetanus for I went sore all over then I don't remember very much until five days ago.'

Fiona kissed him gently. 'You were very lucky that the doctor gave you large doses of antitoxin, just as a precaution, for it cut down the full effects of your tetanus. But let's not talk about your illness. When are we going to be married?'

Robin looked at her for a moment. 'I've got a lot of bits inside me that still have to be dug out. I also want to know if I'm going to walk, and will I be able to support a wife and family? I don't even know if I will be able to give you babies. I can't tell you when, but I will marry you.'

Fiona tightened her grip on his hand. 'There. That's settled.' She smiled happily.

Robin said, 'I think they'll take out my bits and pieces after the King has been.'

Fiona added, 'Then you go for rehabilitation, and that's always tough on the patient.'

'So I hear,' sighed Robin, 'but if they're cruel to me I'll threaten to tell my Fiona.'

'Remember, it's the one with one n and no gh,' she laughed.

His parents returned and his mother was delighted. They had met the surgeons and they were very nice. The older man was a famous Professor in London. The young one was from Lanark, and his mother, Jessie MacArthur, had been at school with Robin's mother, and furthermore, his father was a Sergeant in the Home Guard.

Colonel Hawkins came along to announce that he had a car and driver waiting to take them to the station. As they were leaving, Geoff appeared in the doorway, on crutches, accompanied by a worried looking young nurse. 'Glad I can say hello to your family. I'm having my first walk out with this young charmer.' Robin's mother was gushing as she shook Geoff's hand, so much so, that she slipped into what the family referred to as her 'pan loaf' accent to match his public school speech. He sent his regards to William, called Mr Davidson Sir, and charmed Fiona by saying she was prettier than her photograph, and why would she want to have anything to do with a bad tempered, ill mannered curmudgeon like Jock.

They left and Geoff clumped into the room. 'I'm finished the surgery part and I'm off to rehabilitation this afternoon. I hope our paths cross again. If they don't, let me say I've been privileged to meet you and count you as a friend, an unruly one, mind you.' Jock's tears gushed up again.

All the planning and fussing for Royal visit was finally completed. By 9.30 a.m. everything in the hospital was in order, tidied and polished, and everyone had carried out last minute checks. At 10.20 a.m. Robin was due to be wheeled into an anteroom, and the ceremony would begin at 10.30 a.m.

Just after 9.30, a platoon of Welsh Guardsmen arrived to serve as security guard for the Royal party. Their troop carrier's wheels spun on the newly laid loose gravel and it overturned in a ditch. Most of the soldiers were unhurt but three sustained injuries that required emergency treatment. Sister O'Beirne was called away and Sister Watson from the Rehabilitation Unit took her place as attendant to Robin.

She was thorough and checked the treatment schedule in the nursing notes. She noted that for this ceremony, the patient had been written up to have an injection of morphine to ease the discomfort of being in a wheel chair for a relatively long time. There was no entry in the nursing notes to indicate that the injection had been given, so she administered the treatment and made the entry in the treatment chart.

Later, as she was wheeling Jock to the anteroom she noted what a modest quiet person he seemed to be, contrary to what she had heard about his sharp wit. She was shown were to park Jock in the centre of the room and to stand two paces behind. She was instructed not to speak to the King unless he spoke to her.

Cameramen from the Crown Film Unit switched on their powerful lights and adjusted their equipment. Local dignitaries and members of the hospital staff came in and stood along one wall. Then the Davidson family and Fiona stood in a line to be presented, his father, in his Home Guard battle dress with his Lieutenant's pips on the epaulettes, his mother in her Women's Voluntary Service uniform, William in his Air Training Corps uniform and Fiona in her nursing dress. They all smiled warmly at Robin, but were surprised at his lack of response. He sat with his eyes closed, as if he were distracted by some complex problem which required long deliberation. Fiona was particularly concerned, but before she could do anything about it, the ceremony began. With cameras on, the King and Queen moved down the line talking to each of them as Colonel Hawkins introduced them.

The King and his equerry moved forward to Robin's wheelchair. His Majesty bent over Robin to shake his hand and clasp his shoulder and the equerry began to read the citation. Robin suddenly opened his eyes then said in a clear voice, loud enough to interrupt the equerry's presentation, 'I'm sorry about Holy's face. I hope that didn't spoil the service for you, Your Majesty. He was worried at the impression he might make on you and the Queen. Was his sermon all right?' The King was embarrassed and stepped back quickly while Sister Watson bravely tried to explain this unexpected behaviour by saying that Robin was perhaps too excited at the King's visit. The equerry whispered something and His Majesty went forward and pinned the medal on Robin's chest. He clasped Robin's hand again, then turned and nodded to the family. The Queen joined him, smiled and waved at the family, and they left the room. The equerry had a quick word with the cameraman, finished his reading of the citation, nodded to Robin, then left as well.

Fiona rushed up to Robin, took his pulse and looked closely at his eyes. 'He's had too much morphine, you know. That's what made him confused and talking nonsense.' Sister Watson denied it hotly. Sister O'Beirne who had just entered the room, stated that she had given Robin his injection just before she was called away to Emergency.

Sister Watson paled. 'I gave him another injection. There was no record of your injection.' Sister O'Beirne interrupted, 'The case record wasn't on the ward and I had to rush to Emergency. This young lady's quite right. He has had an overdose of morphine.'

Fiona bristled at her professional status not being acknowledged. 'I am a ward sister and I have had experience of adverse reactions to high doses of morphine. Will you please arrange for stomach lavage.'

Sister O'Beirne wasted no time. She sent one nurse to get the doctor on duty, another to have the Emergency Theatre prepared for stomach lavage. Robin's stomach was washed out, with Fiona at his side, making sure the correct procedures were followed.

Colonel Hawkins, the senior Medical Officer, asked the two sisters and Fiona to join him in his office for an informal enquiry. Sister O'Beirne admitted her error and only just managed to hold back her tears as she recognised the damage that Robin could have suffered. Sister Watson felt she had been slower than she should have been in recognising Robin's confused state, and credited Fiona's initiative in noting the pupillary changes.

Hawkins admitted that he himself had contributed to the mistake. To make sure they were in good order he had asked to have Robin's case records brought to his office just about the time when the injection was due, so they were not available for Sister O'Beirne to write up her treatment. They were back on the ward in time for Sister Watson to see that no treatment had been entered, and thus led to the mistake.

He asked if Fiona wished to lay a formal complaint. Fiona declined and said she understood how the mix-up had occurred, but she asserted that case records should always be available on the ward. Hawkins agreed to change the procedure. He set off to interview Robin now back in bed in his ward, and apparently in touch with what was going on, although a little subdued from the dramatic loss of his stomach contents. When he was asked to recall the events of the morning Robin remembered being hazy, then someone who smelled of cigarette smoke came and spoke to him in a slow, quiet voice. He realised it was the King and he remembered the rugby match in which he had hit Holy Holt on the nose. Holy was to give a sermon to the King and Queen the next day. Robin ended, 'I just wanted to make sure that the King knew that Holy meant no disrespect turning up looking like that. He's a very fine man, even if he is a bit of a terror on the rugby field.' Colonel Hawkins knew of Holy Holt and was relieved that the incident arose from a temporary confusional state rather than a more serious morphine psychosis.

He had words with Robin's parents, while William and Fiona went and sat with Robin. Fiona was able to reassure William that his hero brother was not mad, but just mixed up. The family returned to Hamilton perplexed at what had happened but convinced that it was simply an unfortunate outcome of unexpected events and that Robin's chances of recovery had not been spoiled.

Once the hospital had settled down again, Robin was visited by the surgeon, Professor Sir Ralph McKinley-Taylor and his Registrar, Lieutenant Donald Scott. They examined the wounds and consulted the X-rays, ordered another series of pictures, with a full range of laboratory tests. When Dr Scott returned to do the physical examination, he did everything so formally and seriously that Robin felt he had to prevent pomposity setting in. In a quiet moment while Scott was writing up his findings, he said in his best Scots backstreet vernacular, 'Ma faither's an oafficer an' yours is only a Sairgeant.'

Without stopping his writing, Donald Scott replied, 'Aye, bit ma faither's bigger than your faither, so there.' He stuck his tongue out at Robin. They both burst out laughing. The staff nurse looked puzzled.

Robin had minor surgery to remove the fragments from his shoulder and chest. Three in the abdomen were slightly more tricky, but were dealt with successfully. The snag turned out to be two relatively small bits of metal in the lumbar region which were compressing vertebrae. Their removal involved risks of permanent damage, which would wipe out all chances of Robin walking again. One of them was judged capable of being removed, the other seemed to be too firmly embedded. When they were exposed at operation the reverse held true and after two hours when the easy bit proved intractable a magnet pulled the other one clear within minutes. No one felt inclined to take further action for the moment, so the operation was stopped.

After a period of recovery and another set of X-rays, Dr Scott presented Robin's case at a Case Conference. The inadvisability of any immediate attempt to remove this remaining foreign body was confirmed, but he would be monitored carefully, for any change.

Robin's programme of rehabilitation started with gentle exercises to restore tone to the upper body muscles, chest, shoulders, neck and arms. Sister Watson urged him to action beyond the point at which his muscles had seized up as the exercises became more and more vigorous. He rapidly reached the stage when he could use pulleys to haul himself from his chair to the bed, and back again to his chair. He was impatient with this and wanted to start walking. Sister Watson assured him that his back and legs would be dealt with, all in good time. 'Remember,' she told him, 'Rome wasn't built in a day.'

Robin burst out, 'How the hell do you know that useless bit of information?'

She stood with legs apart, arms akimbo, knuckles planted firmly on her hips and glared at him. 'I read it in my children's encyclopedia.'

He suspected that the rehabilitation unit was preparing him to be in a wheel chair for the rest of his life. He dreaded having to depend on others to help with the simplest things like going to the lavatory, things that everybody took for granted. Robin knew that he, personally, would have difficulty in accepting such a situation. He wondered what career openings there were for a crippled ex-bomber pilot with less than a year of Technical education. He was not sure he now wanted to be an Engineer, and began to turn over alternatives in his mind. He remembered the Dr Kildare film with the wise old physician in the wheelchair. But was this doctor in a wheelchair when he went to Medical School?

To be a medical student, you had to have Latin. He had his Higher Leaving Certificate in Latin. He had done well in English as well as Science subjects, so he could meet the entrance requirements. Would he have enough money to pay his tuition fees, board and lodgings for himself and his wife?

Donald Scott told him about medical education and the progression from classes in the basic subjects to direct experience with patients in clinics and wards. Robin reacted quickly when Donald suggested his wheelchair could be a handicap when he was on the hospital wards. 'But I've no intention of being in a wheelchair all the time. There must be some bloody way of beating the odds.' Scott admitted he did not know, but from the way the rehabilitation experts were thinking it seemed unlikely.

Robin went on, 'Look. I'm not just being over optimistic. For the last two nights I've been feeling restless, especially in my legs. For now, it's a very slight feeling, and I keep hoping it'll get worse so I can report it. I don't want to waste my luck by telling you something that's trivial.'

Donald laughed and called Robin a 'thrawn' bugger, a good Scots description of his contrary, stubborn streaks. 'For God's sake tell them. They'll want to clutch at straws just as much as you do, and they may change their thinking away from wheelchairs to crutches, then sticks, then dancing at the Palais.'

When Robin did not reply, Donald headed for the door. 'All right then, don't bother. Lie there like a mute hero. But I will tell them about your deep secret.'

Within an hour Sister Watson was wheeling him into a small laboratory where they took measurements of the electric potentials of the large muscles in his legs. The scientist in charge stuck a number of electrodes on his back and legs. The wires from these led to a number of pen recorders which produced traces on moving sheets of paper. He was told to relax then to think, just think of himself running, kicking a ball, of climbing up a ladder, of dancing a waltz. 'That's not bad. Now for the hard part. Really do it. Get on your feet and run, kick a ball, do a waltz. Come on. Come on. Do it.'

Robin twisted uncomfortably in his wheelchair. 'I can't do these things. You know fine I can't do them. Don't keep on at me.'

Sister Watson chipped in, 'Doctor, you can't speak that way to Robin. He's a hero, a brave man and he's got medals to prove it. You know what I think?' Robin glared at her, shocked at her disloyalty. She continued, 'I think he likes the wheelchair he's got growing on his bum, and he doesn't want to give it up.'

This was too much for Robin to bear. He rocked his chair then attempted to stand up using his arms. 'For Christ's sake,' he said angrily, 'that's enough.' He took an involuntary step forward. Sister Watson supported him for a brief moment, whispered, 'We'll have that waltz soon,' then helped him to sit down again. He glowered at her balefully.

The electronics man said that he had seen some significant change, and he was going to recommend that the emphasis should now shift to muscles in the lower trunk, thighs, and calves. Robin took this news in slowly. He then realised that the next efforts were designed to get him walking and began to relax.

CHAPTER 30

After a strenuous session of exercises, Robin was lying down when Sister Watson entered, obviously excited. Major Holt had come to visit. She fussed all round him, clucked that he hadn't shaved, straightened his covers and fluffed out his pillows.

Holy was a cheerful sick visitor without being too overpowering. 'Call me Tony. I'm Holy only on the rugby field. I was in the hospital to visit one of my lads who broke both ankles in a bad landing. Colonel Hawkins told me about the incident with the King. I assured him that you really had bashed me on the rugby field, and I wanted to reassure you that my sermon to the King and Queen went well, in spite of the tartan bruises on my face. I was flattered that you had remembered me enough to ask the King how I had done. I'm sure His Majesty had forgotten all about me and my appearance, which was why he was a bit flabbergasted when you brought it up. Now then, how are you after all that?' Robin smiled and told about having been given too much morphine. He went on to tell of his expectations of improvement and of his thoughts of the future.

He said, 'Here's my best offer so far,' and showed Tony a letter he had received from a carnival owner in Bridlington who offered him two guineas a week to appear in his tent show. All he had to do was to sit in his wheelchair, wearing his uniform, and his medals, tell the audience how he got the Victoria Cross and answer their questions. Tony smiled grimly, and told Robin to go for something else.

They talked of Rugby. Tony had played for England against Scotland the previous Saturday. 'I picked up a loose ball, and the thought of being tackled by you brought fear to my heels. Nobody could catch me, and I scored the only try of the match. Corky told me you were to be considered by the selectors, but were in hospital. Then I heard you were up for your medal. Well done. Congratulations.' Robin's news that Taff was in a Prison of War camp delighted Tony who suggested they might spare a charitable thought for the poor German guards who had to keep this Welshman in order.

With some diffidence Robin told Tony about the raid at Kiel, and how he gave thanks to a God he did not believe in. He asked what prayer was, and found that his request was treated seriously. Tony began, 'I deal with a range of chaps from devout to pagan, and they want to know about prayer, especially just before going into action. I have some thoughts, for what they are worth.'

He sat at the end of Jock's bed. 'In its formal sense prayer is part of the ritual in the established church that really determines what the role of the priest, minister or leader of the sect is to be. If prayer is talking to God then it may be argued that the only person who can do so is someone who is ordained, the chosen in Scottish Calvinism, for example.'

Robin was still listening so Tony went on, 'But anyone can pray. In its primitive forms, prayer was simply the repetition of a fixed form of words, something like a spell. Prayer as an outpouring of your inner soul to God, the divine being, came later. Civilised or sophisticated religions, that is those which could claim to be beyond superstition, required awareness of our own inner life as well as a set of spiritual and ethical values. But there can still be superstitious elements.'

He warmed to the subject. 'The prayers we say as children, the "Now I lay me down to sleep" variety, are repeated every night because they obviously worked the night before, when they kept us safe till morning's light. When you talk to yourself when doing a difficult or new job you are basically praying. I remember doing just that on my first parachute jump. I was yelling to myself the whole time, Don't let it swing, haul on the opposite line.' Robin nodded, remembering how he talked himself round the circuit on his first solo.

Tony went on. 'In a way, talking aloud to yourself in that kind of situation is the basic form of prayer to God. Of course, within the established church we tend to have ritual prayers. The Church of England service, for example, has intercessionary prayers in which we ask God to look after the health of the Royal Family. When I was a Divinity student I got into trouble when I said that with all the C of E's praying for them every Sunday, the Royal Family must be the healthiest bunch of people in Britain. I never found out if that was so, for I was chastised for being cynical and flippant.

'In your case, young Jock, you were giving thanks for the most unlikely events which saved you and your crew. You were all the more grateful because you personally had not asked for these things to happen. But you can't dismiss the idea of Divine Intervention simply because you had not put up a prayer to be answered. Someone else on your crew, your parents, your girlfriend, people you had never heard of could have asked for your protection.'

Robin gave credit to Mr Craig who was keeping the promise he had made to pray for Robin and other service-men. 'There you are, then. You were right in giving thanks as you did. Even God appreciates a little bit of gratitude and the way you did it was right for you. In your mind you talked to him in silent prayer, which, I believe, is the most powerful form. For that kind of prayer you don't need any form of guidance other than having something to say.'

Robin was puzzled. 'Now this last time seventeen people were killed and only five survived. I had to concentrate too much on bringing the survivors home. I was too busy to think of asking for God's help. Now I have difficulty saying my thanks for getting back, when so many people did not make it. Maybe it makes me seem more noble than I am, but I decided the only thing I could give thanks for was that I got the other four survivors home. At least I was not glorying in the fact that it was not me that got killed.'

Tony thought for a moment. 'I can understand that, and there's a streak of the Calvinist in you, in that you think it presumptuous to give thanks for your own good fortune, but it's all right if you find that God, in helping you has managed to help others. One function of membership in a Church is to give a balanced perspective between self interests and the interests of others. Watch it, for I think I wrote a sermon on that.'

'But,' Jock objected, 'I'm not a member of the Church. I have no desire to join either. I have no right . . .'

Tony held his hand up to stop Robin's flow. 'You have every right to talk to yourself, and if God overhears you then that's your prayer. Let me leave you with a thought that will take some time for you to accept. You don't have to believe in God to pray to him. Think that over, you wild Scottish wing forward.'

Robin said he hoped that the newly emerging hopes for his recovery could be helped by silent prayer. Tony stood by his bedside, took Robin's hand and bowed his head silently. When he finished, he patted Robin's shoulder. 'There you are, my young haggis basher. I hope the next time we meet, we'll be knocking hell out of each other on the rugby field.' He put on his hat, came to attention and saluted Robin. He winked, said, 'That was for your medal. Let me know how you get along,' turned on his heel and left.

Robin lay for a long time thinking of the message he had just heard. He was rested and relaxed and felt that this kind of inner peace would help him sort out his future. When Sister Watson did her rounds, he told her he would like to talk to her about his future once he had sorted it out a bit more . . .

His immediate plans were to get out of and stay out of a wheelchair. The first stage was being freed from the urinary catheter. He accepted being wheeled to the toilet where he forfeited the male right of standing up to urinate and at nights used a bed bottle if required. It was a simple next step to dispense with the services of the enema expert. Once these preliminaries were taken care of, he set himself targets for walking under his own steam.

At nights after the duty sister had done her rounds, he asked the trainee nurse who tucked him in, to set the visitor's chair at a particular place in his room, initially just at the foot of his bed, then each night a little further away. On waking, Robin would get out of bed and manoeuvre himself into the upright position.

Standing was an odd experience, for with no sensation in his legs, he felt his top half was free-floating. He turned to face the chair by rocking gently from one foot to the other and bending his upper body in the direction he wanted to face. Then, still rocking from foot to foot, but now bending forward then back he began his journey to the chair, then back to his bed.

For the beginnings and endings of these trips he had the bed to hold on to, or even to fall back on. He wanted to increase the distance in which he was in unsupported space until he could catch the back of the chair. He caught sight of himself in the mirror, saw that his arms were up as he rocked his way along. He was reminded of seeing a young child just starting to walk, and he realised he had invented 'the toddle'. He changed the technique so that he could keep his arms lower down, but the effect of moving his hands below his waist to give him balance, was grotesque. He gave a snort of laughter when he suddenly thought of progressing down the corridor in this manner with his face painted with gentian violet, as it once had been. That would have raised a scream or two.

He was pleased at his progress, slow though it might be. He had reached the point at which he had covered three feet to the chair and then back before getting into bed again. He thought that he must have been overdoing it for he could detect a slight ache at the back of his thighs. He suddenly realised that this was a feeling he had not had in the preceding month or so, and lay relishing it. The aches were still there when his breakfast was brought in, so he broke the news to the orderly, who told the nurse who told Sister Watson who came in to check his story, then told Dr Scott who went over him with his rubber hammers and had him sent down to X-ray. An hour later he was back in bed, regretting that his breakfast had been removed untouched, and awaiting news from the X-ray department.

Donald Scott came in, looking pleased, but non committal in his news. 'It looks to me as if that bit of metal we couldn't get hold of has dislodged itself. The great panjandrum Radiologist will be here before lunch and I've put your pictures right at the top of the pile of stuff he's got to read. God knows how it happened. The physiotherapists have just sworn blind that they did not put strain on that area involving your spine.' Robin agreed that was correct.

He leaned towards Scott, 'I taught myself to toddle. Just watch and let me do this on my own,' and he got up to show his unassisted, if undignified, method of progression.

The doctor looked worried but restrained himself from putting out a hand. 'Who showed you how to do that?'

Robin smiled, 'Jimmy McClintock, the wee boy that lives across the street. He was learning to walk when I was on leave the last time.'

Donald looked serious, 'I don't know whether to shake your hand or kick your arse. Promise me you'll stay in bed and rest your back. We might get in and remove that foreign body, but if you shift it back with your cavorting, you'll ruin our chances. More important, you'll ruin your own chances.'

Robin was contrite. 'Right I'll be sensible. When I'm a medical student I don't want to have to fight a hospital to let me on the wards in a wheelchair.'

As Robin was eating his lunch of Spam and fried potato, he was visited by Sir Ralph, still in his surgical gown, accompanied by a burly red-faced major who carried several thick envelopes of X-ray pictures and was introduced as Major Weston, the specialist in Radiology. Dr Scott and another Registrar, Sister Watson, Sister O'Beirne and Nurse Goldie, Robin's cheery little ward nurse completed the party who crowded into his room.

Sir Robin spoke. 'Weston here indicates that your recalcitrant bit of metal is ready to be taken out. Scott tells me you've been jigging about and you must have loosened it. God damn it, man. If you are interested in ever walking about again, don't do that behind our backs. You took a hell of a risk. I hope it has paid off in your favour. I suppose you thought you would just show us how clever you were. If we are to have any chance of fixing you then let us do it without you playing silly buggers. Do you understand, eh?' Robin dropped his eyes, hung his head and murmured that he did.

Suddenly the ward nurse moved forward and stroked his shoulder and turned towards Sir Ralph. 'You've got a bleedin' lousy temper, mate, and you should never take it out on any of my patients.'

Sir Ralph's jaw dropped and his eyes opened wide. There was a terrible silence in the room then Sir Ralph dropped his hand on her shoulder. 'You're bleedin' well right, my dear. I had a ruddy awful time in theatre this morning and was looking for a victim to vent my spleen on. Please accept my apology, Davidson, and thank you, nurse, for sorting me out.'

Nurse Goldie nodded to him. 'See then, you're man enough to admit it. I admire that. Let me shake you by the hand. When are you going to do him?'

He looked at Sister O'Beirne who answered that he had a light list in two days time, and Mr Davidson would behave himself till then under the eye of Nurse Goldie. 'Then that's settled. Do you want to say anything, Weston?'

The major hesitated, 'Just that I'm bloody glad there's someone in this place who can stand up to a loutish St Mary's man.'

'Well, if you've nothing sensible to offer, we'll adjourn for lunch. Nurse Goldie, Mr Davidson. Good morning to you,' and Sir Ralph led the parade out of the room.

Nurse Goldie turned to Robin. 'No more dancing around, eh?'

'Yes ma'am,' was all Robin could say.

The next day a middle-aged major from the Education Corps arrived with Donald Scott, who also had an envelope full of information about the course at Glasgow and the application procedures for the Faculty of Medicine. Major Jones, as his name implied, was Welsh, and Welsh enough to be a devotee of Rugby football. 'Saw you playing for the RAF when you beat the Army by three points only. You finished the Army's chances in the last moment by stopping Holy Holt as he was barging for the line. Great tackle. But to business. Donald tells me you want to go to Glasgow to study Medicine. Let's see if you are eligible.' He picked up a leaflet and read through it quickly. Donald Scott left them to it.

Jones confirmed that Robin possessed the required academic qualifications, and told him to get copies of his school record from the Scottish Education Department to go with his application. He then read through the application form and pronounced it straightforward enough, but suggested a covering letter to tell them about his present situation. 'They'll be tickled pink to have a student with a Victoria Cross and a Distinguished Flying Medal in their Medical School.'

Robin shook his head. 'I got these medals in a war, and I don't need to be a hero in a classroom or in a ward.'

Major Jones conceded, 'All right that's fine, but even if you keep your modest mouth shut, they'll find out about your guilty secret.'

Robin asked if he could be married while he was a medical student.

'Nothing against that, as far as I know, but can you afford it?'

Robin said he wasn't sure yet. He had some money in a Post Office Savings Account. He had some post war tax credits due. He had been told that he would get a pension with his medal.

Jones thought. 'Could your wife work?'

Robin was doubtful. 'I suppose she could. She's a nursing sister. But I wouldn't fancy her bringing in the money. She'd be better running the house like other women.'

Jones interrupted him with a laugh. 'I think you'll find a lot of other women working after this war, so don't reject that possibility. I've heard that Government is working on a scheme to help servicemen get further education and training when they are demobilised. I'll try and find out more about it.'

He wrote to Fiona telling her the outcome of his chat with Jones, and his intention to apply for admission to Medical School at Glasgow University, mentioning, as an aside, his dismissal of the possibility of her bringing money in by working.

On the morning of his operation, Nurse Goldie supervised the preparations. As he was loaded onto the trolley to be wheeled into theatre, the lugubrious enema orderly came to shake him by the hand and wish him good luck, then smiled, an unexpectedly radiant beam.

On the table, Sir Ralph came to inspect him and asked, 'How's my Nemesis, Nurse Goldie? Give her my regards. You'll be pleased to hear that I am as gentle as a lamb this morning.' Then the anaesthetist and the gauze mask over his mouth, 'Deep breath . . . deep breath . . . deep br . . .' Then the taste in his mouth and someone patting his cheek. 'Robin. Robin. Come on, Robin. Come on, look at me,' and it was Sister O'Beirne.

He opened his eyes briefly, then mumbled, 'Hello. I'm just waiting to have an operation. Must have dropped off.'

'You've had your operation, Robin. I want you to wake up now. Come on, Robin, wake up.' His legs were uncomfortable no matter where he moved them. It was like pins and needles all over his thighs and the back of his knees, then down to his ankles. He twisted again to try and get some relief and said how uncomfortable his legs were.

He heard Sir Ralph asking if they were more uncomfortable than they were yesterday. He started to answer then stopped and opened his eyes wide and tried to sit up until he heard the peremptory command to lie still. 'Great, I can move my legs and feel them moving.'

Sir Ralph smiled. 'That's what I wanted to hear. It was a smooth straight forward procedure. Everything went well. Young Scott had the honour of picking the offending metal out.'

'Thank you, Sir, and thank you, Sister two ns and a gh.' Robin lay back and thought about it. He said out loud, 'I am a jammy devil, a jammy devil that's what I am. The feeling is back for good. I won't lose it, will I?'

Sir Ralph replied, 'No, you won't. If you do as you're told, and don't mess us about any more. You have plenty of rehabilitation work before you, and you'll do as Sister O'Beirne and Sister Watson and the formidable Nurse Goldie tell you in future.' Robin acquiesced.

He was taken back to his ward and a delighted Nurse Goldie. She got him settled in bed, then scampered down the hall, spoke to the theatre sister who was coming up the hall and continued to the surgeons' dressing room. She knocked and quickly opened the door to find Sir Ralph enjoying a cigarette. He stood up when he saw her. She grinned and shook his hand. 'I just came to thank you for doing Robin Davidson's back.'

'Oh, I'm glad it went well,' he said. 'Now it's up to you to get him up and walking.'

She nodded and grinned, 'I'll do that, never fear.' Sir Ralph grinned back and she left the room.

Donald Scott put him to bed on the bottle and bedpan regime for a week then allowed him restricted movements for another week. Sir Ralph assured him he was progressing very well and he preened himself when the great man told him he had good healing flesh. With his stitches out, his first days at physiotherapy were devoted to learning how to be on legs again.

CHAPTER 31

Robin got an immediate reply from Fiona. They would get married in August and he could start at Glasgow University in the autumn. The Scottish Education Department were going to send him his school records and the Technical College would provide a letter about his prowess with them. Incidentally they wanted a photograph of him with his medals on to hang in the corridor with their other distinguished former students.

Their wedding would be a simple affair, but it took three pages to give the details, ranging from her wedding veil to the rented house in Hillhead and a tentative offer to her from the Western Infirmary of a position of Sister in charge of Rehabilitation Unit. Robin read the letter several times but found no reference to his firm assertion that his wife would not work. He wisely decided not to repeat it in his reply.

His walking lessons continued and at first he was pleased with his progress. The problems remaining to be overcome were stopping and starting in a fully co-ordinated manner. A dropped right foot meant that he had to avoid catching the toe of his shoe on obstacles such as carpets or doorsteps. He found it easier to start walking by bending his trunk slightly to the left then twisting it to the right. During this lurching movement he could lead off with his left foot. A lurch in the opposite direction, combined with a drop-kicking action with his right foot to flick his toe up gave him his second step. He was concerned that this exaggerated gait would draw too much attention to his disability. While he practised walking in the hospital corridor he watched how other people walked, and tried to remember how he used to walk.

He observed how gait was a highly individual characteristic. Sir Ralph took long strides and propelled himself quickly along the corridor daring anyone to be in his way. Donald Scott bustled along changing step as he weaved his way past other people. The enema orderly had long legs, but took short steps, almost as if his bottom half only was running. Colonel Hawkins marched with measured tread. They all walked in a different manner, and the common feature was their minimal head and neck movements as they strode along. Robin decided he had to eliminate these upper body movements.

One afternoon as he was walking with his mother along the corridor, behind his father and William, he suddenly stopped, saying, 'Look at them. They both walk the same way, and they both lurch.'

His mother was indignant, 'They do not. Besides that's how you walk too.'

Robin replied, 'That's because I had an accident.'

She came back immediately, 'It's nothing to do with your accident. The only thing I noticed from your accident was that you scliffed your right foot very badly as you walked. That's a bit better now, but you still do it.'

She called William and her husband to stop, got Robin and William to walk ahead of her and her husband. Then she and William walked behind as Robin and his father walked ahead. They were discussing the results of these complex comparisons when Nurse Goldie stopped to chat, asking if this was a family row or could anyone join in. She joined Robin's mother while the three men walked ahead. The conclusion was that they all lurched, Robin perhaps a tiny bit more than the other two.

About two weeks later he was told to put on his uniform and report to the physiotherapy gymnasium. It was after usual hours and he wondered what was to happen. The senior physiotherapist introduced him to Elizabeth Watson, who was to partner him in a dance. He had never seen Sister Watson's curly brown hair as it had been hidden, like the rest of her by her stiff and formal nursing garb. Here she was, her hair gleaming and elegantly arranged, wearing tiny pearl earrings and a string of pearls round her neck, and her face lightly made up. She was dressed in a flowered print frock, wearing silk stockings and gold dancing shoes. He was entranced and rose to giddy poetic heights in his admiration, 'You are a real smasher.'

She chuckled, 'Some time ago I promised that you and I would dance.' A record of slow waltzes in the strict tempo of Victor Sylvester was started. He took her in his arms and was delighted at how well and how lightly she followed him in the movements and helped him in the first awkward turn to the right. He settled the matter of his dropped foot by reversing. She nodded her head, and followed his change smoothly. At the end of the music, she curtseyed and he bowed and kissed her hand to the applause of the spectators. 'There, I told you we would have that dance,' she told him.

'I never knew it would be so enjoyable,' he replied, starry-eyed. She asked him to escort her to the door. With her arm through his they walked to the front hall of the hospital, where she prepared to face the brisk winds by changing her dance shoes for heavy brogues and putting on her tweed coat. Her husband was taking her to a mess ball at a nearby Army camp, and she had taken the opportunity of being dressed up to keep her promise of dancing with Robin.

As they waited, he told her of his intention to study Medicine. 'You'll be a good doctor, a surgeon, I would guess. I think you're the same kind of person as Sir Ralph. You're caring, you're intelligent enough to learn what has to be known and never assume you know it all. You can lead others and you won't put up with fools. And I wouldn't want to be in the same room as both of you if the pair of you were in a bad mood.'

'Unless Nurse Goldie was there,' he added.

A car drew up and a tall Major entered. He wore black tie and mess kit with Royal Army Medical Corps insignia. Sister Watson introduced her husband to Robin. He said he'd heard about this wonder patient and was privileged to meet him. Robin enthused about his wife's dancing. The major said that Robin's dance really was a landmark in his recovery, and told him to keep up the good work. He and Sister Watson left, with Robin thanking her once again for their dance. On the way back along the corridor, he intercepted Nurse Goldie and waltzed with her, both of them humming 'The Blue Danube', until she remembered her place and firmly sent him to bed.

The following day he got up and put on his hospital blues after breakfast. He wanted to try himself out on a full day of activity, so he decided to help the nurses out by serving breakfast to the bed patients. Most of the patients recognised him as the chap who had a V.C. and they enjoyed the luxury of breakfast in bed served by a national hero. To help with the conversation he had listened to the BBC news so that he could relay the items to his customers as he set out the tray before them. After three days of this he was dog tired, and aching all over. He was in bed and asleep by 7.30 p.m. and almost missed Alvar Liddell reading the early news.

Robin was living from day to day, making sure that he kept up his gradual progress, and looking forward to his medical board as an indication of his future. On the appointed day as he sat on a bench in the corridor, his future was being discussed inside the Superintendent's office by five members of the Board, all in Army uniform.

Sir Ralph, as a Brigadier was in the chair, flanked by Colonel Hawkins, the Medical Superintendent, and on the other side, Professor George Phillips, the Lieutenant Colonel physician who had treated Jock's tetanus, Major Weston the radiologist, and a young woman doctor, a Captain in the Royal Army Medical Corps.

After hearing the progress reports, Sir Ralph observed that Robin had twice been in and out of the jaws of death, first from being shot up, then from developing tetanus. In the light of this, his residual foot drop was a little price to pay. 'It's still a disability, though. You saw that he was asked to play in an international rugby trial. He's too disabled ever to do that, now or in the future.'

The physician broke in, 'His cardiograph also threw up an inverted T wave. I confess I'm not too sure what that means, but the cardiologists usually tell such patients to keep away from violent exercise. So definitely no rugby football.'

Sir Ralph nodded, 'Let's start by asking if he can go back to operational flying?' The others chorused, 'No.'

Sir Ralph said, 'You need a strong back to haul these bombers about. So that alternative's out.'

George Phillips went on, 'The next alternative is non-operational flying, being an instructor, being in transport command, and so on. This takes us back to the general fitness requirements for pilots. For the next year or so he cannot meet the requirements for the mandatory aircrew medical. The trouble with his back and the inverted T wave on his ECG, would prevent him being selected for aircrew nowadays. That means we can only ground him, and return him to the RAF for non-flying duties, air controller for example.' Weston thought he could favour this recommendation but not wholeheartedly. The others were against it.

The woman Captain spoke up. 'I think we're making this matter more complicated than it is. His back injury, severe enough to give him a dropped foot, plus his T wave anomaly make him unfit for military service, any military service. We would have to bend the rules to keep him in the service, flying or not flying.'

Sir Ralph looked grim. 'That would leave medical discharge as our only alternative. Lead us on that, George.'

The Professor thought for a moment, 'Unpopular though it may be with Davidson, the option I favour is that we recommend immediate sick leave for three months then discharge from the service on medical grounds. He's young enough to go back to his studies in Engineering.'

Major Weston asked, 'How did you know, George, that immediate medical discharge would be unpopular with Davidson?'

The Professor's answer would have surprised Jock. 'I got the impression that this young man has been so successful in the service, being promoted to the highest NCO rank and being twice decorated, that he would want to stay on as a regular, perhaps even be given a commission.' They discussed the option for a time, then Sir Ralph asked for their decision, pointing out that Audrey, the Captain, had stated medical discharge to be the only outcome, painful though it might be for the patient. They all agreed solemnly with her recommendation.

Robin was asked to join them. He already knew the others, and was introduced to Captain Audrey Lewis, a psychiatrist. Sir Ralph summarised their discussion of the various options open to them, ending as tactfully as he could, 'Our conclusion is that we recommend you be given three months sick leave, and at the end of that period you be medically discharged after being reassessed, to establish the amount of the disability pension to be awarded. I am, we all are, sorry that your distinguished career in the RAF cannot continue.'

Robin burst out with a short laugh, 'My idea always was to serve as a flier in wartime only. After my first tour I refused to be recommended for a commission because it would only be appropriate for me if I wanted to sign on as a regular. From what I've read in the Rehabilitation Unit library I'm likely to go through life with a weakened back and the funny T wave on my cardiograph might make it impossible for me to play rugby. But these are not real handicaps. I was planning to go back to being a student, but this time to study Medicine at Glasgow University.'

There was a silence at this news then Sir Ralph apologised for his misunderstanding of Robin's wishes. They all joined in with advice as to what specialties to take up, the most sensible being that from the recent graduate, Captain Lewis, who pointed out that as he went through his training he would find each specialty to have some attraction. In her case she wanted to be a paediatrician, but ended up as a psychiatrist. Sir Ralph closed the meeting by pointing out to her she was far too bloody sensible to be a psychiatrist.

The outcome for Robin was a happy one in that he would have time at home to make the arrangements to matriculate at Glasgow, to find somewhere to live around Gilmorehill, to continue his exercises and to start reading text-books to get back into the role of student. He also had to find out what his mother and Fiona were planning for the wedding. He would, he realised, have to develop some kind of intelligent way of conveying his delight at the selection of curtains, china, bed linen, cutlery and the like.

He was given a farewell tea party by the nurses, which was attended by the

Medical staff who had looked after him. The enema orderly read a poem which he had written for the occasion and Robin replied that he would always be grateful to them for saving his life, for getting him to walk, and for being his friends. Sir Ralph presented him with a facsimile copy of a text by John Hunter, saying he hoped this would inspire Robin in his studies. William, freed from exams, travelled down to escort him and carry his bags when he was discharged from hospital after a stay of almost four months. He was given a letter of referral to the Rehabilitation Unit at Killearn, where the progress of his back could be followed up.

He had asked his parents not to tell Fiona of his arrival. The following day, he took a bus out to the Rehabilitation Unit at Killearn Hospital and handed his referral letter to the receptionist who told him he would have to sit down and wait until the Sister in charge of Outpatients was available. The receptionist heard the quick firm footsteps of the Sister in charge, then her voice crying, 'Robbie, Robbie, it *is* you!' as she rushed into his arms and kissed the new patient enthusiastically.

The secretary sat fascinated by this unusual way of receiving a patient until Fiona came up and asked for the referral letter. She led Robin into her office, stopping only to introduce her fiancé to the secretary. This young lady was even more intrigued when she remembered that she was meeting a real live hero. Fiona announced that she had five days off starting at five o'clock that very afternoon. In the office she made an appointment for his first examination in five days time, so that they could travel back together. Then she began to tell him about the wedding arrangements, all the way home in the bus, then continuing as they ate the special high tea his mother had made for him. He had rung the changes on responses such as 'fine', 'grand', 'nice', 'very nice', 'great', 'smashing'.

When he was asked who his best man was going to be, he immediately replied, 'William'. William put down his cup and left the room hurriedly. Robin followed him and found him sitting on his bed in tears. 'I'm sorry I upset you. I'm just living up to my reputation.'

William tried to smile, 'It's just that I never thought you'd choose me, with all your friends here and in the Air Force. I really would like to be your best man.'

Robin hugged him. 'I wanted you, young brother, and I'm glad you're saying yes.' They went downstairs and Fiona kissed William and said Robin had made the best choice.

Robin found that he was reasonably secure financially from a number of sources, including a Further Education and Training Grant. Fiona remained adamant that she was going to contribute. They found an unfurnished ground floor flat in Lawrence Street, well within walking distance of the Infirmary and the University. New furniture in war time was not high quality so they scoured second hand furniture shops and auctions for traditional solid pieces.

Their wedding was not the ordeal Robin had dreaded. Over twenty of his service friends attended, including 'Whisky' Walker and 'Digger' Drodge, with a DFC added to his DFM. These two had heard that Abie, Taff and Jimsey were still in POW camp. Jimsey was running camp shows at which Abie crooned. Taff ran exercise classes. From X-ray Trigger Selsun, Jonathan Rice and Dave Gray were there but Geoff sent regrets from the United States.

'Chiefie' Woodson and some of his ground crew including the armaments sergeant who frightened Robin stuck together until the music for dancing started. Robin had never seen his mother so animated as after a quick step with the sergeant armourer. Sisters Watson and O'Beirne quietly moved about talking to the other guests. Nurse Goldie in a backless gown seemed to be the centre of attraction for the male guests including Robin's father. Tony Holt was a focus of attention for the members of the Hamilton Rugby Football Club. Mr Craig was awed at meeting a man of the cloth who undertook such glamorous responsibilities and confessed to Robin that he wished he had had such opportunities. Adam found two local teachers who were interested in the work of Grenfell and listened avidly to his description of Newfoundland.

The newly weds honeymooned in Lawrence Street, and got their home in order. Robin found his way around the University, the Students' Union, the Reading Room and the University Library. In the city, the Mitchell Library was a useful additional resource centre. He was asked to join the University Air Squadron as an honourary member. He did so reluctantly, and reminded them that he was medically unfit for flying, but could take some interest in their activities.

Fiona was busy at the Western Infirmary. In addition to the civilians, service patients were being referred to recover from injuries. Robin attended on several occasions to meet these patients and to encourage those who became despondent about their future. A newspaper reporter heard of his attendance at this Unit and ran an account under the heading 'V.C. winner brings hope to wounded soldiers'. A photograph of him at a desk in the Mitchell Library was captioned 'The modest hero catches up on his studies'.

He established a pattern of attending classes, reading in the library, then preparing his notes at home. The biological sciences held a greater interest for him than he would have shown in his engineering days. He enjoyed student politics, and participated in the traditionally vigorous lunch-time debates. With some other ex-service students he formed a committee to foster informed support among the public for the idea of a United Nations which was just being conceived. Thus he addressed public meetings outside the University.

At one early meeting he was making the point that nations would have to work for peace, when an irate lady in the front row stood up and objected to conscientious objectors like him being allowed to air their views in public, when so many young men were fighting for their lives. A number of the audience joined in this objection. The original speaker dared him to deny he was a conscientious objector.

He started to reply to her when another lady stood up and asked the first speaker if she ever looked at the newspapers. The lady said she did, every day. The second lady finished, 'Then you'll have seen his picture in the paper and you should know that the man you're saying is a conscientious objector is in fact a war hero. He holds the Victoria Cross and another medal and was invalided out of the RAF because he was badly wounded. You should be ashamed of yourself.' There was uproar at the meeting and a great burst of applause for Robin, who tried to calm things down. Next day the headline was 'War Hero Calms Unruly Mob', and the photograph showed Robin gesticulating before a sea of waving hands. Robin decided that he did not want this type of exposure and limited his speeches to within the University where he could contend with witty student heckling.

He became apprehensive about the approaching examinations. Compared to the young boys and girls straight from school, who took down every word uttered by the lecturer, he wrote down headings in class, and expanded these into narrative statements in the evenings. The night before his first examination he stayed up late reading and re-reading his expanded notes. Eventually he followed Fiona's advice and went to bed, got up after ten minutes to check on something he did not understand, and came back to bed, only to rise again. He entered the examination hall bleary eyed and worried how badly he would fail. Afterwards he thought he might pass, and by the time of the last examination he had managed to sleep for a whole night. Fiona had shared in these trials and tribulations, so as a special treat, after his last examination he took her to see the film *Mrs Miniver*, and they both fell asleep. When the results came out he had received class prizes in all subjects.

He realised that a good teacher was not just giving a précis of the prescribed text, but was airing ideas and concepts that could be tried out by the student from his reading of other texts and sources. This insight allowed him to enjoy his reading and stood him in good stead in his further studies.

PART FIVE

ADAM

1943–1985

CHAPTER 32

In the Pathfinder Force Adam assumed responsibilities for getting H2S operational. This involved training Navigators in the new system until the Radio Observers graduated from their special courses. At least once a week he would join a Pathfinder squadron on a bombing mission and fly as the H2S operator. It was interesting to observe how different crews reacted to the new technique. Younger crews were receptive, sometimes to the point of blind faith that H2S would give them the answer just by being switched on. Older hands with a large number of missions behind them felt that they had got on well enough, thank you, without a 'magic box' and consequently did not need it.

Within days of being declared medically fit to resume aircrew duties, Geoff Thomas got himself cleared to fly Mosquitoes operationally, and had a Mosquito attached to the Pathfinder Force for special duties. Bennett, with Adam as his navigator, used this aircraft to continue his checks on the activities of his Pathfinders on the various phases of route marking, target marking, incendiary and high explosive attacks. Bennett would be back to meet the crews at their debriefing and would offer comments, harsh or laudatory, just to let them know that he knew what they had been up to.

Although he was uncomfortable in the role of 'snoop', Adam enjoyed flying in this machine and readily accepted the role of being its resident navigator. When other senior officers wanted to use the Mosquito he was automatically asked to take the starboard seat. He considered his flights in Mosquitoes to be among the more memorable of his flying experiences. It was undoubtedly fast, but pilots accepted that it was wise to avoid turning or climbing too fast until you gained height and built up speed. In spite of this apparent instability, the Mosquito was still manoeuvrable and powerful enough to climb on one engine only. The two Rolls Royce Merlins gave it a top speed of 400 mph, but it cruised at 240 mph and landing speed was just below 120 mph. With extra tanks the range was 1,700 miles (7 hours flying).

The Mosquito was planned, designed, test flown, put into production, built and flown in many operations, all in war time. When de Havilland started to meet the need for a fast, light bomber, he chose to build it in wood. The first Mosquito flew in November 1940. Furniture makers were called in to produce them, and less than a year later 'Mossies', as they were nicknamed, were on operational service.

The Mosquito performed nearly every combat job. It carried two-ton bombs to Berlin. It was a day fighter, a night fighter and a night intruder. It flew well at the high altitudes used for photo-reconnaissance, but it could also carry out low level attacks on submarines, shipping, rail and road traffic, and enemy aircraft on the ground. It dropped incendiaries to mark the targets for the Pathfinder heavy bombers.

In addition to its exceptional performance, its wooden construction made it more difficult to detect on Radar than a conventional aircraft. Although hailed as the wooden wonder it could fail in dramatic fashion. Fire was a particularly high risk. In some cases, the wood delaminated, the plywood became unstable and fabric could shred. In the Far East the glue became unstuck.

Geoff Thomas was particularly keen to get information about the German fighter system. He was still smarting at the official refusal to accept his version of the attack using upward firing canon. For some time the boffins had been piecing together information about the German system of night fighter control in the coastal areas of France, Belgium and Holland. From various sources, information was built up about a number of ground control stations, each controlling separate night fighter squadrons. These stations would each use different wavelengths to communicate with their squadron. The next part of the jigsaw puzzle was to identify the characteristic frequency used in radio communication between fighters in each sector.

Geoff and Adam began a series of intruder raids in their Mosquito to discover these frequencies. This was similar to the operation earlier carried out by the unfortunate Fairstone in a Wellington. Now the Mosquito had the speed to outstrip any German fighter, so it could act as a decoy by cruising in an area until an attacker fighter was set on to them. Adam tuned in a sensitive radio receiver until he could read the wavelength which the fighter was receiving. Once they had this information they opened the throttles to speed out of range, often to repeat the exercise in another part of the enemy coast.

With other Mosquitoes operating independently they identified four sectors along this coastline and extending over 200 miles inland. Each sector had its characteristic frequency which did not change during the month of their operations. On one mission to discover the dimensions of the sector that included Hamburg, they found that about 30 miles south-east of this city the frequency changed, suggesting that yet another sector existed.

Adam also observed that their attackers were single engine, single seater fighters, in addition to the more usual twin engine night fighters. It was interesting that the single engined fighters were not in continuous radio contact with any ground controller, as were the twin engined fighters who were being vectored from the ground right from take-off. Bomber crews en route to Berlin reported that single engined fighters would appear from above them, while the twin engined climbed up to engage them. There was no obvious reason for these different tactics.

This most recently discovered sector swarmed with night fighters. This was most probably because Berlin was located within its boundaries, and the Germans wanted to protect its capital city. Following a broad stream of Halifaxes and Stirlings on their way to Berlin, Geoff and Adam became aware of explosions in the air in a region where there was no sign of flak. RAF heavy bombers were being blown out of the air, and as they sped over Geoff suddenly pointed to a Stirling in front of them shouting, 'Look underneath!' Adam saw the dim shape of a Messerschmitt creeping slowly to take position under the Stirling's belly.

Geoff began a shallow dive and fired three short bursts from the nose machine guns. In the reflection of the flames that burst from the Messerschmitt's port wing they both saw the upward pointing cannon quite clearly, then the enemy's nose fell and it went into a flaming spin, out of control. During the dive toward the Messerschmitt, Adam had been aware of several hits on his side of the Mosquito. These could only have come from the Stirling. He told Geoff who said, 'Ungrateful sod,' as he pulled away. 'Any damage?' Adam had just replied, 'We seem fine,' when Geoff pointed at the oil gauge for the starboard engine, which registered a loss of pressure.

He feathered the propeller and shut off the engine, and asked for a heading for home. Apart from the damaged engine the fuel system was intact, the electrical system and all instruments were operating.

'Now we'll see if the maker was right about her performance on one engine,' mused Geoff. 'We caught one of these swine red-handed, dealt it a fearful blow and saved the Stirling from a terrible fate. She repays us by breaking our engine. By God, with you as a witness we can get these Intelligence wallahs to eat their words and accept my version of what happened to Uwe and his crew, and to poor old Bill Prober and Boris Sancerre, good chaps that they were.'

Adam added, 'Don't forget Jock and you.'

Geoff nodded. 'Do you know she's cruising very nicely. Just keep an eye open for fire in that engine. I know she's properly shut down, but we've got all this wood round.'

Adam loosened his harness and had a look towards the interior. He could see some splintered areas towards the tail, some with daylight showing through, but nothing serious. 'So far, so good,' he reported.

Geoff wagged his finger, 'Don't get too cocky, Adam. We won't be able to run away from any fighter with evil intentions.' They each ate a sandwich and drank coffee, then sat quietly scanning the skies, and discussing the merits of various aircraft in a desultory manner.

They were an hour late in returning to base, and were debriefed by the Intelligence Officer who had disbelieved Geoff's story of the upward firing cannon. He was blustering his excuses when Geoff interrupted him, 'I don't give a chuff for your reasons. I want you to send a signal, top priority, to all Bomber squadron commanders warning them about Me110s with their cannons firing upwards. Let me have your draft for approval after my breakfast, then circulate it in time for tonight's briefings.'

In the next week Adam and Geoff went to as many briefings as possible to spread this warning. Then Adam was summoned to Malvern College where Blacklock explained that in spite of the active discouragement of his scientific colleagues, he had continued to develop a navigational aid along the lines of Gee. The system had been code named Oboe and had been tested by a group rather like Ether Atom. Now he wanted Adam to test it in actual operations. He had got a Mosquito aircraft, just had to find a pilot to drive it and had asked for Jock Davidson, but had not heard if Jock would be available. Adam explained about Jock being discharged from the service and being a medical student at Glasgow.

He told the Professor about Geoff Thomas and was surprised at Barlock's reaction of delight. 'Oh yes, I know him. Haven't seen him since we set fire to young Davidson.' He picked up the antique dictating machine and shouted into the horn, 'Get Geoff Thomas to pilot the aeroplane.' He found the ebony ruler and rattled the radiator. His secretary entered, as bright as ever, smiled at Adam and said to Blacklock, 'Geoff Thomas is at the same place as Adam, and they are both at the same place as Bennett, so one phone call from you to your Australian tormentor will sort that out.'

'Right, my love, and while I'm doing that you could show Adam the schematic drawings for the Oboe.' She led Adam into her office, said she would just put her husband through to Mr Bennett, then did so. When Adam said he had not known that she was the Professor's wife, she explained that she had been his University secretary, and had married him in 1936. Their two sons had gone to boarding schools at the beginning of the war and she returned to her role as the professor's secretary as her contribution to the war effort. She showed him the drawings and he could make out a system based on two ground stations, one of which acted as the centre of an arc over enemy territory, the other intersected the arc at a predetermined point, presumably over the target. Barlock finished his call and joined them. 'That's settled. It's simply splendid. Let's have a sherry before lunch to celebrate, my dear. We'll meet you in the flat.' She wrinkled her nose and smiled at him, then said, 'In fifteen minutes time then. Let Adam keep the time.' She left the office.

Adam said that Oboe seemed to be just a copy of the Gee system which had not proved too successful. 'You sound like my disapproving colleagues, and you've missed the two essential points. Oboe works on the detection of range and it uses very high frequencies, a wavelength of nine centimetres to be exact. At this frequency, the Germans can't touch it as they don't have the equipment. And it'll take them over a year to develop it.' Adam nodded.

Barlock continued. 'A bomber flies on a given course until a predetermined point where it picks up pulses transmitted from a ground base in the South of England. In the aircraft the pulses are amplified and transmitted back to the base. The time taken between the transmission of the pulse and its return is a measure of the range of the aircraft from the station. The Oboe system sets up a constant range and signals the pilot to fly along an arc of a circle with its centre at the first ground base. The second ground base sends a signal which intersects the range arc at a point at which the bombs should be released.'

Adam interrupted. 'But the release point depends upon height and speed.'

'Good man, that's right.' Barlock rocked upon the balls of his feet and raised his finger. 'That data can be fed in by the navigator at present, perhaps from the ground in future. In the Oboe system the point of release of the bombs is determined by a ground observer, not likely to be distracted by being shot at. I admit that only a few aircraft can use Oboe at one time, but you Pathfinders are only going to use a few marker aircraft on any raid. The beam coming from the aircraft could attract German fighters, but, as I said, the Germans are not well equipped to handle the frequencies we operate at. Now, young man, you are facing court martial.' The Professor's eyes twinkled. 'You were instructed to be at lunch in fifteen minutes. That was twenty-five minutes ago.' They left in a hurry.

On his way back to Bomber HQ, Adam thought about the question of testing the accuracy of the bombing. The photo-reconnaissance service provided information about the effects of the bombing but often blast could produce damage at a distance from the point of impact, so that the location of the effects of the bomb was not necessarily the place where it had landed.

He suddenly remembered Bishop Sievewright's remarks about getting information from agents and decided to consult this venerable authority to see if on the spot reports could be obtained. The still enthusiastic cleric knew of a group of Belgian resistance workers who had given the location of an isolated work-site where reinforced ramps were being built on a massive scale. It was rumoured that this was to become a launching area for large rockets and they recommended a bombing attack at night when the forced labourers had returned to their quarters in a nearby village.

With their Mosquito fitted with Oboe, Geoff and Adam flew some practice flights to dummy targets in Britain. Adam found the system straightforward and apparently accurate. By the time they were ready for their first bombing mission Bishop Sievewright had recruited four Belgian agents to act as observers. The night chosen proved to be moonlit with slight winds, and Geoff found it easy to fly along the arc at 12000 feet, until they received the release signal.

The information from the Belgian agents was that each of their five bombs had fallen within the target area. They were particularly gratified that the first bomb had fallen on the sleeping quarters for the guards and only a few survivors had been counted. Geoff and Adam were ready to go operational with Oboe and they used it to mark the routes in the next series of Pathfinder raids on the Ruhr valley, nicknamed 'Happy Valley' by the crews.

CHAPTER 33

At his next assessment Adam's shoulder was found to be improved enough for him to be restored to pilot category, but not enough for him to be graded fit for operational flying. He could fly the Mosquito on tests of developments of or refinements to the Oboe system, but only within the British Isles. For his operational Pathfinder duties he continued to act as a navigator.

He joked that he and Oboe came from the same school, Malvern College. To him a Pathfinder Mosquito fitted with Oboe was the ultimate bombing weapon, and he became the accepted, if unofficial, authority on the system in Bomber Command. Bennett used him in this role as more and more Pathfinder aircraft were fitted with the system, and selected crews had to be instructed in how to make the best use of it.

Bennett remained highly committed to large scale continuous bombing of Germany by Pathfinders, and to his expectations of high standards of performance from his crews. In spite of his intolerant and uncompromising attitude, and his surprise sorties over the target to check on their performance, Pathfinder crews held him in high regard. They respected his exceptional skill in the air, and they followed his leadership without question.

Outside of his group Bennett was not well liked by other commanders in Bomber Command. He had been a Pilot Officer on the Reserve, came into the service as a Wing Commander and within a year, at the age of 32, was promoted to Air Vice-Marshal. Thus he was perceived as being brash, jumped up, and disrespectful to his elders and betters. He wanted highly competent crews and deliberately set out to attract the most experienced fliers from squadrons in other groups.

To offset the ill-will that had been generated, Bomber Command eventually decreed that one third of Pathfinder aircrew should come straight from Operational Training Units. These were younger crews, who had volunteered to do a longer tour of duty than the other squadrons. Their rewards were that on passing the tests set by Bennett to become a Pathfinder they were promoted by one rank, and they were temporarily entitled to wear a small metal RAF eagle below their aircrew brevet. The eagle became permanent only at the end of a tour. Bennett also declared that in 8 Group, the Victoria Cross would only be awarded posthumously to any of his Pathfinders. This edict was made in response to the dissatisfaction that arose in the Command with the high numbers of medals awarded and publicity generated in 5 Group, headed by Bennett's rival, Air Vice-Marshal the Honourable Ralph Cochrane.

In late 1943 and early 1944 the growing reputation of the Mosquito led to a large number of requests from pilots and navigators to transfer to Mosquito squadrons. As the Mosquito was not an easy plane for a novice to fly, pilots were expected to have at least a thousand flying hours before they converted to 'the wooden wonders'. This requirement screened out some of the younger volunteers, and gave Bennett the experienced airmen he wanted. The high speed dashing Mosquitoes were being flown by Bomber Command's 'old men', while callow youths straight from Operational Training School were flying the heavies, the lumbering Lancasters, hulking Halifaxes and stalwart Stirlings.

Adam was heavily involved in getting these new crews trained to operate in the Oboe system. However he and Geoff flew on at least two night operations per week, leading the bomber stream by using Oboe to mark important staging and turning points on the route.

In his role as an expert on Oboe, Adam had to attend a number of planning meetings at Bomber Command at which targets of special significance were discussed. Certain names kept coming up, particularly where a number of heavy industrial plants were located. After discussion, the decision was taken whether or not to add a name to the Area Target list, or if it already was on that list whether or not to let it stand.

The city of Nuremburg had been on the list for some time. Although it was out of range of Oboe, Geoff and Adam had earlier led a bombing mission to Nuremburg, but they had encountered a heavier than usual concentration of night fighters, and there was a greater loss of heavy bombers than would justify the slight amount of damage done. In spite of having been bombed eight or nine times, Nuremburg had never suffered serious damage.

Nuremburg was known to tourists as a beautiful example of an old south German city. The Altstadt, in the centre of the city, had a moat and a turreted wall and contained churches, museums and many old gabled houses. The city's best known products were toys, pencils, and carvings in wood and ivory. Thus, when the BBC announced that Nuremburg had been bombed by the RAF, there were protests that important relics of the past and harmless products were being wantonly destroyed.

However Bomber Command's Target List indicated that just outside this picturesque old town centre, plants to manufacture chemicals, vehicles and machinery, had been built at Nuremburg before the war. These had been extended and converted to turn out diesel engines, tanks, armoured vehicles, electrical equipment and other material for the German war effort. The area also contained military establishments, including a large barracks for the S.S. and other official Nazi establishments in the area. Thus, in the area bombing philosophy, Nuremberg as an industrial centre was a strong candidate for attack, but there was another factor, which led it to be described as a 'political' target. After a famous prewar party rally had been held there, Hitler wanted to make Nuremburg the 'Holy City' of the Nazi creed where future rallies and demonstrations of the party power could be held. To house these spectacles, the architect, Albert Speer began to build three large arenas, designed to last for the thousand years of the Third Reich, which Hitler had predicted. These monuments to Hitler's rash promises were never completed. Nuremburg stood out on Bomber Command's list as a target which had not so far been successfully attacked, and which could yield damage to German war supplies, and to German morale.

The Commander in Chief, Harris, held regular morning conferences at which the target for that night was decided. On March 20th 1944, the weather was difficult to predict, but the best guess was that it could hold up for a raid deep into German territory. The bomber stream could take off late, get into a tail wind behind a cold front and follow the associated high cloud.

The target would be visible from the setting moon and the return journey would be made after the moon had set. Harris ended the conference by stating that the target would be Nuremberg, and the raid should be as large as possible. As usual, once the target had been decided, he returned to his office leaving a group of his senior officers to work out the details.

The selection of the route was critical. It could be 'straight in and straight out', with as few legs as possible. This meant fewer turns, kept marking to a minimum, reduced navigation errors, as well as shortening the time in the air, with the decrease in fatigue for the crews and less fuel required. The major drawback of this choice was that as they held to a straight course, enemy nightfighters could anticipate points at which to engage the bombers, particularly as they would have to fly a straight leg of over 250 miles.

The alternative method was to 'duck and weave', following an indirect route with many legs. This left the enemy confused about the target, but lost all the advantages of the direct route. Bennett maintained his preference for this indirect approach, but got no support from the others. They countered that the tail wind meant the bombers would be in the risk zone for a relatively short time. He left the meeting disgruntled that decisions on navigational matters were not left entirely to his Pathfinders, the obvious experts.

On airfields from Cambridge to Middlesborough, squadrons were alerted to stand by with a potential force of over 1,000 aircraft, ready to fly if the weather proved suitable. Not all of this force would head for Nuremberg. There would be diversionary thrusts, such as a mine laying attack by Halifaxes over the North Sea, a route likely to lead the Germans to think that Berlin was to be the target. Others would leave the bomber stream in the Ruhr area to fly towards 'spoof' targets to draw the German nightfighter away from the main bomber force on their long leg. Geoff and Adam were to lead a dozen Oboe Mosquitoes in a 'spoof' raid on Kassel.

While the crews were waiting for the decision to go or to stay, the weather in the south of England closed in, and the betting was that the operation would be scrubbed. However the meteorologists predicted that the cloud would break up over the continent, and word was finally given that the night's 'show' was on. The routine preparations were started, night flying tests, arming and bombing-up, then the briefing where their distant target was disclosed. The crews made their own arrangements and began another long wait for an unusually late take-off time. Eventually they left from airfields over a large area of the country and formed a stream of aircraft over the North Sea, then crossed the Belgian coast to head for Charleroi and the turning point which began the long leg from west to east.

Geoff and Adam, flying above the main force of Halifaxes and Lancasters, were dismayed at the weather conditions. The German nightfighters had two advantages. Firstly, the cold front meant that at their altitude the bomber stream was making very obvious vapour trails. Secondly, these trails and the bombers were easily seen for miles as the moon was lighting up the clear sky above the low cloud. In addition, the navigators were finding that the forecast winds given at briefing were wrong. Instead of being moderate and on the bombers' tails, the winds were strong enough to deflect the bombers from the straight course they had to fly.

The Luftwaffe nightfighters were out in force and, with the almost unlimited visibility, they were picking off the bombers easily. Adam saw over 20 bombers being shot down, by flak or by fighters in the 100 miles or so between Liege and their turning off point for Kassel. From seeing several sudden explosions, he and Geoff knew that the upward firing Messerschmitts were in the thick of the formation wreaking havoc among the heavy bombers.

As the Mosquitoes left the bomber stream and turned to port towards Kassel, they began to drop 'Window', strips of paper with aluminium foil attached. Each strip would be picked up on the enemy's Radar, and the deluge of 'Window' they were releasing would appear on their screens as echoes from a large bomber fleet. In addition they dropped a long line of flares on the way to the target. However these manoeuvres failed to attract enemy fighters away from the main stream. Obviously, the reports from the German fighter pilots attacking the main bomber stream in the bright moonlight had convinced the German operators on the way to Kassel that they were being spoofed. As planned, the Mosquitoes dropped green and yellow target markers on Kassel, then three dozen 500 pound High Explosive bombs. Even this aroused no opposition by flak or by night fighters and Geoff and Adam led their squadron back to base unscathed, but crestfallen that their attempted diversion had fallen so flat.

The bombers continued along the long leg to the turning point at Fulda, the crews cursing the bright moonlight that allowed them to be being continually harassed by fighters. Over the distance of 265 miles 59 bombers were lost. At Fulda the turning point had not been well marked, and experienced navigators had to rework their running plots to get on line for Nuremberg.

Once they neared Nuremberg the earlier aircraft did not see the target markers they had come to expect. There was activity at Schweinfurt and it was assumed that the unexpected strength and direction of the winds must have spoiled the accuracy of target marking. A few experienced navigators ignored the markers and used H2S to find Nuremberg under the low cloud cover.

The fighter attacks had diminished but on the bombing run, they encountered a battery of searchlights and heavy flak. The combination of their bomb bursts and the searchlight sweeps acted as markers for other heavy bombers, but once more, the resulting damage to Nuremberg was slight.

For the whole operation almost 100 bombers were shot down or blown up over enemy territory or crashed when they returned. Some 800 aircrew were killed, injured, taken prisoner or listed as missing. When the losses and casualties were totalled, the Nuremberg raid began to be talked of as 'Bomber Command's worst defeat'. Morale slumped and there was talk that the Nuremberg débâcle had put an end to Harris' dream that the outcome of the war would be determined by a sustained offensive against the enemy's industrial capacity by heavy bombers.

Within Bomber Command, a reappraisal of tactics revived an earlier dispute between Bennett and Cochrane about target marking at high or at low levels. Cochrane reported success with two borrowed Mosquitoes marking at low-level for a heavy bomber force at moderate height. On the basis of this report he asked for two more Mosquitoes.

To his surprise, he was given one of Bennett's Mosquito squadrons. In addition two Lancaster squadrons, which had been taken from 5 Group when Bennett's Pathfinder Force was set up, were returned to his command. This must have been irksome to Bennett. His advocacy of marking from high had been countermanded and his role as sole master of Pathfinding now had to be shared with Cochrane.

Planning of the invasion of Normandy was in full swing, and Bomber Command became part of the large forces under the command of General Eisenhower. Targets set for Bomber Command by Eisenhower had priority over targets set by Harris. Thus Geoff and Adam found themselves back on missions in northern France, Belgium and Holland, all of which were within the range of Oboe. Significant railway junctions and marshalling yards were attacked at low level, airfields were strafed and German occupied barracks and other buildings were bombed from low levels.

Cochrane's group continued to use their low level marking techniques against industrial targets in Germany but as D-Day approached, Harris had to give up his area bombing in favour of missions which would hamper or prevent communications and German troop movements into the area around the Normandy beaches.

Once the Allied land forces had moved out from Normandy to advance through France and Belgium, mobile ground stations could follow them and bring other targets into the range of Oboe. As a result, Pathfinders delivered increasing tonnage of bombs to industrial targets in Germany. In March 1945, a year after Nuremberg the end of the war was in sight and Area Bombing was called to a halt. Heavy bombers dropped food into Holland and other liberated areas, and others ferried freed prisoners of war back to Britain.

At the beginning of May 1945 Geoff and Adam were briefed for an attack on Kiel. When he was informed that the air and ground defences were expected to be light Adam remembered Jock's account of the mess in which their aircraft had returned from this target. Over 100 Mosquitoes attacked in two waves.

Oboe worked like a charm and they were able to place their markers with a degree of accuracy never achieved in earlier raids. As bomber leaders, Adam and Geoff directed the first wave against the port and its installations then circled overhead while the second wave carried out its attack on the now blazing target. When the last bombs had been dropped they flew over the devastated area, took photographs, and confirmed visually that the mission had been accomplished. During the whole raid no defence at all was offered by flak or fighters and all aircraft returned safely.

At the interrogation a number of crew commented that this was how raids should be conducted, with the weather right, the gadgets working and nobody to damage the bombers. A quiet voice countered that the Germans might not agree. There was an awkward silence. As it turned out this was Bomber Command's last war time operation. The official Victory in Europe was celebrated within a week.

CHAPTER 34

Geoff was posted to the United States to take part in an experimental programme which would be used in the war against Japan. Adam celebrated Victory in Europe day in an unarmed Lancaster, flying to Salzburg. Professor Barlock had given him the task of inspecting a German ground Radar installation, which had operated during the later stages of the war from a site in the Salzkammergut region. His brief was to go to the area with a small force, locate the installation and get as much information as possible about the equipment.

He mused that he was following his brief in one respect, in that his force consisted of one man and himself. At Salzburg he met Flight Sergeant Avrum Reichmann, a Radar Mechanic, whose English was too good for it to be his native tongue. He was Jewish and his family had come to Britain from Vienna in 1936 to get away from Hitler. Trained in Vienna in the newly emerging field of Electronic Engineering, he had been dismayed when he could not find an opening in this field in London. To make a living, he set up a small wireless repair shop in the family home. By attending night school, he had obtained the City and Guilds qualifications in Electrical and Wireless Engineering.

The Reichmanns became British citizens. When war broke out, as someone from abroad with a basement full of wireless sets, Avrum was suspected of being a spy. However the British authorities, after a full investigation of his background, decided that he was more an asset than a threat to the war effort, and he was encouraged to enlist in the RAF, becoming involved right away in Radio Direction Finding, installing and maintaining the Chain Home Low system on the south coast of England. The system picked up signals from any intruders who tried to escape detection by flying across the Channel under the normal level of radar coverage.

He had a wide technical knowledge of Radar ground installations and spoke German fluently. Adam was surprised that the service had found the right man for the job, and so quickly. Reichmann was delighted that he had been selected.

For the present operation, Adam and Flight Sergeant Reichmann had no support or backup, not even a map. The Salzkammergut had been suggested as the most likely site. Avrum had spent a family holiday in St. Wolfgang, a famous holiday resort in this area, so they had a vague idea of where to look, but there were so many hills to choose from.

As a first step, they interviewed the officer in charge of the British army contingent in Salzburg. The garrison major, Lawson Langford, turned out to be a tall, languid officer, who wore a handkerchief tucked up the sleeve of his tailored battle dress tunic, which was just a shade darker than the regulation colour, identifying him as a member of the Brigade of Guards. Adam was irritated by the mannerisms, condescending attitudes and the nasal drawl in which this clown confessed to be little interested in this ploy of theirs. 'After all, old boy, even you flying chaps must appreciate that this is not very relevant to my job, which is to weed out all the nasties then shoot the buggers.'

Leaving Reichmann with their kit, Adam went to the US Command Post. He found U.S. Army personnel and civilians bustling noisily through the corridors. Members of a special commission were seeking treasures which the Nazis were said to have dumped in some of the many lakes in the district. Secret service men were following up a rumour that Hitler had escaped from his bunker in Berlin and was in hiding around Salzburg. Rumour was that a special Russian commando group had been formed to find this greatest of war criminals. Not wanting to be left out, the Americans were sending their agents into the field.

In the babble of voices, telephone bells and scurrying feet on the tiled corridors, Adam could not decide which office to approach until he remembered an observation made by his father that if you want someone to listen to your sales talk, find the busiest man in the place. These words came back to him as he was passing an open door. In the room, a small paunchy top sergeant was smoking and chewing a foul smelling cigar, and handing out files to three assistants while telling someone at the other end of the telephone line in his left hand that even with an uncle in the Senate he was not entitled to a limo. He beckoned Adam in with the receiver in his right hand told the caller on this telephone he was mighty glad to be of service then swept both receivers into a drawer, which he slammed shut. He leaned over the desk to shake Adam's hand.

Once he was satisfied that Adam's mission was official, the sergeant opened up a map of the mountain areas. 'D'ya see this place, Gmunsten, on this goddam lake called Traunsee. Well, two things. The good news first. I know real estate, and my guess is that your Radar would be in the Sengsen mountains behind and to the east.' Adam nodded.

The sergeant continued, 'The bad news is that I ain't sure if the Krauts up in them there hills know that their war is over. You better wait until we get troops through.' Adam thought the buildings and equipment they were after could have been destroyed by then and decided to press on.

'OK, that's up to you. What transport have you got?' the sergeant asked. Adam confessed he had none. 'Jeez. Listen to that noise out there. That's a zillion very important guys screaming for transport. You got an uncle in the Senate? You married to Betty Grable? Got a friend called Rockefeller, or Babe Ruth?' Adam laughed and shook his head.

The cigar was still for a moment then resumed its movements. 'I'll let you have a jeep and I've got a guy who'll drive it. One day I'm going to have to bust him down to civilian, but I'll give him to you for your caper. I'll estimate you as being back in three days time, so Petrelli can draw five days rations for the three of you. Go get some chow and be back here in an hour.' Adam was overwhelmed and offered to sign authorization forms, but the cigar interrupted him by pointing upwards and the American said, 'This baby hates goddamn paperwork. I know your name and won't forget it. That's all the record I need. OK? My name is Willard P. Eisnor, Top Sergeant. I'll give Petrelli a piece of paper. That's all the record you get. OK?' Adam nodded his agreement and thanks. 'You don't have weapons so I'll make sure Petrelli carries his. He wants to be Errol Flynn.'

Reichmann had found a British mess which catered to all ranks and they lunched on stodgy cheese pudding and a cup of brackish tea, which became drinkable only with an excess of sugar.

At the U.S. post Adam introduced Flight Sergeant Reichmann to the helpful Top Sergeant Willard P. Eisnor who pointed to a jeep which had just roared up. 'There you go. Tell that sucker Petrelli I hate his guts. See ya.' He shook hands and handed Adam the map. As a measure of his embarrassment at their effusive thanks, he took the cigar out of his mouth for the first time.

Petrelli was a very large Corporal wearing a jump suit and paratrooper wings who got slowly out of the jeep to greet them. He wore the round basin style American helmet and a gun belt with a very large revolver hanging on one side and on the other three nasty looking grenades. A long stiletto knife was sticking from the side of his right jump boot. His dark curly hair was over his ears and his olive complexion and impressive Roman nose made him look brooding and sulky until he smiled, flashing broad gleaming teeth. 'Hi, I'm Pete Petrelli. You're the Limeys who wanna see the mountains.'

Reichmann introduced himself. 'Good to meet you, Pete, I'm Avrum Reichmann. Av for short.' Petrelli shook Avrum's hand then grabbed Adam's hand saying, 'You're the first guy I've met from Newfoundland. How're the igloos up there?' Adam felt his face flushing and started to reply when Pete cut in, 'Forget it, I'm kidding you. I once met a girl in Boston. Came from Newfoundland. Great girl. She told me one of the best ways to get a guy from Newfoundland angry was to ask if he lived in an igloo.'

Adam relaxed when faced with that beaming smile. 'I'm Adam Aitken, and I'm glad you've come to our rescue.'

Pete dumped their gear into the back of the jeep beside two large cardboard boxes. 'You get in the back, Av, and you in the front, Colonel.'

Adam obeyed. 'Call me Adam, and if you must know I'm just a Squadron Leader, a Major, not a Colonel.'

'You can lead my squadron any time, Adam. Tell me where we're going.' Adam pointed out the route to Gmunsten. Petrelli snapped out, 'Got ya, Adam,' then pointed to the window where Eisnor and his cigar were watching and talking on the telephone, shouted, 'I hate his guts,' then slammed the jeep into gear and took off with a screech of tires.

They were quickly out of Salzburg. The road was quiet and the weather perfect for driving. As they passed an inn on the outskirts of Mondsee, Adam noticed a number of men in the courtyard being addressed by someone on the entrance steps. They were mostly in uniform and armed but one older civilian began shouting as he saw the jeep speeding past. 'What was he saying?' he asked Av. 'I think it was that the Americans were here,' was the answer.

In Seewalchen schoolchildren waved in a friendly fashion, and they were soon on their way past farmers pushing small carts filled with root vegetables. They fell in behind a large hay cart drawn by a pair of well matched horses, and travelled at walking pace on the winding narrow road.

A Kraftwagen, the German equivalent of the Jeep, pulled in behind them as they followed the hay cart. Adam noticed in the rearview mirror that it contained four men in uniform. However he could not see any rifles, but they could be carrying side arms. He was concerned that Willard Eisnor's observation could be true. These people had not surrendered and they would certainly not be coerced into surrender by the three of them. When they reached the town of Gmunsten and entered a square, the Kraftwagen accelerated past them to pull up at a large building with a Nazi party flag flying outside. The four uniformed men got out and entered the building. Adam noted they were carrying sidearms.

Pete slowed the jeep to a stop. Adam asked him to unbuckle his belt and put his weapons on the floor under the seat, very slowly. Adam then got out and looked around in as nonchalant a manner as he possibly could. Pete unwound his bulk from the driver's seat and found some giggling girls to ogle. Av squeezed out from the back seat, stretched himself, then wished '*Gruss Gott*' to an old man who immediately snatched off his hat, nodded and replied '*Mein Herr,*' then burst into nervous laughter.

The square was dotted with small groups of people, some women and children but mainly men in uniform carrying arms. The most menacing was a group of 10 men in battle gear, with steel helmets, jump smocks and submachine guns slung across their chests.

Some stalls round the perimeter of the square displayed clothing and shoes, others vegetables. One table had a few sausages, and another had cages with five or six scrawny hens looking balefully at the world. The arrival of the threesome had brought activity in the marketplace to a halt. Even the children stood quietly beside their mothers, who were dressed in dirndl skirts, embroidered vests and neatly pressed aprons. Adam kept his eyes on the men, particularly the group of ten who looked just like the stereotypes of the Wehrmacht he had been led to expect.

A buzz of excitement arose from the crowd when one of the men from the Kraftwagen came out of the building and strode purposefully towards the Jeep. He was wearing rank badges which were most likely those of a commissioned officer, and Adam saw that the flap of his pistol holster was open. The low buzz of conversation from the crowd in the square was stilled. 'I think we're in dead trouble,' said Av in a strained voice.

The officer went straight to Adam. '*Amerikanisch?*' he asked.

'No, Nein, ich bin not but he bin yes.' Adam pointed to Pete who drawled slowly 'Howdy'. Av was pale, but spoke to the officer clearly and rapidly, then explained to the others that he had sorted out their nationalities to the German.

'Austrian,' retorted the officer and his hand moved swiftly to his holster.

Pete dived for the ground yelling, 'Hit the deck.' Av turned his head away and Adam made a half hearted gesture toward the Austrian.

'No, no, not so. See what have I here,' said the officer, 'an emptied out holster without any weapon. I have no harm for you. You are pleased to come with me to meet the Gauleiter, Herr Moser. He has asked for a speech with you.'

He bowed like a headwaiter and swept his arm to indicate that they should precede him. Pete brushed himself off and, with dignity restored, walked towards the building with Av beside him. Adam fell in behind them and was joined by their escort. 'I am Kapitan Stengl. You will be surprised that I speak so good English. Before the War came I was waiter, and learned much English from tourists. I have not spoken so much since becoming a warrior, or soldier. I wanted to practise with the Tommy prisoners in our Oflag but they just told me to sod off.'

At this point they were passing the Wehrmacht troops with machine weapons. The Austrian officer gestured for them to follow and they quietly fell in behind. Here is the firing squad, thought Adam, and we haven't been asked name, rank and number. He tried to recall the procedures laid down in the Geneva convention. Stengl prattled on. 'Today in this Gau, this district, is our busy day for the weapon handing in. It is very important for the fire stoppage, the Cease Fire. All weapons have to be written on the forms and sent to Bad Ischl. Then we can be happy the war is over. My friends and I must do this. But we were late and that is why we went fast past you in the wagon.'

Adam sighed in relief. As they entered the building he raised his voice to address the two in front. 'They're handing in their weapons today. That's why everyone was in the square. I think we're safe.'

'Jeez, I thought we were a goner.' Pete let out a long whistle, then called, 'Hi, sweetie!' to a severe looking young woman in uniform with her fair hair tied back in a bun and wearing wire rimmed spectacles. Her only response was to turn her head away. 'See, it's the old Petrelli magic, Av.' The Flight Sergeant did not answer. The Kapitan asked them to sit down on chairs and he entered a small office. The supposed firing squad walked past them into a large hall at the end of the corridor. One or two of them looked at the unusual trio, but with only passing interest.

Av sat with head bowed. Adam asked him how he felt. Av explained that for a Jew the thought of getting into Nazi hands was a nightmare. He thought he had come to terms with the risk, but was ashamed at how afraid he had been in the square. Pete said quietly, 'It wasn't you flat on your belly out there when that little guy went for his gun.' Av was quiet, then smiled and said, 'Hit the deck,' and all three were sharing their laughter when Stengl returned to take them into the office.

Adam had seen a Gauleiter in a film, a sinister figure, tall, thin, severe, with a sneering face, a rasping voice and piercing eyes, and dressed in an immaculately tailored black uniform. On the basis of this memory of a performance by the great Conrad Veidt, he was disappointed at the small chubby man in well worn leather shorts, who bounded from behind a desk to meet them. 'I am Karl Moser,' he introduced himself, 'and you have met already Karl Willi Stengl.' Adam introduced himself and his companions using ranks but no first names.

Gauleiter Moser explained that he was the senior man in the National Socialist Party in this district, at least until someone else took over. He expected he would have to appear before a special tribunal to be examined on his record. He had heard that this was called being de-Nazified. 'I think I shall look forward to being de-Nazified as a kind of change of life. I would want to go back to teaching. My specialty is British philosophy, Hobbes to Russell. I did my postgraduate training at Edinburgh University a long time ago. But it is of you we must speak, not me. Please sit.'

CHAPTER 35

Adam explained that they wanted to inspect a German Radar installation to find out how it differed from similar Allied stations. Moser had difficulty with the technical terms until Av gave him the German equivalents. 'Now I know what it is you want I can help you. But I am still an official of the party so I must first ask if you have permission to make this search.' Adam produced his letter of authority from the British Department of Scientific Intelligence. Like other British official documents, it was typed on pulped brown paper and was not impressive. Herr Moser seemed doubtful about it.

Pete brought out a single sheet of paper from the US command post stating the Jeep was requisitioned to travel from Salzburg to Gmunsten and outlying areas, for the purpose of reconnoitring Radar emplacements. This carried the imprint of the American Eagle at the top. 'This then is relevant, but whose signature is that?' Herr Moser asked, pointing to a large florid scrawl at the foot of the page.

'Eisnor,' replied Pete and before he could tell how much he hated Willard's guts, the Gauleiter was waving the letter at Willi and inviting him to inspect the signature of the great Generalissimo Eisenhower. Reluctantly handing the form back to Pete, Moser spoke rapidly to Stengl, who then scuttled from the room.

Adam explained that the signature was not Eisenhower's. Herr Moser conceded that with a smile, and explained that he did not want to worry Willi about his involvement in an irregular procedure. He took out a map and showed them the location of the Radar station. 'Your travel there and back and your inspection will take all morning, so you would be better off setting out from here early tomorrow morning.'

Av looked doubtful. 'So why don't we get back to Salzburg tonight and come back tomorrow morning?'

Herr Moser replied firmly, 'I don't advise you to travel back to Salzburg tonight. If you stay here you will save time in the morning. Apart from that, there is the matter of the wolf packs.'

'You mean howling wolves?' asked Pete in some surprise.

'No, worse than that. Gangs of German deserters from the Army live in the forests outside towns. They are called wolf packs because they terrorise the local residents. They steal, pillage and plunder to survive and rape for pleasure. They have recently become more active on the road between Gmunsten and Mondsee and they're just as bad around Bad Ischl. Now that we're taking in weapons they will feel safer and attack more.'

Pete shrugged his shoulders and spread his hands to indicate his acceptance of the situation. Adam acquiesced, but Av raised the issue of where they would sleep. The Gauleiter pointed out that Willi had a hotel, and had gone to prepare their rooms. He did not have much food, but Frau Moser and he would be honoured to give the visitors a meal, although it would not be near the standard required for real Austrian hospitality. Pete silenced him by raising his large hand. 'The cavalry has arrived. We brought enough goddamned food with us, didn't we, so we eat American. Besides, if we went back to Salzburg I'd be back in a bivouac tent and getting bawled out by that bum Willard P. I hate his guts.'

Herr Moser was delighted that they would stay as guests. He turned to Av and asked, 'Do you know that this Radar apparatus was built by French labourers?'

'You mean Jews?' interrupted Av.

'Yes. Many of them were, but there were also captured members of the French Resistance. The SS commandant of the installation is also French. He operated the apparatus with six French military prisoners,' explained Moser.

Adam asked how a Frenchman could be a member of the SS. Herr Moser explained further. 'We have troops who are not from Germany or Austria, including Frenchmen. Rather like the English have airmen from Newfoundland,' he said looking at Adam.

'But we're colonials,' protested Adam.

'The French are the same for Germany,' Herr Moser went on.

'But they're enemies, so they're traitors to their homeland,' Adam broke in.

'Not after we defeated them,' Moser continued. 'Are you not, Sergeant, with your genuine Austrian accent, a traitor to your homeland?'

Av answered quietly, 'I am a Jew. I changed my allegiance when my family left Austria to get away from Hitler. I don't consider myself a traitor.'

Pete broke in, 'I hate to bust up this philosophy stuff, but I see us here getting on real fine with Karl, who I think is still our enemy. I'm a second generation Italian in American uniform. A month ago I could have been killing my cousins, but I don't know. Av maybe was doing the same. Maybe we'll think it was wrong when we get home. But not now.'

After they had taken their kit to their rooms and Adam and Av were looking over the route they would take in the morning, Pete found where the Moser homestead was and drove the Jeep to deliver the food. Frau Moser knew of the town's unexpected guests and batted little more than an eyelid when she realised she was to cook a meal for three extra people. Pete spoke to her in a ponderous, solemn fashion using English words in a German sounding manner, concentrating so hard on his task that he was oblivious to her answers in perfect English.

She was relieved when he showed her the food he had brought, as she had barely enough in store for her own family's dinner. Pete solemnly explained what each can or packet contained in his pidgin German and she acknowledged in perfect English, until he held out a can of Spam and said, 'Piggen Hammen.' This proved too much and she burst into peals of laughter. Her laughter set Pete off in roars. Two little girls came into the kitchen to find out what the laughter was about. Pete showed them the can of Spam and said, 'Piggen Hammen' which set him, then Frau Moser, then the two little girls off again. This was the disarray in which Herr Moser found his family on his return home.

When Adam and Av turned up at the Mosers the house was still ringing with merriment. In the kitchen, Pete had one of the little girls on each of his knees, and was telling a tale of Johnny Wainey and his bing bang gunny. Karl was at the table, enthralled at the story and the mangling of the German language and Lisli was cooking and laughing at the latest outrageous word. When Adam and Av were introduced and duly seated at the kitchen table, Pete informed them that he had mastered the German language in less than an hour.

Lisli groaned and said she would be honoured if they would eat with the family, especially with the food that Pete had brought. With their permission, she would make extra to feed a family where the mother was too sick to cook. Karl remembered a bottle of wine he had laid down for a special occasion, and after conducting a solemn search of a solid wooden cabinet, produced a bottle of pre war Gumpoldskirchen. He set this treasure reverently on the dining table and selected and polished the glasses, with gestures and flourishes worthy of any orchestra conductor.

They went out into the small garden to enjoy the calm of the place. 'It's restful here,' said Pete thinking of the hard slogging fighting he had been involved with in the last year. 'When we marched into Rome I just wanted to set down a while and think it all out. So I went to find my cousin's family, hoping I could have a nice visit with them. They took the cigarettes, the gum, the candies and the cans of food but didn't want to know me. So I left and went back to the airfield where we were bivouacked and got into a fight with a marine. We pasted the hell out of each other for a long time then the police grabbed us and threw us in the slammer. Next day I ached all over but I felt great. That's when I got busted to Corporal.'

Av told of a similar experience when he came through Vienna on his way to meet Adam in Salzburg. He telephoned relatives, but his aunt hung up on him. Adam pointed out that they had found hospitality from people they had never known the day before, even though they were technically still enemies. He believed that people would have to set their sights on relationships wider than the immediate family or nation. The new international organization being talked about – the United Nations – would foster this new attitude.

Karl Moser had heard only a little of this move for world peace, and he confessed to being cynical about its chances for success. He recalled the League of Nations. Although the four of them had quickly reached an amicable relationship quite spontaneously, imposing amicable relationships on nations was a different story. He looked at Av. 'Herr Reichmann, do you think the Jewish people will ever be at ease with the Germans?'

Av shook his head, 'The Jewish people will never be at ease with other people until they are settled in their own country.'

Before Herr Moser could respond, the two little girls came into the garden to announce that the meal was ready, and each grabbed one of Pete's hands to lead him in, arguing who would get to sit beside him. 'Now I see the Petrelli magic,' smiled Av.

From the kitchen came the tantalising smell of browned onions and on the table Lisli uncovered a steaming dish of slices of canned meat covered in onion sauce. 'It is almost, but not quite, *zwiebelfleisch*,' she announced. Karl poured the wine, and asked for the toast. There was a silence then Av stood and offered, 'Friendship.' They sipped solemnly and clinked glasses. The youngest little girl raised her water glass, gazed adoringly at Pete and said, 'Johnny Wayney.'

In the early morning, a mist hung over the mountain tops and the leaves of the trees were dripping. Willi Stengl assured them that the day would be warm as he served coffee, cheese and black bread for breakfast. He wished them well on their expedition and, with Pete's weapons stored under the seat once more, they headed along an uneven two lane highway. A number of farmers already on the road in their horse-drawn carts, raised their hats politely as they passed. Following the map, they came to a gate on a broader well paved road. There was a deserted sentry hut by the open gate.

They set off up the road towards the summit, which was still clouded. Through a break in the trees they caught sight of a large series of girders fastened together. Av explained this was the main antenna, which was surrounded by an array of smaller bristling aerials. Av noted with satisfaction that the outside fixtures were intact and hoped that the control centre would still be undamaged.

They drove along an avenue of pine trees, emerging immediately below the antennae into a square surrounded by a number of concrete buildings. Behind these structures there was a barbed wire enclosure, with a long low wooden hut in the middle. A tower at each corner confirmed that this was a prison camp. The gate facing them hung open. Pete put his revolver on his lap and blew the horn. After a moment, he shouted, 'Hello.' They all looked round, but there was no response. Av got out first saying that he wanted to find the control centre.

Pete's voice had a sudden authority. 'Just wait, Av. You don't want to get booby trapped by a Kraut mine or something worse, do you.' Av stood stock still, peering suspiciously at the ground around him. 'Look for tracks and follow them, but only if they don't have any loose earth. All of us start behind the Jeep and walk along the tire tracks. Get behind me and remember Lieutenant Carson. That's what I'm doing right now.'

Adam asked the obvious, 'Who is Carson?'

Pete answered quickly, 'Who *was* he, you mean. He was a fresh faced kid from Tulsa who led my platoon in the Ardennes until he stepped on a mine.' Adam and Av soberly and cautiously followed Pete's measured pace.

They eventually reached a well trodden path round the front of all the buildings. When they got to the operations centre, Pete led them inside and continued his search, while Av was chafing to get his hands on the equipment. Finally, Pete crossed his fingers and Av went to a master switch and closed it.

Nothing happened for a moment, then a generator switched in, first a startling rumble then a screeching crescendo of power, settling down to a quiet reassuring hum. Av started switching circuits in and out like a church organist. 'It's all working,' he shouted happily.

Pete and Adam went outside to look at the other buildings. They identified a dormitory for about twelve guards, and an adjoining kitchen and mess hut. A more elegantly furnished building had three small bedrooms with shared toilet facilities, presumably for officers and a well-carpeted and furnished suite for the camp commandant. In a corner of the bedroom was a small safe with the door open. Adam moved towards it until he heard Pete say, 'Can it, Carson.' He hesitated and apologised softly, as Pete knelt carefully and peered round the outside of the safe. With his hands behind his back, the American looked carefully at the piles of paper on the two shelves then gingerly removed three bulky folders from the bottom shelf and handed them to Adam. With similar care he cleared the top shelf file by file. He stood clear of the safe and made no movement to close the door, explaining that most people automatically closed a door and that was a good way to lay a booby trap.

Adam opened the first folder. The pages of text were interleaved with circuit diagrams. He called Pete over and his guess was confirmed when Pete exclaimed, 'You've hit the jackpot, old buddy.'

'I think we have got the book of instructions,' said Adam. Pete said he had files of lists and equipment and, he thought, of names. The commandant seemed to be Sturmbahnfuhrer de Malraux.

'That must be the Frenchman Herr Moser told us about, the one in the SS,' said Adam. 'Wonder where he is.'

Pete shrugged expressively. 'He'll be holed up somewhere, I gucss. One thing for sure. He won't be the most popular boy in the school when he's taken prisoner.' Adam was scanning other lists in the file of names, and he was struck by the orderliness in which the names were presented and apparently cross referenced. Both of them were heavily engrossed in the documents until the generator began to slow down. They collected the bundles of files and returned to the operations room, carefully following the path they had taken. Av was methodically inspecting the machinery, and explained that he had shut down the generator deliberately as he wanted to avoid running out of fuel.

Adam could not help savouring the moment as he said in an offhand manner, 'My colleague here,' indicating Pete, 'will pass you a couple of books which might help you in your search, my man.'

Av took the volumes, frowned for a moment, then he exclaimed, 'Well done, your highnesses! These are just what I need. I was cursing that we hadn't brought a camera with us to take a picture of the installation. But look, there are three pages of very good photographs, all labelled. We've been given what we were sent to get.'

Adam showed him the file with the typed lists of names. Av held up two of the longer lists, and explained that these were names of French Jews who had worked as labourers on the site. Some had died in the camp and the survivors had been sent to Dachau earlier in the year for 'correctional retraining'. An explanatory note indicated that de Malraux had travelled to the concentration camp with these prisoners and had stayed until the 'ultimate solution' had been reached.

Pete was perplexed until Av explained that this was Hitler's phrase for killing Jews. 'We take these papers back to the Military Police and set them off after this French guy,' he concluded. Adam remembered seeing a photograph in the office they had just left, and he ran over the clear path to retrieve the framed picture of a sallow faced officer with slicked back hair wearing the dark uniform of the SS, with the swastika armband, posed with jackbooted legs apart, his left hand by his holster belt, and his black cap with the death's hand badge under his right arm. 'If we get Herr Moser to identify this fellow as the commandant, the Military Police will have an easier job to get hold of him and get him to answer for some dirty deeds. He has been up to his ears in nasty work.'

Once they had the papers stowed in the Jeep, Av looked round the camp. 'I have a terrible feeling about this place,' he admitted. 'Perhaps it was because I saw the lists of Jews and what happened to them. But I haven't seen or heard a bird up here. A sunny day and a quiet wooded spot like this and there's no wild life at all. Let's just have a look at the prison camp back there.'

A few minutes carefully following obvious paths took them to the gate, then to the door of the first hut which opened on a room which contained twelve beds. Some blankets and pieces of clothing were scattered on the floor. The other four doors each revealed a similar sized room, but with no signs of recent occupation. Adam found himself trying to place a sweetish smell in the first room. He suddenly remembered a night operation from France carrying a badly wounded agent. He led the other two back to this room. 'I smell fresh blood I'm sure someone in here is bleeding a lot.'

Av spoke quietly. 'There's someone underneath that bed.'

They stood in silence and heard a distinct sob. Pete knelt down with his stiletto in his hand and spoke firmly, 'Out buddy, out.' Another sob. Av spoke in German in a gentler tone and a blood encrusted hand stretched out from under the bed. Pete and Adam lifted the bed and revealed a young man dressed in a tunic with blood stains over it. He spoke in halting German, with French phrases. While Av spoke to the boy, Pete and Adam looked round the room for any others who might be hiding. They found no one else.

Av told them what he had found out. The young man was a French prisoner of war who had been captured by the Germans in 1940. Some two years previously he and another eleven Frenchmen had been moved from the Stalag to this camp. Their duties were to act as guards for the Jewish labourers. In the course of these duties, the French commandant and the two German lieutenants had ordered them to beat the prisoners. He had witnessed several Jews being strangled to death by le Comte de Malraux, a feat the Frenchman used to boast about.

Two days previously, when the news of the Allied advance reached them, the commandant had told the group of twelve that they should take the path through the woods at the rear of the camp and escape. They dropped everything and ran. As they entered the woods a machine gun opened up and mowed them down. This young man, Rene, was near the front and was hit in the left shoulder. When he recovered consciousness he saw that Major de Malraux was moving round with a pistol in his hand delivering the *coup de grace* to those who showed signs of life. Fortunately for him he passed out again. When he returned to consciousness, he found that comrades were all dead. He came to the camp, to get food and shelter then fell asleep but was awakened by the generator starting up. He hid because he thought that the commandant and his lieutenants had come back, but he was relieved to find that he had been found by the allies.

While Rene was telling his story, Pete examined his wound gently. 'The bullet's not in there. But he needs blood. Best we get him to medical help as soon as possible,' was Pete's authoritative conclusion. He turned and ran to bring the Jeep to the door of the hut. Rene was helped into the Jeep and they set off back to Gmunsten.

CHAPTER 36

At the hospital entrance Pete lifted the now unconscious Rene in his wide arms, told Adam to guard the Jeep then hurried with Av into the corridor. They laid Rene on a trolley and covered him with a blanket. Av explained the situation to a nurse who checked the wound and then moved off briskly. She returned with the severe looking blonde girl who had snubbed Pete the day before. With a movement of her finger she indicated that Pete should stand to one side. She looked at the patient and sadly said, 'Oh, Rene.' After some words she sent the nurse off, and started to talk to Pete, but stopped, as she realised he did not understand German.

Av assured her he could speak the language and she continued her examination asking questions of Av who gave an account of how they had found Rene and what he had told them of being gunned down at the orders of the commandant.

He was telling how the commandant had killed the survivors when Pete grew impatient. 'Jesus, Av. Don't just chat to this dame. Tell her to get a doctor, and get on with getting the blood into this kid.'

She was going over Rene's chest with a stethoscope, but she turned quickly and said clearly and slowly in English, 'I am not a dame. I am a doctor. I am not wasting time. The nurse comes now with information of what type of blood Rene himself has.' She turned to the nurse.

Pete looked sheepishly at Av, who grinned slightly and asked quietly, 'Did something go wrong with the old Petrelli touch?'

'I sure as hell bombed out with her,' Pete admitted.

The doctor checked the entry. 'There you are, loud American sergeant. Rene Pichot's blood was checked four days ago by myself. It is quite common.' She pointed to Pete's collar. 'Perhaps you have it.' Pete showed his dogtags, shaking his head.

Av smiled and nodded as he loosened his tie to bring out his identification discs. 'I think I'm your man.' She looked and smiled back at Av, asked about the state of his health and declared that he would be suitable.

She gently rearranged the blankets round Rene. '*Voilà mon petit,*' and patted the patient's cheek then helped to push him into a side room. The trolley was set beside a bed on which Av lay. The nurse put a needle in a vein in Rene's arm, the doctor found an appropriate vessel in Av and, in a very short time the transfusion was under way. Pete went outside to tell Adam what was happening.

When the doctor came to tell them that the transfusion was complete she was more relaxed. 'My name is Janochewsky.'

Adam and Pete introduced themselves. 'Are you a medical soldier?' she asked Pete.

'No ma'am, but we got a lot of training in First Aid in the Fightin' Forty Fours,' he replied carefully and respectfully.

'Have you killed men?' she asked.

Pete frowned. 'I have, ma'am. That was my job.'

She took off her glasses and smiled, 'You did a better job today. You saved Rene's life. We will keep him here until he is better. We can find other blood for him, if we need it.'

Adam asked how she happened to have a record of Rene's blood group. She explained that Rene was a prisoner who helped her when she was called to treat French staff or prisoners at the installation. A little girl in the village had fallen and cut her arm. She had lost blood and Rene had the right blood type for her so he had given some directly. The patient had not needed any more and was doing well. 'Now Rene has had his kindness repaid. My story ends as a fairy tale, eh,' she laughed.

Pete was interested that she was doing civilian as well as Army work. 'That is a long story, which does not have a fairy tale ending, at least not yet. I am not German but Rumanian. In 1940 when the German and Italian troops occupied my country, I am doing my specialist training in Anaesthetics in Vienna. Nobody troubled me until 1941 when I was told that I would have to serve as a doctor for the Wehrmacht. At first I examined recruits, and saw more male organs than I ever want to see again.' Pete and Adam exchanged embarrassed glances.

'Two years ago I was sent here to act as camp medical officer for this new installation. My duties were to look after the health of the officers, the German enlisted men, and the French Prisoners of War who were working on the Radio machine. I was not permitted to treat the slave labour, the Jews, who were doing the clearing of the land, digging drains and so on. They have all gone now, to correction camps, I was told. The old doctor in this place died and I just started to hold clinics down here as well as up there.

'Last August when my country was freed from the Germans, no one made any fuss about it, so I just stayed here treating people and forgetting all the clever things I had learned about Anaesthesia. I'm not sure what I will do. The government of Rumania is not stable enough to make me want to go back. I don't know what will happen in Vienna. I don't have a country to go to. I don't have the career that I wanted.' She shrugged her shoulders. 'I will wait and see what happens tomorrow, or the day after. But I shall make myself gloomy if I talk about me like this. I shall go and get my patients to cheer me up.' She smiled at them, replaced her glasses and strode down the corridor.

Pete and Adam met Av who was looking smug and said he was delighted that Rene was now the possessor of good Jewish blood.

It was late afternoon and when Pete reported to his Headquarters, Eisnor told them to stay where they were for another night. The paratroopers and a company of infantry were setting out at first light to take over Gmunsten formally. By the middle of the morning they would be free to return to Salzburg. Adam then asked to speak to the Commanding Officer of the Military Police detachment. He reported having information about atrocities and killings committed by de Malraux, and his possession of documents to corroborate the assertions. This officer said he would come there in person the next morning to get this evidence and to interview Rene.

Karl Moser said he would be delighted to have them at his home again that evening, and Herr Stengl confirmed that their accommodation was still available.

Adam went to the hospital to enquire about Rene's progress. Dr Janochewsky had gone home to change, but would be back at the hospital in an hour. The nurse took Adam to see Rene who was recovering well and might not even need to have any more blood. He found Rene sitting up, with bright eyes and colour in his cheeks. He remembered being found under a cot by Adam and the others and was grateful for their help. They chatted in French and Adam was satisfied that Rene was willing to give information to the American Military Police in the morning. He left to return to the Moser home and on his way, checked that the documents, files and technical manuals had been removed from the Jeep for safe keeping.

Av and Pete were already at the Mosers and he could hear shouts and yells of laughter from the little girls and Pete's voice booming out a story. He arrived in time for dinner, once more a tin of some processed meat, enhanced by a vegetable sauce. After coffee, Pete confirmed that the documents were in hiding and he left to make sure the Jeep was properly immobilised.

The others began to move the dishes into the kitchen for washing up. They had them piled up and Frau Moser was pouring hot water from the kettle into the washing up bowl, when a voice behind them said, '*Hände hoch*.'

Adam turned to find a dark haired man menacing them with a large pistol. He was just beginning to recognise the Frenchman, de Malraux, when Herr Moser said softly, '*Herr Major*.' De Malraux clicked his heels automatically. He was dressed in the drab uniform of a French soldier and addressed the Gauleiter in rapid German. Av said quietly, 'He wants money, another pistol and ammunition, and our Jeep.'

Herr Moser shook his head, apparently refusing, de Malraux stood beside Frau Moser and put his pistol at the head of the smaller girl, who wept in her mother's arms. He spoke again softly. Av translated that he would kill the child and her mother, if the Gauleiter did not do as he was told. He had just killed a witness so one or two more deaths did not matter. Herr Moser stood grim-faced for a moment then said he would get the keys. As he turned to the cupboard, the kitchen door flew open and Pete stood there looking at the menace offered by the Major.

Pete walked straight up to Malraux. 'You killed Rene, didn't you?' He turned quickly with his right hand out as if to address Herr Moser. In a flash his left hand deflected de Malraux's arm away from the children, and he hit de Malraux full on the nose with a right cross.

The Frenchman was obviously hurt and brought the pistol up automatically as Pete grappled with him. A shot was fired and Pete fell straight to the floor. Adam ran at de Malraux but he tripped over a loose carpet and fell clumsily against a table. By the time he regained his feet, de Malraux was out of the house, had started a motor cycle and raced into the dark. Adam tried the Jeep, but remembered it had been immobilised.

As he went back into the house Dr Janochewsky came running. Adam shouted, 'Come on. Pete's been hit.' When they entered the kitchen, Pete was still flat on the floor and Frau Moser was trying to stop the bleeding on the side of his head. Herr Moser was looking agitatedly down at Pete while trying to comfort the children. A sharp command from the Doctor and he dialled on the telephone and made an urgent request. She was feeling in the bloody area on the side of Pete's head. She looked up and pointed to a hole in the ceiling. 'The bullet. Was there only one fired?' Av confirmed this. '*Gott sei dank*,' she said, 'it's not in his head.'

She explored further with a probe from the emergency bag which had just arrived, then applied a pad soaked in a solution. This slowed the bleeding down and she was able to announce that the bullet had taken off his ear lobe and had gone on to open the skin on his temple.

She got Adam to hold a clamp on his ear while she put stitches in very deftly. He then stretched a flap of skin with forceps while she added more stitches to his temple. She then doused both areas with the solution she had originally used and finished bandaging just in time to hear the flow of curses from Pete as he came round and tried to sit up.

Frau Moser and the children were around Pete praising his actions, and Herr Moser offered a glass of brandy, which Pete drank at one gulp, spluttered and said, 'That stuff sure takes your mind off being shot in the head. Jeez that French louse must have killed Rene. When I went outside I thought there was someone skulking around here, so I went to check that Rene was OK. But I found him dead in his bed. He'd been strangled, I'd guess.'

Dr Janochewsky agreed. 'You're right. I found him dead, and the nurse locked in a closet, frightened out of her wits. She recognised the Commandant and he threatened to do the same to her if she told anyone she had seen him.'

Adam was impressed with the way in which this young doctor performed her tasks. She asked Av to keep Pete under watch all night and to telephone her if he was worried. She talked to the Mosers and reassured them that Pete would be all right. The girls went up to Pete and kissed him goodnight. He smiled and kissed them back. He got to his feet shakily and Av and Adam helped him walk the short distance to the hotel. Willi Stengl was alarmed when he saw Pete with his bandaged face. He produced a bottle of the same brandy that Karl Moser had served and poured a generous measure for Pete.

When Adam went back to the Mosers to make sure they were all right, they were fastening the storm shutters to make them secure. The doctor was still there. Adam walked to the hospital with her in case de Malraux was still skulking around. Together they went round the two wards, looking in cupboards and bathrooms to make sure no intruder was present. She told the nurse to get some sleep and that she and the English Officer would be on watch all night.

As they settled down in easy chairs in her office they exchanged first names and Adam took the opportunity to tell her that he was not English but a Newfoundlander. She had not heard of the place but he realised it would be too stuffy of him to do his lecture, so he asked her about herself, scoring a cheap point by saying in retaliation that he knew nothing about Rumania.

Anna talked about the uncertainty of her future, wondering whether the Americans would treat her as a German prisoner of war or as a Rumanian refugee. For the moment she was reasonably happy where she was, and she was sure that conditions would be worse in the cities where there had been so much bombing.

She asked Adam if he had bombed cities. He nodded but said nothing. There was a pause, then she continued talking about herself. She was doing a useful job here and would be happy to stay, but only for a short time as she would like to resume her studies in Anaesthetics. She had a number of languages, German, French, English, Russian so that she could study almost anywhere. Her father had been a career diplomat and her family had lived in a number of countries. Her flair for picking up languages was an advantage.

Her brother had been killed by the Germans as a member of a Resistance Group. She did not know what had happened to her father and mother, although she had tried to find them over the years. Perhaps they were taken to a camp. Her eyes filled with tears.

In the morning the nurse and Anna bustled about preparing breakfast, stripping and changing beds and handing out medication. Adam helped but was relieved when he heard a loud rumbling from military vehicles in the square. The American soldiers had arrived. There were armoured cars, jeeps, weapons carrier, trucks with armed soldiers disembarking everywhere and taking up position at the outer edges of the square.

A table and three chairs were set out and an American Colonel, flanked by two majors in battle dress and carrying side arms sat at the table. Gauleiter Moser and Kapitan Stengl, in uniform but unarmed, were escorted by a Military Police Lieutenant to stand in front of the table. The Colonel took a sheet of paper from his briefcase and read the order for the surrender of the town, first in English, then in German. After they had indicated that they understood the terms of the order, the Gauleiter and the Kapitan signed copies. The three Americans then signed and a copy of the signed document was given to Herr Moser who saluted, and both Austrians marched back into the building.

The major walked over to Adam, standing with Pete and Av. He introduced himself as Major Berman and listened to their account of finding Rene and the reports he had given of atrocities committed by de Malraux, then his death at the hands of de Malraux. He went to see the body, and confirmed death by manual strangulation. He arranged for the body to be removed to Salzburg for autopsy. Next he questioned Anna about Rene and her knowledge of de

Malraux's misdeeds, and took a statement from the nurse on her experience in being threatened by de Malraux.

Pete went to the U.S. medics to have his wound seen to. Av went back to the hotel room to sort out the technical data and reports from the more incriminating personnel material which would be handed over to Major Harry Berman.

Adam suggested that they look for bodies at the Radar installation and he accompanied Major Berman, his Lieutenant and six military policemen to the site. Adam warned them about the Lieutenant Carson's fate and took them to the areas they had visited, including the hut with the open safe, in which they had come across the files, the control centre and the bunkhouse in which they had found Rene. Up the hill behind the barbed wire enclosure, they came to a clearing which had been heavily trampled down and found seven bodies in Prisoner of War garb in the bushes. All had a number of bullet wounds in the chest, but three had also been shot in the back of the head.

In another clump they found an upturned machine gun on a tripod, and close by were the bodies of two German private soldiers who had been shot at close quarters. 'That seems to confirm the story we got from Rene,' said Adam.

Harry sighed. 'Yeah, I suppose it does. It'll take me some time to sort this whole thing out. I came here to do a ceremonial job of accepting the surrender of a town. Now I've got mass murder, war crimes, atrocities, assault, all on one plate. We'd better send out a description of the de Malraux bastard.'

Adam told him about the photograph they had found. 'Good. We'll get the Gauleiter to identify it as the villain and then get it copied.' Harry detailed the Lieutenant and two men to stay behind to make a sketch of the area noting where all the bodies were, then to have the bodies moved to Salzburg. He and Adam returned to Gmunsten.

CHAPTER 37

Av had sorted out the personnel files and the photograph of de Malraux (certified by Karl Moser and Willi Stengl) ready to be handed over to Major Berman. He suggested that they should leave a written statement saying how co-operative Dr Anna Janochewsky, Gauleiter Moser and Kapitan Stengl had been. This might help them with the authorities if they came before a tribunal. Adam wrote up references for all three and he and Av signed.

Pete added his signature after his visit with the Army medicos. They had taken off his bandages and dressings, laughed at his missing earlobe, admired the stitching on his ear and temple, pronounced all to be in good order and replaced dressings and bandages. Pete took the references off to the HQ truck which carried a photocopier.

Major Berman accepted the original documents from Av and told them they were free to go back to Salzburg, but to stay where they could be contacted. Adam signed a chit for their hotel bill. Willi Stengl was very grateful for the reference they had given him, and the box of groceries left by Pete. Karl Moser was touched at their thoughtfulness in preparing this statement and shook their hands solemnly. He and Willi were scheduled to appear before a tribunal in Salzburg in the next day or so, and he would offer their testimonials to this body. He gave Pete a bear hug for saving his family. Frau Moser kissed each of them and burst into tears in Pete's arms. The little girls curtseyed to Adam and Av then rushed to hug and kiss Pete, their 'Johnny Wayney'. He produced a chocolate bar for each and left, saying he had put a box of 'Piggen Hammen' on their kitchen table.

They said their farewells to Anna. Av was gallant, bowing to kiss her hand. Pete kissed her lips gently and gave her a box of groceries. Adam shook her hand shyly, wished her well and hoped she would get the special training she wanted. She looked at him for a time, then softly kissed his cheek.

In Salzburg, they reported to Willard P. Eisnor. Adam thanked him formally for the use of the Jeep and apologised for returning his Corporal in damaged condition. Eisnor shook his head. 'I never should have let this bozo near a gun without being there to look after him.' Pete grinned and told Eisnor to get supplies of food up to the hospital at Gmunsten, for kids and old folks. Eisnor replied it was against Army policy, and the food would be sent up. The three of them arranged to meet the following morning. Pete returned to his bivouac, and Adam and Av found transit quarters near the airport.

After two days in which Av and Adam were cross-examined by the American authorities about the behaviour of Major de Malraux, Harry Berman returned copies of the personnel files they had given him, including the photograph of de Malraux. Adam felt guilty at sneaking off with the technical manuals and made a mental note to ask Blacklock to make the information available to the Americans.

While waiting for the arrangements to be made for their flight back, Av read these manuals eagerly. A tribunal had been set up and their references for Dr Janochewsky, Gauleiter Moser and Kapitan Stengl had been entered in evidence. They were invited to attend the hearing, which was due to be held that morning.

At the hearing, Av, Pete and Adam were each questioned by an American Air Force Colonel in the chair, a British Commando Major, and a Russian Naval Commander. They were asked about the nature of their duties in this area. Adam simply stated they were inspecting a German Radar station, and had come across the record of atrocities committed by de Malraux. With Corporal Petrelli, they had rescued Rene. He and Av had heard de Malraux admit that he had strangled the Frenchman, and had witnessed the wounding of Corporal Petrelli by de Malraux. The Russian seemed to be irritated that Av could speak German so fluently, and suggested he was a Nazi in British uniform trying to escape. Av quietly revealed he was a Jew. The American chairman and the British Major saw no reason to pursue this line and the Russian conceded grudgingly.

The chairman asked Pete about Dr Janochewsky. 'She fixed me up good,' he replied, turning the bandaged side of his face to the tribunal.

'What is her nationality?' asked the Russian.

'Rumanian,' replied Pete.

'How do you know?' the Russian came back.

'She told me,' snapped Pete.

The Russian gave a snort, 'She told you, ha,' and he smirked.

Pete faced him and asked, 'Are you Rumanian?'

'No, no I'm Russian,' was the automatic answer.

'OK, you're Russian. I know that because you told me,' Pete said quietly and pointed to Anna, sitting in court. 'She's Rumanian. I know that, because she told me.' The Russian glared at him.

When it was Adam's turn on the witness stand he volunteered his opinions about the services performed by Dr Janochewsky. Going round the wards with her he had seen the kind of work she performed and her good relationships with the patients. The Russian asked if he was an expert in Medicine. He admitted he was not but he had become an expert in being a patient when his wound was being treated. He was very impressed by the way in which she had treated the French prisoner of war, and her first aid to Corporal Petrelli had been first class. The chairman nodded his head, the Russian shrugged his shoulders.

The British Major said that the problem facing the tribunal was how to categorise Dr Janochewsky. 'Is she a former member of the German Army or is she a Rumanian national whose country is no longer under German dominance?'

Adam looked at the chairman, 'May I make a comment?' The chairman nodded his consent. Adam looked at the Russian. 'She is not German. In fact, Sir, when your Russian Army defeated the Germans in Bucharest, Rumania declared war on Germany in August last year.'

The Russian raised his eyebrows and nodded enthusiastically. 'Since then Dr Janochewsky has been a citizen of an Allied nation.'

Adam went on. 'At the risk of having my expertise doubted again, I think this is a problem that your tribunal will face time and time again. If you come across a French doctor in a German prisoner of war camp who has been treating Germans as well as his fellow prisoners, you have no problem with his nationality. He is French and is now liberated. Whether or not you think of the doctor as a collaborator is a different issue. He or she could argue that their professional responsibility is to treat and heal sick people, whether they are German, English, American or Russian.'

He saw Anna's head nodding as he spoke. The major thanked him. 'I don't think,' he said with a smile, 'that you have enunciated a new principle of international law, but I detect a valuable dose of common sense in it.' To his surprise, the Russian Commander stood and smiled at Adam, then applauded. The chairman thanked the three of them and asked if they had anything to add. Pete opened his mouth, but a little nudge from Adam convinced him to close it. They were then free to go.

They waited outside until Anna, Stengl and Moser emerged, smiling at having been cleared. There had been no complaints that they had been involved in any war crimes. The decision on Anna took longer because the Russian had recommended her to study in the Moscow Academy, but the American had offered her a post in a refugee camp in the American zone, until she could resume her studies in Vienna. As they said goodbye again, she asked Adam if she could write and tell him what happened. He was delighted and gave her his addresses in London and St John's.

On a routine visit to the Garrison Major Adam was shown a signal informing him that as of a month ago he had been promoted to Wing Commander. For his record on operations he had been awarded a Distinguished Flying Cross and the Air Force Cross for his work in developing navigation aids. The Major had been thinking about this. 'You've been a busy little bugger, eh. Of course you outrank me, you know. In fact you're senior British officer in the garrison now.' Adam pointed out that he was simply passing through. The Major offered him any help he could in carrying out his search for wireless stations. Adam pointed out that he had got all the help he needed from the Americans and his mission was complete.

Adam thought it appropriate to tell a British authority about the war criminal, de Malraux, being at large. The response was characteristic, 'If he's French, then you should tell the French about him. Or better still tell the Yanks to tell the French about him. Bloody Yanks, they've taken over the zone, and they give me dam' all help, you know. However I wouldn't want my masters to know I hadn't offered to assist you. Perhaps I could offer you lunch, eh?' Adam asked if his invitation included his Flight Sergeant. The Major looked shocked at this suggestion, 'Well hardly, my dear fellow. We have to keep up standards.' Adam flexed his new rank and used an expression from his school days, 'Oh, piss orff.' He left feeling a childish satisfaction at his reply.

Back in England Adam and Av went to Malvern to deliver the technical manuals. Professor Barlock was among the first to greet them. He was delighted to find that not only had Adam brought the manuals but had provided someone with the technical background to understand the contents and the linguistic ability to translate them. In his usual fashion the Professor told a Flight Lieutenant to have this valuable Flight Sergeant posted to Malvern. Adam praised the help given by the Americans and recommended that they should share this goldmine of technical information. Barlock led him down a corridor to a small office and introduced him to an American Colonel, who would be working with Av on the German technical manuals.

He attended the last investiture at Buckingham Palace to receive his medals, noted how strained and tired the King looked and felt admiration for the difficult role that this gentle man had assumed because of the defection of his older brother.

Bomber Headquarters was in a state of chaos. It was staffed by so many senior officials that Wing Commanders were considered to be the bottom of the pecking order. Arthur Harris was still on the defensive about his decision to maintain area bombing, and for the apparently cold hearted attacks on innocent civilians. He was embittered by the criticism of Bomber Command, with little recognition of what had been achieved and scant acknowledgement of the high casualties among the aircrews.

The slump in morale was attributed to the disastrous raid on Nuremberg in March 1944. Rumours were widespread about how that débâcle had happened. For example, it was claimed that British Intelligence had found out that the Germans knew the date and time for the raid. But cancelling the raid would let the Germans know that the British could get hold of their secrets, so it was decided, at Cabinet level, to let the raid go on. Insidious rumour of this sort produced a wave of low morale which spread through Headquarters to the Groups, to the squadrons, to the aircrew preparing to resume their lives in 'civvy street' or their careers in the regular service.

Adam was excited at the prospect of returning to St John's and to his business career. His demobilization date was in three weeks, and he had secured a seat on a flight from Prestwick, three days after this procedure. He heard the delight in his father's voice when he telephoned to give the news. He went over to Beaulieu and visited Sister Rodgers, also Eleanor Scrivener, who was about to get married to the General Practitioner. She told him that Deirdre had taken her children back to Ireland, and fortunately she knew the telephone number. When he got in touch with Deirdre, she said she had been out of her mind for weeks after Roger's suicide, but Mike had shaken her out of her self-pity. Their father had died and Mike was now Lord Duingaugh, right out of the service and working happily with the livestock. He was away at the cattle sales at the moment. Deirdre remembered Adam as her special friend and she would expect to see him in Ireland some time. He promised he would visit.

Sir Wilfred was operating in Manchester, but Jessie Rodgers caught him between cases for Adam to have a brief word with him. 'Jessie Rodgers fusses over you like a mother hen, you know. She's told me all about you. She's proud of you, and bugger it, so am I.'

Adam was moved, 'I won't forget what you did for me.'

There was a pause. 'The cutting part is the easy bit. The hard bit is the nonsense I talk to keep the patient from brooding. God bless, young Adam.' Jessie Rodgers showed him letters she had received from Giles, back in Montreal, doing well in his father's firm, and playing tennis and occasionally squash.

He borrowed a car and went to have a look at Tangmere. Some aircraft were there but it all seemed strangely quiet. The cottage where the agents were housed had been sold for a private dwelling. The 'hush-hush' part of the airfield was entirely deserted, so he left. At the Commonwealth Club a letter from Anna was waiting.

She had been offered a place in a teaching hospital in Vienna and was happy to have resumed training. Major Berman had no information about Count de Malraux yet, but the American Secret Service was now involved. She said she often thought about Adam and hoped they might meet again. Adam found that he harboured affectionate thoughts of Anna. He found himself thinking of her eyes. Did she really need to wear these severe looking glasses? She had to wrinkle her nose to keep them up. When she wanted to think before she spoke, she put the tip of her left index finger right in the centre of her pursed lips. How old was she? Did she ever lose her temper? When would he see her again? He began to think of ways to go to Vienna. He answered her letter giving her the mundane details of what he had been doing, then asked her about her glasses.

The day after his official demobilization, Adam went up to Glasgow and took a room at the Central Hotel. He invited Fiona and Jock to dinner at the Malmaison, the hotel's restaurant that had been highly recommended to him. It lived up to its reputation, the food good and simply served on excellent china. The service, provided by distinguished looking elderly waiters, was excellent and restrained. Fiona took to the atmosphere immediately, while Jock fidgeted for some time. Fiona had a glass of white wine, Jock asked for a half pint shandy, which he sipped slowly. They reminisced about Ether Atom and the eccentricities of Professor Barlock.

A man at a nearby table kept casting glances at Jock and leaning forward to speak softly to his companion. As he rose to leave he came over. 'May I shake your hand, Mr Davidson? I recognise you from the papers, and my wife met you during the war. She's too shy to come over.' Jock had frowned at this interruption, but he smiled when he saw the small lady at the next table. He stood up, went to her, shook her hand and asked, 'Did you have A1 sauce with your dinner, Doris?'

Her hand flew to her mouth, 'Oh, you remembered me. The last time I saw you, you were taking off that time you got badly wounded. I thought you were going to die.'

'So did I, Doris.' He led her over and introduced her to Fiona and Adam. 'This is Doris who looked after me in the mess and waved me off on that terrible trip that did me no good at all.' They all stood awkwardly.

'To think you remembered that night,' Doris said.

Jock smiled, 'I won't forget it in a hurry. I saw you waving just before I got cleared to take off, and I thought afterwards that was the nicest thing that happened that night. Thank you, Doris.'

Doris explained that she and her husband were celebrating his new position as a bank manager. They had a new house in Newton Mearns, and she was expecting their first child. Robin and Fiona were invited to visit them any time, and Doris' husband apologised to Fiona and Adam for bursting in. 'Mr Davidson's always been Doris's hero, and she would have been disappointed if she hadn't just said hello.'

Fiona smiled, Adam nodded and the couple left. Fiona kissed Jock's cheek. 'For a medical student, you're a kind, understanding man.'

Adam laughed, 'That's not how I remember him, Fiona.' At Jock's prompting, he talked of Eleanor's happiness at her coming marriage to the general practitioner, and her plan to keep working until they started a baby.

Fiona looked at Adam gently, 'That's what we plan to do, once this dunderhead gets into his specialty training in a couple of years.'

The following day was spent in Troon, visiting the Mackays. Valerie was now a Flight Officer, still in Intelligence, and engaged in the reception of aircrew who had been Prisoners of War. She had become engaged to a young dentist and she was still thinking about entering Dental School when she was released. Mrs Mackay asked if Adam had a young lady in mind. He found himself saying that he had met a young lady doctor in Austria, but he had not discussed marriage with her . . . yet.

Colin was on his demobilization leave. He had decided to go to Glasgow University to pursue a degree in History and then train as a teacher. Linda came home from school, leggy and shy, answering questions reluctantly. She smiled when Adam reminded her about passing the salt that turned out to be pepper.

When she went to do her homework Mrs Mackay explained that she was growing up.

After a meal and a farewell dram with the family, Colin drove Adam in the family car to Prestwick for his flight, this time in a Lancaster converted for passenger carrying.

CHAPTER 38

Adam was back in St John's in September 1945. The war in the Far East had ended in August with two terrible bomb attacks on Japan, leaving the world in a state of moral confusion about the use of atomic weapons, guilt ridden at the death and destruction in Japan, but relieved that no more Allied lives would be lost.

His father and Bridget were delighted to have Adam back with them. At work he found himself interested in how the various sections of the business were interrelated through the St John's office. His dreams of using an aircraft to get around the island in the course of running the business did not last long. The rocky terrain was dangerous for forced landings and the care and maintenance facilities were not readily available for such operations. His father suggested that they should start up an aviation service company to take advantage of an increased interest in air travel, both for passengers and for goods. Adam found himself arguing against it on the grounds that the trend was too early to predict the likelihood of success. His father was amused enough to point out their mutual shift in attitude from their previous discussions on aviation.

In Newfoundland the economic momentum from the wartime boom period was slackening. Support was emerging for Labour as a political force, to some extent influenced by the move to the left in Britain which summarily deposed Churchill. The British were unable to provide financial support, and were trying to encourage Newfoundlanders to think of their future as an independent entity.

The Governor of the day observed that the ordinary Newfoundlanders had no experience of exercising their voting rights. Obviously they needed a spokesman, and Joseph R. Smallwood felt he was the man for the job. He had been born in Gambo, and made much of his outport settlement origins, but he had grown up and been educated in St John's. Before the Second World War, he developed his writing and speaking skills from his varied experiences as a printer, journalist, union organizer and writer in New York and London. He appointed himself President of a Fishermen's Co-operative, in which role he was criticised for his lack of business acumen, and earned himself a reputation as a trouble maker.

Smallwood became the best known radio voice in Newfoundland as 'The Barrelman', a term referring to the man who directed the whaling crew from a position up the whaler's mast. Under this name he commented on Newfoundland matters in terms which appealed to the public. At the beginning of the Second World War he kept his considerable personal and professional skills in abeyance during the temporary upsurge in Newfoundland's fortunes. In this period, Smallwood was a pig farmer in Gander.

In 1946 elections were held for membership of a National Convention, charged with recommending possible forms of future government which could be put before the people of Newfoundland in a referendum. Adam was asked to stand, but declined. The number of candidates offering for election was disappointing and the voter turn out was meagre, except for the district of Bonavista in which Smallwood won and entered the Convention with the largest margin in the whole election.

The proceedings of the Convention were transmitted regularly to the public by the Broadcasting Corporation of Newfoundland. Thus the listeners renewed acquaintance with the 'Barrelman', Joey Smallwood, an accomplished radio performer. He let the country know that he favoured Union with Canada, and sparked off fiery debate in the Convention about whether such a move was constitutional. Diehards argued that the only two options were Commission of Government or Responsible Government, but both of these depended upon Britain for future financial support and there was little evidence of British interest in either option. Smallwood's dogged stubbornness and astute knowledge of the Newfoundland public's wishes, led him to champion the Confederationist cause and to press for a delegation to be sent to Ottawa. He was accused of chicanery at every step and had to deal with cries of outrage.

Some Newfoundlanders, including one or two prominent Water Street Merchants favoured Confederation with the United States, but could never demonstrate that the US would be interested in having Newfoundland join them. In rebuttal, Smallwood had merely to point to baby bonuses, old age pensions, and other welfare benefits that would flow from Canada but not from the United States. Despite Newfoundland's unsettled future, Adam was confident that business prospects would remain good.

Personally Adam was unsettled, and he knew the cause. He was in love with Anna. From the tone of her letters, his feelings were returned. She had successfully completed her training and was engaged in a research project on the administration of prolonged anaesthetics in infants. This work represented an advance over the existing methods and she and her Professor were to attend a meeting in Manchester to present their findings to an international conference. 'I'm excited to know that I shall be nearer to you, but disappointed that I shall not be with you,' her letter ended.

He had recently been appointed to the Board of one of the three General Hospitals in the city and discussed her work with an anaesthetist who dealt with children. This doctor had read two scientific papers by these two Viennese doctors and was excited at the prospects it opened for paediatric surgery. However he could not foresee such research occurring in Newfoundland in the near future. They were still trying to attract anaesthetists to do the routine clinical work. 'If this chap wanted to come out as a locum, to do the ordinary day to day work, we could gladly fit him in.'

'He's a she,' said Adam blushing.

The anaesthetist smiled and said, 'Marry her then, and bring her out here. Solve your problem and ours.'

Adam was silent then he nodded, 'I think I will.'

He told his father about Anna and his feeling towards her and said he was going to ask her to marry him. 'I can't do that by letter, but I'm going to see that new shipper we talked about hiring in Liverpool in three weeks time, when she will be in Manchester, and I'll ask her then.'

Skipper Archie looked serious, 'Are you seeking my fatherly permission?'

Adam immediately retorted, 'No. Certainly not. I'm telling you as my friend.'

Archie beamed, 'Then we'll have a glass each of that Scotch whisky you brought over. Then we'll tell Bridget.' This lady was delighted that her little Adam was going to be married.

'I hoped that's what all these letters with foreign stamps meant. Which room will you want for you and Anna? We'd better get it redecorated before the wedding.' Adam protested that he hadn't asked the lady yet, and went to the den to write to Anna.

His day in Liverpool with the shipping agent proved to be profitable, and he took a train the following morning to Manchester where he had reserved a room at the Royal Hotel. He took a taxi to the University and found the lecture hall where the meeting was in full swing. He was able to stand at the back and listen to a heated exchange between Anna and an Italian doctor who was apparently arguing that babies were quite insensitive to pain. Anna felt that this was untrue and that proper anaesthetic procedures should involve analgesic measures. An excitable Frenchman entered the discussion, then a German, then an American and although the audience was using headsets from a simultaneous translation system, Anna was switching from one language to the other upholding her point of view.

Eventually the Chairman stood up and declared that the session was closed. In thanking Dr Janochewsky for her presentation he commended not only her scientific ability, but her linguistic skills, and the audience applauded enthusiastically. She came towards the door where Adam was standing, her face flushed and her eyes sparkling. He put his hand on her arm and in an imitation of Pete Petrelli said, 'Hiya sweetie.' She turned quickly then flung herself into his arms.

He led her outside the room and asked, 'Will you marry me, Anna?' She nodded enthusiastically.

The Italian with whom she had been having the heated exchange, turned to Adam and with his arms spread wide and a smile on his face, said, 'I was going to ask her the same question. Congratulations to you both.'

They spent the evening talking excitedly, about their future together. She confessed to being willing to give up her career to become a wife and mother. He felt that she could continue as an anaesthetist in the hospitals in St John's and told her about the set up. She was committed to completing her research project in two months time, and she could then come to Newfoundland where they would be married. She was willing to share the large house with Skipper and Bridget and did not mind in the least what colour the bedroom should be. The next morning they bought an engagement ring and she left for Vienna, he for St John's.

The Anaesthetist asked for copies of her professional records and curriculum vitae so that she could be given locum status with the local Medical Board and the various hospitals. Her entry into Newfoundland was covered by her permit to enter the United Kingdom, which was still in effect. In the documents that she sent was a recently dated diploma certifying the award of the Degree of MD cum laude from Vienna for the work she had been defending at Manchester.

Bridget raised a problem when she asked what Anna's religion was. It turned out she was Roman Catholic, but had lapsed during the war years. She would nevertheless like to be married as a Catholic. Bridget beamed at this. Archie and Adam were indifferent as they both admitted they had been lapsed Protestants. They agreed that Adam's marriage to a Roman Catholic would not sully the memory of his mother, and Adam was willing to swear that his children would be brought up in the Catholic faith. So a Roman Catholic wedding was held in November 1946.

Anna was happily busy providing anaesthetics for child and adult patients in the city hospitals. She attended scientific meetings in Canada, and the U.S., and came back restless with ideas, but never complained at the lack of opportunity to carry out intellectually stimulating research projects or to evaluate new techniques. These trips were curtailed when Adam junior (Addie) was born in October 1947, then Annette in September 1949. They could claim that their first child was a Newfoundlander and their second a Canadian, for Smallwood had eventually steered Newfoundland into Confederation with Canada on April 1st 1949.

As the first Premier of the newest province of Canada, Smallwood was responsible for a number of madcap commercial deals which usually involved some reputed expert from outside the province who turned out to be economically inept or even crooked. He had successes in education and one outcome of this was the institution of Memorial University.

Smallwood also started to upgrade medical services throughout the Province. The former American base hospital was converted into a children's hospital and opened in 1966 as the Dr Charles A. Janeway Child Health Centre. Anna was appointed to the Janeway as a child specialist and three years later when the first students were admitted to the Medical School, she was one of the first medical specialists to seek academic status as a clinical teacher.

By this time, Addie was at Harvard Business School and Annette had applied to McGill to do an advance course in Actuarial Science, a field in which she excelled in her undergraduate studies in Mathematics at Memorial. None of the men in the family could last long when she explained her interests, but she would regale Bridget with obscure concepts and ideas and both would appear to be enjoying the interchange. On one occasion Bridget was heard to exclaim, 'But that's just the same as the stochastic process you told me about.'

There was a pause then Annette jumped to her feet and kissed Bridget excitedly, 'You're right, and that's what I've been looking for! You're a genius, Bridget.' A copy of Annette's thesis, entitled 'The Reliability of Short Span Sequencing in Determining Long Term Trends in Actuarial Forecasting', was duly presented to Bridget, and was proudly treasured because Miss Bridget Murphy was acknowledged in the foreword as a valuable advisor to the author.

The bond between the 20 year old and the 64 year old was extraordinary. At one time Bridget would be discoursing to Annette on the complicated family history of the outport Murphies, at another, Annette would be teaching Bridget a rock and roll dance step. Bridget was proud when her Annette graduated from McGill with a Doctorate in Science, but was disappointed when she accepted a Faculty post at McGill as Memorial University of Newfoundland had no opening for anyone with her highly specialised expertise.

Adam had always flown sufficient hours each year to keep his Private Pilot's Licence valid. In the 1960s he bought a Cessna 180 for recreational flying out of the former Canadian Air Force field at Torbay just outside St John's. This 'lightplane' proved to be too light for comfort in windy conditions, so he bought the more powerful Cessna 182 which was rated as 230 horse power and could seat four people. He used it for business trips with occasional week end family outings to St Pierre, the capital of the French possessions in North America.

St Pierre and Miquelon are the two larger of a group of rocky islands lying off the south coast of Newfoundland. Together, as St Pierre-Miquelon they make up a '*département*', a political region of France. Historically the competition for fishing rights led to differences in outlook between St Pierre-Miquelon and Newfoundland and Labrador and more widely between France and Canada. These differences ranged from indifference at times to fierce enmity at others.

Aside from the politics of fishing, Newfoundlanders could go 'abroad' to St Pierre, enjoy French cuisine and return with duty free spirits, wine, tobacco, cigarettes and other goods. The island had a colourful history. Rum-running had been conducted from St Pierre to the United States during Prohibition, and some smuggling continued to the south coast of Newfoundland. On their visits, Adam and Anna would register in the hotel, go for walks or just sit and read, then enjoy a leisurely meal in one of the several restaurants that were being started for the developing tourist trade, then fly back to Torbay airport the following morning.

On one occasion they landed to find an urgent message for them to telephone home. Bridget had found Skipper Archie unconscious at the foot of the stairs. The doctor had got an ambulance and young Addie had gone to the General Hospital with his grandfather. Adam and Anna drove straight there and met the cardiologist who had put in a cardiac pacemaker as an emergency measure. After an hour or so they were able to speak with Archie. His main concern was that he would die before he could thank them all for the happy years they had given him. Addie said that Annette was going to get down there from Montreal as quickly as she could, and he would fetch Bridget. 'Yes, Bridget's been good to us. Will you look after her, Adam and Anna?' They promised readily.

Archie smiled, 'Anna, you've been my daughter for over twenty years. I was fond of you when we first met and each year I've grown fonder. I thank you for the fine grandchildren you and Adam gave me. Addie will do well in the business, and Annette will be a famous professor one day. I'm a lucky, lucky man, but I wish my Lucy had been spared to share these joys with me.' They left him to sleep.

Bridget and Anna went to the Basilica to offer prayers for Archie, and Adam and Addie went to Torbay Airport to meet Annette. They were all with the Skipper when he died. He had smiled at them one by one, but could not speak. They had each kissed him and then stood quietly until he gave a sigh and was still. Bridget and Anna crossed themselves, and they left.

Adam told Bridget of his father's wish that she should stay with them. Anna depended on Bridget and wanted her to stay as a family member. Bridget said that the Aitkens were her family and she was glad they wanted her to stay.

There were new interests for Bridget. Addy announced that he was going to marry a girl called Sheila. Her father was a surgeon, a colleague of Anna's at the Janeway, and she was a kindergarten teacher. Bridget was delighted at the prospect of another baby in the family. Her eyesight was failing and she was becoming frail physically. She would complain that she was a 'poor done old woman' and get indignant if her listener did not strongly disagree with her. Later, when Sheila announced that she was pregnant, Bridget maintained that she would last until she saw the baby, and it would be a boy.

She did see the baby and it was a boy. At a Christmas gathering of the whole family she dandled young James on her knee and talked to him for a long time, using outport expressions and pronunciations. She went to bed early and died peacefully in her sleep. They mourned her passing and Annette and Anna said a special mass for her soul.

CHAPTER 39

The *département* of St Pierre and Miquelon was limited in the medical specialty care it could provide for children. On the basis of an agreement with neighbouring Newfoundland, some French children could be dealt with at the Janeway Child Health Centre in St John's.

In 1977 Anna, as Chief of Anaesthetics, with other doctors at the Janeway, was invited by the French Government to celebrate the Labour Day weekend in St Pierre. The invitation included Adam, so he decided that they would fly down in the Cessna. As always, they enjoyed walking around St Pierre, the town, which was bustling with the weekend's special activities, folk music and dances, games, and sporting events, such as a cycle race, a tug of war and an important soccer match against a team from Newfoundland.

In the evening a banquet was to be held at which certificates of appreciation were to be presented to those from Newfoundland who had contributed service to this part of France. The presentations were to be made by Phillipe de Chabelin the French Minister for Foreign Affairs, who had flown from Paris with two of his senior civil servants.

In the afternoon, a reception was held at which the Minister, flanked by his two Assistants, received the guests. Anna and Adam stood in the reception line behind a loud mouthed Newfoundland politician who boasted that he knew all these people well and would tell them what he thought of Frenchies stealing the good Newfoundland fish. Adam regretted his attempt to persuade him to quieten down when he smelled rum, but all he succeeded in doing was to divert the shouted objections away from the French to the Aitken enterprises.

Two stalwart gendarmes took an arm each and led the noisy oaf across the room to a door, where he increased his struggles and shouted even more loudly. As Anna and Adam stepped forward to be greeted by the first assistant, the Minister turned his head in the direction of the scuffle. The assistant was apologising graciously for the embarrassment caused, when Adam felt Anna stiffen by his side. She hesitated for a moment then stepped forward. As the

Minister turned to shake her hand, Adam was surprised to hear Anna say quite clearly, '*Herr Major.*'

The Minister automatically replied, 'Frau Doktor . . .' then stopped, with his eyes wide open staring at her, his mouth moving but no words coming. The assistant to his right looked at him in a puzzled fashion then at Anna.

The Minister finally spoke, 'It is good to meet you again. On behalf of France, I thank you for your service to my country.' He shook Adam's hand absently, still looking intently at Anna, who had now moved on to be greeted by the assistant.

As they returned to the buffet, Adam whispered, 'What was that about?'

Anna's answer floored him, 'That's de Malraux, the SS Commandant at Gmunsten.'

Adam looked at the Minister, 'But he looks different. His hair is darker and he has a broader nose from the man I remember.'

Anna was firm in her reply, 'Some of your friends use the same stuff on their grey hair, and Pete broke de Malraux's nose, remember? I recognised him because of a scar under his left ear. It is like a crescent, where a skin flap was made, and a little round indentation above, where a drain hole was drilled. These are scars from a surgical technique popular in Europe in the twenties and thirties as a way of relieving pus in children who had a severe infection of the ear, before there were antibiotics. So it is quite a common mark, but in de Malraux's case, the scar is big and knotty, more so than others. I suppose the infection must have spread to the wound before it healed. I had not thought of him for years, but I immediately recognised him from that scar. That's why I called him Herr Major and you saw how he responded. Phillipe de Chabelin, Monsieur le Ministre, is the war criminal, SS Major de Malraux. You and I were there when that judgement was made by the tribunal.' As they spoke Adam saw that the Minister kept shooting glances at Anna as he smiled and shook hands with the other guests.

After the formal greetings had finished the Minister left the room, pleading a slight indisposition. The assistant who had been on the Minister's right, came forward to speak to Anna. After some general comments about the Janeway Hospital, he asked if she had known the Minister previously. 'I met him during the war,' she answered guardedly.

'In Austria, was it, in the Salzkammergut?' he went on.

'Yes, it was,' she agreed.

He pursed his lips and frowned. 'He was there, he claims, as a prisoner of war.' He looked intently at her. She hesitated, and her eyes moved toward Adam who was nearby, speaking to some other guests. Adam saw her glance, excused himself, and came over to find out what was up. The assistant was business like. 'I have put your wife on the spot, I fear. I saw and overheard her brief exchange with our Minister. I understand she met him in Austria during the war.'

Adam nodded, 'I can vouch for that. I was in Gmunsten, but I only saw him once very briefly.' He took Anna's hand and smiled at her reassuringly.

The assistant shepherded them to the far side of the room, had a waiter serve them with wine, and they sat down. He looked all round the room before he spoke. 'Since the Minister was appointed three years ago I have been trying to get some background on him, but unsuccessfully. When he was given the Légion d'Honneur the Sûreté tried to fill in his early life, again unsuccessfully. He said he was in the French Army and was captured by the Germans and taken to a work camp in the Salzkammergut to build a wireless station. At the end of the war, he escaped and got to South America, but returned to France, found his family had all died or had been taken by the Nazis. He worked in the Quai D'Orsay as a clerk and studied in the evenings. He became interested in politics, was eventually elected and entered Cabinet. "From filing clerk to Minister," he likes to boast.'

The assistant was uncomfortable. 'Now to my dilemma, Madame Aitken, you are the first person to say that you met him previously, and it was in the Salzkammergut during the war.' Adam watched as Anna nodded. 'How sure are you that it was M. Phillipe de Chabelin?'

Adam looked at Anna then turned to the assistant, 'Look, Monsieur . . .'

The assistant supplied, 'Charles d'Entremont.'

Adam went on, 'Look, Monsieur d'Entremont, my wife and I have just had a hell of a shock. We may have stumbled into something that could be nasty, and even dangerous for us.'

D'Entremont nodded and Adam continued, 'If that is so, we must be sure of what's happening here. Is your duty to protect your Minister at all costs?'

The assistant replied immediately, 'I give him that protection in his day to day ministerial duties, but I don't have to defend him if he has a doubtful past. In fact if there is something in that past which would harm the reputation of France, my greater duty is to bring it to light, no matter what the consequences may be for him.'

Adam pressed further, 'Tell us candidly what you suspect?'

D'Entremont did not hesitate, 'I think that M. de Chabelin collaborated with the Nazis during the war. If I'm right it is dangerous for us even to talk about it. There is an international organization which is unscrupulous in protecting former Nazis and their sympathizers. I suggest we meet in your room before the ceremony this evening. I had better go to find out if the minister has recovered from his indisposition.' He made a show of rising and smiling his farewells. Adam and Anna chatted to some other guests for a little, then went to change for the dinner and presentations.

Once they had changed, they went over their situation. Adam asked Anna, 'Do you have any doubt that it is de Malraux?'

'None at all,' she answered.

Adam looked at her seriously. 'Then knowing that he has already killed to make an escape, we are in some danger in this hotel.'

Anna agreed, 'But would he leave us alone if we didn't tell M. d'Entremont? I don't think so.'

Adam agreed. 'Our choice really depends upon whether we believe d'Entremont or not. He could be genuinely wanting to unmask de Malraux using the information we supply, or . . .'

'He could be feeling around for what we know in order to protect de Malraux,' Anna finished.

Adam exclaimed, 'There's one precaution we could take. Do you have your address book in that huge handbag of yours?' She searched, then produced it. 'Good. I'm going to write to Willard P. and to Pete. They have copies of the documents we got plus the evidence given at the tribunal, and the verdict of the tribunal. If we don't get in touch within a week they should make the whole thing public, stating that the French Foreign Minister is really a war criminal, called de Malraux. There is a special mail collection here at seven p.m., because of the holiday, so we can get the letters posted when we go down for dinner. Our first move with d'Entremont is to tell him we've taken this precaution. If he is on de Malraux's side it may make him reluctant to have us killed.'

He wrote a quick summary of their situation and the action to be taken 'in the event . . .', then copied it out on another sheet of paper. Anna addressed the envelopes and they took the letters down to the lobby, confirmed that there would be a pick-up in five minutes time and sat on a sofa leafing through magazines until the postman arrived, opened the mail box, placed the contents in his haversack, chatted to the receptionist for a few moments then drove off. Adam got himself a large whisky and under the circumstances ordered a smaller dose of the same for Anna. He took a sip, then laid the glass down. 'None of that, thank you. I'm going to telephone the air control tower to find out the weather forecast for tonight, I'll file a flight plan for home.' He was back shortly and reported that everything was organised for them. They went upstairs, packed their bags and left them out of sight in the wardrobe in the room.

They were joined shortly afterwards by d'Entremont. He reported that the Minister had been upset at meeting Anna, and had explained that her brother had died as a result of the terrible conditions in the same Prisoner of War camp as he had been in. She was obviously bitter that he had survived, but her brother had not. He could understand her feelings, but hoped she would not make a scene.

Adam told about the letters he had sent out to two other witnesses who had copies of all relevant documents and first hand information. Anna explained the basis of her identification of the Minister as de Malraux. Adam talked of Rene's account of the treatment of prisoners by de Malraux, the killing of the wounded Rene, and his attempted hold up of the Gauleiter's office and the wounding of Corporal Petrelli. They both told of the tribunal verdict and of the documents from the camp that Adam had passed to the US Intelligence Service, and the contents of the copies of these documents that he and the other two witnesses still had.

'Dear God, you have everything I need,' d'Entremont said as they finished their tale. He asked if copies of these documents could be sent to him at his home address, and he gave them his card. Adam agreed and mentioned that he and Anna were at risk for the knowledge they had, as de Malraux had already committed murder to conceal it.

After d'Entremont left, Anna and Adam went down to the dining room, and joined the others in cocktails, Adam taking soda water and ice. As the Minister entered the dining room with d'Entremont and the other assistant, Adam asked the owner of the hotel to have his bags brought down at nine o'clock and a taxi waiting to take them to the airfield.

At dinner they were seated with the Janeway contingent, and Adam felt relieved at being in the company of people he knew well. After an elegant dinner, and a speech by the Minister, the formalities began. The certificates were presented by the Minister, with d'Entremont reading the names. When Anna went forward to receive her certificate, the Minister spoke to her briefly. Back at the table she told Adam that the Minister had asked if they could meet afterwards to talk of old times. She had simply smiled politely, but had not answered.

While a small orchestra was preparing to play, Anna and Adam left for the airport. They had an uneventful flight. The tower at Torbay was fully operative and they were home before midnight.

In the morning, Adam telephoned Pete and Willard P. to explain the background to the letters they would be receiving and to let them know that Anna and he had got home safely. He copied the documents, including the photograph and the official tribunal records, and sent them off to d'Entremont. There was a brief acknowledgement from d'Entremont, but nothing further.

Ten days later, the national newspaper carried the story of a scandal in the French cabinet. A Cabinet Minister and his senior assistant had been found dead in the Minister's apartment. It was assumed by the police that this was a murder/suicide between two homosexuals. No suicide note, or other explanation had been found.

An officer from the RCMP Security Branch called on Adam at his office to say that the French police were convinced that this was a double murder. On the same night as the Minister and d'Entremont had been killed, two armed men had been apprehended leaving d'Entremont's apartment. Both had been shot, one fatally, the other lingered long enough to confess to having committed the two murders on the orders of a senior Austrian policeman who had served with the Gestapo. The Sûreté had recovered the documents which Adam had sent to d'Entremont and were not going to release them.

Adam stressed his belief that d'Entremont had not been a homosexual, but had acted courageously to protect the good name of France. He handed over his documents to the RCMP for their keeping.

Anna took him to the Basilica where they each lit a candle in the name of Charles d'Entremont. As they bowed their heads, Anna asked for a blessing on the soul of this young Frenchman whose life had been taken while bringing evil to light.

Anna surprised him one morning at breakfast when she told him that a distinguished British surgeon was going to give a series of lectures in the Memorial University Medical School and receive an honorary degree. The surgeon's wife had written to Anna to ask if she and her husband could stay with the Aitkens. Adam thought it a bit presumptuous of the Medical School to get their visitors to find their own accommodation. Anna agreed and said she would write to Lady Davidson to tell her it was not convenient. Some moments later, Adam put down his newspaper and cautiously asked the name of this visiting professor. Her eyes twinkled as she read from an official notice, 'Professor Sir Robin Davidson, K.B.E., M.Ch., M.D., F.R.C.S.(E), F.R.C.P.S.(G), F.A.C.S., V.C., D.F.M., Regius Professor of Orthopaedic Surgery, University of Glasgow.'

Sir Robin reverted to Jock for a week after the academic commitments had been fulfilled, and was impressed that Adam's shoulder had held up so well. Of the shoulder operations he had followed up from the war, Wilf Chinley's had the best record for long lasting results, although the records showed that immediately post operative, he had a very high incidence of flare-ups. 'In the light of what we know now I think that whatever he did set up an immediate flare up of resistance mechanisms, followed by an immunity.'

The highlight of their stay was a jigging expedition on Conception Bay in a forty-foot work boat with two fishermen from the Aitken fleet taking them to waters where they could lower their jiggers to within 'a foot an' a bit, sir, off the bottom, near heighteen hinches' and jig the line to hook cod. Anna and Fiona preferred to sun themselves on the deck, and talk of the merits of their children and grandchildren. Jock had seventeen middle sized cod in two hours, while Adam had eight.

The older fisherman kept taunting Jock that he hadn't got the big fella yet. Finally Jock tired of defending his catch of seventeen and he handed his line over to the fisherman. The old man drew it in, then quickly scraped the lead jigger until it showed silvery through the dull stain on it. He spat on it then dropped the jigger, gave a few jerks, roared, 'Tunderin' Jaisus. I got 'un!' and hauled in the line to reveal a large cod about four feet long and huge bellied. 'There ye are, me son,' he bellowed at Jock. 'That's what you've been missing all day.'

Jock roared with laughter and retorted, 'Ah, but I haven't got your spit.'

At the end of the day, they hauled into a jetty and went ashore. The two fishermen brought cushions from the boat and spread them for the ladies to sit. Jock and Adam were sent to get dry wood and a chubby lady appeared with a large blackened frying pan and a dish of fatback from pork.

'Now set you the fire just there, me son,' Jock was told and handed a bit of newspaper and a box of matches. 'Mr Adam might give you a hand.' Between them they got the fire blazing. By then six of the smaller cod had been produced and the fishermen were filleting them. The giant frying pan was heated and the fat was sizzling.

Fiona laughed when the chubby lady told Jock to spread butter on the bread.

'I wish his surgical staff could see him taking orders rather than shouting them.'

Jock bowed to the chubby lady and gallantly said, 'I recognise real authority in the matter of bread and butter.'

Adam fetched a picnic basket filled with a variety of bottles. He served white wine to Fiona and Anna, rum to the fishermen and the chubby lady. He and Jock chose red wine.

Jock did the honours, raising his glass to the fishermen, 'Your health, gentlemen, for teaching me to jig for cod. And yours, madam, for that delicious smelling meal we are about to have.' They ate home made bread and butter, with freshly caught and lightly cooked cod, with the sun just reaching the horizon on a glorious Newfoundland day.

Jock reached his arm round Fiona and gave the final verdict on their outing, 'On a day like this, my love, you wouldn't call the Queen your auntie.'

PART SIX

AN ENDING

1990, 1995

CHAPTER 40

Adam celebrated his seventieth birthday. Addie and Sheila and the grandchildren arranged a family party at the Colonial Inn, a well-known restaurant on the outskirts of the city. Annette arrived from Montreal with an intense, garrulous Professor of Mathematical Statistics, her live-in lover, as Anna termed him in her frequent expressions of maternal disapproval. The immediate family and about twenty local friends gathered downstairs, then Adam and Anna were asked to lead the group upstairs. When they reached the top of the stairs they found one table of their private dining room already occupied, by two couples.

Adam coughed tactfully and said quietly, 'Excuse me, I think you're in the wrong room.'

A tall white haired man stood up, blew a kiss to Anna and said, 'Hi ya, sweetie.'

The other man, elegantly dressed and well groomed, shook Adam by the hand. 'I hope your morals are in keeping with your age,' he said in a lugubrious voice, then laughed.

Adam looked over at Anna in Pete's arms, 'It's Jock,' he said.

'It's Pete,' she said.

They moved to the table, where the distinguished white haired lady was Fiona, now restricted in her movements and having to use a cane. A tall statuesque blonde was introduced by Pete as Marlene, Mrs Petrelli the Third. Anna and Fiona were quickly into getting news of each other's grandchildren. Pete told Adam that Willard P. had had his second coronary by-pass and was not allowed to travel. He sent his best wishes to Adam and hoped he would see him on his eightieth. Pete told Adam that he had kept up the tradition and had honeymooned in Europe with the present Mrs P. As with his other two wives, they had gone to Gmunsten and stayed at Willi Stengl's now large hotel. Mr and Mrs Moser had both died, but they had met the two little girls, now grandmothers. Both remembered 'Johnny Wayney', and each had called her first son 'Pete'. Each Pete had a son called Pete, so Petrelli was proud to be well remembered in Austria. He and Willard P. were prosperous. The real estate company which they had started now had offices all through Florida, and the Southern States.

Jock was now officially retired and was writing a monograph showing how the treatment of war time casualties had contributed to the development of orthopaedic surgery. He suddenly asked Adam if he knew that the traditional use of maggots in cleaning open wounds had reached a peak in the Peninsular Wars, but had returned to use in the Spanish Civil War. There was a hush round the table. Fiona spoke, 'Robbie Davidson, you're as old as Adam and you still have not learned to control your mouth. Wheesht man, wheesht.' The great man looked so crestfallen that everyone burst out laughing. He joined in.

The party began with the meal, followed by the toasts. In his reply Adam thanked Addie for bringing Pete and Marlene, Jock and Fiona to this party. He became maudlin when he compared the relationship between himself and his son with the long gap that had existed in the relationship between himself and the Skipper.

For a week after the party, Adam and Anna had the Davidsons and Petrellis as house guests. When they eventually had the house to themselves, Adam confessed to being tired and ascribed this to a change of pace in life. He was sure that a week or so in their usual routine would get him back on an even keel again. The exceptionally fine weather induced him to spend time gardening, and he felt physically the better for the exercise.

He had retired from the firm, secure in the knowledge that Addie would carry on the modern version. Anna was no longer active in clinical work, but she had some light teaching duties in helping postgraduates prepare for their Royal College examinations. Thus for the first time in their married life, they had time to do ordinary things together. They travelled in Britain and Austria, meeting old friends and seeing how places had changed.

Time passed quickly for them and they remained active. Adam was approaching his 75th birthday, and in a year they would celebrate their golden wedding. On a clear spring day they decided to drive up Signal Hill, overlooking the entrance to St John's Harbour, to see the departure of two young adventurers who were leaving to cross the Atlantic in a small sailing boat.

A 30 year old male schoolteacher from Toronto with his companion, a 22 year old female secretary, representing the Canadian Royalist Society were to set off on May 24th 1990 to commemorate the Queen's Birthday by such an adventure. No one seemed to know, or even care, about the society, but a great

Harness and Hatches Secure

deal of publicity was being generated in the press and on the various radio talk shows. Retired mariners and senior members of the Coastguard condemned such ventures by amateur sailors as foolishness and likely to endanger proper seamen who would be involved in the rescue attempts. The teacher's wife was putting a brave face on it, describing the intrepid sailor as a good husband and father, and being unable to comment on his younger companion as she had never met her, adding unconvincingly that she felt she and the girl could be good friends.

Adam and Anna watched the departure of this 30 foot sloop. Accompanied by a dozen motor launches the school teacher had got the mainsail up as they approached the Narrows and was struggling to get the foresail set as they passed through. His crew was at the tiller glancing nervously around as they veered from one side of the entrance to the other. In addition to having wind and tide against them, the foresail was being hoisted upside down. A fishing boat took them in tow, told the teacher how to sort the mess in his sail, and took them into the open sea. A final TV close up showed utter despair on the face of the blonde secretary at the helm.

A radio interview with the fisherman after they had gone summarised the venture. 'None o' the two of them were sailors. They even had the Union Jack flyin' arse upwards.'

Two days later Adam felt he should put in some flying hours, to help convince the licensing authority of the Department of Transport that even with his advanced age, he was still competent. He telephoned the tower at Torbay, heard that the weather forecast was good, and persuaded Anna to make a few sandwiches and a flask of coffee then fly with him to look at the offshore oil installations.

She accepted readily and an hour later they were at the end of the runway, completing the preflight checks. At the appropriate moment she broke in to his recitation to say, 'Harness and Hatches secure.' He smiled and leaned over to kiss her cheek. The controller, who had caught this romantic gesture in his binoculars, interrupted to say that if Mr and Mrs Aitken had finished their smooching they could take off.

They took off and headed over the Janeway and Quidi Vidi village out over the Atlantic. Adam switched his radio to the Marine and Coastguard listening channel. After some time, Anna thought she heard someone calling, with a very indistinct signal. Adam increased the sensitivity of the receiver, and changed his heading until the signal was at its maximum. As the signal grew stronger he heard a desperate plea for help from a tearful voice. The transmitter was being kept on open and it was impossible to break in and acknowledge the repeated appeal for help. However, the open channel had the advantage of giving them a signal to home in on.

He flew lower as the signal strength increased, until Anna caught his arm and pointed to her right. He turned quickly, with the plaintive cries loud in his ears. 'Someone answer me. I don't know what to do. Help me . . .' Dead ahead there was a sloop in the water, sails flapping and tiller swinging. As he flew over he saw someone lying still in the cockpit. Suddenly a blonde head appeared from the cabin and began to wave excitedly. He recognised the former secretary who had left St John's two days before to sail the Atlantic.

While the girl was on deck he circled over the yacht and called to her. 'Don't touch the switch on the microphone yet. Press that switch only when you want to talk, then take your finger off the switch when you want to listen. Do it now. Tell me what I've just told you.'

There was a pause then she came in, 'I press when I want to talk and don't press when I want to listen.' He was about to congratulate her when he realised she still had the transmit button pressed. Then he heard, 'Oh come on, say something. Oh it's me and the silly switch. Sorry.'

He spoke to her quietly. 'That's good. Now don't forget about the switch again. I'm going to get your position so that I can tell the Coastguard where to send someone. In the meantime I'm going to pass you over to my wife who's here with me. You can tell her what happened. Stop every now and then. Other people might want to come in on the conversation.' He circled and took a reading of latitude and longitude on his satellite navigation receiver.

She came back on. 'I've never been on a boat before. I'm frightened. We were both seasick all yesterday and all last night. In the middle of the night he took the sails down, but that made us even more sick. This morning he said his blood sugar was too high so he took a shot of insulin. Now he's lying out there and I think he's dead. Did you hear that?'

Anna replied that she had heard very well and continued, 'You said he had a shot of insulin. How long ago was that? Was it an hour or two hours or longer? Do you know how much he took? Just tell me and then let the button go.'

She was back immediately. 'Right. It was about an hour ago. I'm sorry I don't know how much. Over to you,' and the button was released.

Anna transmitted, 'Well done. That's how to do it. He may not be dead, but in insulin shock. Now you must go and see how he is and smell his breath. Tell me you understand then go to him and come and tell me what you smell. Over.'

'I understand. I'm going to smell his breath. Over.' Adam saw her come into the cockpit and bend over the inert man. She was over him for some time then went back into the cabin and called, 'His breath smells of sick, just like mine I'm sure, but I didn't smell anything else. Over.'

Anna asked if she knew the smell of nail polish remover. When she replied that she did, Anna asked if she smelled that on the patient's breath, she said definitely not. Then she added that he seemed to be breathing now.

Anna reassured her. 'Now we can do something about it. Do you have any honey aboard? What's your name, by the way? Over.'

She replied saying her name was Shirley and she had a jar of runny honey.

Anna told her, 'My name is Anna. I want you to put a lot of honey on your forefinger, pull open the side of his mouth and rub the inside of his cheek with the honey, but watch he doesn't choke or anything.'

Adam took the microphone and said, 'Hello Shirley, this is Adam. I'm Anna's husband. While you're rubbing on the honey, I'm going to climb higher and radio for the Coastguard. Don't worry we won't leave you yet. You'll hear what I'm saying on your radio, but don't interrupt until Anna calls you.'

At 1000 feet Adam called the Coastguard and gave the position of the yacht and an account of the situation. The Coastguard acknowledged and alerted a supply vessel which was returning from the rigs. The skipper came on and said he was altering course. He had not heard any of the previous transmissions because the signals were weak at sea level. He estimated he could be at the yacht in just under an hour. Adam thanked him, then called up Torbay to explain his situation and give his present position. They acknowledged, wished him good luck and reminded him to check his fuel level regularly.

He flew low over the yacht again. Shirley was waving excitedly and the patient, although still lying on the deck was also waving, although feebly. Anna called, 'Hello, Shirley. It seems to be working. Over.'

Shirley was back in a rush. 'Anna, it was great except I had to take out his false teeth. I never knew lover boy had them. I hate them, but I thought he might choke on them. I rubbed honey up and down like you told me and he came round and gave me hell for getting honey on his shirt and for taking his teeth out. I'm considering whether to fling the damn things over the side. That would serve him right. I've had enough of him and his stupid ideas of getting thousands of dollars when we write up our crossing. I heard there's a boat on the way. Over.'

'You're obviously feeling better, Shirley. A supply boat is coming this way. You'll be picked up very soon. We'll have to leave now to make sure we have enough fuel to get back. Over and good luck.'

Shirley replied, 'Thank you, Anna and Adam. I'll never forget what you did for me.'

The skipper of the Supply Vessel could hear this exchange then the Cessna flew over his ship, waggled its wings, gained height and set off toward the coastline. The supply ship reached the yacht shortly after that and picked up the grateful woman and a surly man with no teeth. The sloop was hoisted on deck and secured it with hawser.

On the way in the Coastguard radioed to ask if they had any information about the Aitken's aircraft. The supply ship captain confirmed that the Cessna had left them headed in the general direction of Torbay airport, but after this visual sighting there had been no radio contact.

An amateur radio operator in Tor's Cove to the south of St John's reported that he had had a very faint and indistinct signal, which could have been a Mayday call from a woman. The signal lasted for about 20 seconds, not long enough for him to get an exact bearing, but it was roughly 120 degrees from his station.

An RCAF Rescue Aircraft flew a search along this bearing and sighted what could have been an aircraft in about 20 fathoms of water. The co-ordinates of this position were passed to a rescue vessel with a full diving crew and equipment. It located the aircraft and recovered the bodies which were airlifted by helicopter to the Health Science Centre in St John's for post mortem examination. The wreckage was raised and taken to a hangar at Torbay for inspection by Federal accident investigators.

At the official inquest when the accident investigator presented his official report of his thorough inspection of the aircraft, Addie broke down when he heard that the harnesses and hatches were secure and intact.

A memorial service for Anna and Adam was held in the Basilica. In their honour the entrance was lined by Air Cadets and nurses from the Janeway. The service was conducted by the Archbishop, and the Presbyterian Minister read the lessons. The eulogy was delivered by the Lieutenant Governor, who praised the Aitkens' contributions to the community and the province.

A lone piper played 'The Flowers of the Forest' at the end of the service. After the large crowd of dignitaries from Government, University, hospitals and the staff from the various Aitken enterprises had cleared, a fair haired girl knelt at the altar, and laid two roses, one white, the other red, along with a card on which was written, 'Thank you, Anna and Adam. I'm sorry. Shirley.'